PRAISE FOR
STORM OVER CAMELOT

'A spellbinding reimagining of Arthurian legend and the perfect end to an epic trilogy, *Storm Over Camelot* is lush, luminous and utterly impressive. It shimmers with magic and crackles with intrigue, pulling the reader into a gorgeously written, irresistibly immersive world. Sophie Keetch has given Morgan her voice back and it's unforgettable.'

GEORGIA LEIGHTON, AUTHOR OF *SPELLBOUND*

'A moving finale to a barnstorming trilogy. Sophie Keetch's Morgan is a wonderfully complex creation: every page tingles with her passion and power. Exhilarating storytelling.'

MEG CLOTHIER, AUTHOR OF *THE BOOK OF EVE*

PRAISE FOR THE MORGAN TRILOGY

'Compelling and poignant, Sophie Keetch's prose is as mesmerizing as the ocean's tides... A stunning delight.'

REBECCA ROSS, AUTHOR OF *A RIVER ENCHANTED*

'Keetch's Morgan does not disappoint... Literally fire and a perfect harbinger of the woman Morgan is destined to become!'

STACEY THOMAS, AUTHOR OF *THE REVELS*

'This is the Arthurian legend as you rarely see it: told not by Uther, Arthur or Merlin, or indeed their male champions, but by the complicated woman they condemned... A convincing and compelling read.'

LUCY HOLLAND, AUTHOR OF *SISTERSONG*

'A very real, passionate retelling of Morgan's story, with detail about political and magical lives, and the women who are such a vital part of the tale.'

TAMORA PIERCE, AUTHOR OF THE *PROTECTOR OF THE SMALL QUARTET*

'An utter delight. Keetch blends a deft and convincing historical vision of medieval chivalry and court life with dark and astonishing explorations of British folklore. This is a book sparked through with the gold of British magic; wild and wonderful, a true feminist vision of our oldest stories and sure to be a rising star of contemporary British fantasy.'

EMMA HINDS, AUTHOR OF *THE KNOWING*

'What a page turner! Riveting, immersive, magical and wildly romantic. I loved every dramatic, beautifully detailed page.'

TRACY REES, AUTHOR OF *AMY SNOW*

STORM
OVER
CAMELOT

SOPHIE KEETCH

A MAGPIE BOOK

First published in Great Britain, the Republic of Ireland and Australia
by Magpie, an imprint of Oneworld Publications Ltd, 2026

Copyright © Sophie Keetch Ltd, 2026

The moral right of Sophie Keetch to be identified as the
Author of this work has been asserted by her in accordance
with the Copyright, Designs and Patents Act 1988

All rights reserved
Copyright under Berne Convention
A CIP record for this title is available from the British Library

ISBN 978-0-86154-702-9
eISBN 978-0-86154-849-1

Text design and typesetting by Tetragon, London
Printed and bound in Great Britain by Clays Ltd, Elcograf S.p.A.

This book is a work of fiction. Names, characters, businesses,
organisations, places and events are either the product of the author's
imagination or are used fictitiously. Any resemblance to actual persons,
living or dead, events or locales is entirely coincidental.

No part of this publication may be reproduced, stored in a retrieval system, or
transmitted, in any form or by any means, electronic, mechanical, photocopying,
recording of otherwise, or used in any manner for the purpose of training artificial
intelligence technologies or systems, without the prior permission of the publishers.

The authorised representative in the EEA is eucomply OÜ,
Pärnu mnt 139b–14, 11317 Tallinn, Estonia
(email: hello@eucompliancepartner.com / phone: +33757690241)

Oneworld Publications Ltd
10 Bloomsbury Street
London WC1B 3SR
England

Stay up to date with the latest books,
special offers, and exclusive content from
Oneworld with our newsletter

Sign up on our website
oneworld.co.uk

*To Marina, who always
works miracles*

and

*To Morgan le Fay herself,
for answering when I asked
to hear the whole story.*

Let no one deem me a poor weak woman who sits with folded hands, but of another mould, dangerous to foes and well-disposed to friends; for they win the fairest fame who live their life like me.

Medea, Euripides

1

How easy it was, to ride into darkness.

I had travelled through dusk and midnight, and the forest should not have felt so familiar. Only two days in my life had I ever passed through these woods – once on horseback with a guide, and the other running. Escaping. Between the dense trees, the years gone by and the new route I had taken, I should not have been able to find my way.

But to be bound by magic is no small thing. For my sins, I could have found Merlin's house blindfolded, on the blackest of nights.

As dawn rose, I paused beside a stream so my horse could drink and take a few hours rest. I reclined against a tree but could not sleep, instead watching the brook glimmer over its stony bed, sluggish with the height of summer. My thoughts ran slow with the water, steeped in guilt for my departure the previous day, when I had saddled Phénix without telling a soul and absconded from my house, my valley; Fair Guard as it once was.

Belle Garde, we had called it this past twelvemonth – a tribute to Accolon, my Gaul, my love; the lost half of my soul. He had always referred to our home in his native language and now it could be nothing else. A change as natural as the tides, and as relentless.

The moment, too, had arrived suddenly, without mercy. A year ago to the day, Accolon had died, killed at the hands of my own brother.

The household had wanted to acknowledge the anniversary, hold a banquet and subsequent vigil to mark his passing with the honour it deserved. I appreciated the gesture, even if I could not participate. For them, it would help. For me, I hoped Alys and Tressa at least would understand why I left.

As the morning light strengthened, I remounted and rode onwards, a horde of memories in pursuit. Halfway to noon, Phénix gave a shiver of his muscles, and I knew we were getting close.

I had never fully trusted in the claims of Merlin's death, as one never turns one's back on a wild beast thought tamed. When I emerged into the clearing and beheld his enchanted island, every doubt that had lain dormant reared up. Had Ninianne truly locked the sorcerer in a cave until he died? Or had he managed some final trickery and was now lying in wait, hungering and dangerous?

That cannot be, I told myself. *If Merlin were still alive, you would feel it.*

The gabled house and stone tower slumbered in green shade, bracketed by the enormous elder and oak trees. The rocky moat ran with water but low and calm, not the roaring, deadly rapids it had once been. The marble bridge only Merlin or Ninianne could summon – that supposedly kept intruders out and had kept me in – stood unconcealed above the surface, reclaimed by dried leaves and dirt. *Horses will not cross*, Ninianne had explained upon my first arrival, but Phénix walked the bridge without qualm. There could be no starker sign that things were not as they had been.

Still cautious, I dismounted near the main door. The house was structurally the same but not untouched by time and nature: grass overgrown at the front and climbing plants crowding the windows; unchecked hops vines hanging down, giving out their sleepy yeast scent; the tower almost entirely carpeted with ivy.

Beside it, the giant oak stood mute and resplendent. Once, Merlin and I had buried a white hart at its roots, dead and mangled, brought back to life whole by my skills, my work, my blood. Such a feat had been everything to me, and here I was, chasing the same miracle.

I took the sacks I had brought from the horse's saddlebag and went to the entranceway. The door was swollen from rain and stuck fast, so I laid my hands on the planks and sought the water within, drawing the element forth. The wood contracted with a creak and yielded, letting me inside.

I faced the dim hallway, flagstones echoing under my boots. Spiderwebs hung from the rafters, the air scented with damp and soot, bundled herbs long turned to dust. I paused, letting my senses sharpen to the atmosphere. Beyond my heartbeat, only emptiness. If this was a trap, then it was an extremely well-wrought one.

Still, I could afford to trust nothing.

I began with checking every room. My former bedchamber was eerily undisrupted, the bedsheets thrown back as I had left them on the morning of my escape. Here, I had slept uneasily for over a year, and for three of those nights I had lain unaware, birthing a baby whom I never saw, never heard, never named. Mine and Accolon's son, taken by the sorcerer under Ninianne's unbreakable charm of concealment, eternally hidden from me.

The child was gone, Accolon was gone, every trace that such a thing had happened, gone. The thought made me want to curl up on the dusty mattress, but I forced my unsteady feet to walk away. I was stronger than this; I had to be.

Ninianne's study was still the brightest place in the house, the huge half-moon window letting in a curve of morning. Shelves of manuscripts, cut quills and crystals stood dust-furred but orderly, the long marble worktable empty except for one vase, bearing a few stems of vivid purple foxglove.

The sight of life startled me, until I reached out to touch the flowers and found them hard and cold. They were the same foxgloves that Ninianne and I had turned to stone, her first demonstration of the elemental magic I had come to love, and my earliest, imperfect attempt at recreation. For some reason, she had kept them.

The thought thudded into my gut – that Ninianne had valued our time together as I had, long before she helped my brother orchestrate Accolon's death and turned us into enemies. Now, it didn't matter if we had sat at this table, sharing knowledge and confidences in unusual sisterhood, that we had once transcended our mortal and fairy differences and become closer than either of us could acknowledge aloud. None of it had meant anything.

I put my back to the foxgloves and left the room. I was not here to lament upon the past; I had come to seek my future.

Finally, I went to the long, dim classroom where the sorcerer first taught me, its windows crowded by bitter nightshade. Empty, unchanged, just as the rest.

A cool sweep of draught lifted the hairs on the back of my neck. Only one place remained unseen: Merlin's tower.

The door to the stone stairs stood open. How many times had I made the twisting climb towards wonders and horrors alike? How often had I lamented ever placing my foot on the first step? Despite this, I went forth, up one flight, then another, and the third. It was just another empty room, I told myself. There was nothing to be afraid of.

At the summit, I stopped. The door to the sorcerer's study was shut. *You have nothing to fear,* my mind replied, *unless you are not alone.*

Dread flashed through my veins, but I pushed the feeling away. I was Morgan le Fay and I no longer knew fear.

With a defiant shove, I threw the door open. The room was empty.

Of course it was – what had I expected? To see Merlin behind his huge tree-trunk desk, regarding me with his pointed smirk? He was gone; there hadn't been a whisper to the contrary. Even Arthur's rule had moved on in the five years since Merlin's strings had been cut from the kingdom – the sorcerer would never have relinquished control for so long.

No, Merlin was dead. Ninianne had captured her captor, and the world had continued without him. A year ago, I had walked into Camelot's Great Hall and seen the extinguished black wicks of his life candles with my own eyes.

Regardless, I did not wish to linger. Fortuitously, everything was where I left it: the books and scrolls for my work on resurrection; piles of unbound pages; a few rare and interesting manuscripts on other subjects that my study shelves did not have. I unfolded the sacks I had brought and filled them with as much precious knowledge as I could carry.

I heaved my cargo down to my horse and secured the weight evenly across his hindquarters, then returned to Merlin's lair. Only the final part of my quest remained – the upper tower floor where the sorcerer had watched the stars and hidden his greatest treasures. A place that I had never been permitted to go. There, I hoped to find the miracle I had come for: the Shroud of Tithonus.

A resurrection object of untested but formidable power, the secrets of which Merlin had been trying to unlock to reverse Arthur's prophesied death.

The one thing I needed to bring Accolon back to life.

When I had last seen it, the Shroud lay in Merlin's saddlebag, before he imprisoned me and rode off to Camelot to become the architect of my downfall. Logic suggested that he must have come back to discover my escape, returning the treasure to its hiding place before Ninianne tempted him away to his death.

I ascended the stone spiral, ready to do battle with the threshold, surely locked under magic. Instead, the door flew open at my hand. I felt the scratch of Merlin's mockery; he had never feared me disobeying him, because he believed he held me rapt. The thought filled me with gall.

The mysterious chamber was large and empty, walls panelled in black, highly polished wood. Halfway down, a ladder descended from a closed trapdoor, a route to the tower top and the stars. At the far end, five narrow windows let in barred light, hazy with dust, casting a large lectern in silhouette.

Upon closer inspection, the panelled walls revealed themselves to be doors of large cupboards. I prised one open, revealing a series of smaller cupboards and drawers, studded with silver handles in the shape of dragon heads.

I grasped a handle, expecting magical resistance. The drawer slid open but was only full of sun-bleached bird bones. In a slim cupboard, I found a chunk of smoky quartz, swirling with its own light. Another panel revealed a board pinned with dead butterflies, splayed and bright. A bag of goat horns toppled from a shelf and spilled onto the floor with a clatter. The room was full of Merlin's detritus.

Impatience overtook me from there. Black doors flew open under my hands, drawers wrenched from their sockets, scraps of herbs and twine collecting about my skirts, runestones rattling like teeth as I tossed them aside. I even found the dragon-hilted dagger Merlin had used to slash Ninianne's arm in one of our 'lessons', but no ebony box. No Shroud of Tithonus.

I flung the final drawer aside, pausing to suck a splinter from my fingertip. As I did, my eyes landed on the hulking shape of the empty lectern. In the angled light, I could see the pedestal was carved with carousing dragons, a horizontal shelf jutting proud at the back. On it sat a dark wooden box.

At last. I charged across and snatched up the vessel, throwing the lid open.

A warm, muted glow met my eyes, emanating from a rectangular object within. Reaching inside, I lifted out not the folded fabric of the Shroud, but a book.

It was smaller than most manuscripts, maybe ten inches tall, but thick and weighty, armoured in solid gold. White pearls and blood-red rubies studded the gilt covers, bringing yet more heft, like a cathedral bible. *Substantial*, was the word that came to mind.

Gently, I propped the volume against the lectern. For all the dust, not a speck dared settle on the gleaming surface. Enchanted then – a potentially dangerous prospect. But never in my life had I been able to resist opening a book.

The gold cover was warm against my fingers, parchment creamy and smooth, the most perfect I had ever encountered. On the first page, a star chart had been painted in blue and silver, illuminated at the edges with gold-inked crowns. At the top, Merlin's slanting hand had written a date in early March that had been familiar to me since the first day the skies rendered it significant.

I turned the page. It was blank, aside from two flourishing words.

Arthurus Rex.

Then another, alone beneath.

Prophetiae.

I heard myself gasp. Before me was Merlin's Book of Prophecies for Arthur and his reign, his kingdom, his entire existence. The definitive record of my brother's past, present and future, according to the sorcerer's interpretation of the stars.

Tentatively, I lifted a sheaf of pages, revealing reams of writing in the sorcerer's distinctive script: every prophecy Merlin had made and given to my brother like a poisoned chalice, and used to hold sway over his life.

Within these pages would be the words that led to Arthur's birth through my mother's violation by Uther Pendragon, the dark exchange made for a first-born son; the declaration that Merlin had cast upon the sword in the stone, until Arthur drew it free and first felt a crown on his head. There would be accounts of battles won, of the allies, enemies, and deaths that carved the path to Camelot's creation, the glories and dangers found in the destiny of Britain's greatest king. Then, the final prophecy, powerful and devastating – Arthur's death, and the realm's resulting fall.

And amidst the rest was a prophecy bearing my own name, for a betrayal I was not guilty of, not a prediction of my fall as much as it was the cause. The collapse of my whole life – the loss of my true love, of motherhood, the bond with my brother and my place in his world – all written there with an authority utterly indifferent to the devastation it had wreaked. Morgan le Fay's ruination, rendered in ink.

I would not look at any of it; there was no enlightenment to be had.

I slammed the heavy cover shut and turned away. Chaos greeted my sight – yawning cupboards, drawers pulled out, the floor littered with polished stones, feathers and shards of pottery. I had torn through Merlin's secret world like a tempest.

A vague satisfaction thrummed in my blood, but in truth I had nothing to show for it. Yet surely, if Merlin left his precious Book of Prophecies here, then the Shroud of Tithonus could not be far.

I closed my eyes, letting my mind reach forth. The Shroud's life force had always sung out to me, and my senses, my deepest elemental instincts, had only got stronger over the years. If it was here, then it should answer my call.

A ripple passed through me, subtle but distinctive. Not the comet-tail thrill of a resurrection object, but a disturbance – the pulse of a moving body, whispering robes brushing floorboards, a presence drawing near.

'Morgan,' said a familiar voice. 'What are you doing here?'

2

In the end, it was her light that opened my eyes.

The sight of her beauty was arresting as ever, my eyes so unused to her otherworldly glow and fire-bright hair I was forced to blink away the dazzle.

'Ninianne,' I said. 'I could ask you the same question.'

'I have every right to be here,' she replied. 'It is where I lived for a long time.'

'You don't any more. No one has been here for years.'

Her sigh was impatient, the skim of wind across a lake. Little had changed in her, it being only a year since I had seen her last. That inauspicious day, on the road home from Camelot, with my entire household devastated from Accolon's death, Merlin's former Lady of the Lake had taunted me and galloped off, trying to draw me away from Arthur. It didn't work, but it was an insult that she had even tried.

'What are you looking for?' she asked.

I saw no reason to lie. 'The Shroud of Tithonus. In fact, perhaps you can be of help. Where did Merlin keep it in this puzzle chamber of his?'

'It seems I have helped you enough already,' she said. 'You were using your senses to find it. Fairy skills.'

Those which I taught you, she did not say, but the past hung between us in the illuminated dust.

'I am no fairy,' I said dismissively. 'Just tell me where the Shroud is. As Merlin's *beloved*, he must have shown it to you.'

Her light darkened a shade. 'I know of the Shroud's existence, but Merlin kept a great many secrets from me, as I did from him. Why do you think it is here?'

'The last I saw of it was when your sorcerer took it to Camelot, a few days before I escaped this place,' I said. 'Presumably, he brought it back when he returned.'

She glided towards me through the mess, shutting the cupboard doors with soundless care. Halfway, she paused and said, 'Merlin never came back to this house. After his time at Camelot, I met him outside the city and took him directly to the cave.'

Such honesty was a surprise. 'The cave where you …?'

Her eyes glittered at me, green as spring. An open drawer slid home with a bang. 'Yes. The cave where I sealed him in and brought about his death.'

Instinctively, I wanted to ask her about it, my fascination with her world-altering feat separate from the enmity I felt. That she had dared tangle with Merlin after decades of living with him, learning from him and enduring his obsession with her, was still shocking. How long had she known she would do it? Was she planning his punishment as she sat teaching me how to dance with the elements? What did he do to finally push her too far?

But she would not tell me, and I would never ask. It was too intimate, requiring a level of closeness that we had briefly shared, but no longer. To her, I was treacherous and a mortal enemy to Arthur, whom she had served since his birth. To me, she had participated in Accolon's death at his and Arthur's fateful duel. Ninianne of the Lake had visited as much destruction on my life as she had on the sorcerer's, and I was still alive to remember it.

'Then how did Merlin know I had escaped here?' I persisted. 'Why was he outside my valley, waiting to capture me back?'

She spread her hands in a gesture of obviousness. 'He was a seer, Morgan. One of the very best. Merlin had his ways of knowing things.'

It had the ring of veracity. 'In that case,' I replied, 'you were the last person to see Merlin alive. That can only mean *you* have the Shroud.'

She recoiled. 'It means nothing of the kind.'

I didn't read her as lying, though the air between us vibrated with unease. She always said I shouldn't trust her.

'Why would I believe you? Doing so has only ever caused me misery and loss.'

She stiffened, glancing briefly at the window behind me. 'If that is what you think, Morgan, then so be it. Only one of us in this room turned traitor on her own brother and tried to bring down the entire kingdom.'

'Do not say that, as if it's simply true,' I snapped. '*I* am the one who has been betrayed, in the worst possible ways.'

I heard the heat in my voice and drew a deep breath. She would not have the satisfaction of my lost composure.

'Why *are* you here, anyway?' I asked. 'Quite the coincidence that we meet in this house at the exact same time, no?'

'I certainly did not plan it. I am here on another matter.' She paused, considering me. 'Then again, fairy connections work in curious ways. Perhaps there is something in our being drawn together, on this particular day.'

Her casual reference to Accolon's fateful anniversary flashed fire up my spine, but again I would not let her goad me. She did not know me as she once had; years of love and contentment had mellowed my flame, and though loss had once more made jagged my edges, it had also made me cautious, watchful. Wiser.

'We have no connection,' I said. 'This is nothing but an attempt at distraction, as always. What is it you are hiding this time?'

I looked about the ruined room, to the window where she had glanced moments before. The gold-bound book gleamed back at me from the lectern.

'You're here for Merlin's Book of Prophecies,' I said. 'Or rather – Arthur's.'

The quiver of her light was confirmation enough.

'I see how things are,' I continued. 'Arthur has not asked for your advice, your magic, or even your presence. You haven't been called to fill the absence by his side.'

'It would not have been possible,' she replied. 'I have been busy these past few years, away from Britain. Until recently, I have not had time to often be in the court.'

I shook my head. 'If Arthur felt inclined, he would have summoned you regardless, and you would have gone,' I said. 'But Merlin's death stands in the way – he cannot forgive such an act. However, if you have his Book of Prophecies, his sorcerer's precious words, he might let you do his bidding.'

Her blaze surged, growing so incandescent I had to squint away. Accusing Ninianne of not being mistress of her own destiny had always landed like a scorpion sting.

'To be by King Arthur's side is a gift, not a right,' she replied in a terse voice. 'My actions with Merlin may have caused him grief, but I have always been loyal and was there when it mattered. I saved him from Sir Accolon's sword and your treason.'

This time, she succeeded in lighting the fire in my belly, but I still could not let her win. Instead, I paced back and forth before the lectern, trying to douse my temper with calm.

'I could have killed him, you know,' I said. 'Arthur – at the abbey. He was asleep when I got there. I could have destroyed him a hundred times.'

'I know,' Ninianne replied. 'He told me.'

'I'll bet he did,' I said scornfully. 'Endless verses on his suffering and outrage. Though I showed mercy where he – and you – had none.'

'You *betrayed* him, Morgan. It broke your brother's heart. And not just his. I ...'

She faltered, and it was so sudden, so full of emotion, that I stopped to stare at her.

'After everything you and I shared,' she continued, 'I believed our faith in the High King bonded us, that we cared for the same things and even ... each other. I thought we had an understanding.'

A laugh tore out of me, harsh as a blue jay's call. 'An understanding?' I cried. 'The man I love is dead because of you!'

By God, she had broken me, and so easily. Just my being forced to invoke Accolon's death was enough. I pointed a trembling finger at her.

'You knew I loved him,' I said. 'From the first moment we spoke on Tintagel's headland you *knew* what Accolon and I felt for one another. Your indifference to my feelings didn't even begin with his death. You saw a so-called deal I struck with Merlin in a handful of runestones and took our child away. You *never* cared for me.'

'That's not true,' she protested. 'If I had known—'

'How did you help Arthur?' I cut in. 'The day Accolon died. What did you do?'

Ninianne stepped back, smoothing over her demeanour. Her silence said I did not deserve any answer, but I was far beyond her authority. I flipped open the Book of Prophecies and steepled my fingers against the parchment, a lick of fire flaring in my palm.

'Do not test me,' I said. 'We both know I burn hot enough to turn these pages to ash. And I will.'

Before that moment, I could never have imagined burning a book, but this *thing*, full of Merlin's scrawled assumptions and obfuscations, could certainly prove the exception.

Ninianne made no move; she believed me. 'What do you want me to say, Morgan? Sir Accolon died because that was *how it had to be*.'

Her words bruised my heart, but I pressed my burning hand closer to the page. Good parchment would not catch too easily, but the star chart began to pucker under my heat.

'These pages will not withstand long,' I warned. 'Answer my question.'

Her eyes flicked to the book, then back to my face. 'The battle was ferocious,' she said. 'There were serious injuries on both sides. King Arthur was at risk of death, so ... I took the scabbard from Sir Accolon's belt.'

I closed my eyes against the implication, the nausea that followed. Excalibur's scabbard prevented bleeding and healed the wearer as he stood. When Ninianne snatched it from Accolon, the magical effect would have ended instantly. Everything Arthur had done to him, he would have suddenly felt.

The agony of it rushed through me, how excruciating it would have been, my healing instinct flaring in useless recognition. The thought was unbearable.

My hand fell away from the Book of Prophecies, flames guttering to nothing. In a way, I had known it, had understood the circumstances of the duel from the message Arthur had sent. But I had never let myself apply too much logic to something I couldn't think about without wanting to die myself.

'There was no choice,' Ninianne continued. 'The King was distraught – he insisted they both be taken to the abbey to be healed. Sir Accolon lay there for four days before King Arthur would accept nothing could be done.'

'Four days?' I clutched at the lectern, my body gone cold. 'Accolon was lying in the abbey all that time, when I could have healed him? You knew and didn't *send for me?*'

She paled at once. 'You don't understand ...'

'You *knew* I would have come for him, no matter the consequences awaiting me. I would have flown there on the wind.' My voice was wild, thick with rage and repressed tears. 'Whatever quarrel I had with my brother, Accolon was innocent of it all. You knew better than anyone I would have given my life to save his.'

Ninianne stepped forwards, reaching for my hands. 'Morgan, no ...'

'Don't touch me,' I spat.

With a flick of my wrists, I captured the air between my palms and pushed her sideways. Ninianne collided hard with the cupboards, and I felt the breath knocked from her lungs. She attempted to rise but was too winded to move or access her own magic. I grabbed the golden book and strode past her, skirts dragging through the destruction I had left.

'What are you doing?' she gasped. 'You have no interest in Merlin's prophecies.'

At the doorway, I stopped and looked back. 'No, but you do. If you want to ensure your place by Arthur's side and Merlin's version of the future, there is a tax. Bring me the Shroud of Tithonus, and I'll consider an exchange.'

'I told you – I don't know where the Shroud is.'

'In that case, I suggest you *find it*. You know where I am when you do.'

Before she could right herself, I swept down the small staircase and out of Merlin's study. I rushed through the house, suddenly desperate to be free of the sorcerer's lair, the oppressive walls that still held his essence.

When I reached the outside air, Phénix stood waiting, regarding my panting, trembling form with his usual placidity. I went to him, stowing the Book of Prophecies in the saddlebag, then gathered enough focus to weave a few charms of protection over the manuscript. The silver threads came out kinked and shirred, but they would serve.

Weariness washed through my limbs, so I rested my forehead against Phénix's chestnut neck, inhaling warm scents of hay and horse, not unlike how Accolon used to smell when he came in from the tiltyard, flushed and invigorated, calling for hot water so he could steep his body in a bath. I leaned harder against the horse's bright hide, lest I buckle to the ground. A year he had been gone from this world. How could that be?

'Morgan?'

I turned almost involuntarily. Ninianne stood by the door, regarding me with a quiet scrutiny that felt like sun in my bones. Through her searching gaze I saw myself – drawn face, dark hair escaping my rough braid, the defiant set of my jaw that I felt aching all the way up to my scalp.

She took a step forwards, bearing up her hands; a priestess of ancient days making an offering. 'Take this,' she said. 'Before I change my mind.'

On her palms sat a curved bowl, silver and smooth, thin as a crescent moon. 'I have its identical counterpart, enchanted by my own powers,' she explained. 'If you pour water into the bowl and ask it to seek me, we can speak via the elemental connection – even see one another, if the magic is strong enough.'

I didn't consider touching the bowl. 'Why would either of us want to do that?'

'Just in case. We do not know what the future holds, or how it will change us.'

I looked at her, trying to read the trick, and her beautiful face flickered, the waver in her fairy heart unfamiliar. Ninianne was uncertain in a way I had never known her to be.

However, I could not let myself be drawn. I retreated and put my foot in the stirrup, swinging up into the saddle.

'Keep your spying bowl. I have no need of it,' I said. 'I don't care what the future holds, and it will make no difference to me. Who I am now is who I will remain.'

I turned Phénix away and urged the horse towards the bridge.

'That can never be, Morgan,' Ninianne called, but her voice sounded close, as if she were murmuring into my ear. 'You are water – eternal but ever-changing. There is no final form.'

Her words washed through me with an oblique recognition, but I ignored it and rode on.

It wasn't until I reached Belle Garde the following morning that I saw the cool glint in my saddlebag and discovered Ninianne's silver bowl there, as if I had accepted it after all.

3

I stared at the bowl in disbelief.

Fresh daylight enhanced the silver's definitive lustre, conjuring images of the vessel filled with water. I wondered whether Ninianne and I could indeed communicate through our shared elemental connection, how such a thing might feel.

I brought the bowl closer, tilting my senses towards its power, and the bright metal caught the sun's reflection, searing across my vision. I recoiled, annoyed that Ninianne had managed to intrigue me yet again. Whatever this object was, I didn't want or need it.

'Morgan, you're back!' came a shout across the front green.

I looked up to see Alys hurrying out of the house with Tressa. I slipped the silver bowl into the deep pocket inside my cloak and went forth to meet them.

'*Cariad*, thank goodness.' Alys embraced me as if I had been gone for months. 'We were worried. Riding off like that, without telling anyone.'

'I left word,' I protested, though I knew a scribbled note nailed in Phénix's stall was not good communication.

'*Alys* was worried,' Tressa corrected. 'I tried to tell her that you knew what you were doing. How was the journey?'

I looked around to remind myself I indeed was back in Belle Garde, after so many hours spent in dense, ancient forest. The day was rising blue and warm, songbirds flitting over the treetops, the river trickling its late-summer music. I let myself exhale; I had gone to Merlin's lair and returned, and would never have to see it again.

'Tiring,' I replied. 'Long, even though it wasn't. Strange.'

I went to my horse's side and unbuckled my purloined cargo, slipping the Book of Prophecies from the saddlebag into the first sack. My women followed, arriving just as I concealed the golden covers.

'Did you get what you needed?' Alys asked.

'The Shroud of Tithonus wasn't there,' I said. 'Though Ninianne was.'

'No!' Tressa exclaimed. It distracted them both with a satisfying sense of drama, allowing me to move us away. I wasn't ready to explain my possession of the book that had practically run the kingdom since the day Merlin took my mother's only son from Tintagel.

'What did she say?' Alys asked.

Sir Accolon lay in the abbey for four days.

I cleared my throat. 'She insists she doesn't have the Shroud and claimed Merlin never returned to the house before she locked him away to rot. Of course, anything she says could be a lie.'

'She could be protecting someone else who is in possession,' Tressa suggested.

Such a thought had not occurred to me, but it was a strong possibility. If Merlin never returned after Camelot, he could have given the Shroud to Arthur. Ninianne would never tell me, if she knew.

'Then what of Sir Accolon,' Alys said. 'Does that mean you can't …?'

She trailed off, lips pursed and amber eyes shining. I had become used to that bittersweet expression over the past year – loyal, admiring of my supposed bravery, but sad, regretful there was no elixir to make me feel better. I couldn't tell her that she and Tressa did more than enough; that some days, their love and care was the only barrier between me and the bottom of a lake.

'It's all right,' I said. 'I'm going to start work anyway. I've resurrected birds and restored a mangled white hart with my own hands, so I …'

My voice faltered at the sight of a figure hesitating in the house doorway, his red curls tinted by morning. I dropped my sack and went to him.

'Robin,' I said, putting my arms around his wiry frame. 'How are you?'

'Glad to see you back, my lady,' he said. 'I wish you had let me ride with you.'

He was almost of age now, deep-voiced and taller than us, but since Accolon there had been a droop in his shoulders that nothing could lift.

'I was fine,' I reassured him. 'I needed you here to watch over the household.'

He nodded and drew away, regarding me with eyes bruised with fatigue. The past week had been hard on us all, but whereas I had taken the dubious relief of escape, he had been denied the same, and perhaps yearned for it just as much.

'I'll take the horse to the stables and see him rubbed down,' he said, gesturing to Phénix. I laid the reins across his hand, and he paced away, head bowed.

Alys and Tressa shared my view of the boy's stooped retreat.

'How has he been?' I asked. 'He seems just as despondent as the early days.'

'It was difficult for him to realise it had been a year,' Alys replied. 'People mend, go on with their lives, but his heart is still broken.'

'He's not the only one,' I said. I had not meant to say it aloud and waved the comment off before they could react. 'Will he be all right, do you think?'

'He's finding his way,' Tressa said. 'He spent the last few days building a – what do the household call it?'

'A *carnedd*,' Alys said quietly. 'A tower of stones in Sir Accolon's honour. Apparently, he's been collecting them all year. He finished building it yesterday.'

It struck a blow to my ribs; that Robin had been forced to build a monument to Accolon because I had not. I had given the household no grave, no tomb, no place they could visit to pay their respects, aside from a small shrine I had allowed in the northern valley's chapel, which I no longer attended. For them, I could not even stay to mark his passing, or explain why I was so unwilling to accept that my Gaul was forever gone.

No one but Alys and Tressa knew I possessed Accolon's heart, turned to marble and hidden in my study. Only they understood I could not lay him to rest up at our lake as I had first intended – as he had *wished* for – because of my wild determination that I was going to resurrect him body and soul. Belle Garde's household remained unfailingly loyal, but my inaction must have read as madness.

'Where is it?' I asked. 'The *carnedd*?'

Tressa nodded across the river, to the long meadow beyond.

'The tiltyard,' I said. 'Of course.'

The jousting field Accolon had built and ridden daily, one of his favourite places to spend time. Robin had chosen the perfect location for his tribute to the man he loved as a second father, his guardian and teacher who had offered the knightly future he had dreamed of, only for it to vanish within a strike of a High King's sword.

'He hasn't shown it to anyone,' Alys said. 'He wants you to see it first.'

The thought of walking over the bridge into a domain that was only ever Accolon's – where his hoofbeats and lance splinters, his prodigious skill and exhilaration were steeped into the very soil – brought a rush of dread. For Robin, I hoped I would be able to do anything, but my grief had proven a cruel, inconstant beast. Some days I rose in fire, furious with strength and defiance, and on others I awoke shattered to pieces, drowning in an abyss with no surface to breach. There were times I could barely withstand the joust meadow view from my turret balcony. So much of myself I could simply not predict any more.

I pulled air into my lungs to stop tears from forming. I had not cried in front of anyone since the day I brought the household news of Accolon's death, and I didn't intend to start. It was the least I could do – holding myself steady in public so they could heal a pain to which I couldn't lay hands.

'Morgan?' Alys said. 'Are you all right?'

I tore my eyes from the tilt field. 'I'm fine. I must get these manuscripts to the study. Will you call someone to carry up the sacks?'

'We'll help you,' Tressa said. 'I can find shelf space and put all this away.'

'No indeed,' I replied, forcing lightness into my voice. 'You are both busy. Besides, when have I ever permitted anyone else to shelve my books?'

They hesitated, but did not question me. Alys summoned two lads for the sacks and I left them, heading for the entrance hall and twisting turret staircase that led to my study.

Halfway up, I pushed open a door and entered the dim circular room where I now slept – or tried and failed. The windows were open, casting slim arches of sun across my undisturbed bed. Since Accolon, I had never returned to our long pale-blue bedchamber with its tall windows, secluded courtyard garden and huge carved bed, birds painted on the walls. I could not be there without him.

At length, I took off my travelling clothes and dressed in a clean gown, then retrieved Ninianne's bowl and returned to the spiral stairs. Sometimes, it felt as though my existence had narrowed until the turret contained my entire life, but on my frequent restless nights, it was a relief and a consolation to have my library only a few steps above.

My study looked as I had left it. Recently, Alys, Tressa and I had been sharing the worktable again, attempting to finish our manuscript on women's afflictions, begun long ago. My notes on types of headache were laid out alongside Alys's tincture recipes and Tressa's neatly scribed pages, open balcony door letting in scents of meadow grass and climbing firethorn. The normality of it loosened a knot in my chest.

I headed for my desk and examined Ninianne's bowl. At closer inspection, it was a vessel both light and weighty, thin and solid, surface frictionless as water. I tapped the base and it played a strange, sonorous note. A fairy object and no mistake.

I turned to the alcove behind my desk, cut deep into the stone wall. A pair of impressive tapestries hung over the shelves, woven with depictions of Hecate: one showing the witch goddess at a crossroads under moonlight, then brightly robed and busy at her potions amidst books, braziers and wild animals. Alys had made them as a gift a few years before, and I had enchanted her skilful work to guard my most precious possessions.

Pushing the tapestries aside, I stowed the bowl near the bottom, under where I kept the *Ars Physica* and the chess set Accolon had given me at Tintagel. The uppermost shelf bore only one object – a silver box, containing Accolon's heart in its cocoon of blue silk, turned to stone, waiting for me. I pressed my palm to the lid, savouring the sweet high music of his heartsong. He was still there.

I let the tapestries fall back into place and looked to the worktable. As instructed, the sacks from Merlin's had been left there, so I went across and opened the first one. A confident golden light shone back at me – the Book of Prophecies. I took out the manuscript and laid it on the table. The covers gleamed like the sun, its rubies bloody. I had no intention of reading it, but threw it open anyway.

Arthurus Rex.

The sight of my brother's name brought a feeling I couldn't quite parse, so I turned the page, revealing another gold-crown border and a distinct title.

The Death of Arthur it said, in thick black ink.

Unexpectedly, the Book of Prophecies began at the end. I flicked to the next few headings – Arthur's birth, the War of Eleven Kings, his drawing the sword from the stone. Rather than time, Merlin seemed to have placed his prophecies in order of importance. Where then was my so-called betrayal?

Looking for your own prophecy? I imagined the sorcerer saying in his waspish voice. *Admit it, dearest Morgan – you are more interested in my work than you claim.*

I slammed the manuscript shut again. There was no need to go further: I had heard what was said about me – by the stars and others – and it meant nothing. Picking up the volume, I took it to the alcove and shoved it to the back of the lowest shelf. If I could not see it, then I wouldn't be tempted to read it. Leverage was my only purpose for Arthur's golden book; it would stay in the shadows until Ninianne brought me the Shroud of Tithonus, or I found the miraculous object myself.

If it can be found, came the dark thought, followed by the question that Alys could not bear to ask. *Can you raise Accolon from death without it?*

On the road back, I had spent hours asking myself the same, and the answer had proved unchanging: no matter how remarkable my mind, how good my formulae, or how much of my blood I poured forth, without the resurrection power of the Shroud, raising a dead man whole from only his heart was impossible.

My insides gave an involuntary swoop, but I could not think of that now. I had told Alys and Tressa I would bring Accolon back, just as I had assured the household that everything would be all right again. Failure was not a choice I could make.

The room felt stifling, so I escaped out onto the balcony. From the balustrade, I saw Robin leading his horse across the bridge to the tilt field, for the two hours of morning practice he still kept up – the routine he and Accolon had shared. As he mounted and began his drills, I knew I would not go and see his *carnedd* that day.

Nor would I go the next day, or the one after that, or even when Alys gently pointed out it had been a week and I had not yet been.

Instead, I would do what I had done for the past nine months, to show the household my dedication to our future beyond devastation. I would attend the evening meals with a smile painted on my face, but never take my seat. I would drink an entire jug of wine until my vision blurred and I saw Accolon in the tail of my eye, talking and laughing with others, or sitting atop a table playing the lute, his musical voice ringing in my mind.

After that, fevered and wine-hazy, I would climb to my circular bedchamber and light the candles in a way that made it look as though there was more than one shadow upon the wall. I would lie down on my bed and let my senses conjure Accolon's weight on the mattress beside me, the phantom of his warmth along my body, even if indulging this meant I would turn over to find the terrible gulf where he no longer lay.

A few weeks later, when Alys and Tressa asked if the household could hold a feast in my Gaul's honour for his approaching September birthday, I would agree wholeheartedly to prove how in balance I was. When they told me the revel's theme would centre upon Accolon's various passions, I would advise on his favourite foods, drinks, music and interests and not let my voice shake.

Every day, when my women asked how I was, I would say I was fine, I was well, and nothing more. I could not say that while time and the world moved on, all I did was notice the small, constant abysses created by his absence. I never spoke of the cavern his loss had hollowed inside of me, that only our love could fill.

I told no one that the emptiness he left was so great it had conquered the vast and quiet sky, and there had not been a storm in Belle Garde's valley since Accolon had died.

4

Nevertheless, I had not lied about starting work. It was all I could do.

As with any study, I proceeded in a methodical fashion. First, I drew together my notes from my year at Merlin's – the formulae I had kept hidden from him, and the knowledge I had later transcribed from memory. Next, I began reading, though it meant revisiting the sorcerer's lair in my mind; the memory of my younger self, wounded but still fighting, learning of resurrection as Merlin's obsessive presence loomed. My need for survival, and the guilt it still brought.

Still, I pushed on, making preparations for practical experiment. I asked the huntsman to bring me any perished birds he came across, or hunted and deemed unsuitable for the kitchens. Upon receiving his initial delivery, I felt my spirit rise for the first time in over a year. Here, I knew what I was doing.

I took a hawk-struck wood pigeon with a definitive heartsong and followed my old ways with precision – the same preparations, incantation and drops of blood from my own finger that had brought me past success. But my formula failed to make the bird's nerves twitch, much less return it to life. Next, I picked up a song thrush, a smaller creature with no injuries to speak of. Again, it remained a corpse.

It got no better from there. Bird after bird, I tried to no avail. I tested my methods, tweaked the formula, read my notes again and made additions and amendments, then struck through them when they failed to change anything. I turned to the manuscripts I had retrieved from Merlin's, but the sight of his script only conjured his droning voice in my head.

Look at what you've become, my Morgan of Wonders, he jeered. *A marvel no more, without her teacher.*

The harder I pushed, the louder his voice became and the more pervasive his criticism, a sneering Greek chorus to my inability. One day, I put a goldfinch in a wooden box with feathers and sage, an exact recreation of one of my earliest triumphs, and held the vessel to my chest as I chanted. The lid never rattled. Upon my seventh failed attempt, I threw the box into the fire with a crash.

Watching your failures burn now? mocked the sorcerer. *Face the truth —resurrection has slipped from your grasp. There are no more miracles in you.*

'For the love of God, be *quiet!*' I cried, then realised what I'd done. I had spoken aloud to this entity long dead, my errors recreating Merlin inside my mind in a way so real, it was as if he had sprung to life again. The thought snatched my breath away.

Clutching my chest, I staggered out onto the balcony. It was not the first time I had been overwhelmed by this scorching panic, pinned by the grief that left me breathless, but I had learned to manage myself – to find my way outside, seek cool air. This time, it wasn't enough. My legs buckled and I crumpled onto the stones, dizzy and gasping.

A small weight thudded against my chest, and I looked down to see Accolon's Gaulish coin on its chain, winking in the sunlight. Gripping the gold disc in my palm, I let its tangible presence anchor my senses: to the warm stones underneath my body; the sweet scents of late summer and the blue of a morning sky; the music of water from the river, in the air, in my veins.

My breaths steadied, the heat of panic fading from my blood. 'It's all right,' I told myself, squeezing the coin harder. 'I'm here. Still here.'

I rose and steadied myself against the balustrade. Below, the household was going about its day, its routines comforting and unfailing, bringing clarity to my whirring mind. Belle Garde was healing, and for everyone's sake, I could not risk my weaknesses becoming known. My only choice was to find a new way, accept my work was flawed and stop with the madness of dead birds. More than that, I had to show the world that all was well.

My eyes drifted across the river, and found a familiar sight. Whether I was strong enough or not, it was time.

It was strange to see the joust meadow up close. As I reached the river, I tried not to look at the painted boundary, the quintain, the large black horse waiting patiently by the lance stand, as if Accolon would be along any moment to run drills.

Robin stood before the *carnedd* as he did every day, his brief vigil that put my coward's heart to shame. I forced one foot in front of the other until I stood beside him.

'Lady Morgan,' he said formally. 'I'm glad you've come.'

'I would have been sooner,' I said. 'But I've been so busy, it's—' I cut myself off, shaking my head. 'There's no excuse, Robin. I could have come, and I'm sorry.'

'It's all right,' he replied. 'I understand.'

'You shouldn't have to understand. I should be stronger, better, for you.'

I sounded more fretful than comforting, but he let me put my arm around him, and we looked at the *carnedd* together. The sight of the flat grey stones, balanced expertly, rising from the land, was soothing in a way I didn't expect; the certainty that this monument would still be here, long after all of us were gone.

'It's beautiful,' I said. 'The perfect tribute and place. You should be proud.'

Robin shrugged. 'I'm not sure what it means any more. When I was seeking the right stones, I felt there was a purpose. But now … it's just a pile of pebbles.'

'It's not the stones,' I said, 'but the will in your heart to remember Accolon and how he made you feel. It is the greatest honour you could give him.'

Again came the guilt that I had not offered Robin any touchstone of rest-in-peace. What right did I have to tell him how he should feel, when I could barely govern myself?

I dropped my arm from him so he would not feel me shudder. 'I see you every day, practising the joust,' I managed. 'I'm glad.'

'Sir Accolon always said daily tilt practice was the reason he was so good,' he said. 'That is why I come. And to honour him, of course.'

'Is jousting still what you wish to do? Competitions, travelling abroad as he did?'

He regarded me with a childlike anguish. 'I cannot think of it. Belle Garde needs me. *You* need me, Lady Morgan – you said so.'

'I know, Robin. And I do,' I said, but it was not enough to stop his tears, already rolling down his freckled cheeks. Bravely, he did not look away.

'I'm afraid,' he said. 'I'm terrified that if I think too much on other things, or stray too far from here, I will forget him.'

I put my arms about him again, containing our rising grief. 'It's all right,' I soothed him. 'We will never forget – we cannot. You and I can stay here in Belle Garde, within our memories, forever.'

He nodded and looked consoled, which brought me relief even as I knew I had been selfish. I could not tell him that he could move beyond his sorrow, that there was an entire world open to him outside of Belle Garde that he should explore. I did not know how.

I released him from our embrace and gestured to his horse. 'Sir Accolon would say I should not be taking up your practise time,' I said. 'The tilt field awaits.'

We shared a sad smile, then I left him alone, making my way back across the bridge. As I re-entered the house, I spotted Alys in the dining hall with Sir Ceredig: lists in hand, counting plate, checking on the bolts of Parisian blue fabric piled on the tables for Accolon's banquet.

She caught my observation and raised a tentative hand, her face hopeful, as if I might suddenly walk in and be able to participate. I lingered for a heartbeat, then did the only thing I could – climbed the many steps to my study, with its piles of dead-end notes and voices of my past, the trap of failure I could not escape.

More than a year since Accolon's death, weeks since I had been to Merlin's, and I had achieved nothing. Staggering to my desk, I pressed my fists against the wood and shut my eyes until lights flashed in their darkness.

A patter of water broke through my mood, becoming insistent, along with the noisy complaints of several magpies, flapping about the balcony doorway. I looked up as a sudden rain splashed across darkened windows, the pleasant light from moments ago replaced by a miserable pall of grey.

'It's only rain,' I scolded the magpies. 'We see enough of it.'

They ignored me, amidst anxious caws and batting wings. Exasperated, I went to shoo them, when I caught sight of the lidded basket the huntsman used to bring me perished birds, over on the worktable. Now I had decided to give up, I wanted none of it, but a sparkling trill reached my senses: a definitive heartsong, surprisingly clear at such a distance.

As ever, my curiosity defeated my reluctance. I strode over to the basket, lifted the lid, and peered inside. Only one bird lay there – a large magpie, immediately recognisable. She was one of the original females when I had first come to the valley, now the leader of the descendent flock. She was glossy and whole, resplendent in new feathers, but quite dead.

Her condition seemed perfect, not a mark of violence or illness apparent, but when I took her into my hands her black head lolled. Somehow, she had broken her neck.

I stared hopelessly at her. Outside, the calls of her flock grew in intensity, as if the other magpies knew she was near. It made sense now, why they cried and raged: their matriarch was dead, and there was no good reason why. She did everything for the flock – led them, raised her own broods with her mate, cared for others and defended their territory with skill and vigour. If they did not have her, what might befall those left behind?

Panic burned through me, the healing in my blood igniting like fire. My hands sought damage, and I felt her neckbones knit back together before I could stop it. Repairing bones in a bird hours dead was futile, but her heartsong soared at the golden force. Visions flashed through my mind: of the beech tree's boughs; Belle Garde's landscape from on high; even of me, back and forth on the balcony – traces of a life scored deep beneath her feathers.

In answer, a flock of magpies flew in, generation upon generation, and landed on the worktable, the rafters, my bookshelves, tilting inquisitive blue-black heads at me. Their message was clear – it was not her time, did not have to be, if I could just make myself mistress of the skill I thought I possessed.

'You don't understand,' I told them. 'I can't.'

As I stood in denial, another magpie flew in through the balcony door – the matriarch's mate and companion, whom she had chosen and paired with for life. As usual, he landed upon one of the carved peregrine falcons on my chair back, the opposite side bare in comparison. She had always perched there, beside him.

'All right,' I relented. 'I'll try.'

I grasped for my father's knife, pushing my thumb against its edge. I felt a quick hot pain and pressed the cut against the magpie's breast before any blood could escape, then closed my eyes, taking up the formula's chant. My rational mind wondered why I was even trying, but I could not stop intoning, hope building, unbearable in my chest.

Pressure expanded within my veins, bracing against my skin until I thought I could take no more. In the same instant, a force broke free of my body with a scream. I opened my eyes to see the magpie bursting out of my hands and up into the turret, alive and victorious.

'By the goddess,' I whispered. 'She lives.'

The matriarch circled the study twice on effortless wings, then alighted on my open hands. On her alabaster breast, where the red stain of my blood should have been, was a coin-sized circle of gold. It glowed slightly, as if with the force of new life. What was causing it, I did not know, but just then it didn't seem to matter. I had succeeded at last.

Before I could study her closer, the magpie flew off, landing beside her mate on the back of my chair. They hopped to one another, chattering joyously, as the flock took up calling, a cacophony of celebration from the worktable, the mantelpiece, the gallery banisters. If anyone came up to the turret now, they would assume I had lost my mind.

'I've done what you came for,' I called above the noise. 'You can all leave.'

My order was in jest, but, to my astonishment, the birds spread their wings in unison and took flight, streaming out of the balcony door. Within moments, the room was empty, aside from the resurrected magpie, watching them go.

The shock sat me down in my chair. 'What on earth was that?' I said to myself.

The matriarch flew down to my desk and hopped across my scattered papers, the gold mark on her chest still glowing.

You told them to go, she seemed to say. *And they went.*

I stared at her. 'Did you just …?' I said, then shook my head. 'No, of course not.'

She met my scrutiny with a beady eye. *Call them back*, rippled through my mind.

'This is not happening.' I rubbed my forehead; I was tired, overworked, maybe even mad – perhaps all three at once. 'I don't need any more voices in my head.'

The magpie gave me a long, significant look that did nothing to alleviate the idea she was communicating with me. Inevitably, I could not resist the challenge; in the same way I requested the elements to answer my call, I silently summoned the departed flock.

In an instant, a barrage of dark and light filled the study, as every inhabitant of the beech tree streamed inside again in a flurry of caws, scattering parchment and feathers all over the room, immediately overwhelming.

Enough! my mind ordered. *Leave again.* The birds circled the turret and flew back out of the balcony door. I looked at the matriarch on my desk.

Now do you see? she said. *Then watch.*

Spreading her night-coloured wings, she took flight and followed the rest. The beech tree hove into view in my mind as the bird spied her home again, welcoming the joyous calls of the others. I could see and hear exactly as she could.

Later, I would discover there was much more to this wonder. Through the magpie matriarch, I could understand the mood of her flock and attune my ear to their tidings. I could close my eyes and let her take my mind to fly all over the valley, feel the skim of wind and taste the pure cold air on my tongue. From on high, we could espy the animals and people on the land and roads, living their lives below our collective wings.

Now, as she flew back to my desk, I was far from understanding. No other bird I had raised from death offered me access to its senses, though this had clearly not been an ordinary resurrection.

'But why?' I asked, a hundred questions in one.

For my life, the magpie replied. *We are yours to command.*

5

Despite my success with the magpie matriarch and our incredible connection, I soon realised that whatever I had done to bring her back to life could not be quantified, because I could not make it happen again.

I tried, of course; I had more birds brought, performed the same ritual down to where I was standing and sometimes the same weather conditions, but every attempt failed exactly as before. Feathered corpses were consigned to the fire, and I returned to the torture of an impasse I had sworn to give up, no closer to why resurrection had succeeded for a brief, transcendent moment before disappearing again.

By the time the leaves began to turn, I had spent every day held for ransom at my desk. However, relief arrived one red-gold afternoon, in the shape of Robin dashing up the stairs to my study, his face brighter than it had been in a long time.

'Sir Manassen of Gaul is here,' he announced. 'Come from the Royal Court.'

I rose gratefully from my chair. 'Good. Send him up.'

He left, and I noted his bouncing step with a wash of sadness. He was pleased for our guest's presence because of his proximity to Accolon, yet Sir Manassen too would have to go again, leaving more wounds I did not know how to heal.

I sighed and stepped out from behind my messy desk, as Sir Manassen's tall, lean figure appeared in the doorway. He paused, regarding me uncertainly with his grey-brown eyes, then strode over and dropped to one knee, head bowed. I had to stifle a laugh.

'Get up,' I said lightly. 'I've told you, formalities are quite unnecessary.'

He obeyed and allowed himself a reserved smile. 'Lady Morgan, well met. It is good to be back in Belle Garde.'

'I'm pleased you are here,' I said, and he looked briefly surprised, as if he had forgotten we were no longer at odds.

Before Accolon's death, our rare meetings had mainly involved bickering and dislike, but when we had last seen one another, Sir Manassen had officially sworn himself to me in secret alliance, and was on his way to Camelot's Easter court with my letter of vengeance. Those few months ago, I believed I had come through the darkest hours of my grief, before learning just how wrong I could be. I wondered if time had been the fabled healer for him, or if he too had found his sorrow resurging in sudden, unexpected ways.

'I hope you are well?' he asked.

'In body, yes. In mind, I cannot say with any surety.' My candour immediately seemed too much, but I persisted. 'And you, Sir Manassen?'

'I endure, my lady. This past year has been a confusion of feelings, most of which I never wished to experience. Thankfully, I am otherwise in good health.'

He did look it, in a certain way – he was always neat and in decent fettle by his own standards, but his riding garb was notably fine, boots polished conker-bright, his ash-brown hair and beard sharply trimmed, as if he had been barbered daily. All unspoken requirements, I knew, of attending the Royal Court.

'Some wine?' I offered, gesturing to a jug recently brought. We would need it, I felt, to speak of everything to come.

'No, thank you,' he replied. 'I never partake so soon after a long ride.'

I had forgotten about his strict habits, his carefulness. He was so unlike Accolon it often seemed impossible they were close cousins, and I could never imagine how they spent so many years travelling together as knights errant.

'You will stay to dine, though,' I countered. 'I insist you accept *some* hospitality.'

He smiled in defeat. 'It would be my honour,' he said, and the courteous tension between us dissipated.

I poured myself a goblet of Tressa's apple wine and took a sip. 'You needn't have come to me directly,' I said. 'Your wife must be eager to have you home.'

'Not so, Lady Morgan. My dear wife is visiting her mother some miles up-country and will not return for a fortnight. But I would have come to Belle Garde first in any case. It is my duty to bring you tidings from Camelot.'

I said nothing and drained my goblet. 'Are you not prepared to hear it?' he asked.

'I must listen regardless,' I said. 'Though I've questioned whether I was right to involve you at all.'

Sir Manassen shook his head. 'To kneel to you was my choice. You ask nothing of me that I am unwilling to do.'

I put my cup down and paced back towards my desk, casting my eyes across the chaos of strewn pages and quills I had left there. 'What news, then?'

'The first thing you should know is that the High King has changed where he's holding his Michaelmas court,' he began. 'From Carduel in the north, to Caerleon. What's more, he will be stopping to hunt the forests of your eastwards lordly neighbour, whose manor borders part of yours. Very soon, King Arthur will be riding along your boundaries.'

Of course, Caerleon was one of Arthur's important courts and the closest royal palace to the valley, but my brother always gave my land a wide margin when travelling there. To my knowledge, there had never been fewer than three Welsh leagues between us.

'He has not come so close in years,' I said. 'Nor can he touch a blade of grass in Belle Garde.' I slammed a hand down my desk, rattling a row of ink bottles. 'Why in Lucifer's name would he do this?'

My loss of composure brought immediate regret. 'I apologise,' I said, turning back to Sir Manassen. 'How was his reception of you? Given your relation to Accolon.'

'Unexpected,' he replied. 'The King called for me in private and took pains to assure me my loyalty was not in question. Neither, he said, was Accolon's reputation marked with any treason.'

Again, my anger flared. 'How *dare* he even suggest such a thing.'

He nodded, lip curling as if the memory bore a bitter taste. 'Our exchange wasn't without questions, however. Given he now knows about you and Accolon, I had to confess I never saw my cousin during those years as I claimed, but was covertly seeking him. Which wasn't untrue. The King didn't mention you, only alluded to painful, complicated reasons for why things happened as they did, but said he would not detract from my deep loss. In that way, he seemed reluctant to excuse anything he had done.'

'If he is affecting regret, then that makes it worse.' I sighed, my vehemence dissolving with my breath. 'Not that it could be any worse.'

Sir Manassen hung his head, exhaling hard in agreement. Nothing that Arthur or anyone could say had the power to change the agony of our loss. The sheer emptiness and depth of our shared abyss just *was*.

I leaned back against my desk and he did the same, made weary by memory. At length, I asked, 'What then?'

'The King assured me his sentiments on my loyalty and courage would be shared by the court, and asked for my view on Accolon's memorial tomb.'

'He's building him *a tomb*? After everything—' I cut myself off, squeezing my eyes against a surge of tears until they receded. 'The Devil take him,' I concluded.

'Quite,' Sir Manassen replied. 'He said the tomb in St Stephen's cathedral will be lavish, a monument of great respect. I gave the plans a cursory nod, though Accolon's body should not even be there, he …' His voice caught, thick with more feeling than he had ever let slip in my presence. 'My cousin should be here, with you.'

Without thinking, I put my hand out and gripped his forearm. His eyebrows twitched up and I was certain I had gone too far in our brief time as allies, then his face relaxed into a sad smile that spoke of pure understanding. In this strange, tragic circumstance, we were eternally bonded.

'Arthur cannot erase what he's done with carved marble and a special Mass,' I said. 'The world may forget, but we won't.'

Unexpectedly, he reached up and put a firm hand over mine. 'No, we will not.'

We stayed that way for a long moment, then broke contact, surprised at ourselves but fortified. Suddenly, I couldn't bear to delay knowledge any longer.

'My message,' I said. 'Did you deliver it?'

Manassen nodded. 'I read your letter aloud as written, before the entire court. When I finished, the High King asked for the parchment and studied it for a long time.'

I could see it clearly: Arthur in Camelot's Throne Room, absorbing the fiery force of my words, as I had heard his cold voice through the herald sent to declare Accolon's death. I had lain awake imagining my brother's reaction, the shock and fear I wanted to evoke. Though he must have known I was alive after he saw me turned to stone, I still hoped it shook him to hear Morgan le Fay speak.

'What did he say?' I asked.

'Not a word. Then the Queen asked for the letter and he gave it to her to read.'

My hackles rose at the mention of Guinevere, invading the moment. 'And?'

Sir Manassen regarded me directly, his stillness pronounced. 'She ... laughed.'

It was as if I had not heard it. 'She *what?*'

'When she finished reading, the Queen laughed, as if someone had said something humorous,' he replied. 'She said "My lord, what do we have to fear from this letter? It is lies, the ravings of a desperate, traitorous woman. Queen Morgan of Gore is nothing to Camelot."'

My throat felt hard and hot. 'What did my brother do?'

'The High King considered her, then swiftly stood, declaring it was right for his lady wife to laugh, to show that Camelot will not fear anything, even in the wake of betrayal and corruption. But he looked solemn as the grave. He took back the letter, thanked me, and swept out of the hall. The Queen was shocked but recovered herself, made some jesting comment, and laughed again.' He shook his head grimly. 'The court followed, of course.'

I stared at him but did not see. I was far from the comfort of Belle Garde, standing instead in the midst of the Throne Room, Arthur and Guinevere leading the mirth against my fury and devastation, the court's howls of laughter circling me until I was dizzy with it. My suffering, reduced to the final line in a favourite joke.

Humiliation hollowed my gut, the familiar heat of panic running over my skin. Brushing past him, I charged out to the balcony, forcing my blurring eyes to focus on the view: the front green and meadows beyond; the rows of trees and burnished leaves still clinging to their branches. The river's reassuring rustle guided my breaths until my heartbeat had slowed to a pace that felt less like dying.

I didn't know how long I had been standing there when I felt Sir Manassen's presence at my side. 'I'm sorry, Lady Morgan,' he said.

I shook my head. 'It's not your fault. In hindsight, I'm not sure what I was expecting. What could ever make up for all that's been done?'

His gaze followed mine across the treetops, and we were silent for a long time.

'Autumn,' he said at length, and with that singular word I knew he and I shared one thought. It was mid-September, nearing Accolon's birthday, and we both felt the time of year like a knife edge grazing our skin.

'Autumn,' I agreed. 'The household are planning a feast, to honour him.'

'He would be pleased. My cousin always did enjoy a revel – laughter, music, easy cheer. I never mastered that festival spirit of his, though he often tried to bring it forth in me. How will such a thing feel, for you?'

I shrugged. 'I want it for them – for him. We should always try to celebrate Accolon and what he did here, how he made this place a home for us all. If we are to live in any particular way, then it should be his.'

I wanted to ask Manassen to be there for it, he whose grief resembled mine the most, but I couldn't find the words. We still did not know one another enough.

'What will you do in your time away from the court?' I asked.

'I'll be travelling to Gaul, to check on some private interests,' he replied. 'My own, and … well, your Gaulish estate. Accolon's manor, his lands, everything he earned from jousting or in battle. Unless you wish to use some other agent.'

'My estate?' I frowned in confusion. 'We weren't married. Accolon never had the chance to take me to Gaul. I have no claim over anything of his.'

He regarded me askance. 'Lady Morgan, no matter what words were said in whose church, your life with my cousin was nothing less than a marriage. Anyone who observed you together could see that.'

It was strangely moving, coming from him, a gesture of belief in Accolon and me that I was never sure he truly felt. I smiled, but he averted his eyes.

'I know you think I drove him away from here,' he said. 'But Accolon was a man of wits, of survival. He wouldn't have gone to Camelot, wouldn't have left you, if he didn't believe that it would be a straightforward forty days' service, to affirm my place in the court. He was honourable, driven by his passions, but not a strategic fool. Nor would I have let him go if I thought he was in any danger.'

'I know,' I said. 'He told me you only ever wanted to protect him. I believe it.'

Sir Manassen gave a stiff nod, as if gathering himself against some errant emotion. 'That means a great deal. I cannot express how much.'

He turned and looked at the joust meadow. It was occupied – Robin and his destrier, preparing for his daily drills. Quintain raised, he mounted up and cantered his horse in a loop, warming its paces for the charges ahead. My heart ached at the boy's aloneness, even as his dedication made me proud.

'The day before I left here,' Manassen said, 'Accolon and I were on that tilt field, taking a rest after running trick charges, games we had played as younger men. It was such a fine day. I remember thinking I had never seen the sky so blue.'

The memory of our Midsummers ached. 'They were all fine days.'

'I was questioning him,' he continued. 'How his interests were being managed, how his life here worked. A curse on my head for always focusing on life's practicalities. Now, all I can think of is a thousand more interesting things we could have spoken about.'

His eyes closed, and when he opened them again they were misted. 'It was then Accolon told me – his life was yours, everything he possessed, and if I had any concerns, he would write an official testament that day. It served me right, in a way.'

'I'm surprised you didn't try to talk him out of it,' I said.

'Oh I did, my lady. I tried my hardest to make him see sense. I said "Give her everything? She broke your heart" – as if he had somehow forgotten his own past. I can hear my tone now – so self-righteous, so *certain*. Accolon just laughed and said "Yes, *cousin*, she did. And I broke hers in return. Then she gathered up our pieces and let me put us back together again. Morgan *is* everything."' He smiled with remembered affection. 'It struck the preaching from my tongue. He could always outfox me with his candour – his heart.'

In the meadow, Robin ran his first charge, striking the quintain with a deep thud. The sound carried on the wind, hitting my chest as though the lance had buried itself there. We watched the boy run another charge, then another, the silence between us fathomless, as if Manassen and I had fallen into the same great crevasse.

'Stay here awhile,' I said. 'Do not go back to an empty house.'

He regarded me with glassy eyes. 'Why?'

'Because I do not want for your loneliness,' I said. 'I know how it feels. Sometimes, appearing whole before others is the only thing that keeps us drawing breath.'

He ducked his head, resting his fists against the balcony. I felt the stone grazing his knuckles as if it were my own skin. 'Thank you, Lady Morgan. I think I will.'

He looked again at the view, tracking the path of Robin's destrier, observing the boy's seat, his form, the way he lifted his lance. With a deft tilt, Robin aimed for the mannequin's head – a risky, clever strike, Accolon's audacious showpiece. As the lance connected, I watched Sir Manassen's brow rise in admiration and pain.

On the field, Robin eased his horse to a halt and turned to see what he had done, the absence of praise or advice echoing through his pause. All he could do was couch his lance against the saddle again and set off for another charge. Sir Manassen leaned forwards, anticipating the boy's next attempt.

I put my hand on his arm and it didn't feel strange this time. 'Go,' I said. 'Joust with him, give him your advice, tell him all the stories of Accolon that I cannot.'

He looked surprised. 'Will he want me to?'

'Of course he will. It's all he wants.'

He gave the meadow one more look, then turned to me with a melancholy smile. 'I would be honoured. With your leave.'

I nodded and followed him back inside, watching him retreat down the turret stairs. His footsteps faded, a tattoo of boots on stone recalling one short, unwanted phrase.

They laughed, it said; *they laughed, they laughed, they laughed.*

That night, when I finally fell asleep as the witching hour touched the dawn, I dreamed of a violent sea.

6

Sir Manassen's presence settled upon the household like a soothing tune. In the two weeks before Accolon's celebration, he amused at mealtimes with tales of our Gaul's early jousting career, offered himself up for practical help regarding the feast, and rode out with the huntsman and his lads, bringing his knightly skills to the chase.

Most of all, he continued to spend time with Robin, running the tilt field and practising sword drills, or taking him on long, refreshing rides. Robin began to stand tall again, the verve back in his loping gait.

Sir Manassen and I too found we had more to speak on, and engaged often in companionable discussion on the balcony or walks along the river, keeping me from the obsession of my failures. With him, I ceased to be haunted by Camelot's laughter.

However, Arthur's hunting party was imminent, and I wasted no time in taking control. I rode Belle Garde's edges, casting more protective threads and weaving them closer, until they were tight-knit and strong as a mail hauberk. Three days later, the huntsman brought the first news of Camelot's knights spotted in the wood with horses, hounds and attendants, but by then, the fairy veil was enough to withstand any army.

There wasn't much of a shared boundary before the valley sides rose up and enclosed Belle Garde, yet the hunting party rode through that particular stretch of forest every day. There were no sightings of a High King among them, but the proximity of gold-spurred men felt pointed. In time, he too would come.

On the seventh morning, I awoke restless from yet more dreams of the raging sea against battered cliffs, wild blue waves alive in my blood as I climbed to my turret. A week was enough; I refused to withstand the suspense any longer.

Once the knights had done their usual noon parade along my borders, I stepped out onto the balcony and called the magpie matriarch from the beech tree. The golden mark on her breast was fading, but our connection had remained strong.

'I know he's there,' I told her. 'Find him.'

I had no way of knowing it would work, but she tilted her head as if she understood, then gave a summoning caw that brought another five magpies to her side.

The flock took off at once, soaring towards the east and curving down into the trees like a clutch of arrows. I closed my eyes and saw as the magpies did, my vision swooping between criss-crossed branches and falling leaves. Sounds came through their hearing – other birdsong interpreted, the rustle of potential predators, and, at a distance, what I sought: the steady rhythm of hoofbeats and the alien sound of male voices. I could not understand their words from within a bird's perspective, but felt the magpies' caution, their reluctance to fly too close. Men were hunters, and dangerous.

Soon enough, we spotted the party pacing through the trees, hooves of a vanquished deer just visible, tied to a pole. The magpies settled on a branch further back than I wanted but with good reason: the falcons on their saddlebows were unhooded, still alert.

Distance didn't matter – I saw him like a shaft of sun. A golden figure sitting impossibly upright upon a red bay horse, riding ahead.

King Arthur, set apart from all other men.

As quickly as I had seen him, his image slipped into a bolt of fiery sunlight, and flashing hawk wings set the magpies scrambling up through the trees. I pulled back from the connection and found myself on the balcony again, my body ringing with avian impulses.

Briefly, I wondered if I had seen Arthur at all, or if it was an illusion brought on by my overtaxed mind. Yet the air in the forest had felt like him, and I had sensed his keen instincts, sharp on the breeze. He was looking for me, as much as I was looking for him.

No matter, anyway; this victory was his. Wherever my brother truly was, he resided exactly where he had intended – in my head.

This could not stand. To do battle with mine and Arthur's entire history, I needed more weaponry. Charging back into my study, I went to the alcove, shoved back the Hecate tapestries and pulled out the gold-covered Book of Prophecies. Knowledge had always been my fortress, and now it must be my sword and shield.

It did not take long for me to find what I sought. In fourth place, bordered in gold crowns like the rest, was the prophecy that had secured the downfall of Morgan le Fay.

'Betrayal of the High King', the heading said. Then in the sorcerer's spidery script:

'The Crowned Lion of All Britain shall not fall to the dragon, unless deceived and made weak at the hands of the crowned serpent and the leopard, in great betrayal.'

I read it again, and again. I turned the page to see if the stars had yielded anything beyond these bare two lines, words vague and incoherent, but there was no context, no explanation – just the next prediction important to Arthur's alleged destiny. Nowhere did the stars spell out 'Morgan' or even 'sister'. There was nothing to identify me at all.

For this, I had been exiled from my brother's world. For this, the sorcerer had declared me corrupt and dangerous, causing Yvain to be sent permanently to his father in Gore. For this, Arthur had slain Accolon to punish me because he believed my possession of Excalibur's scabbard was a scheme to destroy his kingdom, rather than what it truly was: a mistake, a stubbornness, a disagreement between two fire-hearted siblings that went too far.

No wonder they had laughed at me in Camelot. I had accepted the destruction of my entire life over words on a page that could mean anything.

Furious, I slapped the pages back to *Arthurus Rex, Prophetiae* and read the rest.

Some events were clear and recognisable – the account of Arthur's birth, his receiving Excalibur, various battles and their outcomes – but woven around these threads of sense was a tapestry of confusion: lists of animals with no obvious counterparts, vague allusions to relationships, miracles, alliances and conflicts. Arthur was a lion, a dragon, a bear; his life's path certain until it would suddenly turn back on itself. Unnamed players shapeshifted as beasts, friends and foes until it was impossible to track any consistency at all.

Here was the shadowy language of prophecy in full force, its meaning decided by a sorcerer said to be sprung from the loins of a demon. None of this was worthy of the power it held over a High King and his entire realm.

For my sanity, I should have stopped reading but I could not, fury and disbelief growing with every word. Upon turning the last page, I went immediately back to the first to start all over again. Sunset passed into evening, then night into morning, as I read hungrily, heat building in my limbs until I was sure I would combust.

An errant gust danced over my skin, raising my head, and I saw the room was cast in a dim grey pall. Above me, the windows in the circular walls had darkened, though the day had not long dawned with clear blue skies. A sensation rippled through my muscles, tugging me out of my chair and onto the balcony. The breeze as I emerged was cool but restive, gaining in strength. Overhead, a thick, steely cloud had formed, scudding around the turret roof and into the beech tree, the air sharp and smelling of life and danger.

I looked up into the cloud's dark belly and an instant, full-bodied recognition jolted through my bones, alive with duelling forces: warmth and cold, water and wind, creation and destruction. Focusing my mind, I reached into the cloud's depths and felt the rain, ready to fall but holding back. Waiting.

The air too was heavy with anticipation, and I realised this was not the first time I had felt it. When I visited Robin's *carnedd*, the sky had been just as clear, but upon returning to my study, upset and frustrated, a cloud of the same iron grey had shadowed the land. Both then and now, my emotions had been heightened with no release, before rain had come.

In wonder, I understood; of the tumultuous skies, I had been the cause.

Tentatively, I raised my arms and took hold of the swirling elements. All of my failures faded behind the tension in my limbs, the rapture of power reverberating through my body. When I shifted my hands, so the cloud went. Another flourish brought down a brief shower of water, so easily it made me smile.

Toying with the weather now, like a common witch? Merlin's voice sneered in my mind, sudden and unwanted, as it had too often. *That isn't even a storm. It's a rain cloud at best.*

Anger surged in my blood, my oldest, most primal power. I thought of the Book of Prophecies on my desk, its lies seeping into the air, and captured the feeling in my chest, sending it through my muscles until my entire body vibrated with its force. Snatching up the air, I drove the heat of my fury up into the cold, pressure increasing as the cloud fought with its changing state. I held firm, exhorting the elements to fulfil their deadly potential.

Then, amongst the pillowy grey came a flash of white light, and a ferocious crashing growl. Lightning and thunder; one following the other as it should.

Wind at my fingertips, I sent the cloud eastwards, a flashing, growling shadow over the treetops. When it was a mile away, I eased the tempest to a halt and drew down the rain, feeling the water descend as a force from the core of my being. I imagined my righteous golden brother, wet and furious, he and his marauding knights chased from my borders, no longer the hunters, but the hunted.

'What say you now?' I screamed into the tumult.

No answer came but the roar of the wind and rain, the sorcerer's voice silenced in the wake of my creation. As my howl of defiance echoed across the valley, with it went my failures, leaving me cleansed. Unleashed.

There had not been a storm in Belle Garde's valley since Accolon had died, but somehow, I had made one.

7

By the time Accolon's birthday came, I had spent most of my free time exploring my newfound skills, testing my link with the magpies, and delving deeper into storm-making.

As with any elemental magic, I had to learn the weather's natural music, the chords and harmonies required to sculpt air and water into vessels of concentrated power. To converse with nature this way soothed me as it had once done with Ninianne, success as exhilarating as it had ever been. When I was constructing clouds, experimenting with their form and how far I could push my creations, I was myself again.

In other arenas, I could not claim such strength. At sunset, the start of Accolon's revel found me in the doorway to Belle Garde's dining hall, unable to put one foot over the threshold. Almost everyone was already inside the room, which had been tastefully draped in his blue and silver jousting colours. Strains of his favourite songs drifted in from the minstrel stage outside, his preferred drinks from Tressa's cider house poured freely. All I had to do was walk in and join the celebration. It was that simple, and that difficult.

'Good evening, Lady Morgan.'

In my paralysis, I had not noticed Sir Manassen's approach. He smiled in his spare, serious way and offered up his arm. 'Allow me to escort you to your seat.'

His artful formality loosened my limbs enough for me to take his elbow and let him guide us to the table. When he pulled out my chair, it made me want to laugh.

'Sir Manassen, I may never have the measure of you,' I said. 'Thank you.'

He looked amused. 'It is my pleasure. Now, if my lady will point me to where I should sit.'

I gestured to the chair beside mine. 'Your place is here. At my right hand.'

'I am honoured,' he said quietly, and I knew he was moved.

As we sat, I glanced to my left – at Accolon's seat, starkly empty. I had forgotten that on feast occasions they always laid him a place, and the sight of his plate, his knife, his empty goblet, was a cold wave I hadn't prepared for.

My breath caught, the room and its familiar faces tilting into a spin. I reached for the gold coin around my neck, but it was not enough this time, inadequate against the sheer force of loss conjured by this day. I gripped the coin harder; I could not do this here, amidst a heartfelt tribute to the man we had known and loved. The last thing I wanted was to let grief tear apart what was healing. Leaving was my only choice.

I made to push up from my seat when a tentative touch on my forearm halted me. I glanced down and met Sir Manassen's steady, understanding gaze.

'We should drink to him,' he said.

He too had seen the empty place setting, and felt what I felt. With him, I was not alone in this, his grief not a feeling I felt duty bound to fix. I found myself retaking my seat.

'We should,' I agreed.

He reached for a wine jug, pouring for us both. 'To Accolon,' he said, raising his goblet. 'Would that you were here to drink with us, cousin.'

'To Accolon,' I said, letting my voice tremble. 'We love you, and we miss you.'

Our goblets touched with a conclusive clink. It was the first time I had raised a cup to Accolon's loss, but Manassen had made it feel necessary, strength-giving.

At length, I said, 'I'm glad you're here.'

'So am I,' he replied. 'I appreciate you letting me overstay my welcome.'

'You could never do so,' I replied. 'Belle Garde is for you as much as any of us. You are always welcome.'

'Thank you, my lady.' He lifted his cup again with a shy smile. 'In that vein, I regret to say I will have to leave soon. My wife is returning shortly, and I must meet her there in preparation for our journey to Gaul. Yet I carry some hesitation.'

'You mean with my brother stalking my borders like a territorial lion?' I said. 'Do not worry – I can handle Arthur. But such things are not for tonight, of all nights. Just know I am sorry to see you go. We all are.'

'That means a great deal,' he said. 'I cannot express how grateful I am for this past fortnight. Not just for this celebration, but the peace, the understanding – for coming to know you better, Lady Morgan. To spend time with Robin, to see how Accolon's skills, his ways, live on … I did not know I needed such a thing, but I did.'

'Robin needed it too,' I replied. 'Watching the two of you gave me hope. You helped him heal, more than I ever could.'

Sir Manassen's shoulders dropped and he looked away, as if the praise was too much to bear. 'It was my privilege, but he did the same for me. It's been so long since I've enjoyed knightly life, or felt truly useful.'

I looked at his face, stern but calm, and could finally read him. He was sad to be going, but his true remembrance of Accolon was on the road, years of laughter and adventure that would sit beside him as he traversed Gaul. At least out there, he could keep moving.

I drew in a breath. 'I have something to ask, Sir Manassen. It is no small request.'

He turned back to me in interest. 'Name it.'

'Take Robin to Gaul with you,' I said. 'When he's ready, knight him on Accolon's behalf.'

His eyes widened; he had not expected it, though to me it seemed the obvious – nay, *essential* – move. Just as quickly, his demeanour softened.

'He is skilled, brave and good,' he said. 'He will be an excellent knight.'

'With your guidance, yes. I will provide everything he needs – horses, arms, clothing, means to live on. The rest – how to be a knight in heart and mind – I cannot give him, whereas you can. Show him the way, hold him steady, instil in him the self-belief to become the person he has always wanted to be. A man like Accolon.'

Sir Manassen bowed his head. 'It would be my honour.'

With his assent came relief, a pressure lifted like a yoke I did not know had lain on my shoulders. Despite my failures, I could do this: for Robin, for Manassen; for the best.

'Keep Accolon's manor for him, too,' I said. 'Do not speak of it yet – let him have his run of the world, then give him somewhere he can make a home. He always has a place here, but Robin needs his own life, as he has always worked for. I want him to be free.'

'As you wish, my lady.'

I held out my hand in an official manner. Sir Manassen smiled and took it, planting a kiss of sworn duty upon the ring I wore – my father's trio of sapphires in gold.

Pledges made, we joined the revel with the others, listening to the music and watching the household dance in the lantern light. Robin stood at the boules pit with the stable lads, laughing and winning the game.

'When will you ask him?' Manassen said.

'You should, if you're willing,' I replied. 'Tell him he has the choice to stay, of course. But he won't need it – he will choose life.'

He nodded, then paused long, his shoulders shifting. Eventually, he said, 'And what of your life, Lady Morgan? Beyond your work, Belle Garde, your pursuit of vengeance on Camelot.'

The question came as a surprise. 'What else is there?'

He said nothing until I looked at him, a streak of colour marking his cheeks. '*Par Dieu*, I am not the right person for this, I ...'

I put my hand on his arm. 'Sir Manassen, if there's one thing I trust and respect in this world, it is your honesty. Never feel you cannot speak freely with me.'

He cleared his throat. 'What I mean to say is ... I knew my cousin, Lady Morgan. He was not a covetous man, nor would he begrudge you a full life. Accolon would not want for *your* loneliness, either.'

It was true – I knew that if he could, Accolon would tell me to seek happiness, to not close myself off to connections of mind or body. *Remember, and choose to live beyond*, he would say. Whether or not I listened was another matter.

'For now, I am happy to change someone else's life,' I replied. 'My own future is still a mystery. Though I appreciate your candour, very much.'

'I'm glad,' he said, still abashed. 'The frankness of friendship is new to us, yes?'

I agreed, but a chill of guilt settled upon my shoulders, the fact I could not be equally honest with him. I wanted to say that Accolon himself should have been the cure for my ever-growing loneliness, but I couldn't tell him about the heart, my intentions or how I kept failing. That every passing day, the truth gained a keener edge: I could not raise my Gaul without the Shroud of Tithonus.

'Go and ask Robin,' I told him. 'On Accolon's day.'

Sir Manassen obeyed and left me, beckoning the boy to walk with him along the silver spring's curved bank. At a distance, I watched Accolon's cousin stop and put a hand on Robin's shoulder, saw the question asked into the evening air.

Robin looked surprised, then glanced across to the joust meadow, where his *carnedd* stood. After a thoughtful pause, he turned back to Manassen with a smiling nod, and they embraced in the manner of knights.

And I, finally, had fixed something.

The day Robin left came too quickly, but the skies honoured Belle Garde with the glory such an occasion deserved. The morning dawned with luminous beauty, autumnal warmth and chill in balance, deep-gold sun tinting leaves blazing like flame.

Robin and I stood alone on the front green, his horses waiting obediently. We looked at one another, and I saw the boy whose shattered leg I healed in Camelot, the young man Belle Garde had part raised, and the valiant future knight he would become. At his hip, he wore Accolon's longsword, its silver horse hilt polished to brilliance. He was ready.

'Lady Morgan, are you sure it is all right for me to leave?' he said. 'I can wait, if the household ... if *you* need me.'

I put my hand to his face. 'All I need now is for you to go and do everything you wish – what you and Sir Accolon trained for, and talked about, and dreamed of.'

His eyes widened in sudden doubt. 'What if I'm not good enough? How can I be sure I will make Sir Accolon proud?'

'You made him proud every day,' I replied. 'You have always been good enough, Robin – he knew it, and so do I. He would only wish for you to be the most honourable knight you can be, and most of all be happy. Life did not always go his way, but Accolon made sure to follow his heart. Promise me you will do the same.'

'I promise,' he whispered, and ducked his head as his tears broke free.

I drew him into my arms and held him tight. Behind us, Sir Manassen had arrived, flanked by Alys and Tressa, the rest of the household streaming onto the cropped grass from all corners.

'There are others who wish to say farewell,' I said into Robin's shoulder.

He straightened, flushing in proud surprise, then looked again at me. 'Thank you, Lady Morgan,' he said. 'For fixing my leg, for Sir Accolon, for Belle Garde. Whatever I become, it will be because of you.'

It was almost too much to bear, but my ability to let him go was the most crucial gift I could give, so I embraced him one final, swift time, then made myself pull away.

'Farewell Robin,' I said. 'I will miss you – I cannot tell you how much. Come back one day and see us. But go, be free.'

He nodded, beaming at me as he had first done as a child, then the household swooped upon him in affection, leaving me standing alone.

Quietly, Sir Manassen came to my side. 'All will be well,' he said.

I nodded, my words hard-won. 'There is one last thing.'

Vision blurring, I drew aside and took a small parcel out of my cloak, wrapped in dense blue silk. I unfolded the fabric, taking in the warm glow of polished gold, and ran one finger over the distinct forked curves.

Accolon's knightly spurs, gleaming and perfect.

I closed my eyes, remembering the care he had taken of them, imagining how he must have felt when he first saw this eternal symbol of knighthood, made for him. In my mind's eye, I conjured Tintagel's Great Hall, low lit for ceremony, Cornwall's sea roaring outside; the sudden weight as Sir Bretel – Accolon's knightly teacher, whom he had squired for, sworn to, and loved as a second father – fixed the spurs to his heels. The race of my Gaul's heart as he felt himself anchored, finally, to his calling.

I had not been there that day, when Accolon spoke his knightly oath and took the blow of honour to his neck, but in turn I saw myself at St Brigid's Abbey, leaning over a volume of anatomy – missing him, but giving flight to a calling all my own. Neither of us knew then that we would find one another again, many times, until we could no longer.

I turned back to Manassen. 'Hold out your hands.'

He obliged, and I placed the spurs on his open palms. A shimmer crossed his face, first of recognition, then an emotion so raw that I had to force myself not to look away.

'Knight Robin with these,' I said. 'He already has Accolon's sword – it's only right he wears his spurs.'

'Of course,' he replied, but when I tried to uncurl my fingers, I found I could not. We stood hopeless, our despair palpable in the air, but the mere act of looking at one another seemed to bring us strength.

In unison, we nodded, and I slipped my hands free, letting everything go.

Sir Manassen and I looked across at Robin, seated on his horse now beside the spring, gazing at the horizon above the trees, ready to ride towards it.

'When the time comes,' I said, 'tell him to swear to no lord.'

8

A short while later, the month turned, roe deer season began, and I was ready.

One fine morning, I gave instructions for the household to keep away from the eastern woods, sent the magpies to confirm that the royal hunting party was preparing to ride out, and spent the morning on my balcony, conjuring a storm.

I well knew the dance by now; I asked the elements to shift, emphasising some and restricting others, until a cloud formed, alive and fractious, full of rain and twitching with heat and thunder. I stood for hours, refining and cultivating the cloud's destructive strength, until it was the biggest storm I had ever made, magnificent and dangerous.

As the hour approached, I marshalled the iron clouds within the wind and made my way into the forest, waiting inside the treeline at the chase meadow's edge. In the distance, the hunting party appeared, a bright gathering of horses and hounds, cantering through the leaf-strewn grass. Men of spurs and rank rode first, flanked by woodsmen and kennel masters, squires following on their rounceys.

It was not hard to spot a king amongst his knights. Arthur rode in the centre of his retinue, his golden aspect and red stallion shining in the midday sun. No matter who surrounded him, how large and impressive and finely garbed his men were, he always seemed taller than the rest, prouder, anointed by a light that could only be bestowed by God.

I didn't need to see any more; I would bring the darkness to him.

Taking hold of my storm, I drew down the cloud. The men looked up in astonishment, faces shadowed as I pulled the dense grey mass lower, blocking the sun. When all eyes were on the sky, I splayed my fingers and let loose the rain.

It was cold and hard, shocking after the pleasant autumn air. Knights shied away with shouts of complaint, pulling their mantles over their heads. None of them had dressed for wet weather. A few shifted their mounts under overhanging tree branches, seeking shelter to wait out what they thought was a typical Welsh tempest. They didn't know the storm would not end until I was satisfied.

With my free hand, I caught the wind and spun it at the group like a ball through skittles. Men and hounds scattered and I pursued them with the rain in icy torrents, the pressure in my blood crackling with the first frisson of lightning. I snapped down a slim white bolt, whipping the hot force against a tree bough. Bark shot off in splinters as thunder roared in answer. Horses screamed and plunged, flinging their riders to the muddied ground.

Arthur's hunter leapt sideways and bucked, but he held firm to his seat. 'Seek shelter!' he commanded. 'Keep to the treeline and ride for the lodge – now!'

The party obeyed, those still mounted gripping their saddles and galloping off, others dashing away on foot, pursuing their foaming steeds. My brother ushered them before him like a good shepherd, watching for their safety until they were all gone. Seeing my opportunity, I pulled down another fork of lightning, slamming the bolt into the ground between him and his retreating men. Thunder crashed in answer, loud as the end of the world.

Arthur's horse reared, shaking him loose. He wrestled enough control to dismount, but his steed tore away from his grip, taking off after the others. He shouted in protest and made to follow, but I brought down a channel of battering rain and blocked his progress as the men charged further out of earshot, leaving him alone.

One more gust of wind was all I needed. I caught a gale in my palm and cut Arthur from his flock as a wolf would a newborn lamb.

As I intended, he dove into the woods, away from the storm's relentless assault, disorientated by reverberating thunder and ice hail that stung like snakebites. My chaos chased him deeper into the trees, further from his knights. It would take a long while for them to calm their disarray and discover their king was missing. I had time.

I tracked him for half a mile, then let the wind drop. Arthur stopped immediately, taking in his surroundings, narrowed eyes scanning for any movement through the trees. A slight quiver reached my senses – not fear, but unsurety. He was hopelessly lost and knew something was in pursuit.

However, nothing could dampen his stubborn bravery, or the forest instincts of his childhood. My brother tilted his head, listening beyond the downpour's hiss for a different, lower roar, following the sound to the edge of a stream that ran between us. As he looked at it, I sensed his wayfinder's relief: he knew the same waterway flowed into the chase and should lead him back to where he began.

Swiftly, he took off along the bank. His long stride was hard to keep up with, but I was in no hurry. Arthur had found the stream and calculated his way out, exactly as I hoped. What he did not know was that I had already made the water flow in the wrong direction.

Consequently, my brother came to a halt in a circular clearing where the valley side rose up, forest floor giving way to a rocky outcropping and sheer high cliff, cut by a blade of waterfall. At its foot, water crashed white and rageful into a round dark pool, foaming with the rain. Arthur regarded the sight with confusion, incredulous that the stone barricade had dared interrupt his passage. He took a few impatient steps one way, then the other, eventually realising there was no way beyond.

'Damn you to Hell!' he roared up at the cliff, then looked back at the unnatural stream, pouring into the pool. As he watched, I let the water return to its true flow, changing direction before his eyes.

'Who is *doing this?*' he shouted. Furious, he swung back towards the stream bank. I was already standing on the opposite side.

My brother started in shock, bootheel slipping on the slick stones. He listed sideways, arms flailing, but there was nothing to grab. Bodily strength alone saved him from plunging into the churning black lagoon.

'Watch your step, Your Highness,' I said. 'If you fall in, you may never find your way back to the surface.'

Arthur stilled, like prey understanding it is finally trapped.

'Morgan,' he said. 'I should have known.'

'What did you expect, charging into my domain?' I replied. 'I thought it was time we looked one another in the eye.'

He glared at me, drawing himself to his imperious height even as his breaths came ragged. 'Your manner of gaining my attention was unnecessary. You put my retinue in danger – they are nothing to do with the trouble between us.'

'*Between* us?' I exclaimed. 'I am in no way to blame for what has been done to me. Or are you finally admitting your part in it all? Your faults – *your* failures.'

He flinched, but put stubborn hands on his hips. 'I am High King. Every wrong, danger and unsolved problem in my realm is a failure of mine. You, sister, are perhaps the greatest threat to the kingdom's peace, and I am guilty of unleashing you upon the world.'

'How dare you,' I said. 'You may rule everyone else, but you do not rule me. I unleashed *myself* upon this world.'

Arthur remained unmoved, his face watchful, superior.

'Is that why you came here?' I said scornfully. 'Desperately haunting my borders, thinking you could solve the problem of Morgan le Fay?'

'I had to act because of your damnable letter,' he retorted. 'Did you think I could let such an aggression go unanswered?'

I scoffed. 'So my letter left you irrevocably threatened? I heard the entire court laughed – that your Queen was particularly amused. Hardly a terror worth avenging.'

'*I* did not laugh,' he said. 'It was a threat to my kingdom, myself, and those I love. Your words have not left my thoughts since.'

I paused, trying to recall exactly what Sir Manassen had said, and realised there was no lie: Guinevere laughed, the court followed, but my brother had walked away.

'Well, here I am, the menace to Camelot's peace,' I said. 'What do you wish to say? That all you visited upon me – slaying my lover, keeping my son from me, painting me as a corrupt traitoress – is akin to your mild feeling of disruption? *Poor you*, Arthur.'

The barb struck home, his countenance darkening until he was unyielding as granite. Rain hit his face, pointed and cold, but he no longer seemed to feel it.

'You could have had peace, Morgan,' he said in a low voice. 'When divine justice turned you into stone, I was contented. Even when I heard you broke free of God's will, I was satisfied to pretend you did not exist. I had no desire to hear from you ever again.'

'Turning to stone wasn't heavenly punishment,' I snapped. 'I did that with my own power. I saved myself and my people from your self-righteous violence.'

'And so you were saved,' he said bitterly. 'Yet you could not keep away, could you? Putting your voice in that letter in all its black bile and rancour. Trying to force yourself into my head in daylight, as you have infiltrated my mind at night. Filling my sleep with images of Tintagel Castle and its relentless roaring sea.'

The words took the air from my lungs, his precise description of my own marauding dreams: a sea blue and wild, crashing over high cliffs I suddenly recognised. How had I not seen it before? The island, the sounds and scents my nights were steeped in came from a place I knew in my bones, my blood. All along, I had been dreaming of Tintagel.

And somehow, so had my brother.

'You know of what I speak, don't you?' Arthur demanded.

The thought tugged at me, a twitch upon an unsevered thread. Except it didn't matter; he had killed Accolon to spite me, and nothing else could hold any significance.

'I wouldn't condescend to creep inside anyone's mind,' I said. 'That was Merlin's way – never mine.' Then, the lie. 'Whatever you dream of, brother, you dream alone.'

Arthur said nothing, but held my gaze for so long I almost gave in and looked away. I felt his disbelief through to my bones.

'If that is the truth,' he said eventually, 'then what purpose, all of this?'

'My letter promised vengeance, and I meant it,' I said. 'I intend to punish Camelot to the full extent of my power. However, there is a way – only one – to prevent it.'

'Which is?'

'Give me what I am owed,' I said. 'The Shroud of Tithonus.'

His face showed no sign of recognition. 'The what?'

'A large piece of white linen, ancient and delicate, once possessed by Merlin. He brought it to you in Camelot in an ebony box, the same month I escaped from him.'

Still no flicker of familiarity, and he had never been skilled at lying. 'It has no use for you, and I can do you no harm with it,' I continued anyway. 'Bring it to me, and I will leave Camelot alone. Tell the court you defeated me. I don't care.'

Arthur scowled, as if the idea was distasteful to him. 'I don't know what you're talking about. I've never heard of this ... piece of cloth. The last object that Merlin gave me was one you traitorously stole for yourself. My scabbard.'

His account of my actions was both true and not. I had hardly thought about Excalibur's death-defying scabbard, but only Alys, Tressa and I knew I had thrown it into a lake to be lost for eternity. The last Arthur had seen of it was when I leapt out of his abbey sickbed window with the miraculous object in my hands.

'Do not think I've forgotten,' he added. 'I will not rest until it is returned.'

'Then you will never rest,' I said. 'You didn't deserve the scabbard, nor appreciated the marvels it was capable of.'

'It belongs with Excalibur. It is mine by right.'

'No one has the right to such power,' I said. 'Any king worth his crown would know that.'

His eyes hardened immediately. 'And you used my property with care, did you, sister? If you hadn't tricked Sir Accolon into carrying it, he would still be alive.'

Despite the chill of the rain, my blood ran cold. In a few words Arthur had cut into the darkest reaches of my grief, my self-hatred, and carved out the tortures I most favoured: what if I had not let Accolon go; if I had followed him sooner; if I had not given him a High King's magical scabbard and told him to keep it close. Even at my mercy, somehow my brother could read the internal scars of my defeat.

We stood frozen before one another, our silence stretching so far the air felt taut with pain, until Arthur almost looked chastened. His lips parted as if he were about to speak – explain, recant – but I couldn't stand more of his cruelty. Instead, he deserved some of mine.

'You might as well forget about the scabbard,' I snarled. 'It will never be back in your possession. I swear it upon my life.'

'That would be a very foolish oath to make,' he said. 'The scabbard is the one means of negotiation left to you. Otherwise, I have no choice but to bring you to justice.'

His enduring belief he was in charge lit up my fury at once. Raising my hands, I reached into the remaining storm and pulled down a shower of thin lightning bolts.

Luckily for him, Arthur's feet were quick. He leapt backwards, staring at the scorch marks where he had stood, the snakes of steam rising from wet stone. His hand went to the gleaming weapon at his belt.

'Go ahead,' I said. 'Even if you could draw that sainted blade before I melted it into liquid steel – it doesn't matter. *You cannot reach me.*'

He hesitated, sword hand falling to his side. I studied him through the steady rain, soaked to the skin, pale-gold hair darkened and dripping, mantle the colour of blood at night. Excalibur's hilt burned brightly at his hip, the only remnant of sun left in the world.

'I didn't have to, Morgan,' he said. 'All I had to do was know you. The moment I rode close enough to your valley, here you are, as if by my command.'

Despite everything, I felt his words, his defiance, within myself. My brother had set a trap for me exactly as I had created one for him, and we had both fallen in. How sharp it felt to discover that we still shared one mind.

The thought was too much, and I could not let it stand.

'I hardly think you are the one in control here.' I gestured to the roiling sky. 'Have you learned nothing? You did not summon me – I brought you to this place with my own power. I made this storm.'

He looked up at the tumult and shrugged. 'It's just weather. I've survived worse.'

'Very well,' I said. 'We shall see.'

I lifted my hands to the raging waterfall. At my request, the element arched forth, looming over my brother in a foaming, muscular channel. He watched it rise and hang suspended, waiting to crash upon him. No matter how strong he was, or that he had been born within Tintagel's seas just as I had, he understood that if I chose this, he would not survive.

Arthur looked back at me, his grey eyes calm.

'Do as you must, sister,' he said.

I savoured the water's force through my body, rippling against my muscles, fierce and deadly. Yet sometimes, I knew, its power lay elsewhere; in the still blue lake, running deep. I would not be told what I must do.

'No,' I said. 'Not like this. I want much more than a swift revenge.'

Carefully, I drew the waterfall down. It obeyed me like an eager young horse, strong but letting me lead the way. Arthur drew breath to argue, but I shook my head.

'Hear this,' I said as I guided the water to the pool. 'What you love, I will take from you – those you hold dearest, the realm's reputation and the faith of the ones who follow you. I want to disturb your peace, your days and nights, disrupt your world until you are hollow with shame and despair. Camelot will feel my vengeance, until you know how it feels to lose everything, as I have. That is my due, nothing less.'

For a heartbeat, Arthur looked stunned, then his face changed, jaw set hard, eyes steel and flashing with challenge, the faint snarl of a smile about his lips. What I read there was not doubt, or anger, but exhilaration.

'If that is a declaration of war, Morgan, then be sure you mean it,' he said. 'You forget, I know this life far better than you. I have never ridden into a battle I did not win.'

'And I have never known how to walk away from a fight,' I said. 'Think of that before you question my purpose. It will save you time.'

Unexpectedly, his smile grew, breaking into a laugh that echoed in the last of the rain. 'In that case, say no more,' he said. 'You have started this, and I will end it. I will do whatever it takes to protect my kingdom. Be warned – it will not be over until I have justice.'

The sound of his confidence ignited in me as competition, a note of similarity between two siblings, both headstrong, both convinced they are right, but utterly opposed.

I gathered the storm again in my hands, thunder growling its own reply.

'Give me your very worst, brother,' I said. 'For every act of war you bring, I will rain down chaos.'

9

A fortnight later, my brother began his war against me.

The first band of knights he sent were spotted on the main road outside Belle Garde as All Hallows' came and went. Camelot's finest approached the valley daily, unable to do anything other than be sent in circles by the protective charms. Their efforts did not perturb the household or limit their movement – there was a secret pass through the southern forest which Sir Manassen always used – but in any case, my virtuous brother did not stoop to order their suppression. This wasn't a siege of anything but his own sister.

What Arthur hadn't accounted for was that I could besiege him equally well without leaving my turret. The storms I created grew stronger: thunderous galleons containing enough rain to flood a fortress; narrow tempests full of pelting ice; black clouds twitching with lightning like whipcracks of fire.

I perfected my form, training in the same relentless way great knights ran drills: practising for hours until my bones ached and muscles screamed, but mastery had become second nature. I harnessed wind and water like chariot horses, until I could drive my savage clouds a hundred miles across the country and call down havoc with a flick of my hands.

If the weather was my armoured warrior, then the magpies were my spymaster, my winged connection to the places I could not go. Through the matriarch, I could see whoever Arthur put on the road towards me, then fly across rivers and forests and over great golden walls, until I had infiltrated my brother's greatest loves: Camelot and his wife.

Both felt the full force of my prowess. With storms, I shattered windows, rained on every hunt; my lightning set fire to wooden stockades the nights before tournaments were due to begin. Every time Guinevere showed her pretty fair head under the open sky, my magpies were there, swooping for her emerald diadem. By the following spring, Sir Manassen brought news that she had cancelled her traditional plans to go a-Maying, and no longer made the public courtyard procession to St Stephen's for High Mass, instead taking the warrenlike passageways with the monks and floor sweepers. Guinevere could walk on no terrace, nor ride any road without a falconer at each corner.

Arthur's fury at my infiltration was clear. Manassen reported the King's abrupt and distracted manner at court, and the knights he sent to bounce off my defences doubled. As expected, he was outraged that I could rattle Camelot's gilded cage, that I knew his heart so well and exactly where to strike him.

Meanwhile, I relished news of the court's fractious and malcontent mood. Many gossiped that the High King looked sleepless; no doubt Tintagel's seas churned as hard in my brother's nightly thoughts as they did in mine. When eventually forced to address his unsettled courtiers, Arthur claimed God was testing their resolve.

But my cause was not divine, and as a year and more passed, the skies absorbed all I had: my endless fury, the black despair for my brutal losses – Accolon's death, my snatched children, the tarnish thrown upon my name – every ounce of my futility and spite.

I was beyond strategy, wedded to chaos, more than the power of creation. I had become the storm.

At least, that was how it felt in the daytime.

In the depths of the night, when I lay sleepless amidst the otherworldly roar of Tintagel's violent tides, there was only me and my solitude, the failures that resided within.

So much I could do, so much noise and fear I could invoke, but I could not hold a dead sparrow in my hands and give it new life. I could not take Accolon's singing stone heart and recreate the man I loved.

Face the truth, my dearest Morgan, Merlin's voice mocked me in the dark. *You are so far from what you could have been.*

Indeed, sometimes it seemed I had overplayed my moves. Reports came that Ninianne had occasionally been seen at court, tales of the strange and beautiful maiden who arrived unexpectedly to cause a stir in the Great Hall and advise the King on some matter, or set in motion a mysterious quest for Camelot's knights to chase. Perhaps Arthur had forgiven her for Merlin, or else had allowed her back into his graces because he was desperate for a more powerful magic to protect his precious city from my disruption.

Either way, the Book of Prophecies sat worthless on its shelf, the Shroud of Tithonus never coming.

'When did you last get a decent night's rest?' Alys said, not long after the second anniversary of my battling Arthur. 'Let me make you a tincture to help you sleep.'

She had offered me such a remedy several times since Accolon's death, but I always refused; even if painful, my body's instincts were all I had keeping me from becoming numb.

'I get enough rest for my needs,' I lied.

'It's just … I can see this is taking a toll upon you in a way it hasn't before,' she said. 'You've … changed.'

It was a strange comment to hear. Due to my protective charms made from fairy magic, all of us who were full-grown and lived in Belle Garde looked only slightly older than when I had arrived seven years ago – myself most of all – in a lesser but similar way to Ninianne's slowness of ageing.

'I'm fine, dear heart,' I replied. 'Sleep will come if I need it.'

I smiled reassuringly until she looked convinced, but later, bored in my bedchamber, I rose from my sleepless bed and uncovered the long mirror I never used in my dressing room. What I saw there was a shock – not out of vanity, but because Alys was right. Looking back at me was drawn, greyish skin, a gaunt and hollow aspect, darkened eyes that were the same deep blue but lifeless and flat. I did not just look older but afflicted, death-shadowed, completely unlike myself. Frequent use of fairy magic may have affected my ability to age, but it was not enough to keep the past three years from my face.

It was not what I intended, and a defeat I would not accept. Despite Ninianne's apparent favour with Arthur, his fraught patience would soon wear out when he realised she could not save him from me. To stay by his side, she would still need the prophecies, her only choice to bring me the Shroud. And when I raised Accolon, I did not want him to find me in any way changed from the day he left Belle Garde.

This, at least, I could fix. Closing my eyes, I let healing gather within me, until my body felt full of light. I drew my hands over my face, across my cheeks and brow and back through my hair, focusing on the golden force until I was a column of restoration. Temples to toes, I shed the weeks and months from my body, undoing the ravages of grief: the missed meals, lack of sleep and frayed nerves that had exhausted all signs of vitality.

When I felt it done, I opened my eyes and in the looking glass saw myself again – or an accurate depiction of the Morgan le Fay I had been on that last Midsummer's Eve years ago. None of this would cure my despair, my secret-keeping and other destructive habits, but I could at least control how my troubles wrote themselves upon the face I showed the world.

Until Accolon and I were together again, I would erase every moment we had been forced to be apart.

Nevertheless, life went on, and sometimes there was good, pinpricks of starlight in the never-ending dark.

A year after he had left with Robin, Sir Manassen came to me and said that his wife was with child, then expecting a second within eighteen months. He named his first son after Accolon and spent most of his time in Gaul, where his growing family were now settled, but still attended every court held at Camelot.

While there, he brought me news, gossip, any rumours he thought would be of interest, but I didn't ask for more than that. Manassen was healing, breaking free of his need for vengeance, and I would not have him take risks for my sake. I was more than capable of bringing chaos to Arthur's door in my own name.

Meanwhile, Belle Garde carried on unheeding of my conflicts, and saw its share of change. Sir Ceredig the chamberlain retired and bid us farewell to live out his latter years with his daughters, leaving Alys and Tressa with complete mastery of the household.

In turn, the huntsman took full charge of the land and stables, as Accolon had always intended. Born and raised in the valley, he was decades younger than Sir Ceredig, proficient with bow, spear and sword, and as fiercely protective of Belle Garde as I was. His true name was Rhisiart, his new title Steward of the Estate, but he called himself neither, refused an offer of knighthood, and was still known to everyone as the huntsman.

To any who enquired who was his lord, he would answer without fail, 'I have none. I serve only a mistress.' I could rely upon every word he brought me, and though it would never be necessary, trusted him with my life.

Elsewhere, the derelict structures throughout the valley had mostly been rebuilt, enlarged and restored where needed, including a marvel that Alys led me to one day, in a clearing just beyond the rising spring. There, a once-ruined, rectangular stone barn had transformed into a whitewashed, high-raftered longhouse, neatly laid with flagstones and furnished with two rows of beds, woven reed screens and washbowls on stands.

'We did it, *cariad*, at long last,' she said, beaming. 'Our own infirmary.'

I wanted to tell her that she alone had done it as I had been only distracted, but she insisted we share in the triumph. The culmination of our vision – originating in St Brigid's Abbey and continued in Gore, when we used our skills secretly to help the women in the village – of healing all who asked for help, now stood before us, firm upon our land.

'It may be ours,' I said, 'but I would not have made it this far without you.'

'Oh hush,' she said sensibly. 'Let's put ourselves to work.'

So we did, and despite my private conflicts, in Belle Garde's new infirmary I found the greatest peace I had ever known. When the sick and injured came, I diagnosed, observed and laid hands to the cases that Alys's herbs and traditional physic could not solve, returned to the challenges and fulfilment of healing without the need to hide my abilities. I was free to use my skills boldly and be proud, in a way I had never before experienced in life.

Soon, word spread, and the valley was busy with people requesting help, problems that I was capable of fixing. Whatever else I could not change, the infirmary was where I made a difference. No one mistrusted me there; I was needed, respected, and appreciated, transcending the corrupted mark that had been put upon my reputation.

'Have you heard what they are calling you around the valley?' Tressa asked, after the infirmary's third winter eased to spring with no patients lost. 'Morgan the Goddess.'

I had heard the name in passing, a moving gesture of faith from those who had willingly bestowed their loyalty. Yet part of me wondered if it was accurate in another way – that I was now a remote figure, existing outside everyday life; an Eris in her high tower, holding her vengeful heart at a distance.

However, not even my fearsome reputation was immune to the shifts of time. After years of attempts, new knights still came from Arthur's various courts, but with lessening context for mine and my brother's long conflict. This lack of enmity let them through the protective charms, into a world of ease and hospitality they had not expected.

Some were injured or lost, others tired from questing for the Crown, wishing only for a soft bed and good meal. A few spoke of Camelot carelessly, irreverently, in a way that would have damned them in years past. They had lost faith in the strict systems, with little guidance or appetite for the virtuous greatness they had been promised. They brought gossip of discontented barons, whispers that the King had become aimless; rumours of factions returning to their strongholds to contemplate a different future. Their talk was amusing, useful, and I hoarded it away like jewels in a vault.

To these knights, I also proved a surprise, a powerful woman far from the humourless, vicious crone they had imagined. Occasionally, where my charm went, their desire followed, and I ate it like sweetmeats, the power honey on my tongue. The first time a knight was brave enough to declare his admiration, I felt it as an even darker revenge, and an answer to quite a different hunger. When I knocked on his chamber door in the violet-black night and he stepped aside with awe, I took him to bed as the goddess of discord I had become, defying the natural order to feed her own wants.

More I devoured thereafter, the knights most handsome and incautious, whose enthusiasm matched my restlessness as I sated the appetites my body did not know how to forget. To lie down with another in carnality, freed from love or consequence, brought a brief oblivion that calmed my senses for the strategic requirements of my days. Amongst other things, it pleased me to return these men to Camelot, gratified and dazed, questioning everything they had been taught, riding back to their oaths and duty in a mild state of mutiny.

They were not the only ones who sought the freedoms of Belle Garde. Women came too, wronged maidens, lovers, sometimes wives, abandoned or jilted in the wake of questing knights. To them we offered harbour: rest and comfort; friendship; an education if they wished. With Alys's nunnery connections, some took the veil, and others helped in the infirmary or were drawn to Tressa's many practical interests – her orchards and cider house, beekeeping, scribework and illumination – then settled in the valley, or took their skills and newfound purpose to share our wisdom elsewhere. In these small but significant ways, Belle Garde strengthened with every healed affliction, each enlightened mind, every soul that came and went feeling better than before.

Within myself, I was not content, exactly, but willing to let Alys and Tressa believe I had settled, returned to the art of physic for my mind, and the pleasures of the body in whatever fleeting way I chose. I had men to seduce, a cause to rail against, and work at my fingertips. To those who loved me best, it seemed a decent start towards my own restoration.

No one needed to hear how I still awoke from my insufficient sleep, Accolon's absence a crevasse in my bed, Tintagel's sea roaring through my body. No one knew that if I cut my heart from my chest and lay it alongside Accolon's, it too would be marble, cold and lifeless, just the same.

Not a soul needed to know me at all any more, outside of my reputation for vengeance and Belle Garde's famed revels and hospitality. While I warred with my brother, sowing destruction throughout his lands, all who came to mine were healed in some way, and I did not mind such a paradox. If enduring rage and my valley's sanctuary was what Morgan le Fay offered the world, I could not argue with such a legacy. For once, I had earned both my bad name and the good.

Regardless, in Camelot, they called my domain the Vale of No Return.

10

When she came, it had been almost five years since our last encounter.

By some measures it was unexpected; Arthur's attempts to invade my valley had tapered off in recent months and life had become quieter. However, I had persisted in my disruption of the Royal Court, so when I was told there was a strange woman at the valley's main entrance asking to speak to me, I found myself surprised that she hadn't come sooner.

'So,' I said, upon reaching the hawthorn grove, 'he finally sent you.'

Ninianne turned, her ever beautiful face solemn through the sheen of my charms. She wore a long cloak in her usual violet over white robes untouched by the dirt of the road, and when she swept her hood down, her sunset hair made me avert my eyes. I was never prepared for the blaze of it, as she well knew.

'Morgan,' she said in her captivating voice. 'No one sent me.'

I scoffed. 'Arthur's hand is writ large upon this. Why else would you stand outside my protective charms? Clearly you come bearing his ill intentions.'

'I haven't yet attempted to pass through to your land,' she said. 'I would not cross your boundaries without permission.'

'How considerate!' I snapped. 'From the woman who stole my child, colluded in my lover's murder, and brands me a traitor. A troubadour couldn't make it up.'

She recoiled as if I had wounded her. The temerity of it brought another flare of outrage, but I bit back on my temper. She would not unseat me so easily.

'Come in, then,' I said, making my voice calm. 'If you are so virtuous, step through the charms.'

Ninianne held my gaze with a peculiar defiance, then picked up her pristine skirts and glided through the veil of protection. The charms didn't quiver.

Fair enough, I thought. *Checkmate.*

'To what do I owe this unsolicited visit?' I asked.

She stopped before me, emanating warmth. 'I wanted to speak with you.'

'I highly doubt that's all.' However, I couldn't deny I was curious. 'I'm very busy. If we must talk, then we will also walk.'

I strode off, unconcerned whether she followed. It was a brisk May morning and I had been reinforcing Belle Garde's magical shield, so I kept moving along the boundary, pausing to pull new silvery threads forth and knit them into the existing veil. Eventually, my work took us along a challenging path up the steep eastern valley side, but Ninianne kept pace with me.

'How are your charms?' she asked. 'Do they still cast easily, and last as long?'

I eyed her with suspicion, but there was no guile in her aspect. 'They form just as usual,' I replied. 'Though I can never get them beyond a week's worth of strength. I assume I have reached my limit with this particular fairy magic.'

She nodded thoughtfully and we climbed the last stretch of forested track. At the top, the trees opened up onto tufted grass and rocky outcroppings, and an all-encompassing view of the valley. We came to a halt on top of a flat rock, jutting over the hillside like a balcony to the world.

'Here it is, my famous Vale,' I said, not without belligerence. 'Belle Garde.'

Ninianne took in the view. 'It's beautiful. I have always been curious to see the place where you chose to settle, and which you protect so carefully.'

'I didn't *choose* as much as I was *exiled*,' I said. 'But I'm proud of my life here. It's worth protecting. Unlike some places.'

She didn't rise to my provocation. 'Your charms are excellent. The boundary is strong – well made.'

'Is that a compliment to me or your own teaching?' I said drily.

'Neither. It is a statement of fact. You truly have mastered these skills, Morgan. Though I warned that using this type of magic every day would change you. And it has.'

'Many things have changed me,' I said, more carelessly than I felt.

'Perhaps,' she mused. 'But this is a profound metamorphosis. You are far more fairy than you were before.'

As always when she spoke of me like this, it resonated in my depths in ways I both couldn't quite comprehend and felt as utterly true. But I would not be drawn by her mysteries; I had enough riddles to solve.

Ninianne returned her gaze to the view, tilting her head as if hearing a faint song.

'Streams, the river, plenty of rain. There is a spring, also.' Her voice was low, hypnotic, the soft lap of water against land. 'I can understand why you were drawn here. The elemental abundance must bring you strength.'

'I suppose – it is an island of sorts,' I mused. 'Though it's not the sea.'

'How long has it been since you have seen the sea?' she asked.

'I cannot remember the last time.'

It took me a moment to realise it because my dreams were still full of saltwater and seafoam, crashing on cliffs; Tintagel in all its wild glory. The night-time visions came so frequently now that I had accepted it as a separate part of my day, a journey to another realm.

'You will return to the waves one day,' she murmured. 'Do you dream of it?'

'Yes,' I replied, and my honesty surprised me. I had told no one else. 'Often.'

I wondered if Arthur still dreamt of our birthplace too, if that was why Ninianne wanted to know. I felt her studying me, as if her fingers were skimming my face.

'There is something more,' she said. 'You have ... a lake.'

One mention of Llyn Glas and our strange peace shattered. I saw it all: Accolon under the willow, swimming in the sapphire depths, lit with sun; my Gaul above me, beneath me, all around me; his voice in my ears, the scent of his neck, his touch on my skin as the weeping branches skimmed the water's edge. The silence that hung across the lake now, as if all joy had taken its leave. Whatever I had let her bend within me felt ready to snap.

'Damn you, Ninianne,' I said. 'You talk as if we were old friends filling in the gaps of our lives. Tell me what you want.'

It was the first time she looked truly offended; she despised being rushed, or told what to do. In that we were the same.

'Speak now, or leave,' I urged.

'You know why I am here,' she said tersely. 'Your antics with Camelot – disrupting the court, harassing the Queen. The magpies. The storms. Your confrontation with King Arthur in the woods when you threatened to drown him – you should not have done that. Your mastery of weather is interesting, but the way you are using your skills, for mischief and conflict, is beneath you.'

It was both surprising and boringly prosaic. I felt laughter stir in my chest.

'A scolding!' I exclaimed. 'Ninianne of the Lake sent to tell off the terrible Morgan le Fay like a nursery child. Is this what your great King Arthur has you doing to show your worth? What a glorious purpose it must be to serve him!'

Her face didn't flicker, but such apathy didn't fool me. She was right that over the years my senses had become finer-tuned, and I felt her motives as one fairy to another.

'You wouldn't come all this way just to tread on my tail,' I said. 'Why are you really here?'

Again Ninianne offered no response, so I walked away from the edge and began to conjure new charms in the air. She followed, watching me work in silence.

'Very well, if you won't answer, I will tell you what I know,' I said. 'The mood of the country has been wavering. Some factions are tired of Camelot's ways, the lavish celebrations for every occasion, its obsession with virtue and focus on individual knightly glory, rather than the kingdom's collective concerns. I know that Guinevere has recently turned thirty years of age and still no heir from her belly. Arthur will be frustrated by the criticism, worried for his legacy and desperate for answers, and there is only one way to soothe him. You want the Book of Prophecies.'

'I have never pretended otherwise,' she replied. 'I assume by now you have thoroughly read it, so I thought you could return it to me.'

'Indeed, I have read the book and found it wanting,' I said. 'I'm not interested in Merlin's mutterings, and I thought they would be beneath your concern. You have enough wisdom of your own.'

She looked mildly flattered. 'It is more than that. The High King is facing new threats from Saxons in the north – there will be war. I need the book to see if there is anything I must seek to counteract.'

'You believe you can change a prophecy?' I said. 'I thought Merlin's predictions for Arthur were unquestionable, immutable.'

'You know I have never thought it so straightforward,' Ninianne replied. 'That it's a matter of potential, and the ways of the mortal world – emotions, desires, mistakes – can divert destiny's path.'

'In which case, what is the point of the prophecies at all, if they are so vague and malleable?' I countered.

'I see you still believe that life is fuelled by individual decisions, actions we choose and are responsible for,' she said. 'It may oppose Merlin's view, but is no less strict.'

The suggestion I was the sorcerer's mirror image made my skin prickle. Overhead, a cloud darkened, shadowing the daylight; it was possible my mood had done it.

'What I *know* is Merlin's betrayal prophecy wasn't about me,' I said. 'So either the entire book is full of lies, or Arthur needs to look over his shoulder for the true traitor. Other than that, I spend little time thinking of the fates of so-called great men. But good luck in your quest to try and stop the future from happening.'

I abandoned the charm-making and dusted off my hands, turning towards the mountain path.

'I need the book, Morgan,' Ninianne called out. 'For the sake of us all.'

I paused, looking back at her. 'You need it for *Arthur's* sake,' I corrected. 'Why should I care? If things are going wrong for Camelot – good. *That is what I wanted.*'

'You are not being fair,' she insisted. 'There are others involved now, lives at stake. This is important, it … It's not a game for me.'

An involuntary flush spread across her face, the first true intrigue she had given me. It was rare for Ninianne not to have complete control of her body.

'What "others"?' I said. 'Since when do you hold concern for anyone beyond yourself and Arthur?'

She didn't reply, but our connection quivered with a new sensation – fear, mixed with stubborn courage, and a bursting need to express herself. She wanted desperately to share what she felt, and to keep her secrets close.

'Something is different with you,' I pressed. 'Your heart beats too fast. You wear uncertainty like a sable cape. At Merlin's, you told me you had been busy abroad. What has changed, Ninianne?'

Another pause stretched between us. I was about to turn away when her voice came, halting, unsure.

'I–I am a mother,' she confessed. 'Since Merlin's death, I've been away from Britain, living in seclusion. Raising a son.'

I would not have guessed it given five thousand chances. 'How? Can you—?'

'No,' she cut in. 'The markings on my thighs, my own protective charms, remain unbreakable. I still cannot lie with a man and beget a child that way.'

'Then how did you ... beget one?'

Her face took on a dreamy look. 'He came to me, as if brought by an angel. Or as if he *were* the angel, bestowing himself upon my heart. A child of twelve – a born prince – well aware of his own mind, able to choose me as his guardian. For ten years now he has let me love and guide him.'

Her reverence was like nothing I had seen, a lavish sort of poetry I didn't think possible in her. It was overwrought, unmoored, irrational – it was human.

'I'm not sure I understand,' I said.

'It was during the resurgence of war in Benoic. His father was slain, his mother claimed sanctuary in a convent. He was running from armed men and found himself trapped at the edge of my lake. I didn't think – I just gathered him into my arms and took him into the water, to my home where they could not reach us. I kept him safe, gave him all I could, until he was ready to venture into the world.'

When the weight of her words hit me, the pain was rib-crushing. She had gained a son with the same speed that I had been deprived of both of mine.

'Are you ... happy?' I asked.

'More than I've ever been,' she said. 'The day he first called me "Mother" ... I never knew my soul could soar, until then.'

I could not bear to hear any more, yet I could not stop. 'Where is he now?'

'He has taken knighthood in Camelot,' she said. 'My son has suffered much heartache, but his honour runs deep and his talents are prodigious. He wishes to be the greatest knight this kingdom has ever known, and he will succeed. He will carve his name upon this world.'

'Benoic is still a country of influence,' I said. 'What of his family, his titles?'

'He knows who he is, but has chosen to set it aside. Before he left our home, he asked if he could take my name.' Her light grew until she held the pride of summer sun. 'He is of the Lake now.'

Bitterness rose in my throat, but I would not give her the satisfaction of my undoing. Defiance was all I had.

'Then I'm surprised this new happiness hasn't given you greater perspective,' I said harshly. 'Yet here you are, begging favours, prostrating yourself for selfish kings.'

Her light surged in annoyance. 'Always you accuse me of not having my own mind. Of doing only what others demand.'

'You know what they say, Ninianne. If it slithers along the ground and hisses with a forked tongue, most likely it is a snake.'

'I am no snake,' she said. 'Nor anyone's servant. You of all people know that – or Merlin would still be alive.'

It silenced me as always, the undeniable enormity of what she had done.

'That choice I made alone,' she added. 'Even if no one will ever understand it.'

But I understood, and she knew; perhaps I was the only one who did. To my mind, she had ended Merlin's reign of control, she was justified, and I would never claim otherwise.

'Why did you do it?' I asked. 'After all those years.'

She sighed, relenting. 'I could tolerate my own life, but his actions in pursuit of the prophecies, what he did to ensure things happened as he thought they must – it was never easy to bear. What he visited on you alone … It had to come to an end. For good.'

I regarded her sharply. She was speaking of my stolen child, her involvement that she insisted was a trick of Merlin's. She saw my resistance to her regret and looked away.

'It took years to plan,' she said. 'I had to consider every angle, accept that a world without Merlin was less governed, more prone to the whims of the human heart – but a truer world, a freer one. I had to find the cave that would hold him, withstand his magic. Convince him to go there with me.'

'Weren't you worried he might suspect?'

Her glow dimmed, as if someone had blown out a row of candles. 'At times, Merlin had led me to believe he could read minds,' she said. 'I was terrified.'

There was nothing I could say, haunted too as I was by memories of Merlin, his voice still in my head. Ninianne had risked herself and done what I had wanted to since childhood. In this she was a heroine.

I released my breath and she did the same, an echo containing every moment of our past.

'Your brother is a good man, Morgan,' she said quietly. 'Whatever you insist on believing. Let him travel freely and fight the kingdom's battles without your interference.'

Part of me wished I could just agree and let myself rest for a while. But I was fighting my own solitary war, and Ninianne was still on the opposing side.

'I don't see why I would,' I replied. 'I haven't been offered a reason to agree. You know my terms for the Book of Prophecies. I cannot give it to you.'

'Just peace, then, for King Arthur to do what he must. What would it take?'

Her willingness to negotiate caught me unawares, but the answer came to me at once, clear as a falcon against a bright-blue sky.

'Tell me of my sons,' I said. 'Both of them. That is what it will take.'

'You know I can tell you nothing of the baby I delivered from you …' Ninianne faltered, then understood what I was asking. 'Only that the charm of concealment still holds, regardless of Merlin's death. It was my magic, and I know its power. Yours and Sir Accolon's child is promised a good, happy life, but you cannot – will not – ever meet.'

I expected no other answer and believed her, but I had needed to make sure, one last time. 'And Yvain?' I said. 'What of his status now, his place in Arthur's plans?'

Again, she hesitated, the thought of her loyalties shadowing her face.

'Do not evade me,' I warned. 'This brewing conflict is in the North – Yvain's father will be called upon to fight. I need to know what will happen to the son I can hear of.'

She exhaled and I felt the guilt in her – another blossoming mortal trait – and a new affinity I never expected us to share: we were mothers.

'Yvain is squiring age,' she said. 'Soon to be fourteen – you know that, of course. Given Camelot's instability and the impending war, he has recently been sent to continue his knightly training in Garlot. To the royal residence there.'

'To Elaine?' I exclaimed. 'My sister's household?'

She inclined her head. 'Queen Elaine and her husband have full care of him. They send reports to Camelot and his father, but aren't otherwise overseen. That is all I know.'

It was more than I had hoped for, though the news split me inside, twin rivers of joy and agony. Yvain was with my family, but I still could not look upon his face.

'I have done my part,' Ninianne said. 'Will you promise to keep King Arthur free of chaos?'

I glanced away, towards the path that led down into the shielded depths of my valley. How I wished to be alone again.

'You have my word,' I said. 'Now leave my land and go back to your king.'

11

The first thing I did when I reached the house was write a letter to my sister.

My middle sister, to be exact – my prudent, even-handed Elaine, Queen of Garlot. Her country was of the same reserved attitude as herself, with an easy alliance to Arthur and modest ambitions of only keeping its own peace. For this reason, since I had been run out of Camelot, I had not sought contact with Elaine, so as not to taint her contented and carefully balanced existence with my she-devil reputation.

But Ninianne's news had struck differently, bringing a fervent yearning that, out of necessity, I had long tried to keep buried. Arthur's decade-old Royal Decree had prevented me from contacting Yvain by threatening his knightly future, but during my final catastrophic trip to Camelot six years ago, I had looked into my son's hurt, angry face and chosen to leave him to his happy and successful life, now fully in motion.

Yet Elaine was my sister and my son was in her household. I was more a woman of free will than Fate, but some signs could not be ignored.

I drafted my message on a wax tablet a hundred times before I committed it to parchment.

E, it said, *I have heard that something precious of mine is in your hands. Due to my mistakes and the world's cruel ways, I have not heard news of what I cherish for many years, but it has never left my mind. I will not ask for more, but all I wish to hear is – how does my treasure fare? M*

For caution's sake, I did not sign my letter in full and added a magnanimous afterthought. *Burn this note and do not reply if contact is of any risk to you. I will understand.*

Then another postscript, less careful but deeply felt: *I cannot bear to cause any pain. He should not know I ask about him.*

I sent the letter by fast horse messenger, and never let myself expect a response. It was too much to ask of my sensible sister, and she would be right not to indulge me. So determined was I to pre-empt my disappointment, that when Alys entered the study a fortnight later, idly holding out a sleek folded packet to me, I did not make the connection.

'What's this?' I said, glancing at the red wax bearing the image of a heron.

'I don't know,' she replied. 'It says your name, but I don't recognise the seal.'

Nor did I, so I tore it open and unfolded the letter – good, expensive parchment, covered with a hand that was legible, but belonged to no scribe. My eyes went directly to the neat, upright signature at the end. The first and last letters of the name were emphasised, a trait I recognised even through the long halls of time.

'Elaine,' I gasped.

She had replied and even signed her name, the heron seal not Garlot's standard but her personal arms, a symbol of nobility and patience. In other words, Elaine to her core.

Morgan, the letter said. *You always were so dramatic. I will not hide or pretend I do not have sisters. You have every right to ask about your beloved one, and I am sorry that this is the only way you can. If I had known they were keeping him from you in private as well as in public, I would have sought to change it earlier.*

It was her calm voice, as clear as if she were standing in our old nursery chamber, sighing over some careless act of mine. Tears welled up, but I held them back so Alys would not see and took the letter out onto the balcony.

Your son is strong, healthy and full of life, it went on. *Quick of mind and body, with an easy nature and good humour, which brings us much amusement. He excels at his knightly training – quick-witted at lessons, adept at the courtly requirements – and charms every tutor. Skilled with sword and horse, I am told. Handsome, of course, but without vanity. Sometimes his expressions remind me of Father.*

He has your eyes. And your boldness, occasionally. His sense of loyalty is strong, and he fights for what he believes is right. When something matters to him, he is not afraid to speak the truth – as he sees it – to authority.

A tear fell and splashed on the parchment, then another. Every day I had ached with the effort of trying to envision my growing child, and Elaine had anticipated exactly what I wanted to hear. Suddenly, my mind's eye could see Yvain, sense him, understand him. In a few brief words I knew my son again.

Even if I had never been told, my sister wrote, *for those reasons, I would have known he was yours.*

I wrote back, still cautious but hopeful, and Elaine replied again at once, until our network of messengers were retained solely for our correspondence, and letters flew back and forth as quickly as their fast horses would allow.

Our replies grew longer; I asked more, shared more, hungry for every word of Yvain, and eager to tell my sister my own truths. We spoke upon our interests, family memories, our lives since we were in Cornwall. I told her of my time at Camelot, Belle Garde, even my breach with our brother, with the caveat I was not seeking her to take sides.

However, on the story of my marriage, Elaine was not without opinion.

I met your erstwhile husband not long ago, she told me. *Despite his good looks and superior airs, he is surprisingly unimpressive. I see why you chose to run as far away as you could. Knowing you as I do, I assume he bored you to tears.*

She made me laugh, she made me cry, but I lived for every one of her words.

Meanwhile, Arthur's war in the north had begun. Belle Garde grew quiet: no knights came seeking to capture me, though the infirmary continued to gather patients and renown. As promised, I didn't send storms, birds or any other disruption as Arthur led his army up-country, less out of obedience than the thought of my son, training hard in Garlot; what Ninianne had given me that could be taken away. Moreover, I wouldn't have compromised Elaine for anything.

Such as it was, I tried to direct my attention towards other things. I wrote, I read; Alys, Tressa and I finally decided to call our manuscript on women's afflictions finished, then immediately began a second volume. I no longer tried to raise dead birds, but I did quietly study my resurrection formula, refining it with the Shroud of Tithonus in mind. One day, I even saddled up Phénix and set out for the cave where Ninianne had ended the Age of Merlin, putting my cheek to the sword-scarred stone that blocked the entrance to his tomb.

'What say you now, you pile of bones?' I demanded, but for once the sorcerer's voice was silent, and no thrill of vitality answered. If the Shroud of Tithonus had ever been there, then it was dust, along with Merlin himself. A victory and a defeat, all at once.

Soon after, the news came. Following two years of failed treaties and hard-fought battles, Arthur's war was over.

The war of Saxon Rock has finally been won, Elaine wrote. *My husband and eldest son, and most of our knights, have returned safe and well. An agreement was made with the rebelling faction, and the High King declared victory and a new peace in the name of Camelot. From what we hear, dissatisfaction with the Crown has quietened, and a sense of unity has been restored throughout the kingdom.*

Much of this I had already gleaned from the knights out questing again, some who ended up at Belle Garde's infirmary or dining hall, or occasionally beneath candlelit bedsheets with my restless self. My instinct was to return to my former campaign, to disrupt the celebratory tournaments, banquets and hunts that were being thrown by the Royal Court at a near-constant rate, but Elaine's next missive gave me pause.

I am sad to say that your son is due to leave us, she wrote. *Now the war is over, he will go to Camelot and squire for King Arthur for a while, a great honour ahead of his knighthood when he reaches eighteen. His time here has been a pleasure, and I will miss him, as much as I will miss sharing his progress with you. Be assured that I will make every effort to hear of him and keep bringing you news.*

So for Yvain, my son, rushing towards his knightly future with unfathomable speed, I left Arthur and his court in peace, revelling and carefree, amidst what they were now calling Camelot's Golden Age.

Two years, more training – which my sister kept diligent track of – and many letters later, the day finally came.

Your son was knighted today by King Arthur, at Camelot, Elaine said. *Myself and my husband were in attendance, and all were made proud. Yvain stood tall and handsome and took his oaths with admirable grace. There was a great feast and much celebration.*

Upon seeing it in matter-of-fact black ink, I did not know what was more torturous: the parts of the ceremony that I could picture – Camelot's Throne Room, my brother in his kingly robes, regal and serious – or the aspects my mind's eye would not provide. What Yvain wore to receive the accolade, whether he trembled to stand before so many people; my son's face, changed from boy to man in ways I could barely imagine.

However, my sister had more, an uncertainty creeping into her usually steady hand. *Now, I must make a confession,* she wrote. *I pray to God what I have done does not cause trouble between us. Before we left Camelot, Yvain asked me of his mother. Of you.*

My heart lurched with a hope too painful as my mind provided every possible disaster such an action could bring. I forced myself to read on.

There were questions – where you reside, how you live, who you are as a sister and woman. I did not have time for much thought, so for the first time in my life, I took the risk and spoke of you, the truth from my heart. He is a man now, old enough to know beyond what he has been told. I do not regret it, Morgan, even if you are angry with me.

I gazed at her letter in wonder. For my sake, Elaine had defied me and her own careful nature, her love and bravery humbling in its quiet power.

Never has there been a sister of such wisdom and selfless grace, I wrote back. *You have done more for my life than I knew how to do myself.*

Then, my own leap of faith, the kind I had long not trusted myself to make.

I ask only one last thing. If you speak to my son, explain where Belle Garde is and how best to reach it. Tell him that he is welcome here, and I will always be waiting.

But Yvain never came; of course he didn't. Six months after his knighthood, in the bleak hollow of winter, the only arrival was more news from my sister, her tone apologetic.

Three months ago, Yvain swore fealty to his uncle as a knight of Camelot and joined the Royal Court officially. Word has it, he has donned the plain white silks and been inducted into the Order of Queen's Knights.

I stared at the parchment. To imagine Yvain serving Guinevere, obeying her, protecting her, burned through every shred of hope I had let build within me over the past few years. Camelot, as ever, was winning: much as I had tried, no one had been punished for Accolon's death, not a soul shamed for the lies and wrongs thrown upon my name. I stood by as the realm's unity continued to strengthen and the kingdom returned to peace, while my son was stolen from me all over again. Arthur did not even send his men to bring me to justice any more. I was beneath my brother's notice.

It was the first and last time I ever threw one of Elaine's letters into the fire.

12

The following spring, Sir Manassen returned, bringing distraction from the problems I could not solve.

We had not seen him as much in recent years – he had been fighting in Arthur's northern war, and since then had been back and forth to Gaul with increasing regularity. Nevertheless, whenever he was in Camelot he came to Belle Garde, this time breaking away from Easter court as the valley filled with blossom and the scents of spring.

Manassen spent the first several hours greeting the household, catching up on the months since he had last visited. He was heartily welcomed: everyone wanted to hear of his life and knightly adventures; of Robin and how he was faring in the ten years since he had ridden off to achieve his spurs. An afternoon banquet was arranged in celebration, so by the time he and I climbed the turret stairs to my study, the sun had almost set.

We took up our usual discussion spot on the balcony, wine in hand, watching a cloud of starlings pulse across a pink evening sky. He told me that his wife suspected they were having a fourth child; his forays into horse breeding were proving successful after advice from Belle Garde's stablemaster; and Robin was in Brittany, jousting to great renown and thinking seriously of marriage.

'I'd like to say it's far too soon,' I said. 'But time has swept us along, hasn't it?'

'At an alarming pace,' he agreed.

With his sigh, I felt a flicker of portent. Life was about to change.

'What is it?' I asked.

He smiled ruefully at my prescience. 'I have asked the King for leave to relinquish my place in the court and move permanently to Gaul. He has granted my petition.'

It landed hard in my gut, but my happiness for him outstripped the swoop of loss. 'I'm glad for you,' I said. 'It is the right thing to do. When will you go?'

'Me, my lady wife and the children will sail before Pentecost.' He looked at me doubtfully. 'Though, as your sworn knight, yours is the leave I should truly ask.'

I reached out and squeezed his hand. 'You owe me nothing. But I will miss you deeply, Sir Manassen. I admit.'

'I will miss you too, Lady Morgan. If there ever is anything you need, at any time – send for me. Upon my honour, it will be done.'

A thought struck, and I opened my mouth to speak, then closed it again.

'Is there something?' he asked, but I shook my head. It was too much.

'All I ask of you is that you ride off to your homeland and not look back,' I said. 'Promise me, Manassen of Gaul.'

At my deflection, he glanced away and cleared his throat, casting his gaze upon the joust meadow. 'You do not know this, but when Accolon died, the fealty I had sworn to you was all that kept me rising each morning.' He spoke slowly, as if afraid his voice might break. 'There would be no future, no happiness, no freedom for me and my family, if not for my oath to you. That day you rescued me on the road, when you told me dying was too easy and accepted my service, you saved my life. In more ways than one.'

When he looked back at me, his eyes were bright but calm, more serious than they had ever been. 'I swore my duty to you, as your faithful knight,' he said. *'Call upon it.'*

The words tugged in my chest, knowing it was the last time he would speak them. From the day he had awkwardly kneeled and insisted he become my knight, through a decade of secret alliance and navigating our shared grief, we had found mutual respect, then friendship; another soul with whom to walk through the fog.

'My son,' I said. 'Sir Yvain. You and I have never discussed him, but he is not long knighted and I ... Have you seen him, in Camelot?'

Sir Manassen smiled softly, pleased I had trusted him. Taking my hand, he kissed my father's ring then released me with a bow, formal and courteous to the last.

'I have seen Sir Yvain,' he said. 'We have spoken on occasion. A fine young man – personable, good-humoured. Skilled as a knight and well liked, by all accounts.'

My heart ached more than I thought possible. 'Thank you,' I said. 'Was he there, this time? Before you left.'

'No, he was not in attendance,' he replied. 'Which is probably for the best, given the unrest in the court.'

'Unrest?' I echoed. 'Is Yvain in trouble?'

'Of course not,' he said. 'I believe he's spent the past few months questing abroad. I meant it's better he has not been present for the recent disruption.' He regarded me in disbelief. 'Have you not heard?'

I shook my head. 'Only of the kingdom's great unity and faith in the King since the war. Camelot's glory and renewed strength.'

'*Sacredieu*, I thought something such as that would have reached even here.'

'By the Devil – tell me,' I exclaimed. 'I can hardly bear the suspense.'

A gleam came to his eye, the pleasure of bringing me something important. 'The High King and Queen have been living apart,' Manassen said. 'He sent her away and declared them divorced.'

It hit like a thunderstrike. 'He … *what?*'

'I know – it sounds unbelievable,' he said. 'Given my time in Gaul, I hardly know the full story myself. But from what I've heard, King Arthur declared that Queen Guinevere was false, and their marriage was rendered invalid because of some deceit she had perpetrated. She's been gone from the court for a year, banished upon pain of treason.'

'*Treason?*' For once, the word brought a thrill of satisfaction, and something else thrumming beneath – a low note of potential. 'This cannot be true. It is too fantastical.'

'Oh, it is true and strange both,' he replied. 'Though now, he has called her back and wishes her to be Queen again. If, of course, she can prove her innocence to the court. He has summoned his most prominent knights and powerful lords to Camelot to bear witness.'

'Bear witness to what?' I asked. 'How will she prove her innocence?'

'The usual way when one is accused of treason,' he said. 'Queen Guinevere is being put on public trial for her life.'

'*No*,' I gasped.

'Yes,' replied Manassen. 'A trial by combat. She will be found innocent, of course – her champion knight is famed for his fighting prowess and will be impossible to defeat, as King Arthur is well aware. However, rumours say this incident has caused chaos in the royal inner circle, and it has certainly unsettled the unity fostered during the Saxon Rock war. By making the trial public, the King hopes it will put the matter to rest.'

'Will it work – to restore her reputation?' I asked.

'Who can say,' he said. 'King Arthur still has a hold over the people's hearts and minds, but Queen Guinevere has waxed and waned in popularity. Not all were upset to have her branded an imposter and sent away.'

There was a certain satisfying poetry to it, imagining Guinevere thrust into exile quite as abruptly as she had done to me. Better still, Camelot's claims of strength, the story that both court and realm were more unified than ever had been a subterfuge, denial of a serious royal problem. That Arthur had sought to hide such instability was a subtle weakness, but obvious to one who knew him as well as I did. The golden castle's walls had not yielded to my efforts at disruption, but perhaps its foundations were where the fissures could be found, ready to be exploited.

'When and where will this trial be held?' I asked.

'In Camelot, on May Day itself. The King wants a large crowd, to …' He trailed off, casting sharp grey-brown eyes at me. 'You should not go.'

I smiled. 'Whoever said I was?'

'I know you, Lady Morgan. Of course you will want to see the Queen who wronged you publicly tried. But you should not risk it – they have never stopped being alert for your presence and will surely expect you for this.'

The idea of my dreaded arrival rather pleased me, but I made no reply, instead picking up the wine jug to refill our empty goblets. Manassen watched me pour, then took his cup from my hand with a sigh.

'I'll escort you there,' he said. 'As a good knight should.'

'There is no *there*,' I insisted. 'You are a good knight – nothing will change that – and I would never risk getting you in trouble. Because we are friends, are we not?'

It raised a wry smile in him. '*Oui*, I suppose we are. In that spirit, I must be bold and say again – for your own sake, you shouldn't go.'

'I don't fear them,' I said.

'I know, and that is not what I mean. Under no circumstances would Morgan le Fay be able to ride into the city. They fear *you*.'

As well they should, I thought.

I looked up at the deepening night sky, last sunrays gilding the spring bloom. The longest days would soon be upon us, but light or dark, midsummer or midwinter, every moment for the past ten years had felt endless. I was due some relief.

'Don't worry, Sir Manassen,' I said. 'Morgan le Fay won't be going to Camelot.'

13

'So what does it entail?' Alys asked. 'This – what do you call it?'

'A glamour,' I said. 'An enchanted image worn about your person, so what others see is different from your true appearance. I will cast the illusion and maintain it as necessary.'

It was mid-morning on a stuffy grey day and we had been riding since dawn, after staying the night in the priory of which Alys's former study sister was the Reverend Mother. We had been given a warm welcome and godly hospitality, and had confessed to not a thing about what we were doing.

Inevitably, we were on our way to Camelot. Where I had persuaded Sir Manassen I would not attend Guinevere's trial, Alys had not been so easily convinced.

'You won't fool me, Morgan of Cornwall,' were her exact words, before insisting I must not go alone. Tressa agreed to manage Belle Garde in our absence, and the decision was made. Now, I was glad for Alys's company, but I didn't know what trouble we were riding into. Magical intervention seemed the only way.

'How long can we wear this "glamour"?' she said.

'For as long as it's comfortable. It's not a garment, but if worn too much it can chafe, and fidgeting weakens the effect.'

'Isn't it tiring for you to maintain?'

I shrugged. 'It's more important I stay composed. To keep our false image strong, I need to hold myself with complete calm, and not get distracted.'

'At Camelot?' she exclaimed. '*Iesu mawr*, we will never manage it.'

I laughed. 'Such lack of faith! I've been practising, you know. Hours on end.'

'So that's what you've been doing,' she said. 'Shut away by yourself.'

I ignored the shiver that skittered across my skin. The time I had spent immersed in Merlin's favourite magic haunted me, reading his writings, following techniques he had once used for purposes that still made me nauseous. To revisit his deceptive arts meant inviting his voice back into my head, making me wish I had resisted, found another way.

You will never be free of me, was his refrain.

'It was necessary to keep us safe,' I said to Alys, half to assure myself.

At the curve of the road, the trees suddenly receded, revealing a wildflower meadow stretching into the distance, to the foot of a steep-sided hill. On the summit stood a sprawling golden edifice, turrets and spires breaching the heavens, its gleam undimmed even under cloudy skies. The seat of the realm's power, great and terrible; the kingdom's own sun.

Eleven years, almost, since I had seen it last: the place I had once escaped to, then run away from. More than a decade since I turned my back on its gilded walls and knew it was rotten to the core.

Four thousand empty nights since I had walked away from Accolon's slain body with his heart in my hands, changed from what I had once been, into whatever I was now.

My body turned cold, then hot as flame.

'There it is,' I said. 'Camelot.'

I cast the glamour upon us in a clearing not far from the city walls.

I kept Alys's general physicality the same, but made her hair a strawberry blonde and scattered freckles beneath her newly blue eyes. For myself, I would go much further, choosing a stout, greying woman, rosy-faced and benign, advancing upon her twilight years.

'It feels like a heavy sort of shroud, but I can see through it.' Alys toyed with the end of her obscured brown plait. 'How can I touch my own hair?'

'The effect is only for the eyes of others.' I batted her fussing hand away. 'Just believe in it, and be natural.'

How much I sounded like him, the sorcerer in his lessons. *The key to any glamour skill is belief. Believe you want to disappear. Intend to exist out of mortal sight.*

My hands shuddered as I concealed my own image, bringing a blood-deep chill.

No, I told myself; *you are not Merlin.*

Knowledge was about intention, and the way I used my skills was nothing like the way the sorcerer had wielded magic. Invoking this spell was self-protection in a world that scorned and hunted me; using his arts did not make me like him.

We entered the city through the western gate. Camelot was busy: clusters of people crowding the squares; street traders offering refreshments; latecomers finding no luck with lodgings. Determined not to miss this spectacle, I had sent a fast messenger to secure rooms in a comfortable inn before the trial news became widespread.

May Day flowers garlanded buildings and posts, incongruous against the serious mood and street criers announcing the Queen's inauspicious return. There was vexingly little about the actual charges against Guinevere, Arthur's influence writ large across the city's information. The trial would take place at noon in the large arena just outside the castle walls. The same pavilions and jousting field where Accolon and I had sparred and challenged one another through Camelot's first tournament, on our way back into each other's arms.

My bones hollowed at the memory. It all felt like yesterday.

'Are you sure about this?' Alys asked, as we reached our inn and dismounted.

'As much as I can be,' I replied. What I didn't say was that I was seeking not catharsis, but a new game of vengeance, ways to disrupt Camelot from within.

We left our horses with the ostler and joined the band of visitors that snaked out of the city towards the jousting arena. The stands were starkly undraped, the only colour Arthur's red-and-white dragon banners hanging from the Royal Pavilion. A single golden throne stood in the middle of the platform, casting its long shadow.

Realisation hit like a wave on the shore: I was about to see my brother again, a decade since we last laid eyes on one another. It was the longest we had ever been apart.

Alys and I found a spot in the public stands nearest the empty court pavilions as the crowd filled up around us. I wondered where

Guinevere was, and it occurred that I had never heard of any protocol for the trial of a queen. The thought struck with unease; would this too be my fate if justice caught up with my chaos? Who, then, would fight for me?

I tore my eyes from the field. 'Stay here,' I told Alys. 'I'm going for a walk. The glamour will hold.'

I was out of earshot before she could argue, squeezing through the crowds and drawn behind the raised court stands. The Royal Pavilion beckoned me inexorably closer, where I once held a seat of my own. Without knowing why, I put my foot on the first step.

A pair of shadows loomed around the corner, so I slipped off the steps and under the pavilion, behind the thick canvas that concealed the supporting struts.

'I must speak with you,' said a woman's voice. 'Now, quickly.'

Dislike prickled up the back of my neck in recognition. The first shadow travelled across the drapes and along the pavilion's inner side. I followed the dark outline until it stopped, then peered through a break in the fabric to a narrow grassy lane that ran between the stands. Several feet away, facing me, stood Guinevere.

'There's no time,' a man replied. 'The herald will make his call soon.'

His voice was deep and clear, exquisitely court-trained and compelling, but the Queen merely waited with an insistent look on her face. She was uncrowned but still swathed in sumptuous ivory samite, not looking much like a woman on trial.

A weary sigh followed, then the man hove into view before her. He was a knight of tremendous stature, shoulders broad and carved across a muscular triangle of back, narrowing into a sleek, sword-belted waist and long legs. I could not see his face, but he wore his dark hair jaw-length and shining, tucked behind his ears, and was clad in highly polished mail under a pristine white tunic. Without a doubt, this was Guinevere's much-lauded champion, and the tension between them was thick as pollen in summer air.

'You don't have to do this,' she said to him. 'Three knights – it's madness.'

'Three, six, a dozen, send them all,' he replied. 'The King wants you exonerated, and I will fell them for this cause. Given it is what you want, too.'

Guinevere glanced away, a gleam of tears on her lashes. 'The trial only requires one duel. Sometimes, I wonder if you are trying to …'

'What? Die? With a sword in my hand?' His tone was firm but not harsh. 'You know I cannot come to harm if you do not wish it so. All I want is for your happiness.'

Such candour was outlandish, even for a close Queen's Knight, but to her it didn't come as a surprise. She made no reply but fixed him again with her pale-green gaze.

'What I have done is for you,' the knight insisted. 'Do you not believe in me?'

'You know I do,' she said fiercely. 'That doesn't mean I understand this.'

The feeling in her voice seemed to cow him. His shoulders dropped, and they were silent for so long it felt as though time held its breath. Suddenly, he stepped towards her, so they were barely a hand's width apart.

'Listen to me, then,' he said, with a fraught gentleness. 'When I go out there and defeat one man in your honour, you will be vindicated. When I defeat the second, it will prove *once again* that in God's eyes, you have done no wrong.'

He swept her hands into his, as if about to take a holy vow. My breath caught with the quick intimacy of it, how he presumed to touch a queen; another man's wife.

'When the third man falls to my sword,' he continued, 'I will have completed the most astonishing feat ever seen in a trial by combat. And that greedy, questioning crowd – they will only remember my victories, how well I cut and parry. Every ounce of unfair shame and doubt put upon your name this past year will be silenced. They will no longer speak of you with carelessness, or recall why this trial was held. You will only be High Queen again, in honour and glory. Exactly as you should.'

Guinevere's expression softened as he spoke. 'You would do this? After everything that's happened?'

In a swift, furtive movement, the knight brought her hands to his chest and drew her closer. To my amazement, she allowed it, leaning in to him so far their bodies must have been touching. His voice shook to its depths.

'*Anything* for you,' he said. 'You know that.'

This time, the gasp escaped me, indiscreet and too loud, catching on Guinevere's consciousness. She wrenched away in alarm.

'We can't be here like this. It is too much.'

Her champion remained still, regarding her with the same directness. Hesitantly, as if she could not help it, she raised her hand and put it to his cheek.

'My true knight,' she said. 'I don't know what to say.'

'Say nothing,' he replied. 'I know your heart, and you know mine.'

Softly, he lifted her hand from his face, and slowly kissed first her skin, then the emerald ring on her fingers. There was only one, I noted, not the pair she had always worn.

'My Queen,' he said.

They stood there for so long I began to feel like the interloper I was, but I could not risk withdrawing, nor pull myself away. Somewhere beyond this strange moment, a bell rang. Guinevere separated from him, then paused in her retreat, doubt written across her face.

'Go,' the knight told her. 'It's time.'

She left in a sigh of silken skirts, her companion heading in the opposite direction, past where I stood. I shrank back, holding my breath as he went by, then immediately peered out, desperately wanting to see the man who Guinevere let come so dangerously close.

But he was already gone, his long stride carrying him to the battleground, where he would serve his Queen far beyond what was required of any guiltless heart.

'Where have you been?' Alys said when I returned. 'It's about to begin.'

'Nowhere in particular.' Telling her would have to wait until I had gathered my own thoughts. First, the performance of Guinevere's innocence had to play out.

There was none of the usual opulent fuss: trials by combat were judicial and solemn, their ceremony spare. The Queen sat in the former joust judges' pavilion, looking suitably grave, but unperturbed. She had nothing to fear, after all.

Three heralds trooped onto the field to announce the High King of All Britain. Arthur's arrival too was understated – instead of parading through the field, he appeared from the back of the Royal Pavilion with no accompanying retinue. Still, it held the quality of an entrance, the crowd falling to silence as he strode forth, swathed in blood-red silk and ermine.

The difference that had been wrought in him by the years was obvious, but hard to quantify. He looked older, but not in any particular way, and stronger, though I could not have said how. The crown around his temples was larger than the one he had favoured in years past, but still modest for a king of his power and reputation. Nevertheless, he looked *greater*, as if his increasing legend had taken root in his chest and grown from within.

He offered no speech to his subjects, and no one joined him. King Arthur took his throne alone, poised as if seated amongst thorns.

A second herald stepped forwards. 'Now entering the battlefield, the High Queen's champion,' he announced. 'Sir Lancelot du Lac.'

The name elicited sounds of appreciation and reverence around the stands. All eyes turned to the arena gate as Guinevere's champion cantered in amidst a blaze of white – his destrier and spotless tunic, armour so bright it shone like star fire. The closed helmet he wore was crowned with a crest of snowy horsehair, like a Roman commander.

The knight dismounted at speed, handed off his horse to a squire, and bowed – first to Arthur, then separately, deeper, to his Queen. Formalities dispensed, Sir Lancelot du Lac stalked a large impatient circle, as if his opponents were already wasting his time. In the same moment, the air filled with the sound of bells – Camelot's cathedral, marking the hour.

'Three worthy warriors defend the charges brought by the Crown,' declared the third herald. '*Bring out the first challenger.*'

The crowd gasped at the news of three duels; unlike many men who talk of great feats, Guinevere's champion had not exaggerated. The first knight stomped out onto the field, wielding a two-handed greatsword.

No names were declared, and it soon became clear why: whoever fought was irrelevant to the matter at hand.

In a calm, sleek motion, Sir Lancelot drew his sword, then ran towards his opponent's heavily swung weapon. He carried no shield, but as he pushed and danced and struck, it was obvious such prosaic tools would only have slowed him down. The first man had barely managed to land a blow on the champion's blade before he lay unconscious.

As the first challenger was carried from the field, the white knight demanded his second. This fighter proved stronger, cleverer, with a pent-up aggression in his strikes that seemed to ignite something in the Queen's defender. Sir Lancelot increased his speed, using all parts of his sword to bludgeon and smash his adversary. After a lengthy melee, the beleaguered second knight blocked a dramatic upswing, but the force knocked his sword out of his hands. He had no choice but to yield and stagger off, stunned.

By the time the final duel was called, the champion looked almost bored, handling his third challenger with the proficient grace of an exhibition fighter. The crowd began to talk: words of awe and praise for the magnificent feat of arms; the knight's strength and prowess. After the first rout, Guinevere was innocent, then their undisputed High Queen. By the third, no one mentioned her at all – exactly as he had predicted.

As the last man fell to a blow that would have floored a giant, a great clamour took up – the bells of St Stephen's ringing again, marking an astounding, definitive victory. The entire battle had taken less than an hour.

Guinevere's saviour turned immediately to the judges' stand, but his Queen was gone, already emerging beside her husband in the Royal Pavilion. When Arthur placed her crown on her head and offered his arm, beaming with pride as she laid her hand atop his, I knew then that Sir Manassen was right. Everything had gone as my brother intended.

Thus reunited, King and Queen beckoned to the shining white knight, an invitation to join them in their new harmony. Sir Lancelot du Lac only stood motionless, closed helmet concealing whatever expression his face held. With sudden decision, he knelt, crossed himself swiftly, then rose and strode off the battleground.

The crowd drew a shocked breath, but Arthur and Guinevere just watched the knight go, their expressions clouded, strangely alike. Immediately, the heralds began to clap, breaking the audience's pause until applause flowed unabated around the arena.

'That was quite something,' Alys commented above the racket. 'The Queen is lucky to have such a champion.'

'Yes, isn't she?' I mused, then I took her arm and turned our backs to the tilt field. 'Come, we've seen more than enough.'

14

Before the sun had a chance to set on the rucked battle arena, and the crown of All Britain had settled uneasily back on Guinevere's head, heralds were dispatched into the streets to make several royal declarations.

First came confirmation of the trial by combat: Guinevere was innocent of treason and had been restored to her throne. Secondly, the Royal Court had been temporarily dismissed, its members told to keep to their lodgings or chambers. Lastly, the castle was closed, its public halls shut for a brief but unspecified time. A gesture of peace, the King's messengers were at pains to impart, to let the city's loyal subjects rest after the rigours of the trial – a generous act from their benevolent High King and Queen, now devoted once again.

It meant nothing to me. I wasn't finished with Camelot.

After a wakeful night, I rose at dawn's first gleam, dressing surreptitiously as Alys slept. I was donning the previous day's glamour when her drowsy voice came.

'Must you do this now?' she asked. 'The castle is locked down.'

'Not enough to keep me out,' I replied.

'Cariad.' She sat up a little, taking me in with her steady amber gaze, then said nothing more. She knew better than anyone that nothing held the power to change my mind.

'I need to see, Alys,' I said quietly. 'Alone.'

Reluctantly, she nodded. 'I know.'

Leaving her and our lodgings, I walked the periphery of the slumbering city until the outer walls met those of the castle. As expected, muted bells soon rang for the guard change, and I slipped easily through an unmanned side gate, tracing a labyrinth of paths to a cloistered courtyard and an unassuming door at the back of St Stephen's Cathedral. So many years since I had lived in Camelot, and I had forgotten not a single shadowy corner.

I entered silently, hurrying past the Lady's Chapel and into the large, stained-glass apse that stretched cavernously behind the central altar. The mausoleum of fallen knights held a place of prominence opposite the King's private chapel, guarded by railings twined with golden laurel leaves. Inside, tombs of white lined the edges, pale effigies slumbering atop marble plinths, armour-clad, gripping swords that would never more be drawn.

A pause on the threshold was all I allowed myself. Sir Manassen had told me the tomb was cut into the cathedral's north wall, the most prestigious position at the head of the shrine. I saw it immediately, under an ornately carved arch, bracketed by lit candelabras. Marble angels flew above, their heads tilted in reverence towards the long sarcophagus.

It felt as though I walked for an hour, every footstep faltering. When I could go no further, I exhaled long and let the glamour fall away. Before him, I would only be Morgan.

I looked down, and my gaze landed on Accolon's white, dead face.

Horror jolted me back. I had not expected the effigy to look like him.

Icy panic flooded my body, snatching at my breath. I shut my eyes tight, hand reaching automatically for the Gaulish coin, squeezing it in my fist until its solidity marshalled my bodily reactions enough to let my mind resume control.

This block of stone was not Accolon. He wasn't here, in this cold tomb, in any way that mattered. His presence, his soul, was safe in Belle Garde.

Holding his coin to my pounding heart, I looked again.

On a second glance, the effigy did not resemble him. It had shades of his bone structure, his handsomeness, the style of hair he had let me cut for Camelot. The sculptor was a near-Grecian master of the art – probably the most expensive Arthur could find – but he had not known his subject in life, and therefore could never capture him with any accuracy. Accolon embodied vitality and grace, his beauty illuminated by joy, humour and the pleasure he took in living. What lay before me was a lump of stone in the approximation of a man.

Becalmed, I studied the rest of the pure white marble. The effigy lay, as they all did, on its back, dressed in a tunic bearing the Royal Standard over full mail, hands laced across a sword hilt. An image flashed before me: Accolon's body in the same position on the altar just beyond, before I had snatched his sword and spurs away and left my slim mark on his chest, where I had liberated his heart. Nothing of my love and pain was written here.

Instead, I read the words others had bestowed upon him. *Sir Accolon of Gaul*, it said on the side of the tomb, beneath the date of his death; harsh, stone-cut confirmation that such a thing had happened. No shield of arms, because he had never been given one.

Then above, within the host of attending angels:

Fell valiantly in an honourable duel of swords.

The first lie.

Beneath, more lazy epithets, grandiose and empty, related only to what he was within the world of kings and men. Knight. Warrior. Joust champion. Brother-in-Arms. Nothing to say how adored he was by those who knew him best; how good a man he had become through his own efforts; the unfailing honour with which he lived, faced his troubles, and cared for others. How tender, strong and dedicated a partner he was, in life and in love.

Robin's *carnedd*, Manassen's eldest son carrying his name, fond tales the household still told at the feasts they held to celebrate him; the fact that we called my valley Belle Garde, because he had made it our home. Our lake, where he and I had lain beneath the willow tree. Even the endless tides of my grief were more of a monument to Sir Accolon of Gaul than this tomb could ever be.

Nevertheless I put my hands over his stone fingers, and found myself speaking to the barren edifice.

'I haven't given up,' I said. 'I can fix this – all of it. I will bring you back, find a way. I will cut those who wronged us to the bone, seek their weaknesses and rain down true vengeance. I will not stop, even if the world ends. Or the Devil take me.'

The words echoed back: artificial, dishonest as the façade I had worn to find my way to his tomb. Again and again, I had failed him.

The thought drove into me and I folded, until my forehead touched the hard chill of the effigy's chest. Against my skin, I felt the upraised relief of Arthur's dragon, all claws, teeth and boundless power.

A long, deep cry tore from my lungs: my own dragon roar of fury and defiance against the world, the past; against myself. The sound brought me strength and I lifted my head, forcing my shoulders back and my entire body upright, refusing my own prostration.

'No,' I declared to the cathedral's bonelike arches, the indifferent God whom I was long past praying to. 'Never again.'

This place, Arthur's great creation, had broken me once, so badly I thought I would never find my shattered pieces. Camelot would not defeat me this time.

I took one more look at Accolon's insufficient marble face. Whatever lay here, it wasn't my Gaul. His essence was where it belonged, at our home, where I should be.

I stood up, preparing to restore the glamour and leave this forsaken place.

'Is someone there?'

The voice was low, church-hushed, but I knew it well. Through the gold railings, I saw a figure emerge from the southern transept, patrolling in his impatient way. Quickly, I drew the glamour down and my hood up, and hurried towards the gilded gateway.

There, I came face to face with Sir Kay.

He stood several feet away, hands on his hips, trying not to show his irritation. His face was livid with bruises.

'Madam,' he said. 'There is no court today, nor is outside business being dealt with. The castle is closed under Royal Order, to afford a period of quiet reflection.'

'As it should be, after yesterday,' I replied. 'I'm well aware.'

He bridled slightly at such a retort from what appeared to be a genteel elder lady. 'Perhaps I'm not being clear,' he said. 'I am the Seneschal, in charge of the High King's household, and you cannot be here.'

He sounded so officious I couldn't resist the opportunity to rattle his world-weary attitude. Lifting my hand, I drew off the veil of glamour, revealing my own face.

Sir Kay's eyes widened for a heartbeat, then his expression relaxed into its usual sardonic resting place.

'I knew it,' he said.

15

My spine uncoiled at the familiar dryness in his voice.

'Don't be absurd, Kay,' I said. 'How could you possibly have known?'

He offered his crooked smirk of old, as a sudden bell rang through the sepulchral hush. 'The monks are still praying the hours,' he said, beckoning. 'Come with me and hide your face.'

Without considering whether it was wise, I pulled down the glamour and followed him, out a side door and into a warren of servant passages.

Kay glanced at me sideways. 'I pride myself on being a rational man, but that disguise is unsettling. You look nothing like yourself.'

'I could say the same for you,' I replied. 'I can barely see your face for bruises.'

He grimaced. 'I assure you these are far less magical.'

Otherwise, he was largely the brown-bearded, curly headed knight I had known, with his mother's eyes and a harried expression. More frown lines on his forehead, perhaps. At length, we emerged into a familiar gallery and he ushered me towards the Seneschal's Chamber. The room was also unchanged – shelves full but orderly, walls painted with trees and woodland creatures, the long table at the back spread with parchment, detailing whatever lavish event Camelot was planning next.

I dropped the glamour and became Morgan again. Kay looked on in mild amusement, then walked stiffly to his desk. His gait had been laboured all the way, but I now saw he was trying to conceal a pronounced limp. Soreness came off him in waves.

'You were one of the knights,' I said. 'In the trial by combat.'

'So you saw it. Wonderful.' He gave a sour smile that tugged at a split lip. 'Second to fight, second to fall.'

I recalled the white knight's flashing sword, his dominance, the relentless speed and strength as he cut and battered his way to victory.

'God's blood,' I said. 'You should be in bed. I can feel your pain on the air.'

'I'll live,' he replied. 'Camelot doesn't stop because I ache.'

He shuffled a pile of papers to no purpose, then looked up at me, suddenly serious. 'Eleven winters, and not the slightest bit different from the last time I saw you. How can that be?'

'To a *rational man*, it would sound like madness,' I said. 'Let's just say, time and experience have changed me in ways this world cannot understand. How did you know it was me, in the cathedral?'

Kay leaned his palms against the desk and sighed. 'I saw you in the mausoleum. By a particular tomb.'

'Oh,' was all I could say.

'On our last encounter, Lady Morgan – everything happened so quickly. I never had a chance to express …' He pushed himself upright, regarding me directly. 'Sir Accolon was a great knight and a good man – even I was fond of him. I am sorry for his death, and that you were parted.'

'Thank you,' I said. 'I wish I could say it was a long time ago, or that he is blessed to be with God – but I cannot. Better he was still here, sinning with me, than turning to dust in our brother's crypt.'

There was no reply Kay could make, so he gestured to a chair. I took one and he attempted to sit opposite me, but the pains in his torso screamed so fiercely that they flared on my nerves as heat.

'You took quite the beating yesterday,' I said. 'To guess, at least three of your ribs are broken. No one should be walking around in such a dangerous state. Let me heal you.'

He limped back towards his desk, clutching his sides. 'I shouldn't.'

I stood up, strangely irked by his refusal. 'Are you afraid I'll put you under some witch's curse?'

He regarded me with such reproach that I felt immediately scolded. 'Of course not,' he said. 'But if you heal me, then I will be better. The bruises will vanish from my face, and I'll once again be able to frolic these halls like a newborn foal. How would I explain that to my fellow knights and brother King, who all saw me get pulverised barely a day ago?'

I blushed at my overreaction. Kay did not fear nor hate me, and had never been afraid to show it.

'Forgive me,' I said. 'Though I'm not deterred. I can leave what's visible, but let me fix your ribs, check you are not bleeding within. You will at least be able to sleep and suffer less discomfort. And not die unnecessarily in the middle of drafting a memorandum.'

His face broke into a cynical smile. 'What a glorious thought. King Arthur's Seneschal dead, with not a sword in his hand but a quill, while reprimanding some ill-behaved Round Table knight.' He lifted his arms in surrender. 'Go ahead.'

I grinned and put my hands to his ribs, savouring the golden force rising in my blood. Kay flinched at the pressure, trying unsuccessfully not to squirm.

'How is Lady Clarisse?' I asked by way of distraction. 'I have missed her wise companionship.'

'My mother is well, Lord be thanked,' he replied. 'Though she retired from the Queen's service several years ago, preferring to be at home in the forest.'

'Why, if her sons are here?'

'Things have changed. Camelot is larger, grander, busier than ever. The growing court brought a shift in mood that she didn't much like.'

He forgot to fidget, and I found his damage: several broken ribs and a few blots of internal bruising. 'How so?' I encouraged.

'Oh, ambitious types arrived, along with a mania for questing, increased competitiveness, complicated loyalties. The Queen's ladies kept changing. Nothing feels as it did at the beginning.' He flinched as a jagged rib slid back into place. 'I miss Mother, but I'm damned glad she didn't witness this past year.'

The last interior bruise dispersed, no more than a flourish of my fingertips. I stepped back with satisfaction. 'There. All fixed.'

Kay embraced his sides in astonishment. 'By God, it worked! You are as good as you claim, my lady. Not that I had any doubts.' He regarded me with unexpected regret. 'You are a loss to Camelot – I don't care what anyone says. I wish things had been different.'

'So do I,' I replied with a sad smile. 'How on earth did yesterday come to pass, Kay? Why did Arthur send away his own wife?'

'I cannot comment on what happened between the King and Queen,' he said. 'Their marriage isn't my business.'

The thought felt unfinished, so I waited. He sighed and gestured to the chairs again, where he now sat down easily.

'After Sir Accolon and your escape from custody, there were a few strained years,' he said. 'Dark portents, brewing feuds, unsuccessful policy – all clouds that hung over Arthur. Then the Saxon Rock war came, we won, and it brought the kingdom together. Broken bonds were healed, alliances made, but within Camelot … I don't know. There was tension, an odd mood. The King and Queen had a … disagreement.'

'So he and Guinevere divorced?' It still sounded too outlandish to be true.

'Whatever rumours you've heard, it was a mistake, and it's over now,' Kay said firmly. 'But, accusations of dishonesty were made, and despite Queen Guinevere's upset and outrage, Arthur would not see sense. She was sent away, and Sir Lancelot – her trial champion – left with her. They went to his castle in the north.'

'They *lived* together?' I exclaimed.

Kay raised an eyebrow. 'He remained in the Queen's *service*,' he corrected. 'Arthur was upset that his best knight left Camelot, but you know how he is. He ground his heels into the flagstones and bid them good riddance. It took a year, but eventually he realised his error and brokered a peace for his marriage.'

The story had artfully little detail, but I understood it was as much as Kay could give. He was still Arthur's brother, after all, and unfailingly loyal, with limits that even I could not push. However, his information was useful, confirming my suppositions about the cracks in Camelot's foundations, trouble deeper rooted than I had imagined.

'As usual, a powerful man can lose his mind for an entire year with no consequences,' I said drily. 'Still, I'm surprised you chose to fight yesterday, against the Queen you have spent your life serving.'

Kay's response was a dark laugh. 'God's teeth, I didn't *choose* that,' he said. 'I know myself, Lady Morgan – I can be abrasive, sharp with my tongue, and can be goaded into argument on occasion. It's even been said I'm a good fighter, when my blood is up. But I'm not foolish enough to enter into a doomed situation. I was picked by my opponent.'

'Sir Lancelot chose you? Why?'

'The Queen's brave champion doesn't *like* me. And when something in the world displeases him, his solution is to duel with his troubles until they submit. Of course, given he is Arthur's favourite, I am the only soul on this earth who holds this view.'

'*Arthur's* favourite?' I said. 'He was fighting for Guinevere against his cause.'

Kay shook his head. 'Nothing is against Arthur's cause when it comes to his wife. Our brother needed a way out of his mistake, and Sir Lancelot provided it. You'd be surprised how many things work this way since the *great du Lac* came to Camelot.'

The notion was curious. Arthur having knightly favourites was not unusual – indeed Accolon had been one of them, before my brother decided he must die – but due to Merlin's constant warnings, and the natural isolation that came with being a king of his stature, he had always found it difficult to trust. For Arthur to hold such an intimate faith spoke of an affinity beyond anything I could have expected from him, and a potential weakness. Clearly, he had not seen how the same knight spoke in private with his Queen.

'What of Guinevere?' I asked. 'If her champion is Arthur's man, how could she rely upon him?'

'Oh, do not mistake me,' he said. 'Sir Lancelot is close with them both, but he was Queen's Knight before he was anything. Even more so now, after this. His breach with the King is far from healed.'

'Arthur cannot forgive him for leaving with Guinevere?'

'That would make the most sense, wouldn't it? But no, somehow Sir Lancelot's saintly heart is the unsatisfied party.' Kay rolled his eyes. 'He intends to leave soon, perhaps break from Arthur. Our brother is trying to convince him to stay, of course.'

'Interesting,' I said, but Kay's face defied further speculation. 'So everyone is an admirer of this knight but you, Lord Seneschal?'

He assumed a pious look. 'You know me, Lady Morgan – I am too busy to think of who duels best, who is the most virtuous, or sends the most defeated knights to kneel at the Queen's feet. I care that Arthur is pained by this falling out with his *great friend*, but otherwise I don't have time to hold a particular opinion on Sir Lancelot of the Lake.'

His words landed on me like cold water. He was lying – there wasn't a speck of life that Kay didn't hold an opinion on – but that wasn't what struck me.

'He is "of the Lake"? That's how he styles himself?'

'Yes,' Kay replied. 'Sir Lancelot du Lac, but it's all the same.'

Somehow, I hadn't spotted the translation, but now I felt as though an unseen hand had tapped me on the shoulder. 'Where is he from?' I asked.

'Benoic. Raised around Brocéliande forest. By a lake, I suppose. Any more and you'd have to ask our dear brother.'

It could not be coincidence. The orphaned child who had captured a water fairy's elusive heart had also honoured her name by taking it as his own. *He is of the Lake now.*

Sir Lancelot du Lac, Guinevere's champion, Arthur's favourite and Camelot's best knight, was Ninianne's adopted son.

Kay frowned. 'What is it?'

'Nothing,' I said. 'I'm just surprised that Arthur puts so much trust in one man, when his own brother commends him so little.'

He gave a heavy shrug. 'So it has been all my life. Sir Lancelot represents perfection to Arthur, his vision for the kingdom in virtuous knightly form. Whereas I only bring him childhood memories of the scrawny earnest boy he was, or the dull lists that come with the administration of kingship.'

In this, we would always find our bond – as the rare counterpoint to our brother's insistent idealism.

'You do far more than that, Kay,' I said. 'You bring Arthur unconditional loyalty, true brotherhood – the comfort of being seen as just a person. He cannot find that elsewhere.'

'Maybe,' he conceded. 'Even if he complains my honesty is too brash. I know he loves me for it, in his way.'

I smiled. 'A thankless task, being family to a king. As I well know.'

Kay hesitated, as if suddenly remembering this was not a typical day with us set about some courtly task, but a forbidden meeting under the shadow of treason.

'Why are you here, Morgan?' he said quietly.

I shrugged. 'I wanted to see the chaos.'

He gave a slow, accepting nod. 'And what will you do, now you've seen?'

Take what I have learned and seek vengeance. As I swore to Accolon I would.

I opened my mouth, seeking a more appropriate reply. 'Well, I—'

'Kay, did you hear about …' A tall, auburn-haired knight strode into the room with an authoritative air. At the sight of me, he stopped as if he had seen the dead rise. Dark-blue eyes assessed my person, a shrewd mirror of my sister Morgause.

'What in God's name is this?' demanded Sir Gawain.

Kay and I leapt up at once, and I cursed under my breath. Of all the people in Camelot, it had to be someone who knew me.

'Well met, nephew,' I said. 'No greeting for your own blood?'

Knightly courtesy forced a brisk bow. 'Aunt Morgan,' he said. 'This is a surprise.'

'For us both,' I countered. 'How is your mother?'

'She is well, last I heard,' he said, but my diversion couldn't hold him for long. He swung back to my companion. 'I assume you have availed the King of this, Lord Seneschal, and not simply idled here gaining your own information.'

Not a soul would call Sir Kay into question in his own domain. 'Information is my business,' he replied. 'I know to a *knight of action* such as yourself that everything is a quest to be dashed after like quarry in the hunt, but running the realm cannot always be steeped in adventure. Sadly.'

By the end of his response, Kay's voice was so dripping in sarcasm that Gawain's neck had turned red as wine. The Seneschal's talent for offending his peers was still unmatched, my nephew now distracted from everything but the insult to his manners.

I did not fear him regardless; Gawain had his own hot-headed righteousness, but my rank was a complicated prospect, and I was of his blood, which the Orkney clan took more seriously than most. Moreover, in our shared first year at Camelot, he had showed an interest in physic, and I had taught him some basic herbal remedies, quick diagnosis, how to stitch a wound. As such, we had never crossed paths in quarrel.

Yet he wasn't wrong: I was an Enemy to the Crown and Arthur should have heard of my presence immediately. Kay's civility towards me was a courtly liability.

I stepped between the two knights. 'The Seneschal was just about to take me to the High King. We were merely settling the terms of Safe Conduct, were we not?'

'Yes,' Kay said without hesitation. 'Within my duty and *authority*, which some might say should not be questioned. In any case, the court has been ordered to keep itself to private chambers. Are you some great exception, Sir Knight?'

My nephew held up his hands. 'I will take my leave of you,' he said. 'Lord Seneschal, Aunt Morgan – I commend you both to God. You may need His grace.'

Shaking his head, Gawain stalked out. Kay turned to me and exhaled. 'You had better leave, and swiftly. Draw down that disguise of whatever-it-was.'

'You can't let me go,' I said. 'Releasing me will make you look like a traitor, and I won't let you take the fall for this. Can you secure me Safe Conduct?'

Kay rubbed a hand across his bruised jaw. 'I think so. After all that's happened, I can't see Arthur wanting any more unrest.' He looked at me, demeanour suddenly soft, resembling Lady Clarisse. 'But to face him now, after all this time …'

I put a hand on his arm and forced a smile. 'It's all right. It'll be … enlightening for me to see him.'

The word *him* hung between us, sounding larger than it should have, as if we were referring to a capricious god.

'We must go, before word travels,' I said. 'Take me to Arthur.'

16

We walked along the Seneschal's hallway in silence, Sir Kay two paces ahead.

Eventually, I asked. 'Where are you taking me?'

'To the private throne room,' he said. 'I assume that's where Arthur will want to receive you. If he doesn't just have us thrown in the dungeon.'

I wanted to tell him not to worry; the Arthur I had known would not argue with Kay's judgement. But if our brother was so different that I could not imagine it, I might be in more trouble than I thought.

'I didn't know he had a private throne room,' I replied.

'I told you, things have changed.'

Eventually, Kay led us past the King's Council Room and Great Chamber, then through a crown-embossed door into a rectangular, sun-filled space. A dais rose up at the end, upon which stood the usual pair of golden thrones. Behind, a slew of dragon banners hung from the wall.

'Wait here,' he said. 'Don't get up to any … mischief. Please.'

'I'll try,' I said faithfully. He gave me an ashen smile, then hurried up the dais steps and disappeared through a door in the back wall.

I circled the small throne room. For Camelot it was understated, ceiling painted red-and-white, a row of windows along one side glazed with restrained images of swords and lances. There were no window seats, alcoves or benches to rest upon – no furniture at all apart from the thrones. Nowhere to hide.

A large tapestry hung opposite: an image of Arthur on his coronation day, surrounded by knights and lesser kings. Merlin stood off to the side, rendered in dark threads, waiting to tell the young High King of his true birth.

I was contemplating using an unravelling charm on it when the dais door opened and an immensely tall, broad-shouldered knight entered, a silver-hilted longsword at his hip. He was clad in mail so high-polished it glittered like stars, overlaid with a tunic of the purest white samite. His chest, wide and deep as a church door, bore no device – the plain livery of Camelot's order of Queen's Knights.

He strode across the dais and came to a halt between the thrones, turning to face me in an elegant, disciplined movement. He was dark-haired and stern of expression, and the most objectively beautiful man I had ever seen.

To look at him directly was to stare at the sun: fascinating and tempting, but difficult to withstand for long. There were Roman statues in Arthur's courtyards that would have shattered in envy at the classical lines of his face, the carved muscular strength in his upright, symmetrical stance, singing of equal beauty in the body beneath.

Yet his remarkable aspect and godlike stature were not all that made him, but an intangible, resonating gleam, beyond his silk and mail. His hair shone like obsidian glass, jaw length and tousled, pushed behind his ears, next to skin that upon reflection was less sun than moon: its light subtle, cool, celestial in its own right.

'You're Sir Lancelot du Lac,' I said.

He cast his gaze down upon me, eyes ice-blue as a January sky. His perfect mouth, full and sulky, twitched slightly at the corners, but he did not speak.

I needed no answer. This was Guinevere's avenging angel champion, the dazzling, relentless warrior of sword and steel; he who had clutched the Queen's hands and vowed he would risk anything to restore her reputation.

I smiled. 'Since we are getting along so well, I should introduce myself. I'm—'

'I know who you are,' he interrupted. 'Morgan le Fay.'

His voice was deep and clear as I had heard it with Guinevere, but with none of the tender, impassioned tone. He had spoken my correct name, at least, but the severe way he said it – like a dagger on bone – sparked in me, an affront and a challenge.

'A pleasure to meet you,' I replied. 'I saw your impressive performance yesterday. I daresay I enjoyed it almost as much as the Queen herself.'

He looked as though he might rise to my bait when the dais door opened and drew his attention. I braced myself for a royal entrance, but instead came the familiar figure of Sir Kay, his ears so red it looked like they had been thoroughly boxed.

'What's wrong?' I said. 'Is Arthur coming?'

'*King* Arthur,' Sir Lancelot snapped.

I met his savage, handsome glare with a grin, and he averted his eyes as if he had stumbled into Medusa's lair. Briefly, I wondered how it might feel to climb such a tree.

Kay cleared his throat. 'Upon discussion ... the King says he honours Safe Conduct, but will not be accepting an audience.'

Heat ran up my spine. 'My brother is *refusing* to see me? How will I explain that you haven't done anything wrong?'

He spread his hands in defeat. It hadn't been my plan to get caught in Camelot, but now I felt something had been stolen from my grasp. I had set my mind to a meeting with Arthur, and like any knight with his blood up, I would have satisfaction.

'He cannot just dismiss me. It's not good enough.' Turning on my heel, I charged up the dais steps towards the interior door. Kay rushed after me, but Sir Lancelot got there first in two unhurried strides, putting his body in the way of mine.

'*Let me pass*,' I said.

My demand seemed to amuse him, his lovely mouth rising in a smile of utmost confidence. 'Absolutely not,' he replied.

His arrogance lit me up like a torch. 'If you think I need permission from you ...' Curling my hand, I struck my fingers against my palm. Fire before his exquisite face would show him who he was dealing with.

Nothing happened. My concentration was more scattered than I thought.

Kay stepped between us. 'Perhaps I should try asking again.'

Sir Lancelot pulled his eyes from mine, snapping back to seriousness. 'You heard what was said, Lord Seneschal. The High King has made his decision. Nor does my lady the Queen deserve to be further distressed by this incident.'

In the heat of our confrontation, I had forgotten about the gleaming knight's less official attachment to Guinevere: what I had seen and heard, secluded between the pavilions.

Anything for you, he had said. *You know that.*

So quickly had she leapt to his thoughts now. What had sparked in my mind at the trial crystallised, became certain. He was more to her than Queen's Knight.

I took Sir Kay's arm and drew us away. 'Go back to Arthur,' I murmured. 'There's something I need to tell him urgently.'

Kay frowned. 'All of a sudden? What is it?'

'It's only for his ears. But he will want to hear this, I promise.'

'Lord Seneschal.' Sir Lancelot's cut-glass voice raised our heads. 'I respect your office and the rank you carry here, but King Arthur wants peace in Camelot, and has refused the request. I'm sure you would agree there is no negotiation to be made beyond that.'

His tone was not strident but commanding, impossible to ignore. Beside me, I heard Kay's sigh of impatience, though I knew him well – it was also a concession. No threat could make him retreat, but the thought of his brother, the loyalty running deeper than blood, spoke the loudest. For me, he had tried, but Arthur came first.

'Come, Lady Morgan,' he said. 'I'll escort you to the castle gates.'

'No.' Sir Lancelot strode between us, his starry mail sounding a faint music. 'I will escort her. To the *city* gates, and ensure this task is completed properly.'

'Do not inconvenience yourself, Sir Knight,' Kay said tersely. 'I'm sure you are busy preparing for your imminent departure.'

His barbed tone bounced off the champion like an arrow on stone. 'I always have time to ensure Camelot's absolute security,' Sir Lancelot replied. 'In addition, when you were making excuses to the Queen, I suggested to King Arthur that he should understand what happened today – how an Enemy to the Crown and fugitive from justice was given Safe Conduct so easily. By you.'

Kay closed his eyes, nostrils flaring. 'Du Lac, so help me *God*—'

'I wouldn't delay, Lord Seneschal,' the knight interrupted. 'His Highness awaits your explanation.'

Kay looked at me in doubt, but I shook my head; I had already caused him enough trouble. I mouthed a silent apology and he nodded, smiling faintly in forgiveness.

Sir Lancelot cast his winter gaze upon me and pointed to the door. 'Come with me, Morgan le Fay.'

The shining knight ushered me out of the small throne room, past Arthur's Great Chamber and Council Room, until we were beyond my brother's vicinity altogether.

His long stride left me struggling to keep up, so I slowed to an obstinate, comfortable pace, taking in the bright murals on the ceilings and new stained glass, yet more impressive tapestries garlanding the walls. My supposed escort was several yards away before he noticed.

'Stay within my reach,' he warned.

'Then I suggest you slow down,' I retorted.

With a huff of irritation, he stalked back to my side, where I could study him at close quarters. He was just as astounding in profile but easier to look at, without being in the direct beam of his beauty. Perfection was often boring, but not in his case: every expertly rendered piece of him gave something upon looking.

Sensing my scrutiny, he glanced down in disapproval. His handsome disdain only made my blood flare.

He looked away again. 'Do you have a horse?'

I wasn't about to tell him of Alys and our city lodgings. 'Just outside the western walls,' I lied.

'Then I will escort you to the Welsh Gate. Once you are without, I would strongly advise you to stay there.'

I laughed. 'Threats! How quaint, if not very knightly.'

'I do not speak on my own behalf,' he said. 'I serve at the pleasure of the King.'

'And the Queen,' I replied. 'Do not forget *her* pleasure.'

A slight tension flexed in his jaw, but he didn't otherwise react. Wordlessly, he led us into Camelot's Entrance Hall, empty aside from a skeleton of guards. At the sight of Sir Lancelot, they stood taller, straightening their pikes as if he had ordered them to. He strode across the atrium, acknowledging each man courteously as we passed.

Halfway to the centre, I froze.

My escort stopped abruptly. 'Come along. I do not have all day.'

I ignored him, my eyes fixed upon the tiled floor, and the vicious red dragon encircled with white. The memory formed, quick and brutal: a long bier thudding onto the beast's spiked back, draped with Arthur's banner; the terrain of a body underneath, unmoving and unseen; my brother's cold words echoing through the hall, seeking to tear me apart.

Sir Accolon of Gaul, slain by my own hand.

It felt like centuries ago and yesterday all at once. Or maybe I had never truly escaped this spatter of blood-red tiles, hearing that the man I loved was dead.

'What is it?' Sir Lancelot's voice broke into my reverie, softer than before.

'I lost someone,' I heard myself say. 'He was killed, and they brought him here.'

'I know,' he replied. 'A righteous punishment for your treason, I am told.'

His bland tone ignited my pain into a fresh white fury. 'Good God, you have the measure of everything, don't you?' I snapped.

He recoiled, as if the dragon beneath our feet had risen fully fleshed and scorched his skin. My temper had shocked him, which brought me a gall-black satisfaction.

'Come away,' he insisted, but his voice had lost its self-assured tenor. He changed course, keeping to the room's edges and leading us out of the main door.

Warm wind circled the courtyard with an eerie cry, white cherry blossom gusting across us in sweet-scented puffs. I felt a sudden relief to be back out under the sky.

The knight forged ahead, marching us through the gatehouse and across the castle moat, past gliding swans and petals on the water. In the pearlescent afternoon he was even more remarkable: a star brought to Earth, carrying his own light.

Of course. Sir Lancelot was born to mortal parents, but raised to prominence under the fairy care of the Lady of the Lake. His gleaming presence was formed by her love.

'I know your adoptive mother,' I said. 'Ninianne and I have a long history.'

He pulled an unimpressed face. 'From what I've heard, you have a *long history* with a considerable number of people.'

'Yet more you know about me,' I said. 'I'm rather flattered.'

He scowled. 'Keep walking.'

We continued down the castle road until we reached the crossroads leading to the city's four major gates. He paused and let me move ahead, testing to see if I would remember the gate I had claimed to be leaving through – a subtle chess move that left me impressed. There was more to Sir Lancelot than swordfights and the appearance of a god.

I smiled and sauntered off towards the west. The city was quiet, its squares almost empty, with just a few curious eyes upon us amid snatches of coy laughter. If Sir Lancelot noticed the attention, then he didn't show it, striding forth until the towering Welsh Gate appeared before us, carved with stone dragons. He halted only when we had passed under the portcullises and stood officially outside Camelot.

'Let it be known that from now, Safe Conduct is no longer in effect,' he declared.

'My thanks to you for escorting me,' I replied. 'You performed your duty with great thoroughness. I'm sure your dear Queen will reward you.'

Sir Lancelot crossed his arms, frowning handsomely along the road. 'You asked how I know so much about you,' he said. 'It is because, after all you have wrought, I made it my mission to learn as much as I could of your treasons and reputation, the threat you pose to the kingdom's peace. What I discovered is that you stand in opposition to every lesson, every tenet, every person I hold close to my heart.'

I studied him as he talked, enjoying his speech, the seriousness that rendered him almost divine. When I made no reply, he glanced down at me.

'The disrespect you have shown to King Arthur and this realm made us enemies long before we could ever meet,' he continued. 'And we will remain so after you leave this city and my sight.'

'What if I don't leave?' I asked. 'Word has it, in a few days you will have left Camelot yourself. You can watch me walk out of these gates now, but you cannot stop me from coming back in.'

For the first time in our brief acquaintance, Sir Lancelot smiled in full force, his face so transformed and devastating I had to look away and back again.

'You believe that, I'm sure,' he said pleasantly. 'But let me put it in terms you understand. There is no place so far I cannot return from. No circumstance that can prevent me from protecting this realm.' Unfolding his arms, he stepped closer, his shadow blending with mine. 'Think of a locked door, guarding the heart of Camelot. The strongest, most impassable boundary between Morgan le Fay and the High King and Queen. *I am that door.*'

I smiled wide at his arrogance, gazing up at his astonishing face until I felt lightheaded; not quite his adoptive mother's dazzle, but fairy enough. I had no idea if he was aware of his effect on others or not.

'Is that so?' I said. 'I assumed the King and Queen wouldn't need you at all, considering their renewed union, and your great rift.'

His flinch was no more than briefly clenched teeth. 'You should go now,' he said.

'Of course, good Sir Knight,' I replied. '*Anything* for you.'

My words travelled across him like a cloud, familiar, provocative. Obediently, I walked away, but a few yards down the road I felt the irresistible impulse to look back. The great du Lac stood in the same place, framed by the gateway, his eyes on me like first frost.

I held his gaze for one long breath, and another, then turned away. This knight, the High King's favourite, believed he had outplayed me, but it was what he did not know that would be his undoing. Morgan le Fay held more complications than he could imagine, but from one overwrought speech and flex of his jaw, I had learned exactly where his weaknesses lay. And in any game of strategy, everything began with understanding one's opponent.

Sir Lancelot was not the locked door to Camelot, keeping me out – he was the key.

17

Alys and I left Camelot that day, and she scolded me for several miles for what had transpired in the castle. She was justified, but I had no regrets: between Sir Lancelot and Guinevere's embrace, Kay's information and the secret cracks beneath Camelot's façade, I now had a stronger footing than ever to build my vengeance upon.

Back at Belle Garde, I set upon forming a new strategy, though what that plan should be proved more difficult. Supposedly, Sir Lancelot would soon leave the Royal City, but I didn't know when or in which direction he would go. For over a week, I sent magpies out to seek his path, but they found nothing. There was no trace of the champion knight at all.

Strange and frustrating as it was, I could do nothing but wait and trust he would leave Camelot as planned, so I returned to my daily rhythms and counselled myself in patience. There was no rush to exploit my advantage; I had waited ten years, after all.

Then again, it is said that to make plans is to hear the gods laugh, and it happened that my game was ready to begin whether or not I made its first move. Late one afternoon, I was reading alone at my study desk, Alys, Tressa and the household having gone up to the northern valley to attend an early feast for Pentecost. I was just contemplating joining them when the turret gave a great wrenching shudder, as if shaken by a giant. The gallery shelves rattled, jars of quills toppling on the worktable. A clay bowl shuddered off the edge of my desk, scattering polished hematite across the floor.

I leapt up and ran onto the balcony as another tremor took hold, vibrating the entire world before my eyes. The disruption wasn't emanating from the land – not an earthquake or subterranean collapse – but from the air itself.

Instinctively, I looked across the treetops, towards the east and the valley's main entrance, and saw my protective veil quivering, silver threads coming apart like bad stitching.

'What in all Hell …?' I exclaimed.

Another shudder shook the horizon, and what was left of the charms tumbled, dissolving into nothing, until the entire eastern boundary of Belle Garde was as bare as the day I had arrived. Somehow, my unbreakable fairy magic had been destroyed.

Limbs coursing with shock, I ran back inside and careered down the spiral stairs. Before I got halfway to the main door, a huge bright figure charged in, halting my running body in its tracks, just ahead of a mutual collision. Stunned, I blinked at the blaze of silver-white armour in my entrance hall.

'What in the name of Lucifer is this?' I demanded.

Sir Lancelot of the Lake recoiled, disdain settling across his fierce beauty. I raised my chin in anticipation of his retort, when another breathless knight rushed through the door.

'Du Lac, thank God,' the newcomer said. 'You ran off as if pursued by demons.'

'There are no demons here,' I said. 'Only trespassers.'

Sir Lancelot fixed me with a cold, pale stare. The second knight bowed with immediate courtesy.

'Lady Morgan,' he said. 'I am Sir Galescalain, Prince of Garlot. Queen Elaine's eldest son.'

'Oh!' I exclaimed. 'That would make me …'

'My aunt, yes.'

I had never met Elaine's children, but the descriptions from her letters matched him exactly. Galescalain stood taller than his father and less slight in a wiry, knightly-training way, but was otherwise a perfect mousey approximation of my sister and her husband.

'In that case, you are welcome, nephew,' I said. 'Though I cannot offer the same greeting to the wild-man you travel with. If he has caused the slightest scratch to anyone in my valley, I would have every right to kill him where he stands.'

Sir Lancelot clapped his hand to his sword in outrage, though we both knew his knightly tenets precluded him from drawing it. Galescalain put a placatory palm on his companion's shoulder.

'Our apologies for the manner of our entrance, Aunt Morgan, but no one has been harmed. We are not here to seek trouble.'

'Then why are you here?' I asked.

'Where is he?' Lancelot interrupted. 'What have you done with him?'

I cast a sardonic gaze upon him. 'Where is *who?*'

He glared at me as if to say *You know who.* 'Sir Gawain. He's been kidnapped.'

'And you think *I* have him? For what reason? I have no argument with Gawain.'

'Your grudge against the High King extends to all of those loyal to him,' he said. 'You pursue Camelot's sworn knights, seeking to disrupt as many noble quests as you can.'

I laughed, I couldn't help it. 'I don't even know who all the knights of Camelot are! What a waste of my time, chasing after any of you.'

Lancelot's jaw hardened. 'Yet my brother-in-arms is missing, and you like to keep men trapped here. Rumour has it he's being held captive in a cursed land, perhaps in a tower. Where else but your Vale of No Return?'

'This valley isn't cursed,' I said. 'And I do not *keep* anyone here. Knights happen upon me, just as you have – though with considerably less fuss.'

Sir Galescalain stepped between us. 'There's no proof of foul play, du Lac. She is Sir Gawain's aunt, as she is mine. My mother says Lady Morgan would not act against her sisters, and my mother never lies. I trust her word above all else.'

Sir Lancelot gave his companion a long look, then took his hand off his sword. Praise was due to Elaine for passing her unfaltering evenness onto her son.

'In the interest of helping our shared relative,' I told my nephew, 'I may have some information about this so-called cursed vale. You must rest here the night, and we will speak on it. If your friend can find his way to civility, of course.'

I extended my hand to Sir Lancelot; he regarded it as if my skin were poisonous. At Galescalain's urging look, he gave a growl of reluctance and swiped up my fingers.

As soon as his skin touched mine, another tremor rattled through my bones, the same sensation from the turret but radiating from inside my body; a forceful, nauseating weakness. Shocked, I reared back, causing his grip to tighten. A second quake rippled through me, less violent but profound, snatching at my strength like an illness. I tried to give myself a burst of healing and found the golden force dry as a drought-hit riverbed.

Alarmed, I struck fire in my hand to scorch him off, but nothing sparked. My skills were silent, unreachable, every sense dulled by the low, sickening absence pulsating through my body. I could not access magic.

I pulled away and caught sight of Sir Lancelot's hand as it fell. On his middle finger he wore a flat-banded ring, dull grey and set with an unassuming brown stone, plain to the point of ugliness. Something so unappealing could only be an item of great sentimental value. Or an object of power, trying to go unnoticed.

First the protective veil and now this; it was Lancelot's fault – it had to be.

The shining knight drew back, his eyes on my face. Though our connection was broken, the draining effect remained – lesser than by direct touch, but still potent. No doubt there was a distance at which my powers would return, but I needed to know how far.

My nephew took up my hand next, allowing me time to gather myself. 'We appreciate your hospitality, my lady aunt. Both of us.'

'You are welcome.' I beckoned them to the reception room and gestured inside. 'Please, take a rest while I make arrangements for your stay.'

Leaving them settled, I exited the house and headed for the stables. Within a few hundred feet, I felt my strength rushing back, and by the time I mounted my horse, I could once again wield magic to my full abilities.

From there, I rode through the hawthorn grove and to the valley's main entrance. Shredded charms carpeted the ground like gossamer, a great scorch mark left where Sir Lancelot had charged in. In experiment, I drew a few charms forth and wove them together successfully, but I was sure enough: the ring he wore held some sort of enchantment and had caused the quaking, bringing down the protective veil when he came into contact with it. It also explained why I could not find du Lac through the magpies before he was upon me. The ring must protect him from magic.

Whether the knight knew as much was still in question, but when I arrived back at the house, Camelot's champion was standing alone in the entrance hall, watching me as I came through the door. He studied my windblown aspect with a slight amusement, as if he had guessed where I'd been.

'The meal is ready to be served,' was all I said. 'Though there is one courtly rule here – no swords at my dinner table. I assume that won't alarm you, Sir Lancelot?'

His face shifted to a cool, imperious look. With slow hands, he unbuckled his weapon belt and rested his silver-hilted sword against the wall.

'I fear nothing from you, my lady,' he said. 'Shall we?'

He gestured to the room where my nephew still sat, brown stone winking dully in my direction. I concealed a shudder of weakness, but du Lac noted it, perfect mouth curling up in satisfaction. He knew exactly what the ring meant for me.

I did not have as much power over Sir Lancelot as I thought.

The three of us sat down to a private dinner, my nephew even-handed and talkative, Sir Lancelot displaying surprisingly good humour and manners, though part of me missed our attempts to get under one another's skin.

'You look like you haven't eaten well for days,' I said, as they tore into a second plate of seeded bread.

Galescalain nodded. 'We slept a few nights in the woods. Some manors are tired of hosting knights on quests and don't open their doors. Though my friend here possesses charms that I do not.'

He grinned at Sir Lancelot, who responded with a look of mild reproach.

'If you are tired then stay longer,' I offered. 'To truly restore your strength.'

And give me chance to understand the brown stone ring, I did not say.

'Impossible,' Sir Lancelot replied. 'The matter we are pursuing is urgent.'

'Ah yes, the rescue of Sir Gawain from kidnap,' I said. 'Forgive me, but if this quest is so dangerous, just the two of you doesn't seem a very robust rescue effort.'

'That opinion is my lady's prerogative.' Sir Lancelot gave a tight smile; his every politeness held a razor's edge. 'Indeed, we were travelling with a third knight, but …'

He stopped, halted by a glance from Galescalain – a cautionary look, but ultimately calming. My nephew seemed as good at soothing his companion's fire as Elaine had been at dousing my hot temper as a child.

'What third knight?' I asked, hoping to needle du Lac regardless.

Sir Lancelot ignored my bait. 'It doesn't matter – he was wise enough to move on. But if you do have knowledge of where Gawain is being held, best you share it now.'

'The land you seek is about a day's ride away,' I replied. 'Said to be cursed, but mainly plagued by bad luck, worse weather, and an unpopular lord. His residence is a rather forbidding place – dark stone, difficult to enter, with a tall, isolated barbican that would make a good prison. Locally, it is known as the Dolorous Tower.'

'That is the place,' Sir Lancelot said to Galescalain. 'I'll be on my way at dawn.'

'Wouldn't it make more sense to inform the King of this?' I asked. 'He would be able to throw an entire army behind the rescue.'

Du Lac regarded me severely, but I was used to it now. 'Sir Gawain is my brother-in-arms, and I was there when he was taken. It is my task, upon my honour.'

'*Our* task,' my nephew said quietly.

Lancelot was quick to concede, putting a brotherly hand on his arm. 'Of course, my friend – forgive me. We will all bring him home.'

Galescalain smiled, and beyond my own warped lens, I could understand why so many knights were drawn to Camelot's lofty champion. His air of superiority was pronounced, but his sense of brotherhood was genuine. Suddenly, I believed that Sir Lancelot would indeed risk his life to rescue anyone in peril, and never surrender.

'More wine?' I said, as the meat platter arrived. The food distracted my hungry guests' attention, so I took our goblets to the side table and poured three generous cups. Covertly, I drew a narrow vial from my sleeve and unstopped it. A slightly foetid scent drifted up, but with a spoon of honey it would not register on the tongue.

Henbane and opium, a grind of lettuce seed – a concoction potent enough to drive the strongest man into a ravine of sleep. I added a few drops to Lancelot's cup; he had been imbibing it all evening, and now was the time to push him over the edge. For all he claimed to know of me, Lancelot had forgotten I was capable of more than just magic.

Back at the table, I watched him pour the wine down his gleaming gullet until I could feel his senses spin. When the meat course was finished, the shining knight sat back in his chair and gave a yawn so loud that my nephew regarded him in astonishment.

'We should retire now,' he declared drowsily. 'Rest is of the utmost importance.'

I beckoned to the serving lad. 'Show Sir Galescalain to the yellow chamber off the north gallery,' I said. 'Sir Lancelot, your room is in the west wing. Come, I will show you.'

It raised no qualms in him, the henbane as effective at dulling his edges as I had hoped. Du Lac bade a sleepy goodnight to his companion, then bowed to me.

'After you, my lady.'

We proceeded by candlelight and the greenish glow of a three-quarter moon. I eyed Lancelot through the twilight, watching for the effects of the sleeping draught. Cooler air had sharpened his awareness, but his gait had slackened, a slight swaying in his shoulders.

'Here.' I pushed open a door and led him inside a well-appointed bedchamber. The woody scent of a newly laid fire filled the room, candles making tall our shadows. 'I hope you will be comfortable.'

He laughed in a careless way, his lack of concern impressive. So accustomed was he to commanding every situation that he moved through the world completely without doubt or fear. I could only imagine how sweet such freedom must taste.

'I never thought I would say this, Lady Morgan, but your hospitality is excellent,' he commented. 'Not quite the Circe's island I was expecting.'

'An insult or a compliment – I will not ask which,' I replied. 'Though you are no Odysseus, Sir Lancelot.'

Suddenly, he looked down and captured my gaze, eyes serious beneath heavy lids. Softened by candle flames, his beauty was almost too much to bear. He smiled, lazy but calculated, and for the first time he seemed aware of the effect his face could have, and was enjoying testing me.

'I will sleep, then,' he said.

'Yes, you should,' I replied. 'I bid you goodnight.'

I held out my hand and he took it, raising my wrist to his lips with a drowsy courtesy. I wrapped my fingers around his, feeling for the brown-stone ring. His extremities would be numbed and tingling by now – enough delicacy and I could slip it free.

As his kiss touched my skin, a rush of sucking, negating power told me I had found it, along with a harp-flourish of light behind my eyes: the unmistakable call of a fairy enchantment. My guess was correct – the ring was powerful and sentimental both. Ninianne had made this object and given it to her adopted son to keep him safe from magic. And I would take it from him, to prove I was better.

I braced my thumb and forefinger against the metal and pulled. An instant, searing pain screamed through my fingertips, as if I had picked up the wrong end of a forgemaster's tongs. I reared back, trying to bring the ring with me, but it was immovable, hot as hellfire; the more force I applied, the harder it resisted.

'What are you doing?' Sir Lancelot snatched his hand from mine, but I could not let my discomposure sober him up. If he suspected, I'd never get near the ring a second time.

'Nothing,' I said. 'I'll leave you to your rest.'

I turned and walked away, but felt the press of his gaze along my spine.

'I will come for you,' he called after me.

I stopped and looked at him. 'I beg your pardon?'

The light in his eyes had changed – still glazed, pupils black and liquid with the drug effects – but no humour in them anymore.

'I look beyond your wrongs now only for Sir Gawain – for my quest.' He sounded his words with precision, avoiding the instinct to slur. 'The King still wants you to answer for your crimes, and I intend to make it so. Soon, I will return here, arrest you as Enemy of the Crown, and convey you to trial in Camelot. For King Arthur's sake – for the kingdom's – I will bring you to justice.'

As ever, his arrogance made me smile. 'I would very much like to see you try.'

To my surprise, he smiled back – handsome, magnetic, the most lethal of traps. 'Many have tried and failed, I know,' he said. 'You have the world convinced that no one can reach you within your *Val Sans Retour*. Yet I rode through your magical boundaries without pausing for breath.'

His hubris was a strategy, desiring my shock, my anger. But I was not here for his gratification; he was intended for mine. My immediate focus had been to secure the brown-stone ring, but his presence was a gift from the Fates, and I wanted so much more.

'You look tired,' I said. 'Take a rest. Things may seem different in the morning.'

His stubborn, astonishing face – his surety that he was master of the situation – did not waver. Regardless, he would soon learn. The next time he saw daylight, it would be through the high windows of a prison.

'Sleep well, Sir Lancelot,' I said, and shut the door.

We were playing my game now.

18

When he awoke and discovered his imprisonment, Sir Lancelot of the Lake made the most enormous fuss I had ever heard from man or beast.

In the hours before the henbane wore off, I had been busy. I dealt with Sir Galescalain first, putting him under a sleeping spell and having the stable lads ride him to a meadow some miles off, waking beside his armour and horse, refreshed and unscathed. A slight memory charm meant he would have no knowledge of how he got there, but feel convinced that Lancelot had galloped off towards the cursed vale as promised.

Your eldest son is a credit to you, my next letter to Elaine would say. *Please accept my apologies for the mild trick of the mind I used upon him.*

Secondly, I rode Belle Garde's boundary and spent the hours of dawn recasting the protective charms, until they hung silver and woven like mail again. Later, I would give Alys and Tressa a truncated account of all that had happened while they were out of the house, and assure them my actions were necessary. I told them Sir Lancelot carried a ring that compromised my magic, and I needed to secure it for Belle Garde's safety. All true, if not the full scope of my intentions.

Before that, I had the still-sleeping Sir Lancelot put on a horse litter and conveyed to one of Belle Garde's restored buildings near the northern valley: a small hunting lodge easily secured, nestled in a secluded hollow. He would be kept in the building's central room, a high-raftered hall now furnished as a comfortable bedchamber, with heavy doors and unreachable windows. The chamber was overlooked by a lofty minstrel's gallery, accessible only through two locked antechambers and an outside staircase. From there, I could safely view the wildcat in my menagerie without the need for magic.

Hence the hour of noon found me concealed in the shadows above, waiting for my eminent guest to wake up from his haze of drugs.

The first indication he had awoken was a tremendous crash as Sir Lancelot threw himself against the door.

'Morgan le Fay!' he shouted. 'What have you done? Show yourself!'

My name in his full-throated roar sent a thrill up my neck, but I resisted the command. More noises ensued, loud bangs and heavy scrapes, the creak of splintering wood. When the racket didn't stop, I edged towards the minstrel's gallery balcony.

Already the room was in chaos – bed hangings torn down, furniture dragged out of place, unlit logs thrown from the hearth. As I watched, Sir Lancelot snatched up a chair and flung it at the door, where it crashed into pieces without troubling the unyielding oak.

He stopped dead, as if the action had alarmed him; I could sense his guilt swirling with the dust. Gathering himself, he went and pressed his ear to the door, but no sounds answered his disruption. Eventually, he sagged against the planks and slid to the floor, his silence seething around him.

'At last, you've quietened,' I said, and felt his nerves jolt. 'I was afraid I'd never get a word in.'

I stepped to the front of the balcony, where he could see me clearly. His face was a glorious sight – a warlike Achilles, full of shock and rage. He scrambled to his feet and marched beneath the minstrel's gallery.

'What is the meaning of this? *Let me out.*'

'A pleasure to see you again, Sir Lancelot,' I said. 'Despite the circumstances.'

'How dare you,' he snarled. 'Where is Sir Galescalain? Is he also trapped in a hell of your making?'

'My nephew is safe and on the road to Sir Gawain, in the belief that you have run on ahead,' I replied. 'The only one in Hell is you.'

He dragged a hand through his hair, muttering furiously to himself. 'Why didn't I see this coming? Accepting your hospitality – how *stupid* could I have been?'

Without warning, he ran at the door again, throwing himself bodily against the wood amid bellows of frustration.

'There's no point in trying to vault through the woodwork,' I said. 'It would also be easier if you didn't destroy all of the furniture, to make your stay more comfortable.'

'My stay?' he exclaimed. 'How long do you intend on keeping me here?'

'I don't know yet,' I said. 'That depends on how well we get along.'

He shot me a ferocious ice-blue look. 'Save your breath, Morgan le Fay. There is no peace to be had between us. Presuming you can even hold me.'

It wasn't an idle threat. The lodge was as secure as it could be, but according to various tales, Sir Lancelot had been in a hundred traps and sprung every one. To keep him contained while I considered his purpose, I needed to be in full possession of my magic.

Still, I had my bravado. 'Oh, I can hold you for as long as I wish, *Lancelot du Lac*,' I said. 'No one outside can hear you, so shouting and crashing about is a waste of strength. However, if you hush and obey what I ask, we can quickly resolve this.'

I may as well have asked a tiger to let me play with its claws. He glared up at me, breathing hard. 'I will *never* negotiate with you.'

Difficult, I had expected, but not quite so intractable. I arched over the railing to consider him and a glint of light caught my eye against his heaving chest, flashing green and gold. Amidst his exertions, a silver chain had fallen out of his shirt, carrying a shining object that had hung hidden around his neck.

I did not need to look twice to know what it was. Sir Lancelot was wearing Guinevere's missing emerald ring.

A rush of power jolted through my chest. Unknowingly, he had just conceded a major piece in his game, but I would not snatch it away yet. I must take my time, decide how best to use my advantage.

'As you wish,' I told him. 'I will leave you.'

I stood upright, retreating, and his brow flickered with surprise; he had wanted more of a fight.

'Enjoy your thoughts, Sir Lancelot,' I said. 'They are all the company you will have until you and I can speak reasonably.'

With his renewed roars of protest in my ears, I put my back to him and walked away.

I left Sir Lancelot alone for three days. Food and drink were delivered through an anonymous hatch in the wall, but otherwise he saw and spoke to no one.

At first, the huntsman reported a great deal of crashing and shouting within the room. By the end of the second day, our guest had quietened, though from the magpies I learned he paced all day and night, never succumbing to rest. On the third day, however, only silence, so I returned to the minstrel's gallery that same evening.

Sir Lancelot was awake, the thud of his footsteps echoing through the room. When I approached the balcony, he stilled like a cat at the sight of prey, tracking my movements. One arm reached for an unbroken chair.

'Any tantrums and I will leave this instant,' I said. 'Or you can find out the situation you are in. Your choice.'

Slowly, he dragged the chair towards him and rested two hands on the back. He tilted his chin up, and I saw the emerald ring's chain wink at his collarbone.

'I am ready to listen,' he said. His voice was surprisingly measured, and he attempted a polite smile. I didn't trust it in the slightest. 'How long do you intend on keeping me here?'

'That is up to you,' I said. 'Your stay depends on how willingly you cooperate.'

I offered a smile back, sweet and edged with mocking, but he held my gaze. His eyes could have cut diamonds.

'Cooperate. With. What?' he said, jaw tight over every syllable.

I rested my elbows on the balcony rail, taking on a confidential aspect. 'All you have to do is tell me something of yourself and swear to God that it's the truth.'

'That doesn't sound too difficult, if it's not breaking a confidence I have promised to another.' He made a show of considering it, then stood up decisively. 'Come down here to me. I will kneel before you and make my oath, as a knight should.'

He sent up another, more powerful smile, and the sudden light it brought to his beauty, the sheer handsome audacity of him, almost made me want to succumb.

'Much as I desire to see you on your knees before me, Sir Lancelot,' I said, 'unfortunately I must decline. You might feel compelled to throttle me as a godless witch.'

His pleasant expression dropped a few notches. 'I would never do that. Whatever *you* have done to others, it is beneath my honour to cause a woman harm.'

I believed it – courtesy towards women was one of Arthur's tenets that all the knights of Camelot swore to, and not even Sir Kay questioned Lancelot's dedication to his code. However, putting myself within reaching distance was impossible. I feared no harm from him, but without my magic, he could easily contain me then escape with little effort.

'How gallant,' I said. 'Put your hand over your heart, and we'll call it the same.'

He scowled, but raised a large, strong hand and lay it across his chest. 'What is it you ask of me?'

'Confess who you are in love with, and I will set you free.'

I have known what it's like to turn into stone – figuratively on the inside, and literally, through the power of the earthen elements – and the way Sir Lancelot hardened from head to foot was as if I had cast him into marble myself.

His oath-taking hand dropped. 'Oh my lady,' he said, as if my foolishness was astonishing. 'If it happened I fell in love, you would not hear of it from me.'

'Don't play coy,' I replied. 'That is not enough to earn your freedom. Tell me who you love, and swear upon it.'

Of course, it was not so simple – mere verbal confession would not be enough to rattle Camelot. But if I could get this famously pious knight to speak his sins aloud to the Lord now, I was halfway to persuading him to put his and Guinevere's betrayal in writing.

Sir Lancelot considered me hard, then covered his heart once more. 'If you want an oath, I'll give you one. By Almighty God, I swear – that will not happen.'

'You have no choice, if you ever want to see your secret beloved again,' I said cheerfully. 'Imagine, your entire lives wasting away while you hold your tongue.'

'No, my lady. *Your* life will be gone before I ever speak a word about it.'

I laughed aloud, enjoying his annoyance much more than his restraint and charm. Like this, he was ready for battle, and my blood rose to it in answer, thrilling for a challenge.

'In that case, make yourself comfortable,' I replied. 'Until you give me the truth, this will remain your prison.'

His response was to pull the chair to his side and sit down with his arms crossed. 'Then I will be staying,' he said. 'I am not here to satisfy you.'

But I was satisfied; already I felt more alive than I had in years. I could have remained on the minstrel's gallery all day, duelling with him and enjoying his irritation.

'A few simple words, Sir Lancelot, and you will be free.'

My provocation elicited nothing, so I slipped back into the shadows. Another stretch of waiting would do him good.

I was halfway out of the door when he called after me.

'Who, then, will rescue Sir Gawain?'

It halted my steps; a new manoeuvre in our conflict. I returned to the gallery edge.

Sir Lancelot was still in the chair, eyes raised and piercing. 'You must be content that your nephew might easily die,' he added.

'He is also a respected and skilled knight, of far more years' experience than you. No doubt he has faced many a dire situation and survived.'

'Most knightly escapades are not as dangerous as being held prisoner in the Dolorous Tower.' Sir Lancelot uncrossed his arms and pushed up his shirtsleeves, shoulders shifting like rockfall. 'He will require rescue, and without me, my brothers-in-arms will fail.'

Perhaps it was true – I had seen his prowess with my own eyes – but his attempts at persuasion intrigued me. He could not be fool enough to think I would just let him go, yet here we were, conversing around the subject.

'What are you suggesting?' I asked.

'I could go and rescue Sir Gawain, then return to your custody.'

It caught me off guard, and I laughed. 'Do you think I've abandoned my senses? I'm hardly going to release you after I went to all the trouble of taking you prisoner.'

'This is not about me,' he insisted. 'It's about a knight and a friend. One of the men I love best, and your own blood. I will accept any terms you impose – just let me save him.'

The obvious move was to demand once again that he name Guinevere as the woman he loved, but his adamant refusal suggested I should not knock directly on that door again. I would have to be cleverer.

'A knightly oath means little to me,' I said. 'However, for the sake of Sir Gawain, I am willing to accept a different pledge. Give me the emerald ring you wear around your neck, and I will keep it as a guarantee of your return.'

He paled. 'I don't know what you're talking about.'

'Deny away,' I said. 'I saw the ring days ago. I also know who gave it to you.'

Abruptly, he reared up and turned his back, suddenly unable to face me down. It was the first true sign of discomposure he had shown since throwing his body at the door.

'My lady,' he said hoarsely. 'I will swear any oath that you wish, but only death would part me from this ring.'

'More excuses!' I threw up my hands in exasperation. 'Do you believe you make the rules here? That you can keep refusing until I give in? *You* are asking something of *me*. I need to trust you, and if I leave this building unsatisfied, you will never save Sir Gawain.'

He swung back, his eyes blazing with outrage, as if just realising this was the one room he did not command. I let my demeanour cool.

'I do not wish my nephew harm,' I said reasonably. 'Offer me *something*, Sir Lancelot. You are wearing another ring – what of that?'

He lifted his fist, contemplating the brown stone. The moment stretched, my pulse pounding so hard I was sure he could hear it. Then, in a quick, decisive movement, he pulled Ninianne's ring off his finger and tossed it in a high curve, grey band whirring towards me.

I reached out and snatched it into my palm. In an instant, a weight I didn't know my body was carrying lifted, renewed strength surging into my limbs. My stature felt like it grew to twice its size. Once again, I was in full possession of my power.

Sir Lancelot had chosen to return my ability to wield magic, and confirmed that Guinevere's token was more important than keeping himself safe from the worst punishments I could rain upon his head. He was risking his life to shield her and their love.

The realisation thudded into my gut, dulling the edge of my triumph. I had known that kind of wild, self-sacrificial love once, and it was taken from me, by the same people that Lancelot fought so hard to protect. If I held any remnant of doubt over my actions, in that moment, it burned to cinders.

'Wise choice, Sir Knight,' I said. Out of curiosity, I sent a whisper of sleep down, and he yawned, eyelids drooping. I watched him shake off the sudden fatigue before returning his insolent gaze to me.

'That ring is my oath, upon my honour,' he said. 'Release me.'

'It shall be done,' I agreed. 'First, I will tell you how I intend to help your quest.'

He rolled his eyes. 'I don't need any help. Especially not from you.'

'Your attitude to my kindness is disappointing,' I said lightly. 'Nevertheless, you are mistaken if you believe one paltry ring and a so-called promise is enough to earn my trust. To ensure your return, you will also share your journey with a young lady of my household.'

'No,' he said. 'Company will slow me down.'

'Not this maiden,' I replied. 'She hails from the same vale as the Dolorous Tower and knows a shorter, less perilous route. With her help, you will reach Sir Gawain much faster. She is exceedingly beautiful and of charming spirit, and requires only your protection. Unless … you wouldn't dare take up such a responsibility?'

Sir Lancelot cast impatient eyes to the heavens. 'Don't tell me what I would not dare. Just bring my horse, my arms and this damsel, and let us speak to one another no more.'

'Good,' I said. 'In the morning you'll be on your way, and free of me awhile.'

It was only half a lie.

19

While Camelot's prized knight took a generous meal and armed himself ahead of his journey, I went to Alys and Tressa's rooms and informed them of my intention to ride out. They had their misgivings, but I hadn't told them the full extent of my plans so there was little opportunity for discussion.

Within myself, at least, my intentions were clear: allow Sir Lancelot his heroic rescue and simultaneously have my 'damsel' charm him into ease and conversation, playing on his breach with Arthur to gain information on the royal instability and, with any luck, his treasonous connection to the Queen. Then, I would bring him back to Belle Garde softened, and persuade him to make official the confession to strike at Camelot's very foundations.

What I needed now was the 'damsel' herself. The hour before we were due to leave, I went to my empty bedchamber and regarded myself in the looking glass: small in stature, deep-blue eyes, hair a black river about my shoulders, my face no different from the last moment Accolon had seen it. All this would have to change.

How should this young lady look to gain Sir Lancelot's trust? Similar enough to Guinevere that he would be stirred to intimacy, but not so much that he would close himself off in regret. Fair hair, then, but paler gold, and an arrogant prettiness that would echo in his chest just enough. Her eyes I made an arresting light blue, near identical to the knight's own. Sometimes, all a man wanted was to see his reflection and imagine himself understood.

Drawing the glamour down, I watched myself change, the last of my own image shimmering behind the lie. I made the maiden a little taller, then touched my throat.

'Pleased to meet you, Sir Lancelot,' I said experimentally. The sound was delicate as birdsong, and as pleasant to hear. When the damsel spoke, he would listen.

It seems my arts do have their uses, the sorcerer's voice drawled in my head. *How many times before you admit that my ways are your own?*

I didn't care, I told myself. For now, I was someone else.

But, when I looked again at the damsel's unfamiliar face, a deep sea-blue looked back – my own eyes, unchanged. A fault in my casting of the illusion, perhaps, but seeing their true shade brought a flash of defiance. Why should I vanish entirely? Sir Lancelot would never notice, and I had lost enough of myself in my war with Camelot.

I deserved to remember who Morgan le Fay truly was.

The sight of Sir Lancelot ready for a quest was enough to take anyone's breath away.

He stood outside his lodge-prison, armed and upright in silver mail, a fierce star under the morning sun, not a trace on his tremendous figure that he had barely slept, or spent half his time flinging himself at doors. I savoured the glorious vision of Camelot's best knight, and felt the urge to break him like a new pane of glass.

However, I could not indulge my impulses. My damsel must be innocent, charming, beguiling. She must appeal to his masculine sensibilities in a way my true self would never condescend to.

The first thing my knightly companion did was stride over and bow to me, in a manner so absurdly graceful that I felt a flush up my neck.

'Pleased to meet you, my lady,' he said. 'I am Sir Lancelot du Lac. It is an honour to have your company.'

I accepted his politeness, offering him my hand and some girlish name. He kissed my fingers, then took my palfrey's stirrup and handed me deftly into the saddle.

'Lead the way,' he said, after mounting himself. 'I am in your capable hands.'

We rode off through Belle Garde's northern valley. The glamour was comfortable, stronger than it had been in Camelot, requiring less of my direct focus. Merlin's demon magic yielded to practice like every other skill, and I was getting better.

My first words were to ask Sir Lancelot of his quest. He explained Gawain's rescue in succinct detail, without deviation from the reasoning he had given to me as Morgan.

'A noble endeavour, saving a friend,' I replied. 'I feel fortunate to have such a knight as you by my side.'

I wondered if it was too much flattery, too soon, but my compliment gave him no flicker of pause or doubt. He was clearly used to hearing a great deal of praise.

'What has your mistress told you of me?' he asked.

'Very little, aside from I am to show you the way to the Dolorous Tower, and return with you to Belle Garde. Why, what should I know?'

'Nothing, my lady,' he said lightly. 'I am your knight, and you are my guide. That is all we need.'

I didn't want to raise his suspicions, but our rapport was friendly, and patience had never been my strength. 'Travelling companions often seek to know one another better,' I countered. 'I've heard you were raised in a lake.'

He gave an easy-going shrug. 'Maybe I was. Though it is a little early in the day for life stories. Ask me again later.'

We travelled a while longer, until I guided us off the road and into an airy wood carpeted with bluebells. 'How do you know the way?' Lancelot asked, as we rode under birdsong between shafts of sun. 'Are you from near the Dolorous Tower?'

'Maybe I am,' I said coyly. 'Ask me again later.'

I had never heard him laugh, and the sound was a music I could not have imagined, low and unguarded, clear as spring rain.

Our eyes met and we smiled at one another. Dazzled, I looked away, and he courteously returned his gaze to the road. In my senses I felt his nerves settle; the damsel being flustered had shown her as natural, uncalculated, allowing him to trust her a little more.

We passed a while talking on inconsequential things. When not fraught with anger or dislike, Sir Lancelot was good-humoured, friendly and surprisingly modest, with a confidence that landed naturally as charm.

'May I ask questions yet?' I said, just past noon. He inclined his head in assent. 'Tell me of your life in the Royal Court. It seems such a faraway place, as if it isn't real.'

His hesitation was barely a heartbeat, but I felt it. 'It is as real and magnificent as you can imagine,' he said. 'Though my life is the same as most sworn knights. Sometimes I have duties in court, for the King and Queen, and other times I am questing, or doing battle for the glory of the Crown. All is an honour.'

At my urging, he continued, amiably expanding upon the pleasures of his knightly life. He even began speaking of the love he held for Arthur and Guinevere, though when I looked interested he retreated from the subject, as if he had pressed upon a bruise.

'What of you?' I asked instead. 'The man within the knight?'

To my surprise, he flushed, as though he was unused to considering his inner self. Beyond his appreciation for horses and swordcraft, time with his brothers-in-arms, I managed to extract that he occasionally read poetry and had mastered several musical instruments.

'Chess,' he added. 'I like to play. Or I did, with the right partner.'

The answer was a kick to my sternum, bringing memories of Accolon and myself in Tintagel, first bonding over a chessboard, our connection growing strong.

'I know little of chess,' I said; the damsel was not me, after all. 'I had a paramour who played, but I could not learn.'

Sir Lancelot regarded me with interest. 'What became of him?'

Again, I fought with the image of those earliest days, the happiness and thrill of being with my Gaul, feeling that the world would bend for whatever we wished to become.

'He is long gone,' I managed. 'It was not meant to be.'

Lancelot gave a slow, sad nod, as if he understood, but still the past ached through my bones. I needed to take hold of it, make my pain useful at least, and now was my chance.

'Do you have a beloved, Sir Knight?' I asked. 'Someone to return to?'

I expected at least resistance, but he answered. 'I thought so, once. I loved and was loved in return. Now, I am not so sure. Things change.'

'Love doesn't change without reason,' I said. 'What happened?'

That gave him pause, and he was silent for so long I assumed I had over-reached. Suddenly, he turned, his pale-blue eyes locking with mine.

'*I* happened,' he said. 'The way I ... am made, how I can be. The circumstances – it is too complicated. My feelings remain, but I am not what she needs.'

I had not anticipated any answer, much less one of such honesty. 'I'm sorry,' I heard myself say.

He sighed. 'It is my own fault. Some say I feel too much. Love, anger, despair, the need to break free. At times, it leads me into trouble.'

His words echoed to my core, so apt they could have come from my own lips. 'You are not your flaws,' I told him. 'To feel things strongly is nothing to be ashamed of.'

'That is kind of you, my lady, even if it is not so simple.'

He smiled sadly and cast his gaze away, leaving me faintly adrift. For several miles we rode on in quiet, while I wished he would keep talking. I wanted to hear more of him, keep seeking the strange similarities I never expected us to share.

Late afternoon, we paused by a stream to let the horses drink and graze. Sir Lancelot refilled our waterskins, then we sat down amongst a haze of bluebells.

'How long until we reach the cursed vale?' he asked, then flushed. 'My apologies. I should not speak thus of your homeland.'

I waved it away. 'Not too much further. We will have to pass the night somewhere, then the Dolorous Tower should be within reach by tomorrow noon.'

I plucked two of Tressa's apples from my saddlebag and offered him one. He accepted the fruit with a melancholy smile.

'Sir Gawain loves apples,' he said. 'Wherever he goes, he seeks them out.'

He took a short knife from his belt and cut into the fruit's flesh, eating a slice from the blade. 'We must pray tonight that he can hold on.'

I bit into my own apple, cold and wine-dark. 'If Sir Gawain's situation is so dire, would King Arthur not come to the rescue?'

'It's not for me to say,' he replied. 'When I left, the King had promised the Queen he would stay by her side.'

'She could join him,' I said. 'It is said they've never liked to be apart.'

Sir Lancelot frowned, thrusting the edge of his blade hard into the apple. The bright steel slipped with the force of it and veered out, slicing into his left palm.

'Blood of Christ!' he exclaimed, rearing to his feet.

I leapt up in genuine surprise; in all the insults he had slung at Morgan, I had never heard him curse before. He stared at me, aghast with himself.

'I'm sorry, my lady. That was inexcusable.'

'It's all right,' I replied. 'Let me see your hand.'

He shook his head. 'It's nothing. A flesh wound.'

I reached out anyway. 'Here.'

At my insistence, he followed me to sit down again and let me draw his hand into my lap. He was right – the cut was long but not too deep, a row of ruby beads shining along the slim, clean line. My blood prickled in response, eager to heal.

'It shouldn't need stitches,' I said. 'I have muslin and a salve that might help.'

A slight tension girded his shoulders. 'Did your mistress teach you this?'

'No,' I said quickly. 'Lady le Fay is too busy to condescend to teach.'

His hand relaxed, my instincts straining to repair such a simple injury. I traced my thumb along the laceration and a drop of his blood sprang loose, marking my skin.

A rush of vitality shot up my arms, a pure, white-gold pleasure. The sensation careened around my body and glittered through my mind, formless and wild, different to mine, but instantly recognisable.

Sir Lancelot had healing in his blood.

It was all I could do to stop the wound from closing in an instant. With a gasp, I pulled away hard, as if trying to halt a runaway horse.

The knight regarded me in concern. 'Is something wrong?'

'No, I …' My voice was faint, breathless. 'Clean your hand first.'

He obeyed, pouring the contents of his waterskin on the wound as I fought to recover my composure. Reaching for my saddlebag, I drew out muslin and a pot of chamomile ointment. The soothing scent rose up, but it didn't help calm my racing pulse.

'I can tend it myself,' Lancelot offered. 'You don't have to—'

'It's all right,' I said, beckoning, and he lay his hand back on my open palm.

Salve on my fingers, I prepared myself for the effect, and as I touched the open injury, his blood sang out more clearly. His natural affinity was not as strong as mine; whatever he held felt dormant, without the clarity brought by years of practice and medicinal knowledge. Still, it was there, running through his body like a river in the sun.

I let my fingertips circle his palm and drew steady, careful breaths, allowing our connection to flow through me without answering its call. I was in control now, as sure of my power as I was that Lancelot did not know of his.

A quiver of observation prickled over my skin, and I raised my gaze to find him looking at me intently. All of a sudden, keeping the damsel's eyes as my natural colour felt like a mistake I should not have made.

I lowered my eyelids and reached for the muslin, methodically bandaging his palm. His attention remained on my face, so keenly it felt like touch.

I relinquished his hand with a shiver of relief. 'All done.'

'Thank you,' he said. 'I am in your debt.'

'You will have to be careful with it for a while. Palm injuries are tricky to heal.'

Lancelot raised the bandaged hand to his chest. 'It won't take long. Fortunately, I have always been a very fast healer.'

Perhaps he knew about his blood after all. 'Why is that?' I asked.

He shrugged. 'A blessing from God, maybe.'

Of course that's what he thought. Outside of his knightly prowess, his life had never given him cause to need other talents. He was lauded enough by the world he inhabited.

Better that it be this way, I decided; no matter that this was a further similarity between us, a connection rare and powerful that I had never felt with another. I had my own purpose, and he was the road, not the destination.

'Evening approaches,' I said. 'We should find a bed in which to pass the night.'

Briefly, Lancelot hesitated, then swung up onto his horse, glancing off through the trees at the fiery sunset.

'Yes,' he replied. 'I think we should.'

20

'This is the only chamber we have, but you are welcome to it.'

After some procrastination, Sir Lancelot and I had been left with no choice but to stop at the first building we found, before darkness fell entirely. The manor house was very small, but presided over by a vavasour who was abundantly happy to give us food and lodgings for the night. It wasn't until we had dined and were taken to our sleeping quarters that we understood his reference to a singular bedchamber was literal.

'I'm sure you don't mind sharing,' our host added. 'Given your relation.'

My knight-escort swallowed and said nothing. It had been his idea, not mine, to avoid questions of our virtue by claiming we were brother and sister.

'Of course,' I said. 'We are honoured by your hospitality.'

The vavasour bowed and departed, leaving us alone. Lancelot remained motionless just inside the doorway, so I took the taper he carried and walked around the room, lighting the candles until the chamber was bathed in soft yellow light. In the middle stood a large, richly draped bed, fit for any noble guest, and a far less auspicious pallet against the wall, meant for smaller squires.

'This will suit us well enough,' I said, but my companion didn't move.

'I'll find somewhere else,' he declared. 'It's my lie that put us in this situation. I'll sleep in the kitchens if I have to.'

'Don't be ridiculous,' I said. 'It's late, we've been riding for hours, and there are two beds. Stand there all night if you wish, but I'm going to undress and go to sleep.'

It was bold behaviour for any lady, but the chafing glamour had me too restless to mind the damsel's delicacies. Lancelot nodded in vague agreement and I disappeared behind a nearby screen, letting the illusion drop from my body with a sigh of relief. Recast, it should last a few hours while I slept, then I could rise before dawn and restore my disguise.

Methodically, I began to undress, savouring my liberation with each piece shed. Boots, belt, the blue serge surcoat, heavy and practical over my gown. I let down my own hair and shook the dark locks loose, massaging away the tension in my scalp.

A low sound reached my ears through the room's peace. I paused, listening to the rapid murmur of words, recognisable by a familiar rhythm.

Hallowed be thy name.

Sir Lancelot was saying his prayers.

I dropped my hands to my waist, unlacing my under-gown to the rise and fall of his voice. *Forgive us our trespasses.*

When I stood in my loose linen chemise, I drew a deep breath and cast the glamour once more, making sure it reflected the damsel's ready-for-bed appearance, my tousled hair turned golden again about her shoulders.

Lead us not into temptation, I thought, and stepped out from behind the screen.

Lancelot looked up from where he knelt beside the large bed. He had disrobed to his breeches and billowing undershirt, fingers woven together in prayer.

Slowly, he rose to his feet, toying with something at his throat. Guinevere's emerald ring fell from his hand, glittering like envy.

'Amen,' I said, when he failed to conclude. 'What's that?'

He glanced down, and the sight of the green stone seemed to deflate him. 'Nothing,' he said, tucking the ring back into his shirt. He gestured to a wine tray that the vavasour had left us. 'Shall we share a last cup, before retiring?'

I nodded and he went to pour, returning with two goblets. I lifted mine aloft.

'What shall we drink to?' I asked, then saw an opportunity. 'No – let us make a wish. What do you want, Sir Lancelot, more than anything on God's earth?'

He fell still, and I could feel his heartbeat across my senses like a songbird's wings. Confession laced the air between us.

'To perform a miracle,' he said.

His declaration caught me off guard, startling and sincere.

'What sort of miracle?' I asked.

His shoulders shifted in a slight shrug. 'Something remarkable,' he said. 'Beyond the skills I am known for, that which is expected of me. A pure act of wonder.'

I thought of his healing blood, how he didn't know what ran through his body; the power that did not require a sword. How easily I could give Lancelot his miracle, teach him to harness the wonders within and change his entire existence.

Before I could offer a response, he drained his goblet and said, 'It doesn't matter. Perhaps for me, such things are not possible. Your turn, my lady – what is your wish?'

His quick self-dismissal left me intrigued, but he left no room for further questions. 'I wish …' I mused, then trailed off, eying the man before me, his demeanour both open and evasive. I put my cup down and stepped closer.

'I wish you would tell me what you hide, Sir Knight.'

He said nothing, so I reached for the silver chain between his shirt laces, seeking the ring. Lancelot's hand fell on my wrist, soft and quick as a cat's paw.

'I told you, there's nothing to see,' he said. 'We should rest.'

He moved his hands to my forearms and, with a delicate force, sat me softly down on the luxurious bed. In any other circumstance, a man trying to handle me this way would have been torched with my fury, but he did it with such gentleness that I allowed the presumption.

'That mean pallet will never fit you,' I said. 'There's plenty of room in—'

'Do not say it,' he interrupted. 'For both of our sakes.'

His voice did not convince me; I put my hand on his wrist this time, and sat him down at my side. Lancelot complied without resistance or reproach. Our knees touched, and he did not prevent it or move away.

'Take the good bed,' I said. 'You are the one who has to do battle tomorrow.'

He smiled, tired but unguarded. 'I cannot. What kind of knight would I be?'

'One who is rested, and lives.' I lifted his bandaged hand, still in mine. 'You only have one good arm, after all.'

His gaze roved my face, lingering on the dark-blue eyes I hadn't changed, and I felt a warm, exposed sensation, as if he had seen through my disguise and recognised me. Part of me wished he had.

Without thinking too much about it, I sent a flush of healing through my fingers and felt the knife cut in his skin mend. It was so subtle I never thought he would note it, but a ripple of awareness passed through him as the cut vanished, a sensing of change.

'What is all this?' he said in a low voice.

'I don't know,' I replied. 'I could not speak it aloud.'

'Speak it in my ear, then.'

Tilting down, he leaned towards my lips, so close I could see the leaping pulse at his throat. His breath scored a hot path along my neck.

'There is the way things appear, or how they really are,' I said. 'You choose.'

He drew back and considered me with a quiet intensity, as if a secret accord had passed between us. 'Things must stay as they are,' he said. 'There is no other way.'

So we were decided; Lancelot had chosen denial.

Folding his fingers across his healed palm, I pressed his hand to his chest and stood up, relinquishing him and the comfortable bed. When I reached the narrow straw mattress, he hadn't moved, a sculpture of indecision, sitting with his bandaged fist curled to his heart.

'Go to sleep,' I told him, and though I shouldn't have, I raised my arm, captured the air within my fingertips, and extinguished the candles in one dark sweep.

By the time the new day had fully dawned, I had risen and restored the damsel's glamour, and met Sir Lancelot's arrival at the manor's entrance. The bandage on his hand, I noted, was gone.

We rode the rest of the way in a thoughtful but companionable quiet, and reached the so-called cursed vale mid-morning, dismounting in an aspen grove beside a river, half a mile from the Dolorous Tower.

I watched him fuss awhile, checking his horse's legs and saddle before strapping on his pauldrons and greaves with ruthless efficiency. For a moment, he paused at the sight of his unblemished hand, then pulled his gauntlets on and came over to me.

Reaching to his back, he drew out a sleek dagger with a handle in the shape of a wildcat, spun the weapon on his palm and offered me the knife, hilt first.

'I don't need it,' I said. 'I can protect myself.'

'Take it anyway,' he replied.

Reluctantly, I took the blade and he nodded briskly. 'Some rules,' he said. 'You will wait here and stay out of the tower's view. For this quest to succeed, you must trust I will return, according to my oath.'

'I take no issue with that,' I replied. 'Though if you are not back by nightfall—'

'Midnight,' he cut in. 'If I do not return by then, come for me – the moon will be full enough. I will heed you, even if I cannot heed myself.'

In a sudden impulse, he took up my free hand and kissed it, then left me, leaping onto his horse from the ground and wheeling his mount in the direction of his next battle.

As I watched him canter off, I wondered if he was not only heading towards Gawain's rescue but escape – if I had fallen for a ruse and given all my advantage away. My blood flared, but I felt the ghost of his kiss on my knuckles. I would trust him, for now.

I didn't see Lancelot liberate the Dolorous Tower, but I heard of it from a passing shepherd who had borne witness. It seemed the famed du Lac went about his task with his usual strategic flair and ferocious will, and the entire campaign was over by mid-afternoon.

Meanwhile, I had become bored of watching the river and making the wildcat dagger levitate, and my compliance had begun to feel like a weakness, so I conjured a concealing mist and walked, until the granite edifice of the Dolorous Tower appeared beyond the woodland boughs. The castle indeed looked newly captured: shutters were flung open; the former lord's banners torn down, a few knights patrolling the gateway. Unseen, I settled against a rowan tree and waited for something to happen.

I was conjuring a small rainstorm and wondering whether sending it across would speed things along, when the ground vibrated and a train of large horses thundered over the opposite horizon, bearing heavily armoured men and red-and-white banners. Amongst them, gold-armoured on a pristine white warhorse, rode Arthur. The Knights of Camelot were too late, but the High King had come.

The procession halted, Arthur riding to the front and dismounting before the lowered drawbridge. A shining silver figure was already striding forth: Sir Lancelot, still present, coming to meet his lord.

They stopped a few yards apart, regarding one another, an endless pause stretching between them. Then, finally, Camelot's champion dropped to his knee and bowed.

Arthur looked strangely relieved. 'Congratulations, my friend,' he said. 'I commend you to God for your courageous feat.'

When the knight rose, I expected them to embrace as brothers-in-arms usually did after battle, but instead, Lancelot turned and walked back into the vanquished tower, leaving his King in his silent wake.

When night fell, Lancelot had not come.

It was long before midnight, but Arthur's arrival sat uneasily within me. At first, their obvious tension was proof of the breach between King and knight, a more serious fissure than Kay had described. Yet as the hours wore on, the delay took on a different cast. Maybe my oathbound prisoner and Arthur had talked, resolved things. Lancelot was unpredictable, and I would not lose him now, not this way.

Shrouding myself in mist, I walked the few hundred yards to the tower, the royal flag now flying over the ramparts. A communal meal had not long been called, so I waited until all were settled to their food, then slipped through a side gate and kept to the shadows. Eventually came the goodnight murmurs of men retiring to bed, window-light snuffed out, and the building exhaled with collective sleep.

It was too risky to conjure fire in my palm, so I proceeded by torchlight and the generous moon until I found myself in a small stableyard, just as a towering figure emerged from an open row of stalls. His head was down and his presence belaboured, as if he were exhausted to his very bones.

'I heard of the tower's liberation hours ago,' I said.

Lancelot did not flinch, only gave the damsel a weary nod and leaned heavily against the nearest wall. Faint runnels on his cheeks suggested tears, but his eyes were dry.

'It's not yet midnight,' he replied. 'I've broken no oath. I was ensuring all was settled before I returned.'

'And is it?' I asked. 'Settled?'

He shrugged. 'As far as it goes.'

Whatever plagued him, I knew he wouldn't speak on it here, so I let it pass. 'In that case, I am here to summon you,' I said. 'You must honour your agreement with my mistress and return to her vale.'

He cast sharp eyes up at me. 'Your mistress, is it?'

It was an open question, but I couldn't be sure what he was asking so I said nothing. His pale stare held me rapt, disbelieving and inescapable.

'I know what this is,' he murmured. 'Who you are.'

It came forth with certainty, but no threat. 'Is that so?' I replied, and he gave a slow, definitive nod. In his gaze, I felt the same thrill of recognition as the night before, along with a different rush, hot and alive through my body in a way I hadn't felt for years.

'No more pretence,' Lancelot said. 'Show me.'

In the instant he said it, I knew it was what I had wanted since looking in the bedchamber mirror and leaving my eyes their own shade of blue.

Exhaling, I let go of the glamour, pushing the illusion away. The disguise fell away in layers, dissolving into curls of silvery smoke until I was Morgan again.

Lancelot made no sound or movement, so I edged closer, letting him take in my true face for as long as it took. His heartbeat pounded slightly faster, but he did not recoil or show any signs of horror, just kept regarding me keenly, as if nothing had changed.

'Well?' I said. 'What will you do now?'

He considered my challenge, glancing up to the darkened tower, then back at me. At length, he sighed deeply and said, 'Let us ride out. We do not have to go far, just …'

He stopped, biting his lip. *Away from here*, he did not say.

'Agreed?' he said instead. 'I can guide us safely by the moonlight, if you trust me.'

I took him in, his weighted posture, the flexing tension in his temple and jaw, as if he were experiencing a persistent pain. My fingers twitched in anticipation, but the parts of me that knew grief recognised that this was not an ailment curable by healing.

'I trust you,' I said.

Decisively, he pushed himself up from the wall. His armour and sword hung nearby, sparkling like new, the scent of vinegar on the air. While the others were feasting, Lancelot had chosen to spend the hours polishing his armour like a punished squire.

Lifting his mail hauberk, he eased it over his head, then slipped on his muddied, blood-speckled tunic, a contrast to the perfect sheen of his mail. Lastly, he picked up his weapon belt and drew it around his waist, but his hands shook on the buckle and it slipped from his grip. Cursing, he tried again, but the judder of his nerves overcame him, belt falling to the floor with a crash. I had never seen him so unmade.

I went to his side and retrieved the belt. 'Let me do it.'

To my surprise, he stood like an obedient horse while I passed the leather around his waist and girded him with his sword. I had just secured the buckle when his hands covered mine.

'I need to see someone, just briefly,' he said. 'Await me here.'

Before I could prevent it, he pulled away and strode off. A bolt of doubt shot through me; I wondered if he was going to raise the alarm or even rouse Arthur. Perhaps Lancelot's sense of justice was greater than their rift. I drew the glamour back down, waited three more heartbeats then followed him into the tower's inner keep.

Halfway along a twisting passageway, I spotted his bloodied silk back slipping into a nearby chamber. I tiptoed to the door and sharpened my hearing.

A familiar voice spoke, gruff with sleep and an Orkney burr. 'What is … du Lac?'

There came the sound of creaking bed slats. 'If you're going to wake me in the middle of the night,' Gawain said, 'at least have the good grace to be a willing paramour.'

It elicited a soft laugh from Lancelot, then his tone fell to seriousness. 'My friend, listen. I have to go – tonight. In the morning, just tell the King I am gone. I know they will look for me but please, delay them if you can.'

'What are you talking about?' Gawain's voice was filled with concern. 'Where are you going?'

'That I cannot say.' He drew a deep, echoing breath. 'Stand in for me, will you, as Queen's Knight?'

I felt Gawain's hesitation. 'Lancelot, should I be worried?' he asked.

'No,' he replied, but it was half sigh. 'Do not fear for me. Goodbye, my friend.'

'Nay, it is but farewell, surely?'

No answer came, but I heard the slaps of a brotherly embrace and approaching footsteps, so I slipped swiftly back to the stableyard. When Lancelot returned, he noted the damsel's reappearance with a bare nod, then wordlessly retrieved his horse, checked its girth, and helped me into his saddle. Without pause, he swung up in front of me, my body pressed against the hard relief of his back. We set off through an unattended postern gate, following the rustling river to the aspen copse.

'The moon is strong and still rising,' he said when we had stopped and dismounted. 'We can reach the valley by morning if we don't stop.'

It was as we had agreed, but not as I expected. Like any good knight, Lancelot held my stirrup and hand as I climbed aloft my own horse then remounted himself, gesturing for me to lead the way. All along I had anticipated a fight, some trick, an attempt at escape, yet here we were, about to ride back to Morgan le Fay's Vale of No Return.

We spoke little on the return journey. My knightly companion was not uncivil, but kept up a pensive quiet, and neither I nor the damsel could think of a way to surmount it.

When we reached the lodge in Belle Garde's valley, as a soft blue dawn breached the sky, Lancelot relinquished his horse, dropped his sword belt where he stood, then strode into his prison chamber and shut the door behind him without saying a single word.

21

I slept an entire day and night, longer and deeper than I had in a decade.

When I awoke the following morning, my first thought was of Lancelot. I had ventured under the shining knight's façade, seen the hidden places where he kept his flaws and quieter charms, the damage he carried beneath his haughty perfection. In the midst of it all, I had found a heart larger and more complicated than I could have imagined.

My next recollection was of our journey, how we had recognised one another in myriad ways, discovered similarities that neither of us could have guessed. Lancelot's blood ran with healing as mine did. He had chosen to return to Belle Garde instead of running back to his King and life of duty. He had seen my true face and not looked away.

What it meant was not for me to decide alone, but the connection we had shared under the moonlight felt natural, powerful, a current of potential that maybe we owed to ourselves to explore. Lancelot wanted to work miracles, and I could show him how.

All I knew for certain was, I had to see him.

I rode up to the lodge in the soft morning light, eschewing the minstrel's gallery to go directly into his room. Lancelot was awake and pacing, dressed in a clean shirt and breeches, his bed undisturbed. He had his boots on, as if he thought to go somewhere, but the buckles flapped loose, his every step a metallic crack.

'Good morning,' I said, closing the door behind me. 'I commend you for keeping your word and returning.'

He regarded me in the searching way I had become accustomed to, taking in my well-rested aspect, the sleek midnight gown I wore, my hair that I had brushed so it shone more than usual. In contrast, his eyes were dark with lack of sleep, cold as a winter dawn.

'What in God's name are you doing?' he said.

I had not been expecting friendliness, but the severity of his tone and forbidding demeanour halted me outright. I adjusted to an attitude slightly more circumspect.

'I've come to hear of my nephew's rescue,' I said.

'I'm sure you know everything you need to,' he retorted. 'From your *damsel*.'

So this was how he intended things to be – evasion and hostility. I let the allusion blow past me. 'Only you were at the Dolorous Tower's liberation. What happened?'

'There is nothing to tell.'

'Not even that Arthur was there?' I said. 'Or that you could hardly face him and his praise? It was only a few weeks ago you were telling me you were the door that stood before your beloved King. Now you cannot bear to look him in the eye.'

Lancelot flushed a sudden and guilty red. 'Assumption is not knowledge. You don't know anything about my life in the Royal Court. You don't know anything about *me*.'

His voice was still hard, but a weariness had crept in. I edged closer, until I could see the jump of pulse between his collarbones.

'Don't you find it exhausting for us to lie to one another this way?' I asked. 'My grudge isn't with you, and I don't believe your real troubles lie with me. I see you more clearly than you like to admit.'

He let out a heavy breath but did not move away. Unexpectedly, he was listening.

'We share more than our differences,' I continued. 'In fact, what we have learned of one another these past few days holds great potential. An opportunity for us both.'

Lancelot's gaze sharpened. 'What do you mean?'

'You ran out of Camelot to break free,' I said. 'You returned here from the Dolorous Tower, to Morgan le Fay herself, without even attempting to escape. You came back for a reason, perhaps more than one.'

'I came back because my honour demanded it,' he said unconvincingly.

'That is not what you told Sir Gawain.'

For a moment, he looked stunned, conflict flashing across his face between what he knew but could not admit to himself – that he and I had gone to the Dolorous Tower and back together, and had found ourselves mutually drawn.

'You dare put words in my mouth,' he said. 'When all I did was fulfil my oath to return to your captivity and am once again at your mercy. Nothing more.'

His voice was studiously bland but uneven beneath, both goading me to argue and willing the conversation to be over. To push him now felt dangerous, a dance on the edge of a cliff, but how much I wanted to try. How badly I wanted to light this fire and feel us burn.

'What is it, Sir Lancelot?' I murmured. 'Are you afraid of wanting something you believe you cannot have?'

His mood, already stormy, turned dark. He stepped closer, his heat cloaking my skin, and I looked up at him, taking it as the challenge he intended.

'Tell the truth,' I said.

For a moment, he seemed about to retreat, but it lasted only the span of a breath. 'Very well,' he said. 'If you want the truth, then I have some honesty for you.'

His words came through a taut jaw, as if he was forcing them out. 'When Sir Galescalain and I dined with you, I'm sure you remember he prevented me from speaking of a third knight in our company, who did not enter this valley. Do you know who it was?'

I frowned. 'Why would I?'

'You claim uncanny instincts. Use your *great insight* to see what is obvious.'

It didn't take long for his implication to dawn. 'Not—'

Lancelot nodded, his mouth a cruel curl. 'Sir Yvain. He was travelling with us, in pursuit of Sir Gawain.'

I stared at him. 'My son was at Belle Garde?'

'Almost. When he returned to Camelot, he heard of our previous encounter and was intrigued. He asked of you, and for his sake, I said you were charming enough – a flesh and blood woman despite your demon reputation. My words got him all the way here. Nevertheless, when he stood on the edge of your *Val Sans Retour*, he decided he could not bear it. He preferred to ride on alone, towards danger, than set one foot closer to his mother.'

I swallowed, all wit struck from my tongue. 'Was he at the Dolorous Tower?'

'I won't discuss that without his agreement,' came the sanctimonious reply. 'From what I hear, you have not earned the right.'

That he discerned my deepest wounds with such accuracy was as surprising as it was agonising. 'So you use Yvain as a weapon against me,' I managed. 'How honourable.'

'You asked for the truth and I gave it to you. Moreover, I will speak to what Sir Yvain cannot. *Your son deserves better.*' He regarded me with an angel's disdain. 'You know it's true, Morgan le Fay, deep down.'

I knew it was a tactic, that he wanted my hurt and fury to distract from the true nature of what smouldered between us. To keep his world in perfect balance, I could not be the charming damsel, a wounded mother, or a woman of fascination drawing him towards new freedom. I had to be the corrupt sorceress, the traitor, his enemy. To absolve himself, Lancelot needed to hate me and wanted to make me hate him too.

And in that moment, I did. He had won.

'Enough of this,' I snarled.

With a sweep of my arm, I cast a spell of containment and flung it upon him like a poacher's net. He resisted falling but thrashed madly against the magic's strength, bellowing in anger. Unwilling to hear it, I wrapped an invisible gag around his mouth.

'How dare you goad me with my losses,' I said to his struggling form. 'As if I don't know what they are, or feel them as glass in my skin, every moment of every day.'

I put my fingers to his neck and found the silver chain beneath his shirt, dragging out the emerald ring. Lancelot gave a cry of protest deep in his throat.

'Perhaps you should learn what it is like to lose what is precious to you,' I said. 'How it truly feels to be Morgan le Fay.'

With a hard tug, I snapped the chain and snatched the ring into my hand. He made a furious lunge within the magical bonds and managed to break towards me, but I avoided him easily. A click of my fingers brought him to his knees.

'Oh, hush,' I said above his muffled roaring. 'How you love to make a fuss.'

I stepped out of arm's reach and unbound Lancelot with a careless flourish. A brief demonstration of my power was all he needed, though it had tired me to contain such a force as he. Bondage was a showy spell, far costlier than using the elements, and I should not have used it. Still, I had enjoyed tying him up.

My captive knight was less pleased. He scrambled to his feet and pointed a threatening finger. 'We made a deal. I gave you my other ring so I could keep the emerald. You have no right to take it.'

'I have every right to do whatever I wish,' I shot back. 'I make the rules here, not you. I decide when they change.'

'This is the Devil's work, even for you,' he said. *'Give me my ring.'*

He glared at me with such ferocity that a lesser being might have combusted into ash. To me, it was a bowl of oil thrown upon a raging pyre.

'Damn your ring!' I cried. 'It is lost to you.'

'You don't understand,' he insisted. 'It is all I have left.'

'And now you have nothing,' I replied. 'Painful, isn't it? Get accustomed to the feeling, as I have.'

The harshness in my voice repelled him better than any magic, my playful insults and threats something he had not taken seriously. For the first time, Lancelot du Lac believed in the true strength of my fury.

'Tell me what you want for the ring,' he said desperately. 'I'll do anything.'

'I want nothing from you,' I said. 'Keep your charms, your persuasions, your handsome, beguiling pain.' I held up the emerald ring between my forefinger and thumb. 'How is this for a difficult truth – the name *Guinevere* is carved inside the band.'

He stood rigid, trying to form a strategy, but I felt his mood as one I knew intimately: the rage coursing through his miraculous blood meant he couldn't see straight, let alone form rational thought.

'I see now it never mattered what I knew,' I went on. 'That the Queen fell for the knight in her service and ran away to live with him for a year. It was irrelevant what I saw behind the pavilion – what I *heard*. The lengths you would go to. *Anything for you.*'

I paused to take in his shock, and it was as searing and satisfying as a hot bath on a cold day. 'As long as you kept quiet, I could do nothing. Until I beheld this ring, the answer to everything. Confess or do not, it makes no difference. The two of you are adulterous – treasonous – and I have my proof.'

'It only proves the emerald was given to me,' Lancelot argued. 'Believe what you wish, keep me here forever, I don't care – but if you have any decency left, you will honour our deal and give my ring back.'

'God's blood! My ring, my ring, on and on! I am *so bored of this*.' I held the emerald out to him, tantalisingly within reach. 'Forget your oaths, the deals we made. If you want your precious ring, then come and take it.'

With breathtaking speed, Lancelot lunged for my hand, displaying a sweeping grace where his honour denied him brute force. He took hold of my left wrist, just below where I held the ring and I allowed it, letting his obsession become his downfall. Right hand at my belt, I whipped out my falcon-handled knife and pressed it to his throat.

In an instant, he wrapped his free hand around my knife-wielding wrist, but even with his strength, I could easily slice two major vessels in his neck before he could move. We were fused in a vicious stalemate, breaths hard and aligned, as if we shared one pair of lungs. Our faces were so close I could have reached up and bitten his bottom lip.

I could cure you of her, I thought. *Given one long night, I could make you forget her name and sing my own.*

It was a dark notion, selfish, as much a cry from my body's own hunger as my wish to push Lancelot to his limits. His eyes widened as if he had heard it, the memory of our journey rearing up: Lancelot's confession of a desire to work miracles, beyond who the world thought he was; the glamour falling from my face and his acceptance. Our quiet, determined ride back in the moonlit dark, away from the life he knew, and towards a different future.

'It doesn't have to be this way,' I told him. 'What you believe of yourself isn't true. There is so much more for you to know, to achieve, if you set yourself free.'

He fixed me with his piercing blue look, unfaltering even with a knife at his throat. For several pounding heartbeats we seemed inevitable. Then, all at once, Lancelot dropped his grip from my wrists and held his hands apart in surrender.

'I am not a faithless knight,' he said.

He did not pull away from my knife, so I let the blade take its pressure off, leaving a pinprick of red on his skin. His healing blood called out to mine, the miracle he would never know he possessed.

'This could all be different,' I replied. 'If you just let yourself be stolen away.'

Lancelot shook his head. 'I am not a faithless knight,' he said again. A useless oath that no one needed to hear but him.

'Then that is your choice.' I lowered my knife, sheathed it, and stepped away from his hard-breathing frame. 'The consequences will be yours to bear.'

He didn't flinch, but said, 'What does this mean for me?'

'Are you asking if I intend on killing you?'

'I don't fear death,' he replied. 'I just want to know my fate.'

So do I, I thought. *But I will create my own.*

'I'm not going to kill you,' I said smoothly. Summoning the door open, I let my feet carry me towards it, away from our shared, feverish heat. Lancelot sprung forwards as if to prevent me, but stopped dead when I turned to look at him.

'I don't need you at all,' I continued. 'I have more than enough to destroy Camelot by myself. Guinevere, Arthur, your adoring brothers-in-arms, your fairy mother who helped ruin my life – they can all feel what it is like to suffer for love.'

I slipped the emerald ring on my finger, admiring it at a distance. 'It suits me, don't you think?'

Lancelot stared at me in horror, frozen, incandescent with beauty, as I swept out of the room and shut him back in. It wasn't until I was securing the iron bar that I felt the slam of his shoulder against the door – a futile attempt to escape, or perhaps feel something other than defeat. I pressed my spine to the oak planks as the collisions kept coming, savouring his rage through the wood, reverberating deep in my body.

Taking off Guinevere's emerald, I rested the shining band on my thumbnail and flicked it up in the air, catching it neatly in my palm, again and again, green and gold whirring before my eyes, drawing my next move into focus.

The ring was enough to strike lightning through Camelot, and maybe start a fire after that.

22

The court was no longer in Camelot but at Westminster, so it was there I went, to the same white-stoned, crenellated fortress where my brother and I had first met.

I knew the palace well: Arthur had thrown his usual luxury upon the public halls until everything was brightly painted, gilded and hung with sweet-smelling garlands, but the snaking passageways and narrow staircases were the same as when I had crept around them as a child. Now, as then, I was hiding, concealed once again beneath the glamour of Sir Lancelot's damsel. How little had changed since my neck was under Uther Pendragon's boot.

To my relief, I found the Seneschal's chambers closed. Sir Kay didn't like the London palaces, I knew; he preferred to see woodland out of his window, and if there was a quest he could convince Arthur to let him take, he always made it coincide with the court being summoned to the crowded, noisy cities along the Thames. Though I would miss his cynical face, no part of me wanted to cause more trouble for him.

I drifted through the courtiers milling around the main entrance hall, and approached a pair of heralds near the Throne Room entrance.

'I must see King Arthur,' I said. 'It is urgent.'

The senior of the two looked mildly irritated. 'Young lady, you cannot simply speak to the High King. His Highness will make no Royal Appearance today. Sir Bedivere the Marshal is dealing with public matters – you may bring your petition to him when court convenes this afternoon.'

'You don't understand,' I said impatiently. 'I have news of Sir Lancelot.'

It was as if I had told them I'd shared wine with Christ Himself. 'You've heard of his whereabouts?' the second herald exclaimed.

'I've seen him with my own eyes. Indeed, I carry a message from the knight's very lips, and must only speak it to the High King before the court.'

Nothing further was needed. One herald hurried off towards the King's chambers, while the other ushered me into the Throne Room and before the dais. Within moments, bells began to ring, calling the court to assemble. As fast as they could muster, knights, lords and ladies swept into the vaulted hall, whispering in fervent speculation.

When the room was almost full, a third herald appeared on the dais. 'Arthur, High King of All Britain and Lord of the Seven Realms calls this court to order,' he declared.

The royal party entered without further ceremony, bringing the room's bustle to attention. Sir Gawain hastened in first, tall and russet as an autumn oak, taking Lancelot's usual place between the thrones. Behind him strode my brother, swathed in red-and-white silk, Guinevere on his arm in gold, looking pretty but drawn. Arthur guided her to her seat, then took his own in preparation.

Silence fell. I was so close to the dais the thrones loomed over me, as if I stood at the foot of Olympus. Raising my chin, I met my brother's gleaming grey gaze.

He recoiled, just barely. I had forgotten that as a mere subject, I was not permitted to look him directly in the eye until he invited such a privilege. Already, I was presumptuous.

Swiftly, I ducked my head and dipped to my knee. 'Your Highness, a thousand thanks for meeting with me. I am humbled by your presence.'

Arthur chose graciousness. 'Please rise, my lady, and I commend you to God. I believe you bring an important message for the court.'

The expression he cast upon me was benevolent, and so reassuring that for a moment I felt comforted, as if he were truly my High King whom I was pleased to serve. It had always been one of Arthur's greatest powers, his ability to capture others within a moment of his own making; as though you were the only person in the room, the one voice he needed to hear. A regal deception, of course, but a potent one.

'Yes, my lord,' I replied in my delicate voice. 'A knight of your Royal Household bid me come here. But first, I beg you to bear me no ill will for the sad news I must deliver.'

'My lady, you are doing us a great service,' he said. 'I guarantee with all my heart that you will not suffer punishment for anything you tell us here. This room, this court, is a safe haven.'

His assurance landed as an ache in my chest. It had felt like that, once, to be under my brother's protection, made safe by his power, his lofty ideals. For a time, we had been happy in one another's high regard, our familial love mutual, a feeling I could be sure of.

'Thank you,' I managed. 'My lord is generous.'

He inclined his head courteously and I felt myself soothed. Then, he flicked his eyes back to Guinevere and the feeling was gone, blown away by the reality of our intervening years: the long shadow of exile; Arthur's part in Accolon's death; his wife's hatred and threats; the betrayals that led to the loss of both my children. Everything those unpunished wrongs had left behind – my need for revenge, honed to a knife edge.

'I bring news of Sir Lancelot of the Lake,' I declared. 'He will not return to the court, and will never again bear sword and shield.'

My invented words had their effect, a collective exclamation emanating from the audience. Both King and Queen paled to the colour of bone.

How does it feel? I thought bitterly.

Gawain stepped forwards. 'I'll set out immediately,' he said to his uncle. 'I will bring him back.'

His control of the situation was quick, but it didn't halt the escalating shock. Before Arthur could calm the room, Guinevere stood abruptly and turned to leave.

Her husband leapt up and caught her elbow. 'What are you doing?'

'I cannot hear this,' she protested. 'It's too much, this so-called *testimony* ...'

I felt the room jolt, silenced by her loss of composure.

'Darling, this maiden has come to us,' Arthur said in a low voice. 'It is our duty to hear what she has to say.'

'This *maiden* ...' She extended a brocaded arm at me. 'What proof is there that she speaks the truth? You know how Lancelot has been pursued against his will. She could be another spurned pretty face.'

Arthur gazed at her hopelessly, then Guinevere swung away, stalking off with my advantage in her sweeping skirts. The moment was slipping from my grasp.

'King Arthur,' I called out. 'If your lady Queen doesn't stay, then I cannot tell you the rest. And I am far from finished.'

He glanced at me, discerning my conviction against his wife's.

Then: 'Guinevere!'

At the sound of her name without title or endearment, the Queen stopped, regarding him over her shoulder with pale-green coldness.

'Come back to your seat and let us continue,' he said simply. I had heard him use the tone many times – utterly reasonable, but somehow defying disagreement.

With slow, deliberate obedience, Guinevere retook her throne. Arthur surveyed the room until it settled, then returned to sit beside her and addressed me once more.

'As you can see, our entire court regards Sir Lancelot with deep affection. Tell me – where does your news come from?'

'From the knight himself,' I replied. 'He recently came to my mistress's house, grievously injured. She took him in, tended his wounds as best she could – even put him in her own bed.'

Guinevere's gaze tightened upon me like a turned screw. I resisted the urge to smile. 'Unfortunately, his injuries were too great,' I continued. 'We hoped God would gaze down in healing, but Sir Lancelot believed quite certainly he would die. Because of this, he decided to make his final confession. He insisted my mistress's household be called in to hear his greatest sins told. That is how I came to bear this message.'

My brother leaned forwards, eyes keen. He did not suspect what was coming, and I wanted it to ring in his head like a sword against a steel helm.

'My lord, need we hear this now?' Guinevere's voice interrupted, high and strained. 'When we do not even know if our best knight lives?'

The court again took up in whispers, the odd groan of suspicion. Arthur did not heed his wife's last-chance distraction from her deadliest secret; his focus remained on me.

'Did Lancelot die?' he asked.

His voice cracked just barely, indiscernible to any ear but mine. I understood then that Arthur feared the answer to this question only. Of Guinevere, he suspected nothing at all.

'Time has passed while I travelled here,' I replied. 'But he still lived when I left.'

'Then this is not over,' Gawain insisted. 'I will ride out at once and get him. Put him on a litter if necessary, bring him to our best healers.'

Arthur's face flickered unexpectedly, a chord played along my spine. He was thinking of me – his clever sister with death-defying skills at her fingertips; the one person in the entire kingdom whom he could not ask, or command, or summon to his aid. Five hundred of their 'best healers' could not replace one Morgan le Fay, and my brother knew it.

'Excuse me, my lords,' I said. 'But Sir Lancelot said that if he survived, he would take to the road and doesn't wish to be found. He swore on my mistress's crucifix that he would wander barefoot, wear rough clothing beside his skin, and never again bear arms.'

My fabricated description sounded so much like Lancelot's bouts of martyrish despair that I knew it would ring true. Arthur sagged back as if he had heard du Lac himself speak, and the room's knightly cohort murmured in similar conviction. Even Gawain's sceptical brow rose in recognition.

Only Guinevere resisted the charms of my shrewdly drawn portrait. 'I still do not see why we should believe any of this,' she said. 'We do not know this fair damsel from Eve. Again I contend she may have been rejected by Lancelot's virtue and has come to cast shadows upon his reputation.'

Her refusal to be shaken, the strange astuteness she had always shown at times inopportune for myself – the fact that all ears listened intently when she spoke – burned in my gullet like vinegar. Worse still, I had limited myself: the damsel was an obedient, respectful messenger, possessing neither the rank nor the disdain for the court that Morgan le Fay did. Unlike me, she was not hungry to bring the news that could break an entire nation.

I forced nervousness into my false voice. 'My lords, my lady. Sir Lancelot knew you might question my intentions, so he sent proof. He said I should seek Sir Gawain.'

'I'm Sir Gawain,' my nephew declared at once, to Guinevere's obvious chagrin.

'Good Sir Knight.' I greeted him with a curtsey. 'Sir Lancelot told me that if my truth was held in doubt, that I should repeat to you the words he spoke to you on the night after he liberated the Dolorous Tower.'

The royal pair looked at him in enquiry. 'He came to me before he left,' Gawain confirmed. 'I remember it exactly.'

'Tell us, young lady, please,' Arthur said.

I recounted the story with care. 'Sir Lancelot said that when he told you he was leaving, you asked where he was going and he replied that he could not say. He asked you to stand in for him as Queen's Knight.'

Gawain ducked his head. 'Go on.'

'You said "Lancelot, should I be worried?" and he told you not to fear for him. Lastly, when he said goodbye, you urged him it was surely farewell, but he made no reply.'

'Well?' Guinevere demanded. 'Is this true?'

My nephew looked up, his eyes misty. 'That's what was said.'

A pervasive hush fell, the terrible realisation that Lancelot might never return or be seen alive again. Fairly easily, I had won over the court, but it wasn't their belief I sought. I cast my eyes back to my brother.

'My lord,' I said. 'Can I trust that I am now believed as a messenger of truth and integrity? Because there is still Sir Lancelot's confession, which he wished spoken aloud.'

'My sincere apologies for our doubts,' Arthur said. 'Please continue.'

A pall of sadness had fallen across his face, but I had not done all this for him to focus on the wrong tragedy. It was time to drive a lance through Arthur's shield and send Camelot into freefall.

I looked at Guinevere, her eyes lowered, fingers picking at the spray of seed pearls sewn across her skirts.

'My lady,' I said. 'This confession is also a message for you.'

She raised her head, looking pleasingly wretched. I drew a deep breath, the sweet taste of vengeance on my lips.

'Queen Guinevere,' I said. 'Sir Lancelot gives to you his deepest love, and thanks you for your love in return. He wishes to confess his treason, and beg God and King Arthur for forgiveness. As your faithful knight, and lover in adultery.'

23

There was never a more satisfying sound than when the court gasped at my declaration. For all my magic, the skills I possessed, the wisdom I had learned – I always felt at my most powerful when I was telling the truth.

The Queen didn't move, a doe caught in a lioness's sights. Arthur shifted on his throne, digesting my words like a heavy course at a banquet, surprised at the discomfort it brought. Too late for him now; he had eaten what I had served him and must suffer the pain.

Gawain was the only one who could speak '*What* did you say?' he demanded. 'Explain yourself, madam, and quickly.'

I tried to sound more afeared than I felt. 'I beg your pardon, my lord. In his final confession, Sir Lancelot said he had no choice before God but to admit to his adultery with the High Queen of All Britain. I swore an oath to him that I would respect his last wishes.'

'This doesn't make an ounce of sense,' my nephew muttered, then fell silent too, either in shock or because of his natural respect for oath-taking. I took it as a sign to embellish at my leisure.

'Sir Lancelot confessed that he loved the Queen from the moment he saw her, and has lived in mortal sin ever since,' I continued. 'That he has dishonoured his King, his King's wife, the Crown, and himself, as a knight and a man. I respected his bravery and godliness, so I promised I would bring his words exactly as he uttered them.'

I returned my focus to Guinevere. She hadn't spoken for a long time. In the hall, new whispers took up, multiplying until the air hissed with burgeoning scandal.

Arthur's eyes flickered across his congregation, then came to rest on his wife, waiting for her next, impossible move.

In a sudden jolt, Guinevere stood, silencing the room at once.

She paced right up to the dais edge, and for a heartbeat I thought she was going to keep walking, off the raised platform and beyond – leaving the room, the palace, her entire life. But she stopped just short, gazing out at the court's upturned faces as they waited for denial, or her own confession.

Instead, with a sudden cry, the High Queen of All Britain burst into tears.

Before us all, she put her head in her hands and wept, shocking, uncontrolled sobs, as if she wasn't in public, much less revealing herself to the kingdom as an adulteress with her husband looking on.

Nevertheless, Arthur flew from his throne and put protective arms around his wife, drawing her away and against his shoulder. He leaned in, speaking softly into her ear, but my fairy senses captured every word.

'What is this?' he asked her. 'Why do you lament in such a way?'

Guinevere raised bloodshot eyes to him. 'Lancelot may be dead, or in so much despair he will never return. Can you truly hear such news and not feel your heart breaking?'

I expected disgust from Arthur, if not outright fury – the nerve of her to ask for sorrow in the face of his humiliation, when she should have already been chased from the Throne Room in shame and indignity. Yet he took in her words with slow, indulgent nods, as if she spoke the very essence of truth.

'I know,' he said. 'It is hard to hear. But—'

'And the rest, in their judgement,' she cut in. 'They do not understand. No one ever could. Though God knows I deserve better than this.'

Arthur stepped back and gripped her elbows, making her meet his steady gaze.

'If you have something to say,' he told her, 'then address them.'

His understanding seemed to bolster Guinevere; she raised her chin and drew up to her statuesque height. By the time she turned again to the room, her shaking hands were still, her face flushed and eyes agleam, one of those rare and infuriating people who look beautiful when they cry. Anyone who looked upon her would want to forgive.

Still, they could forgive, but Arthur's entire reputation balanced on fair and equal justice – not a month ago, he had put his wife on public trial to prove the same. For the kingdom's integrity, he would have to act. I let the air out of my lungs and waited.

With a poise well-honed, Guinevere gazed over my head, to her court, her subjects, those waiting to see if she floated or sank. This was different from the mild disapproval she had encountered over the years: whether she dressed too finely or spent too much; whether her easy talk with the King and his knights was charming or inappropriate; her continuing childlessness and who was to blame. For her, adultery was treason, punishable by law, and the champion she relied upon for deliverance was locked in my Vale of No Return.

Despite all of this, the High Queen of All Britain was determined to speak.

'Whoever wishes to spread ugly tales,' she began, 'you may go ahead and talk. You will hear no denial of the love I bear Sir Lancelot. He is the most beautiful man, and the best of us in his goodness. There is not a knight in our Seven Realms by whom he is outdone. I have loved him since I first knew him and will continue, with everything I possess.'

Her confession thrilled in me, every word a victory for the anger and despair I had known since the day she guessed at my pregnancy and demanded I leave Camelot. This was the peak of my hard-fought battles, like a great rock pushed up a hill at the moment of suspension, before it rolled easily down the other side.

However, the crowd didn't seem to be absorbing the significance of her speech. Their faces were rapt, not scandalised. The High Queen had admitted her love for a man not her husband – it seemed impossible that outrage wasn't written across the room.

With slow emphasis, Guinevere added, 'As a Queen should.'

She glanced at her husband, and Arthur came immediately to her side. I had the sudden tilting sensation that I needed to wake up from a dream.

'We have *all* loved Sir Lancelot,' she said. 'For his prowess and deeds, his perfect heart and unwavering honour. Since he first joined this court, he has made us better and proven himself to be the greatest of men. If I, or my lord husband, had to recount all of the virtues he possesses, our tongues would fail before we had reached the end of the list. It is my duty – *our* duty – to love him for all he has given to this realm.'

To my utter disbelief, Arthur nodded in support. Fresh anger rippled through the glamour, a tremor across my disguise. The more out of control I felt, the more Morgan le Fay I became, and I couldn't be her now. I couldn't let her fight her way through.

Meanwhile, Guinevere kept talking; she couldn't seem to stop.

'But within Sir Lancelot's great virtue,' she went on, 'we see a single flaw. He has shown himself to be the pinnacle of high-mindedness, and from this comes his one error – he is prone to overstatement.'

The crowd took up murmuring, but it was all nods and sounds of agreement. They were as used to Sir Lancelot's particular intensity as I had become.

'To him, as Queen's Knight, the regard he holds for me is the greatest of loves, as his unmatched loyalty demands,' Guinevere said. 'Therefore, through his own goodness, *of course* Sir Lancelot would assume that his love for his beloved King's wife must be forbidden. What else would he do but confess it before God *just in case* we had fallen to such an unwitting sin? His last heroic act was to ensure the salvation of our souls.'

She thrust out a silken arm, and to my annoyance I jerked immediately to attention. 'If he knew this woman had reported his courageous words as an unspeakable act of treason, he would throw himself upon his sword at once. You all know it to be true.'

It was a very pretty speech, made more convincing by the force in her voice, the growing presence of her beauty as righteousness took hold. The court immediately began to applaud, as if witnessing an incredible performance, which I supposed they had.

Perhaps she even believed what she said. Maybe she didn't know that their sins had left Lancelot broken, so shattered that he gave up his safety from dangerous magic just to hold on to the emerald ring she had given him as a token of consolation.

The ring, my mind interrupted; *of course.*

I was losing, but I still had one piece left in play. I slipped the emerald off my thumb and into my palm.

'My lord, my lady,' I called above the clapping. The court quietened, eager to hear more. 'Sir Lancelot had one last request concerning the High Queen.'

Guinevere's face froze. I held out the ring.

'Sir Lancelot says you gave him this ring as a symbol of your love. He accepted it with feelings equally powerful, but it represents the adultery you committed with one another. He asked me to return it now, in the hope that you can both beg forgiveness for the betrayal you have wrought upon the High King, and the kingdom itself.'

The room sprang to life, courtiers and ladies surging forwards to see the object in my hand. Before anyone else could touch her precious trinket, the Queen took two long strides towards me and snatched the ring from my fingers.

As she did, the matching ring she wore caught the light, both emeralds shining in perfect harmony, like the true pair they were.

She turned away, but in a swift, surreptitious flourish, I summoned the air and sent a small jet through the gap in her hand. The ring fell and skittered across the floor, coming to rest at Arthur's feet. Guinevere rushed across, but he scooped the ring up, holding it between his fingers. Their eyes locked over the twinkling stone.

'Is it his?' he said. 'Is it *yours?*'

They stared at one another for an endless moment, Guinevere's expression pleading with him that she should not be made to say more. My brother held firm, armouring himself with the cold strength I knew so well.

The Queen lowered her eyes, breaking free of his scrutiny.

'You know it is,' she said.

I wish I could say that I felt the slightest remorse, but I was far beyond such a virtue where Guinevere was concerned. Mine and Accolon's lost child, my place in Camelot, the belief that my brother and I should be kept apart – it all began with her. There were many at fault for how my life had ended up, but she had cut the first stitch of my unravelling.

Arthur made no move. *This is your doing*, his expression said to her. *You must be the one to undo it.*

It took Guinevere less time than me to decipher her husband's silence. She reached out and plucked the ring from his fingers.

'It's true,' she declared to the Throne Room. 'I gave Lancelot the ring and will deny nothing about it. I gave my Queen's Knight a token of my affection and gratitude. For his service, his presence by my side, and his loyalty when I needed it most.'

It was a swipe, gentle in tone but deeply meant – her husband had abandoned her for a year, and his right to question her was still in flux. Arthur looked away, but this time she did not let him yield.

'Indeed, I have shown favouritism, and reproach me if you will, but I feel no shame.' She slipped the second emerald ring back on her finger and pointed her bejewelled hand at the court. 'Let God and everyone in this room know, there has *never* been a guilty love between myself and Sir Lancelot du Lac.'

Still my brother said nothing, but I could read the discomfort twisting within his body, the thorned vines of keeping a nation's peace.

'Well?' his adulteress Queen demanded of him now. 'Can *you* profess to love Lancelot any less than me?'

The look between them held for an age. Then Arthur moved, as he so often did: quickly, decisively. The stability of his Crown depended on what he said next, and how he chose to say it.

He turned to the room, smoothing over his demeanour to reassuring authority. 'My wife speaks her true heart,' he said. 'And I commend her for it.'

Though I had expected his saving face, I still felt the world shudder, my old quake of panic.

'This maiden does not know Sir Lancelot, or his honour, as we do,' Arthur said. 'Nothing the Queen has said perturbs me, nor should it any of you.'

Reaching out, he took Guinevere's hand in his, and lay the other over his heart. 'As God is my witness, I regard Sir Lancelot with such respect and great love that I would gladly see my lady wife marry him, if it meant he remained my own companion for life.'

The oddness of the comment struck like an ill-tuned bell, bringing me back to clarity. In truth, it was not the damsel who was the stranger here, but me. I had lost track of this world – Arthur's court had become a tangle of love and hate, oaths and jealousies, honour and dishonour, a labyrinth only navigable by those who had stayed within. All at once, I realised how deep my exile had cut; how far away I felt from my own brother.

To what end had I even come to this place? I claimed I did not fear anyone here, yet I could not even appear before them as myself. Was this what Morgan le Fay's heart stood for, or had my purpose been lost, adrift somewhere behind the mist of glamour?

Whatever the truth, for now, for me, this was over. The game was forfeit; all I could do was return to Belle Garde and decide where my next move lay.

Wordlessly, I turned and retreated from the dais. Three steps were all I managed before Sir Gawain called out. Wearily, I looked back.

'You haven't taken leave of the King,' he said, not unkindly.

I almost scoffed, unable to remember the last time I had imagined obeying arbitrary court rules, or asking permission of a king for anything.

'Forgive me,' I said. 'But I have a long ride back to my mistress's house. I beg Your Highness's leave.'

'By all means,' Arthur said graciously. 'Do you have an escort?'

'I came alone, my lord. I do not need one.'

'I insist,' he replied. 'It took much courage to come here. You will be protected on your journey back by one of my finest knights. My conscience will have it no other way.'

I knew from experience that doing battle with Arthur's conscience was a futile endeavour. Whoever it was, I would wait until we reached the forest, then give them the slip.

I bowed my head in tired acceptance. By the time I looked up, Arthur had beckoned a knight forth, now standing before the thrones, but turning to face me.

A shaft of sun caught on his dark-gold hair, the light on his profile rising in my chest like a wave cresting towards the sky. His eyes were the deep blue of a Cornish sea, like mine, and my father's before me.

'A pleasure to meet you, my lady,' he said with natural good humour.

'With no knight in my service will you have safer travels,' Arthur said. 'By the grace of my Crown, I give you into the care of Sir Yvain.'

24

How I kept the glamour about my person I will never know.

I hadn't even known he was there, I thought, as Yvain walked beside me to the palace's main door. Shock had stolen my ability to speak, along with the sheer force of concentration needed to keep the veil of illusion intact. I contemplated running away; I had planned to escape any escort Arthur chose, and the idea of riding concealed beside the son I had not seen since he was eight years old seemed a punishment too great for both of us.

But as we waited wordlessly for our mounts to be brought, I couldn't help but steal a look at him, then another, and again – at his grown man's face, new but reminiscent, the even features and handsome aspect that he wore with ease but not arrogance. On my fourth glance, he caught my gaze, smiling with a companionable kindness. I knew then that even if doing so was torture, I would stay by his side for as long as I could.

'Are you ready, my lady?' he asked, as the horses came.

I nodded, too afraid of my true voice coming forth to utter a word. When my son held out his hand to help me into the saddle, I hesitated for a moment then did what any typical lady would do – I took it.

The warmth of his palm swept through my blood as an ache. I wanted to take him into my arms, stroke his hair in the way he had loved as an infant. He was a head and a half taller than me now, and broad-shouldered like his father, though his figure carried more deftness than Urien's brute bulk. Nevertheless, I could still see the child beneath – a primal instinct for the son I had carried and birthed and nursed. No matter how old or changed he became, no matter how far we had been separated by time and kings and my own grave errors, Yvain was my baby and would always be so.

The glamour shivered with my erratic heart as I settled into the saddle, so I drew the hood of my travelling cloak up. Yvain mounted and we rode out of the palace courtyard, along a path beside the river. The tide was in and I reached for the water's essence, letting the element play its soothing, ancient song in my veins.

A polite cough drew my attention. 'Apologies, my lady,' Yvain said. 'It might be helpful if you tell me which direction you are travelling in.'

His smile was sleepily charming as it always had been, but with a self-contained calm that sang of my own mother. He had never known his grandmother, Lady Igraine; the last I had seen her was in this same palace, when he was barely a glimmer in my womb. That he smiled her way was innate, and too much to bear. How many pieces of mine did he carry?

'West,' I croaked.

We rode along the river until we left the city walls behind, trekking beyond flattened farmland onto a wide, forested road. Cathedral bells rang in the distance, the second set we had heard; over an hour had passed and I still hadn't managed another word.

In the end, it took my son's grace to do what I could not. 'I beg your pardon, my lady,' he said. 'Perhaps we have not been well enough introduced.'

'Sir Lancelot asked me to keep my name a secret,' I said quickly. 'So no one can use it to find him.'

He nodded consideringly. 'Then it is a pleasure to meet you, Lady of No Name.'

It made me laugh, regret quick at its heels. I would have to escape at some point – I could not lead him within ten miles of Belle Garde. He had already stood at the entrance to Morgan le Fay's enchanted vale and knowingly turned the other way.

Still, I had always been weak for the wants of my heart. However long this lasted, I wished to know him as much as I could.

'Thank you, good Sir Knight,' I said. 'I would gladly hear more of you.'

He bowed his head courteously. 'I am Sir Yvain. Son of Urien.'

My blood ran cold in an instant, tendrils of nausea spreading through my body.

'Is that what they all call you? An extension of your father?' It came out harder than I intended, and his brow furrowed. 'I mean, I thought you were a knight of Camelot,' I added. 'Part of King Arthur's ... Table, is it?'

'The Round Table,' he supplied. 'I'm not a member of that knightly order, yet. One day, I hope – when I have proved myself worthy.'

It came as a surprise that Yvain hadn't been inducted into the King's most prestigious order of knights. Urien, cowardly rakehell as he was, had a seat, yet Arthur had denied his own nephew?

'Why have you not been deemed worthy?'

He regarded me with sudden uncertainty. 'My lady, you ask bold questions.'

His waver made me even more curious, but I held to the damsel's decorum. 'Very well, something simpler,' I conceded. 'What does Sir Yvain of Camelot do for amusement?'

The change of subject relaxed his shoulders. 'Jousting, hunting. I like to spar with my sword. I enjoy singing, if there is enough wine at hand. Any game involving a ball, some might say. Oh, and falconry – that is a great passion of mine.'

The latter revelation knocked the breath from me. 'How so?' I managed. 'Did your father teach you?'

I was surprised Urien had let him indulge a pastime his mother had enjoyed at all. Or, more likely, my ignorant husband had not known that about me.

'No,' he replied. 'My father is a king and busy, and has little interest in birds. We had a good falconer in my childhood home – Kit. He taught me.'

The memory struck with loss and affection: Kit, the young deputy falconer at Castle Chariot, whose sister Elisa I had saved from death. He knew my love for falconry and had given the gift to my son. So many people I had been forced to leave behind.

I wanted to question him on what he learned, whether his teacher mentioned the same affinity in his mother. Disingenuous, all of it, but I could not help but seek out our joint traits, and wonder whether Yvain knew what we shared.

Yet it was untenable, too much to ask. I was a lie, a stranger behind a counterfeit face. I had no right to any of his past.

Forcing my curiosity aside, I returned to the present. 'So now we are acquainted,' I said. 'Why are you not yet worthy of the Round Table?'

Yvain sat back in the saddle and regarded me intently, for so long I wondered if the glamour had held. Eventually, he sighed and returned his eyes to the road. 'Before I begin recounting my not particularly interesting tale, perhaps you could answer a question I have?'

My heart took a yearning leap. 'Yes?' I said nervously.

He considered me again, then shook his head. 'Never mind. It's nothing.'

'Sir Yvain, if I am to trust you as my escort then you must speak freely.'

A slight flush bloomed across his face. 'Just about where, more specifically, we are headed. It is my honour to escort you anywhere, but I confess I have another purpose. I … thought you might lead me to Sir Lancelot.'

Relief flooded my body, half disappointment. 'I see,' I replied. 'But Sir Lancelot said he did not wish to be found.'

'I know, but someone will go and seek him – King Arthur won't want Lancelot far from his side for long. Even if he has left your mistress's house, I thought perhaps I could learn the road he took, and follow his route.' He cleared his throat. 'It sounds rather impulsive, now I've spoken it aloud.'

His determination to question accepted wisdom struck me with pride. Here I was in his blood – his mother's rebellious spirit alive in his burning desire to solve a problem, save his friend. His father never had half as much spine as our son was showing now.

'You and Sir Lancelot are friends?' I asked.

'I love him as though we were brothers. I cannot count the occasions he has saved my hide. I'd like to be the one to find him this time – to return the favour, and …'

'Because it would put you in good stead,' I concluded. 'With King Arthur.'

He smiled, flushing again. 'There you have me caught. My reputation at Camelot will prosper, yes, but I miss Lancelot too. All I ask is to be taken where you saw him last, and by my faith, I will be your knight forever.'

Another blow landed upon my weakened heart. *You are already mine forever,* I thought. *Even if you will never suffer to know it.*

'You speak of your reputation as if it needs improvement,' I said. 'Why?'

He looked down, fussing with the laces on his gloves. 'A while ago – well, not that long – my uncle ... King Arthur, he ... banished me from his court.'

Motherly outrage reared in me like a woken dragon, but I managed to stop my own voice from breaking through. 'Goodness!' the damsel exclaimed. 'What had you done?'

For a moment, he looked slightly mutinous – another sliver of myself reflected. I wondered if Yvain had ever unleashed his Morgan side upon his father.

'A handsome mantle was sent to Camelot as a gift for the King,' he said. 'But it was poisoned, deadly. God be thanked, its danger was discovered before he could wear the garment, though by causing the death of the unfortunate messenger who brought it. However, the King declared that it was my mother who sent the mantle to cause his death. This did not sit well with me, so I stood up and argued that she could not be to blame.'

I gripped the saddlebow lest I slip sideways. 'You didn't think she was guilty?'

He shook his head. 'There was no proof – certainly not enough to make such a declaration. To begin with, she is far cleverer than that, and it did not seem like something she would do. The King took my words as defiance, and sent me from the court.'

My first impulse was to cry out he was right, that for all the chaos I had inflicted upon Camelot, sending a piece of clothing to murder Arthur was not one of them, and I indeed was wiser than such a faulty scheme. I wanted to assure my son he had acted with honour and courage, and no king could ask for more. But I was either an unimportant damsel or his wayward mother who had left him behind; neither of us had the privilege.

Instead, I swallowed my feelings and asked, 'How long were you banished?'

'A year,' he replied, and another flash of anger crackled through me.

'I don't understand,' I said. 'What you did was a noble act. Does the King allow for a knight's mother to be maligned without answer?'

'It wasn't only my defence of her, but speaking her name at all. My uncle ... she is the blood link between us, but he forbids any mention of her in his court.'

'His own sister?' I exclaimed, as if what he was saying sounded completely bizarre. It did, I supposed, from the perspective of an outsider. So much of what had happened – the war Arthur and I had been fighting in the strangest ways, my status as Camelot's sworn enemy, first unfairly then later well-earned – I had just accepted as part of my life, but I had never paused to consider how *peculiar* it all was.

Yvain nodded, as if he understood my confusion. 'They were once close in heart and mind. She descended into corruption and was exiled, but before that my uncle held her in his highest regard.'

'He has spoken to you of this?'

'Not him, but others have,' he replied. 'About the past, better tales of her, things I am not supposed to know. Even from within the court itself.'

Sir Kay, I thought with a surge of fondness, sceptical of absolutes and always happy to offer the contrarian view. Elaine too; my middle sister did her part and would have given the fairest account, my flaws and merits both.

'You have an open heart,' I said.

'Maybe,' he replied. 'Or perhaps I simply do not believe her capable of so much maleficence in the way it is claimed.' He looked at me directly, so sudden I had to hold fast to the glamour. 'Is that wrong of me?'

'N-no,' I quavered. 'It is the decent and fair-minded view. Things are always more complicated than they seem.'

Yvain sighed. 'But she did betray my uncle, terribly. Ran away from Camelot, threatened the kingdom, tried to destroy him to snatch his throne. Some say it broke his heart – others claim he expected it due to a prophecy. My father says her punishment was well-deserved and mere exile wasn't harsh enough. In any case, her name is the only thing we cannot utter in the King's vicinity. As I discovered when I tried, and found myself banished.'

'What did your father say? Couldn't he argue your case?'

'Yes, he could have, and perhaps it would have been different,' he said. 'As it was, he agreed with the High King.'

If I ever saw Urien again, I would burn him anew for letting his hatred for me hurt our courageous son. What good was he, if he could not save Yvain from unjust punishment?

'You should be proud,' I said firmly. 'You defended your mother's honour.'

Yvain's brow creased. 'At first, I thought I was protecting my own honour, but now I don't know. My mother brought me forth to life, after all. I cannot escape that. Nor will I be ashamed of who I am. She is part of me.'

If I had died in that moment, my son's words would have been enough. Yvain had gone against what he had been raised to believe and formed his own feelings about his mother. It had cost him, to stand in my defence – he must have known it would – yet he had spoken up anyway. To my shattered heart, it was as much of an absolution I could hope for, even if I could never deserve such a thing.

When I didn't reply, he gave a rueful smile. 'I don't know why I have told you all of this. Though perhaps you see now why I wish to be the one who finds Sir Lancelot.'

'You do not fear him … gone?' I asked. 'For good?'

'Lancelot – dead?' He shook his head vehemently. 'No, he cannot be.'

The fervent belief Lancelot conjured in his peers was still perplexing, but I understood it better now. Most days, the way he carried himself suggested that if Death came for du Lac, he would buffet the hooded one on the skull with a sword hilt and take his pale horse as a prize.

'Regardless, it is no use,' Yvain added. 'If Lancelot is alive, he will be long gone by now. Without knowing the road he took, I'll never catch up with him.'

He sighed deeply, so defeated that I wanted to put my hands to his face, look into the eyes that I had given him and say everything would be all right. The afternoon light was already fading into a lavender dusk; our time ran short.

'My mistress's manor sits in the shadow of the two highest mountain peaks in south Britain,' I said. 'Just off the Roman road that leads through Cymri lands. If Sir Lancelot has recovered and departed as he swore he would, where do you believe he would go?'

Yvain considered it, then shook his head dismissively. 'I don't know, I—'

'You know your friend,' I encouraged. 'I'm sure you could make a good guess.'

'I suppose,' he said hesitantly, 'I'd say Lancelot would ride the Roman road north to Chester or so, then turn north-east and keep going to the coast. He has a castle in that part of the country – it makes sense he would go there.' By the end of his thought he had grown in surety, sitting taller in the saddle. 'Yes, I'm certain that is what he would do.'

'There, you see,' I replied. 'Already you have a plan. You will find him, Sir Yvain. I have faith.'

He offered me his bright, hope-giving smile. 'Thank you, my lady. If I succeed in my quest, it will be in no small part due to you.'

His gracious words tore at my heart, the weight of my deception crushing any happiness I might have felt. I couldn't bear to lie to my son any longer – to hide myself, my love or my regret from him for another moment. Nor could I tell him the truth.

My only choice, once again, was to let him go.

As the sky began its tilt towards twilight, I gathered my courage. Reluctantly, I cast a whisper of a sleep charm across him and watched him yawn.

'You are tired,' I said. 'Let us stop. You can sleep, and I will take first watch.'

Yvain opened his mouth to protest, but another yawn stole his words. 'I insist,' I said. 'I promise I will wake you for the slightest disturbance.'

I led us off the road to a grove of oaks. At my urging, Yvain settled back against a trunk with his mantle drawn across his body and closed his eyes, slumbering deeply within ten breaths. I had not seen my child fall asleep for so many years, but he was just the same: quick to succumb, trusting, an abandon that still spoke of an innocent heart.

I watched him a while longer, then cast a web of invisible protection over his sleeping form, so he could not come to harm. The thought of leaving him was unbearable. If I could, I would have ridden at his side forever.

But for his sake and my own, I could not stay. Silently, I retrieved my horse, whispered my farewell into the air, then galloped off by the blue light of the moon, and didn't stop riding until I had reached Belle Garde.

25

I returned to my valley in the bare dawn, free of the glamour but aching, still wearing the weight of my lies like a cloak of steel.

Heavy with tiredness, I went to my bedchamber and lay down, but sleep would not come. My head was full of Yvain, every guilt and regret, things I should have said and done – on the road, in the past – pressing upon my soul.

In turn came visions of my disaster in the court, and a conclusion I never imagined possible. The emerald ring was my one move to secure my vengeance, and now it was gone, leaving me with a moody and unpredictable prisoner, admittedly fascinating, but more of a distraction than perhaps was wise.

The thought of Lancelot made me rise from the bed, circling the room to burn off the restlessness pricking at my body. First of all, I needed to keep away from him. He was never going to confess, and our potential had turned to ruins, defied by the knightly vows he wore like a hair shirt. All he could offer me now was temptation and wasted time. What's more, Midsummer's Eve was approaching, along with Belle Garde's annual feast, our most beloved celebration because it had been Accolon's favourite. After that would be the anniversary of his death and his birthday revel, all occasions that deserved my full attention. With instant certainty I knew – du Lac could not be here for any of it.

Even so, the thought of simply releasing him was a battle my stubborn heart could not lose. I had kidnapped Camelot's champion knight for a purpose, and just because my revenge had failed didn't mean he shouldn't be of use. There had always been one guaranteed way for eminent knights to earn their keep.

A jug of fresh water had been left for me, so I grabbed it and marched up to my study. Sweeping aside the Hecate tapestries, I retrieved the silver bowl and carried everything out onto the balcony. The water reflected the rising morning as I poured, lively in the light and awaiting my request. I leaned over the settling surface.

'Ninianne,' I murmured. Then, firmer, *'Ninianne.'*

Immediately, the liquid began to pulse from its centre in concentric circles, as if struck by a constant raindrop. It did not take long before the reflection changed from the sky above me to a large pale stone room, arched ceilings dappled with coloured light.

'Morgan?' came her low, enrapturing voice. 'Is that you?'

She did not come into view, but her presence resonated through the water. I could sense her broken concentration beneath the continuing scratch of a quill; she was deep in study, and for a moment I wanted to ask what she was working on.

'Of course,' I replied. 'How many enchanted silver bowls do you have out there?'

She ignored my sarcasm. 'I never expected you to use it. I am pleased.'

'Save your satisfaction,' I said. 'I bring difficult news. I have your son.'

The quill scratching stopped. Her face appeared, shocked and gleaming. 'What do you mean?'

'Sir Lancelot is my prisoner, with no hope of rescue. I will only give him to you.'

She paused to study my expression, her green eyes glittering, then settled on belief. 'It will take me a while to get there,' she said. 'I am across the sea. I need your word that nothing will happen to him.'

'You are in no position to make demands of me,' I replied. 'This is a ransom. If you want Lancelot back, unharmed and in all his glory, you must bring me the Shroud of Tithonus. Soon – before Midsummer. I won't wait indefinitely.'

'Morgan, I've told you before,' she began. 'I don't have—'

'This is not a discussion,' I cut in. 'Farewell, Ninianne.'

In the midst of her protests, I lifted the silver bowl and poured the water over the balcony. Her pleas echoed, then dissipated, flying away on the wind.

In truth, I didn't know if Ninianne could get the Shroud; I was relying on a suspicion that had scratched at me with little proof for years. However, if anything would bring her to my door, it would be her son.

The thought brought a vision of Yvain, of his good humour and generosity that had allowed me to learn of him, his troubles and hopes, as we rode side by side. In an effort to ward off my sadness, I sent for a fresh horse and retrieved a large gyrfalcon from the mews, intending to disappear for a few hours flying. I was leashing the bird to my saddlebow on the front green when Alys happened upon me.

'You *are* back – thank goodness,' she said breathlessly. She was drawn and dark-eyed, as if she hadn't slept. 'There's a problem with Sir Lancelot.'

Who else? I thought tiredly. There never seemed to be any escaping him.

'What's he done now?' I asked.

'He's stopped eating.'

No one noticed at first, she explained – he was sly about it, throwing his meals into the underground channel that led from the lodge's privy, or into the fire. Once it was discovered, he simply declined food outright, leaving it to fester in its hatch until someone took it away again.

'It's a protest, or a play for sympathy,' I said. 'Tell the kitchen to keep sending food. He'll eat when he's hungry.'

'It's more than that,' she said. 'Since you left, he hasn't taken wine or water.'

I stopped still. 'No liquid at all?'

She shook her head, toying anxiously with her braid. We both knew what it meant: Lancelot was determined to die.

'It doesn't make sense,' I said. 'He is dedicated to his knightly vows, not to mention God-fearing. He would not meet his end this way.'

There were many shameful ways for knights to die and they were desperate to avoid them all, but self-destruction was by far the worst, a mortal sin regarded as an act of utmost cowardice. Lancelot had many faults, but lack of bravery had never been one of them.

'Five days, Morgan' Alys said. 'I don't know how much longer he can—'

In my chest, my tired heart started to pound. I thought of Yvain, his love for his brother-in-arms, the friend he missed, and new guilt hit me like a winter flood.

'It's all right,' I told her, easing up into the saddle behind the falcon. 'I'll fix it.'

The morning sky was afire as I rode to the lodge – an ominous portent, so the shepherds said. Leaving the hooded falcon dozing on my saddlebow, I retrieved an ignored wine jug from the hatch, filled it with fresh well water and let myself into Lancelot's prison.

The large chamber was dark and stuffy. I opened the shutters with a gesture, filling the room with brightness and fresh air. Unusually, my captive was not stalking the room, or glowering at me over his chessboard, but still in bed. Or at least, he was a lumpen form laying on it, in his shirt and breeches. I could tell by his breaths that he wasn't asleep.

I strode across and put the pitcher on a side table, then stood over the so-called best knight of the world.

'Lancelot,' I said, 'are you really going to let yourself die like this?'

Slowly, the jumble of limbs turned, sunken eyes squinting into the light. Heat came off him in waves, the body's urgent response to preserve its remaining water. A dark scruff of beard shadowed his jaw.

'My lady, please,' he croaked. 'Leave me alone, I beg of you.'

'Do not try to get around me with politeness,' I said. 'It's beneath us both.'

My voice was not harsh but held a hint of challenge and Lancelot stirred at the sound, his bloodshot eyes igniting. I lifted the water jug and poured a gobletful. The liquid's song drew his attention, but when I held out the cup he looked away.

'You need to drink,' I said.

'No,' he croaked. 'It is futile – everything. A day or so more, and I will be no trouble to you. All I ask is for you to send my body to the nearest holy place, so I can be buried in the name of Christ.'

His self-indulgence lit a fire in my gut. 'Damn you,' I cursed. 'If you think I'm going to let Camelot's best knight die on my land and take the blame for something else not my doing, then you are mistaken. End your life anywhere else, but not at Belle Garde.'

Unexpectedly, he moved, hoisting himself up onto his elbows to better stare me down. 'I'll do what I want,' he growled. 'You cannot watch me every moment.'

If I could provoke him into argument, perhaps there was hope. 'I will if that's what it takes,' I replied. 'I'll lay hands and heal you if I have to.'

He managed a scoff through cracked lips. 'I'd rather you cut off my head.'

The fierceness on his face brought me a healer's satisfaction. Somehow, I had goaded him back to life. I held out the cup.

'Then drink,' I said.

We glared at one another like two feuding bulls, but in the end, my threat prevailed. Lancelot propped himself up on an elbow and took the goblet, sipping slowly, the relief of refreshment closing his eyes. I let my senses follow the water as it ran down his gullet and into the tributaries of his body.

'Good,' I couldn't help but say.

His eyes snapped open, severe but already clearer. He thrust the empty goblet back at me. 'It's just delaying what is inevitable.'

'You might defy God, but you won't defeat Morgan le Fay,' I retorted. 'And I will not bear the responsibility of letting you die.'

'It is *not your choice*.'

Pushing both fists into the mattress, Lancelot tried to force himself to his feet, but the exertion was too much and he collapsed forwards, breathing hard. I caught his shoulders to stay his fall, and his afflictions flew to me in unison: an aching, shrunken stomach, organs strained to their limit, a relentless, devastating thirst. The cup of water had barely begun to relieve what he had visited upon himself. His entire body was made from pain.

I eased him back against the pillows. 'If you won't let me heal you, we need something more.'

His response was a glower, so I returned to the jug and passed my hand over the rim, asking the element to gain in potency, as Ninianne had once done for me at Merlin's. The water quivered, clarifying until its goodness glittered through the liquid like diamonds.

'What are you doing?' Lancelot asked.

'This water will restore your strength,' I said, pouring another cupful. 'Your fairy mother taught me this trick, so that should prove I'm not here to harm you.'

Invoking Ninianne gave him pause; he rolled his eyes and took the goblet. 'You'll do whatever you wish, you always have,' he said, after several refreshing gulps. 'You are the most disloyal and treacherous woman in all Britain.'

Insults; this was more like it.

'Only Britain?' I said carelessly.

He scowled between sips. 'Perhaps who has ever lived.'

'And you are the "Flower of All Knighthood",' I said. 'Yet unable to withstand the slightest of my provocations.'

He glared at me, then leaned over and swiped the jug from my hands. Briskly, he refilled his own cup and drank with a furrowed brow. Again, I sensed the crystal liquid flowing through him, his strength returning with every drop.

'Why do you, of all people, care about keeping me alive?' he asked. 'What do you want from this?'

The question struck me, mainly because I had little idea how to respond. I wanted Lancelot gone from Belle Garde and Ninianne was on her way, but my ransom plans had brought no satisfaction, nor cured the restlessness that still scratched beneath my surface. When I tried again to capture the feeling, it flew out of my reach.

'I don't know,' I confessed. 'Perhaps nothing, any more.'

'Everyone wants something,' he said. 'Even if it is impossible, or an act of faith.'

His words resonated within me, the revelation sudden as a peregrine dive. What I wanted was not to perform my own act of faith, but answer one.

I simply do not believe her capable of so much maleficence in the way it is claimed, Yvain had told the damsel. *Is that wrong of me?*

My own son had offered the only faith I needed – his belief that I was better than how the world painted Morgan le Fay. All I wanted was for Yvain not to be wrong, and for me to deserve such a blessing. And what my son most wished for was to be restored in the eyes of the court. Lancelot did not need to be ransomed; he needed to be found.

'What if I let you go?' I said suddenly. 'With conditions, of course.'

Lancelot's face leapt to surprise. 'If you think you will get me to tell you—'

I held up my hand. 'No more will I ask whom you love. But say I will release you from my custody now, if you swear me a different oath. All you must do is stay away from the Royal Court until Christmastide, take the exact route I give you on the Cymri roads, and travel directly to your own castle in the north-east. Would you agree?'

Lancelot studied me again, suspicion writ across his face, gaunt but with his colour returning. His inner strength was almost restored.

'No,' he said slowly. 'I would not.'

It hit me like a joust strike. 'It's barely half a year. You don't want to be free?'

'Not on those terms.'

There had never been a refusal so absurd. 'Then you will rot,' I said, incredulous.

With an insouciance I did not know he had, Lancelot shrugged. 'So be it.'

I stepped back, regarding him in disbelief. His gaze met mine, cool and serious, as if he sensed the chaos in me and refused to let it entangle him.

We stayed that way for what felt like an age, a true stalemate in the great chess game that had started the moment we met. Something needed to change.

I sighed. 'This is getting us nowhere. Come with me.'

26

I expected resistance, but he didn't display any appetite for more argument. Heaving himself off the mattress, Lancelot pulled on his boots and accepted his outdoor mantle from my hands. It billowed around his frame and I saw how much his suffering had diminished him, though he still cut a finer figure than most men.

Without ceremony, I returned to my horse, slipping on my leather gauntlet and unleashing the gyrfalcon. My prisoner followed me outside, blinking into the sunlight.

'Aren't you afraid I'll escape?' he asked.

'Not in the slightest,' I said. 'I don't need doors or chains to contain you. I could strike you dead faster than this falcon on a rabbit.'

He looked at me in disdain, but for once, his beauty didn't stun, dimmed to the point where I could now withstand its effect. Or else I had just become accustomed to him.

'A fine creature,' he commented, as I encouraged the bird onto my fist. 'Prestigious. I was taught only kings can possess a gyrfalcon.'

'One cannot truly *possess* a preying bird,' I said. 'But I will fly any falcon I wish.'

He pulled a considering face. 'She must be heavy for you. I'm happy to carry her, save your struggle.'

It was such a delicate balance between courtesy and insult that I was impressed anew at his wit. 'Ah, those celebrated noble manners,' I replied. 'Unfortunately, I wouldn't let you bear her if Christ Himself made the petition.'

I slipped the bird's hood off. She regarded Lancelot sharply, lifting her wings in disapproval. I stroked her breast and turned her away from having to look at him.

'She doesn't like you,' I said.

He eyed me coolly. 'I'm not elated by the company myself.'

I laughed, the usual pleasure I took in our sparring, but the falcon shivered. She was sensitive, too alert, her nerves put on edge by mine and Lancelot's way with one another. It wasn't fair to expect her to fly between whatever he and I conjured in the air.

'Unfortunately, I have no choice but to tolerate you, but I will not make her do so,' I said, leashing the bird to a hitching post. 'Let's go.'

We walked beyond the lodge's walled garden, where a wide stream flowed towards a meadow speckled with cornflowers. Blossoming apple trees ran along our path, tinting the air with sweetness.

'I want my emerald ring back.'

His voice was sudden, decisive, catching me unguarded. 'I no longer have your ring,' I replied.

'Do not lie. You and I are beyond such pretence.'

Heat flashed along my spine. 'I am many things, but a liar isn't one of them,' I said. 'Your ring is back in the hands of your dearest Queen, as she bravely awaits the return of her lover in adultery. You.'

'I don't know what you speak of,' he said by rote. 'Whatever witch's third eye you have, it does not see clearly.'

'I do not need a third eye when I saw enough with my own God-given pair at the Royal Court a few days ago.'

It stopped him, drawing down his gaze. '*You* saw the King and Queen?' he exclaimed. 'Impossible. You are wanted for trial – King Arthur wouldn't have you in his sight, much less let you walk away.'

I smiled enigmatically and made to move on, but he caught hold of my forearm. The skin was bare of sleeve where he held me, and an involuntary thrill glittered across our nerves. I watched him feel it, then gather himself.

'I went in disguise, aided by magic,' I replied. 'No one ever knew it was me.'

My pointed words flickered through him, another reminder of our journey to the Dolorous Tower and all we had learned of each other. That I had given him every opportunity to break his oath without dishonour and escape, but instead he had followed me home.

'Well?' I added. 'Aren't you going to ask me what I said?'

He shook his head. 'I have no need to know what you wrought. I have failed all those I love in ways you cannot comprehend. Whatever ill they think of me, it is deserved.'

His sheer inability to see his life with clarity lit me like a bonfire.

'God's blood,' I said, pulling away from his touch. 'You don't even know what you have, do you? Hear this – I stood before the entire Royal Court and told them everything. That you love the Queen and she is adulterous with you, betraying your King. It didn't matter – they all have so much blasted faith in you that it didn't change a single thing.'

I turned from him, gathering the control I didn't wish to lose. I could feel his curiosity like sunbeams on my face.

'They didn't believe you?' he asked.

'That's right,' I retorted. 'All they cared about was where you were, if you lived. Sir Gawain wanted to leap on a horse and gallop out after you. Guinevere defended you with such passionate rhetoric, she had the court agreeing that your love held no shame. Arthur wished only for you to return to his side. My own son was banished for speaking his mind, when you are praised, believed and valued, given the benefit of every doubt. Worse still, you refuse to see that you succeed because of this privilege *every day of your life.*'

For a moment, Lancelot looked shocked, and I saw my own anger reflected in his eyes, then he swung away, storming towards a hollowed tree trunk beside the stream. He kicked out, boot connecting with a heavy crack. I felt it hurt him, but he didn't show it.

I marched after him. 'Don't you dare run away from this. You won't wallow in self-pity, not now. *Look at me.*'

Unexpectedly he obeyed and turned back, his expression drained to one I had not seen yet – a deep, yearning sorrow.

'My lady, I can't go on this way,' he said.

The intensity in his voice arrested me; firm but desperate. 'What do you mean?' I asked.

He looked at the stream, water-light oscillating across his melancholy, remarkable face. For the first time, I considered that it might be a curse to be in possession of such beauty, to distract when sometimes all one needed was to be seen in the truth of our pain.

'I thought I knew my own mind,' he went on, 'but your presence, what we are doing to one another ...' He glanced back, his gaze meeting mine. 'This torment will be the death of me.'

His confession sapped the anger from my chest, leaving only my fluttering heartbeat. His eyes were so piercing I felt I had been pulled into a star.

'It's *you*,' I said. 'Do you not know it? Between here and the Dolorous Tower, there were a hundred chances to escape and you ignored every one. I offered you freedom and you refuse. You won't let me be.'

At my words, he turned to me fully, a frown of question shadowing his brow.

'Either go and be at liberty,' I persisted, 'or if you want to stay and explore everything I spoke of, then find your honesty and *say it*.'

He stood almost rapt, body still but poised. Finally, he shook his head. 'I can't.'

When his answer came, I felt suddenly unstitched, vulnerable, exposed to the light in a way I was not used to. My voice came hard, but I could not hide the tremor in it.

'What is it?' I demanded. 'Am I not enough for you?'

Lancelot didn't baulk, his eyes clear as the stream and direct, as if once again looking into the centre of my being.

'You,' he said, 'are too much for me.'

I tasted the words, finding disappointment. I had heard it before, so many times. I said nothing and looked down, abandoning our shared gaze, his decision.

Amidst my silence, Lancelot sighed. 'I will take your deal. For my freedom.'

I found no victory in his reversal. Nodding, I moved to step away, but he caught my hand in his, holding my palm to his deep chest. His pulse felt like thunder in my blood.

'I swear this oath to you and before God, that I will obey your exact terms,' he said. 'To stay away from the Royal Court until Christmastide, and follow the route you command.'

I cleared my throat. 'There is one more thing. Yvain will be the one who finds you. When he does, if you speak of this, say I released you with mercy. Swear it to me.'

He nodded solemnly. 'I will. Upon my honour.'

We stood there awhile, both joined and severed, then I drew my hand from his body and turned on my heel, heading back the way we had come. In my wake, I felt a shiver of his confusion, but he soon caught up to my side.

'I assume you wish to depart immediately,' I said.

He eyed my new briskness sidelong, then nodded. 'I would, but I cannot ride, fight, or withstand travelling in the state I am in now.'

'I can heal you, if you let me lay hands,' I offered, though the idea rippled with unease. 'You could be on the road by the morning.'

'Absolutely not,' Lancelot replied. 'The taint of your devilry would bring about my eternal shame.'

I was grateful for his swipe, bringing us back to the safety of our antipathy. I smiled, baring teeth; he regarded me with a handsome hauteur.

'Bring me food, and I will eat it,' he said. 'Give me access to the gardens and I will regain my breath and muscle. I will restore my own strength, then leave. Thereafter, never again, Morgan le Fay.'

I didn't know what he was vowing against, but accepted it nonetheless as we reached the entrance of his former prison. The gyrfalcon sat calm on her perch, resplendent as the moon. She gave the knight a savage glare.

'Then we are concluded, Lancelot du Lac,' I said. 'Fly away home.'

It did not take my guest long to find his way back to strength.

According to reports, he kept his pledge and ate well, exercised, and schooled his horse in the nearby cornflower meadow. He transformed from a despairing jumble of bones, determined to die in a strange bed, back into the champion knight he had sworn to remain.

I was there for none of it. When Sir Lancelot of the Lake armed himself and rode out of Belle Garde through the northern valley, it was only from the word of others – and the slightest shiver of absence across my senses – that I learned he was gone.

27

A week or so later, the huntsman brought the news.

'There's a woman at the boundary, my lady, claiming you summoned her. She says you'll know what it's about.'

I noted he looked faintly dazzled. 'I do,' I replied. 'Let her in.'

Gathering all I would need, I prepared the entrance hall for her arrival and waited. Soon after, she swept in, a blaze of impatience in the cool, quiet house.

'Where is my son?' Ninianne of the Lake demanded.

'You know,' I mused, 'the last time that phrase was uttered between us was when I discovered you had snatched mine and Accolon's newborn child. How things change, but ultimately remain the same.'

'Only I did not snatch your son,' she retorted. 'Whereas you did take mine. Where is Lancelot?'

'Then I assume you have come to meet the terms of our exchange,' I said evenly. 'Firstly, where is the Shroud of Tithonus?'

She lowered her voice to its most alluring pitch. 'I told you – I do not have the Shroud. Nor do I know what Merlin did with it.'

The light from her skin settled, turning deep gold and reaching across the space between us. Her warmth was the quality of a perfect evening: a long walk under the sunset; good wine generously poured; one's true love waiting open-armed in bed. Pleasures of life she had also stolen from me.

My nerves pulled taut but I held fast to my self-control, sharpening my senses to her presence. Waves of silver-bright vitality flowed off her, calling out to the healing within me. She lied; the Shroud of Tithonus was somewhere upon her person.

I let her bodiless embrace soothe me for a moment longer, then shook it off as though it were a wet cape.

'I don't know what's worse,' I said. 'That you still do not appreciate the depth of my intelligence, or you think I have time to waste.'

Her light dimmed, withdrawing. 'I am not here for the pleasure of refusing your request. I am here for my son.'

If I had worried she would sense my lies about Lancelot's liberty, I knew then she could not. Her powers of reading me had diminished, and to realise it was odd, empowering.

'The son whose handsome neck you are risking with your denials,' I replied.

'I know you, Morgan,' she said. 'I have held my hand on your heart. You would not do that to me.'

'Yet much has changed since then, any closeness we shared so long in the past.' I put my palm to my chest. 'What would you feel now, do you think, if you put your hand to the shattered pieces of my heart that you and Arthur left behind? Would it spare your son?'

She stepped towards me, her glow expanding, threatening to combust.

'Careful,' I said. 'Any moment now, you may decide that you wish to dominate me with your far greater magic. Remember, the moment you allow it, you will be dragged out of this valley by my protective charms. I will not permit you entry again.'

'Why are you being this way?' she said. 'I know you have been grieving these past years, but what you are doing and saying is not who you are.'

'How dare you,' I said. 'I have not been grieving – I still am. And I will keep *being this way* until what I lost has been restored.'

'This is beneath you,' she insisted, her vehemence rising to match my own. 'Suspicion, destruction, control – I didn't risk my life to rid the world of Merlin for you of all people to become just like him.'

'I am *nothing* like Merlin!' I shouted.

The sound snapped throughout the hall, echoing my anger back to me, the trap Ninianne had tempted me into. I pulled back on the reins of my fury.

'This is a ransom, nothing more,' I said in a controlled voice. 'A simple exchange widely accepted in knightly circles. It is you who vacillates over saving your son.'

'Lancelot doesn't need me to save him,' she replied. 'But kidnap, ransom, threatening his death? I came here because I was concerned about your state of mind.'

'How bold of you to question *my* rationality,' I scoffed. 'I've never threatened Lancelot with death. Indeed, I have already saved his life once.'

I had never seen Ninianne pale so fast, not even when Merlin had sliced open her arm to prove that I could heal it. She drained to the colour of bonedust. 'What do you mean?'

'The only danger to his person has come from himself, throwing his body at destruction at every opportunity. Just recently, he refused to eat or drink and almost perished. I was the one who brought him back from the brink.'

'He wouldn't,' she said, half to herself. 'He is too …'

'Honourable? Courageous? Beloved? Yes, that's what I thought. Yet when I found him, he told me to leave him to die. I said I would never let that happen.'

I advanced towards her, until we stood within arm's reach. The silvery force of the Shroud thrilled through my body like a lover's whisper, reminding me of its presence.

'Above all, I am a healer,' I said. 'But I am not omniscient. You can walk away now knowing I won't slay Lancelot, but with his disposition, I make no guarantees I can keep him alive.' I paused, holding her dimmed green gaze. 'Place your hand on my heart now and see if I am telling the truth.'

She made no move. *I know you are*, her mind said to mine.

'A wise choice,' I replied aloud. 'Perhaps your son cannot escape the confines of his inner troubles, and I sympathise, but he can be freed from Belle Garde.' I held out my hand. 'Give me the Shroud.'

With a glittering reluctance, Ninianne reached into her cloak and drew out a red-and-white silk bag. Seeing Arthur's colours surrounding the precious object put my teeth on edge. I grabbed the bag before she could change her mind, turned away and reached inside.

The Shroud looked and felt the same as before – bleached soft linen, the shade of old bones. Greedily, I clutched the fabric, running the linen through my fingertips, looking for damage, falseness, fairy traps.

A symphony of vitality shot into my blood in reply, scattering bright goodness throughout my body. No counterfeit charm could recreate the pleasure of it, or my unique connection. In my hands, I held the true Shroud of Tithonus.

I smiled at Ninianne over my shoulder, victory singing in my veins. 'It's about time,' I said. 'Stay exactly where you are.'

I went over to a table by the fireplace, and the provisions I had made before she arrived. A reliquary of blue glass and silver stood waiting within a cage of protective charms. I opened the hinged lid, folded the Shroud with delicacy, then placed the marvel inside with a rush of satisfaction. At long last, I possessed what I most wanted; there wasn't a person in the world, armoured with magic or steel, who held power over me any more.

'Our deal is done, Morgan,' Ninianne said. 'Bring me my son.'

Slowly, I turned back and faced her. Perhaps what I had done was fraudulent, even theft, but she had stolen from me first. She had lied to me countless times.

'Lancelot,' I said casually, 'is not here.'

She recoiled, then charged forwards, snapping like a she-wolf. *'You lie.'*

'Spoken by one who knows how,' I replied. 'Nevertheless, I have no reason to, now I have what I want. Sir Lancelot has left my *Val Sans Retour.*'

'He is here, I can feel it,' she insisted. 'You cannot fool me, Morgan. I have ways of knowing where he is.'

'Maternal instinct, I suppose?'

She bridled at the bitterness in my voice. 'A ring he wears that I gave him. The enchantment acts as a link to his presence.'

'Ah yes! The ring that also protects against magic.' I reached into the top of my bodice, brandishing the dull grey band. 'This one, I believe.'

Ninianne's eyes grew wide at the sight of the brown stone. 'How did you get that? No one but Lancelot is able to touch it.'

'I know. It thoroughly scorched me when I tried. Impressive work from you, as ever.' I flicked the ring up on my thumbnail and caught it in my palm. 'Your magic didn't fail. He gave it to me.'

She shook her head fervently. 'That is not possible.'

'Then how do you explain my possession?' I said. 'Or why you were sure he was still here, when he is truly gone.'

Ninianne cast her gaze about the echoing hall, as if hoping Lancelot might leap out from behind an arras to carry them both off to safety.

'Search the entire manor if you wish,' I said. 'You won't find him.'

She turned sharply back to me, her light fierce. 'How do you have that ring, Morgan? He would not part with it willingly.'

'Oh, it wasn't *willingly*,' I said. 'I will say this for your indomitable son – you have raised the stubborn fairy side of him to perfection. But there is a mortal heart in that deep chest of his, scored with honour and love. Sir Gawain was in peril and he wished to rescue him. I generously agreed to it, if he gave me his other ring to guarantee his return. He couldn't bear the thought, for obvious reasons, so he gave me your magical gift instead.'

'What other ring?' she asked. Unease shimmered through her, but I couldn't tell if it was due to knowledge or lack thereof.

'You know well enough. The square emerald in a gold band which Lancelot wears around his neck. A token of love from one who favours such stones, with her royal name carved within the band. *Guinevere.*'

This time, Ninianne could not hide her shock. It came off her in waves.

'And you *dare* speak to me about betrayal,' I said.

'I don't know what you mean,' she protested. 'I ... I—'

'Then let me explain it to you,' I cut in. 'Your darling son, the most honourable, eminent, perfect knight of the realm, is the greatest traitor this kingdom has ever seen. Sir Lancelot and Queen Guinevere are lovers. If Merlin's precious predictions must be believed, *they* are the betrayal that was promised, not me.'

I returned to the table and unwrapped the final object I had brought: the Book of Prophecies. I picked up the golden volume and opened it to the page I most wished to burn.

'Here,' I said, thrusting it towards her. 'Read the prophecy that Merlin decided was definitively about me. The one that Arthur and you chose to believe.'

She caught the open book in her hands, and I paced back and forth while she diligently read, as if she didn't know exactly what was there.

'Show me where it says my name,' I demanded. 'Where *anything about me* is written.' I stopped and slammed my finger onto the page. 'Nowhere does it say "Morgan". Or sister. Or even a woman of magic. Merlin's cursed prophecy was never speaking of me – I've said it ten thousand times. Read what he wrote and tell me who it is truly referring to.'

Ninianne made no reply, reading and re-reading the prophecy, flicking to further pages, her presence mired in confusion. I couldn't tell whether she was learning of all this for the first time, or was gathering her thoughts because I had discovered her son's secret.

I reached out and took the Book of Prophecies from her hands. She didn't protest, only closed her eyes with a pained expression.

'Where did he go?' she said. 'My son. Where is he?'

At first, her reaction surprised me, just ahead of understanding. For her, this was not about me, the Shroud, nor even the prophecies. It was about Lancelot – the love she had let into her life. She was a mother now, protecting her son from harm. No matter how strong or famous, how formidable he became, she would always fear for him.

I felt myself relent. 'I'll tell you where he isn't. In Arthur's court.'

Her eyes snapped open. 'Why not?'

'As a condition of release, he swore not to go near the court before Christmastide. I told him to ride to his own castle, and laid out the exact route he was to take.'

'Which route?' she asked immediately, but I shook my head.

'I will not say, for my own good reasons. But he accepted my terms, and there was no trickery or purposeful danger to where I sent him. That I will swear to.'

I expected a thousand more questions, but Ninianne merely nodded. She believed me, suddenly, without qualm – a feeling she had not bestowed for a very long time. We regarded one another, time stretching around us as if it could not move on until we did.

I held out the Book of Prophecies. 'Take this. You have earned it.'

She did not reach out or speak, only looked at me quizzically.

'I promised you an exchange for a son, and he's not here,' I said. 'It's only fair.'

Tentatively, Ninianne raised her hands. I placed the book on her open palms but didn't let go. 'This does come with one last request,' I admitted. 'Do not seek Lancelot yet.'

'Why not?' she asked.

'I put Yvain on the same road. Because of me, his reputation was damaged in court, so in exchange for the prophecies, I ask you to let *my* son find Lancelot, and be the one to return him to Camelot. It's not his fault that his mother is Morgan le Fay.'

She paused, then nodded. 'I will do as you wish.'

I took my hands away from the Book of Prophecies, leaving it with her. Ninianne looked at the golden covers, then back at me, her eyes searching my face. I felt strangely exposed, as if I was about to confess something.

'Is it truly not you, Morgan?' she asked. 'Are you not the betrayal prophecy?'

'No,' I said. 'I never was. Which is partly why I cannot believe anything written in that book. If not for Accolon ...' My head dropped at speaking his name, but I forced my chin up. 'Everything I have done since he died – every act of chaos and revenge I have rained upon Camelot – they are treasons and I regret nothing. But I did not betray Arthur first.'

Astonishingly, Ninianne kept believing me, her light as soft and enrapturing as years ago when she said she couldn't teach me, then did so anyway.

'Can we speak?' she said suddenly.

Instantly, I wanted to, but my reaction galled me, the way I was still compelled by her. To talk peaceably to one another felt natural and apt, and an indulgence I couldn't afford.

'Why would I do that?' I asked.

She gestured at the Shroud, safe in its glass box. 'Because you won,' she said.

To her credit, she always knew what I wished to hear.

28

I led us to the reception chamber, not quite sure what I had agreed to or why.

Ninianne entered the room, immediately drawn to a curved window that overlooked the edge of the rising spring. She stepped closer to the glass, trying to see more.

'Water calls to water,' I commented.

'It does.' Her eyes stayed on the silver pool. 'Are you still dreaming of the sea?'

'Yes,' I replied. 'When I do manage to sleep. Though I have never minded it.'

I didn't know I would tell the truth until I had spoken. Ninianne turned, flickering with intrigue. 'King Arthur dreams of it, too,' she said. 'Perhaps there is something in that.'

I had never told her I knew of Arthur's dreams. That his visions had persisted alongside mine was a surprise, but I expressed nothing more. Ninianne would not use me to interpret my brother.

'Or there is little significance beyond coincidence,' I said carelessly. 'No doubt we could argue the point all day.'

She stepped away from the glass and sat at the small table in the window recess, placing the Book of Prophecies before her. With careful fingers, she opened the cover, turned past *Arthurus Rex*, and started to read.

Taking the seat across from her, I watched the parchment shifting under her hands, her eyes moving swiftly over Merlin's script. I sensed her immediate absorption in the sorcerer's words and felt a ripple of some surly, unnameable emotion.

'You look older,' I said. 'Far more than I would have expected. I first noticed it at Merlin's house. I didn't think it was possible for you to age so quickly.'

It wasn't entirely meant as insult, and I expected it to bounce off her regardless. However, she looked up in shock, then swiftly away, as if caught hiding behind a curtain.

Her evasion hooked me at once. 'I'm right,' I said. 'Something has taken its toll. Magic, maybe – a form complex and risky. What was it?'

Ninianne leaned back in her chair and sighed.

'Lancelot,' she said simply. 'He was so damaged, in need of such comfort. I wanted to spend more of my life as his mother – teach him everything he wished to learn, give him the love and assurance to heal his losses. There were never enough hours or days, so … I changed things. For him, I slowed time.'

To anyone else, it would have sounded absurd, but I knew such things were possible. When I first saw her when I was a child, she had paused time to ensure my escape from Merlin's notice, and years later, as we rode to the sorcerer's house, she had stretched the sunlight when the journey should have taken us through the night.

'You made more hours in the day?' I asked.

'No – creating time is impossible,' she replied. 'It's more of a … bending. I slowed the march of the hours so we spent longer within them. Lancelot had more time to enjoy life, to gain his knightly skills and try to move on from the horrors of his past. Physically, he is his born age, but his mind and instincts have travelled far beyond his years. In effect, he has lived twice as many days under my care.'

Knowing him, it made an odd but perfect sense. 'And this aged you faster?'

'Time resists change,' she said. 'The cost of holding such an enchantment, duelling with that force so often … it visits itself upon the body. Mine.'

Ninianne put a hand to her face, which was still dazzlingly beautiful, but better inhabited, more seasoned goddess than eternal nymph. She carried herself more gently, as if she knew what it was to ache.

'Quite the motherly sacrifice,' I said. 'I told you there was potential for your heart. Other sorts of love. You discovered the protective, selfless kind, wanting your child to flourish at all costs. If my life here has rendered me more of a fairy, then your past fifteen years have made you—'

'Weak?' she cut in, green eyes flashing.

'No – human,' I replied. 'The Ninianne I once knew would have never brought me the Shroud, or given her immortal body to battle with time, all for the sake of another.'

She tried to muster offence, but her light softened at the thought of him. 'I gave Lancelot what he needed. It was worth it – every moment.'

The sentiment echoed within me; I had expressed the same to her long ago, about bearing children. I felt myself harden, turn cold.

'And now, if you believe your precious golden book, your son's actions will lead to the destruction of the entire country,' I said harshly.

Fear flared on her face. 'We cannot be certain. As you said, the betrayer isn't named, nor are all the prophecies equally worthy.'

'Is that what you were looking for?' I said. 'Where Merlin placed the betrayal prophecy in his order of importance? It is fourth. Far from insignificant.'

'Merlin ordered King Arthur's prophecies by the ones *he* believed to be most valuable,' she protested. 'You can hardly claim there is a significance when you have never trusted in his predictions at all.'

'I had no reason to believe anything in that book, when I knew the betrayal could not pertain to me,' I shot back. 'Yet all this time you've conveniently believed me a traitoress and wanted Arthur's prophecies. Why, if they are suddenly untrue?'

'None of this has been *convenient* to anyone,' she replied. 'It has caused so much hurt, far beyond what you imagine. I never said the predictions were not true, just …'

She trailed off, then suddenly, decisively, closed the Book of Prophecies. 'I did not expect to be given this, nor did I want to argue with you.'

'Then why did you ask to speak to me?'

'I wanted to talk as one elemental entity to another,' she replied. 'Much is happening to affect this country's future, far beyond the stars. Whatever has gone between us, you are the only one I feel will understand.'

Her admission struck an odd chord, a deference that was unlike her. I leaned forwards and rested my elbows on the table. 'Very well,' I said. 'Try me.'

Ninianne drew a deep breath. 'Magic is waning in Britain. In the land, in the air, the water. It is getting harder to charm, to enchant, even call upon the elements. The damage has been progressing slowly for years now. The natural, the conjured – all is in decline.'

I didn't know how to receive such a serious declaration, but questions were a scholar's candle in the dark. 'Not to invoke him,' I said. 'But beyond his faults, Merlin was still a strong diviner. Surely he would have foreseen something so cataclysmic?'

'Remember, Merlin possessed no natural power. This loss was not for him to feel, nor for the distant stars to know. The effects are most felt by those whose magic connects to nature. Those of us with the elements alive in our blood.'

My mind sparked with recognition, tracking back to my failures with the resurrection magic I had once performed so easily; the dead birds thrown in the fire because I could not answer their heartsong. Aside from the magpie matriarch and my flourishing healing skills, what she spoke of resonated deeply. Even my protective charms did not last as long as they had ten, even five years since.

Ninianne noted my pause. 'Have you felt it, Morgan?'

I did not wish to lie or confirm the truth. 'What's causing it?' I asked.

'One cannot be sure, but my theory is, as the age of men gains in strength, the damage done through war, bloodshed and other unchecked power takes its toll.'

'What a surprise!' I said. 'Practitioners such as Merlin, allowing monstrous men like Uther Pendragon to harness magic for brutality and dominance, has led only to destruction. No stars were needed to predict that.'

She let my bitterness pass. 'It's true the decline cannot be reversed, though King Arthur has done much to slow the rot. Even when Merlin stood beside him, he was mainly kept as an advisor, especially after revealing the circumstances of your brother's birth. Since then, the King has relied on his actions, his sense of responsibility, his heart. He has never asked to use my skills for might, or to bend a cause to his will.'

I was in no mood to hear her preach upon my brother's courage and goodness, though I could not dispute it in part. Whether Arthur ran the kingdom perfectly was a matter of opinion, but he had never spoken of magic as a kingly tool, or sought to use sorcery to solve a problem. His reverence for prophecy was his weakness, and that was because he had been inured to it since boyhood.

'But even Arthur cannot stop what is already happening,' I said.

Ninianne shook her head. 'Eventually, for me, this realm may no longer sustain.'

The regret in her voice plucked at my sympathy, but I owed it to myself not to let her play with my feelings. 'That sounds like a fairy quandary,' I said offhandedly. 'I thought you said this wasn't your realm anyway.'

'In some ways, but it is complicated,' she replied. 'My lake in Brocéliande is my *realm*, as you call it, but it became visible to this world due to the needs of raising a mortal son. As a result, it is vulnerable – to unrest, hardship, death. The more man-made destruction that seeps into the earth, the less power I can hold. If the major prophecies prove true and the kingdom falls, whatever is wrought will all but destroy magic in this land. I, and others like me, will not endure here.'

'Where will you go?' I asked.

'There is a place. An island off the Welsh and Summerland coasts, outside of time and beyond mortality. A sanctuary for those of us touched by fairy magic. Avalon.'

'Avalon,' I repeated. The name landed softly, echoing deep as if I long knew of it, though I had never before heard the word spoken.

'To some – your Lady Alys and most of this household – it would be *Ynys Afallach*,' Ninianne continued. 'Isle of Apples. The apple, of course, representing knowledge, wisdom. It is a place of study and nature and peace. When the time comes, for those of us who live by magic, it will become our home for all eternity.'

'"Those of us"?' I said. 'There are more like you?'

'Of course. There are more "water fairies", as you call us, other ladies of other lakes. Some of my learned counterparts have already left these shores.' She leaned towards me, her eyes bright and serious. 'But they are not my concern. Do not forget, Belle Garde is kept safe by fairy charms. Where will you go, Morgan, when the magic dies?'

'Go?' I said. 'I will be here, where I have always been. I won't be chased off this land by the world of men.'

'That's not what I mean,' she replied. 'Avalon is a haven of freedom, of choice – a place to keep learning, expand further into knowledge, to better explore our own power. It is a home for those of us who never quite fitted this world, who feel evermore alien as time goes on. A woman such as yourself.'

Ninianne wasn't wrong that the world had never understood my ways, and I had felt thus since the day I was born. However, I was no fairy.

'Why are you telling me this?' I said. 'There's no place for me on some mystical island full of virtuous immortal priestesses.'

She beheld me with mild amusement. 'None of us are perfect. I tell you this because I wish for us to be honest with one another. You are one of the best minds I have ever encountered. Your love of knowledge feels closer to my own than anyone I've ever met. Avalon is made for you.'

'I've heard of these "fairy otherlands",' I said. 'I wouldn't know the first thing about reaching there. What's more, I have loved ones I would not leave. I'm not like you, Ninianne – for one, I am mortal, with all the weaknesses that come with my flesh.'

'You would need myself as guide, of course,' she replied. 'Nor is Avalon a prison. You would be free to travel back and forth to see those left behind. And when the souls of our loved ones leave this world, their spirits are at liberty to seek Avalon, where the veil between worlds falls away, and join us there. But anyone touched by fairy magic can make passage. Your two women, for example, who have been saved from death by your healing, and have lived years within your protective charms. They too are scholars, and would be welcome.'

The idea was intriguing. As a woman of many exiles, to seek a different freedom by choice, to live for knowledge, my skills, with endless time to study and explore, would always be a seductive thought. Yet life had never been so simple for me.

'This is beyond comprehension,' I said. 'When you arrived here, I was a traitor. I may not be the betrayal prophecy, but I have gone far beyond treason since. I kidnapped your own son, yet you offer me sanctuary from the world's destruction and an eternity to learn? None of this makes sense.'

Ninianne offered only an enigmatic shrug. 'I am aware of the contradictions,' she replied. 'But if you are truly not the betrayal, then a great deal begins to make sense.'

'*If* I'm not the betrayal?' My cultivated calm chafed, starting to wear thin. 'Once again, your belief is conditional. It's clear that this offer comes with a cost.'

She shook her head. 'You misread me. I would never offer you Avalon at a price. The offer is genuine. But—'

'Ah, here it comes,' I said. 'What do you *want*, Ninianne?'

She frowned at me in rare annoyance. 'Again, nothing I have said is conditional,' she insisted, then put her hand on the golden book. 'But you have read these prophecies, no doubt studied the words from every angle. You have ten years of insight into what's here.'

'I have also deemed what I saw in those pages as misleading, vague to the point of irrelevance,' I countered. 'Which is why I gave it to you – it has no purpose in my life.'

'I don't mean only what is between these covers, but other instincts you have,' she replied. 'Things you have heard, your knowledge of King Arthur, confidences he might have shared. Words in this book not written in plain sight.'

'I have no time for your riddles,' I said. 'What are you saying?'

'Nothing specific,' she said quickly. 'All I mean is, if you are not a traitoress, and you truly believe this book is leading the country in the wrong direction, then let us put the power of our minds together, bring King Arthur the truth.'

I laughed in disbelief. 'What truth? Camelot's walls would turn black and crumble before Arthur's precious pride would let anything I say change his mind.'

'I can bring you together,' she persisted. 'He trusts my word and would agree. With time, he will seek to forgive. A great deal is changing – there is no better time for you and he to find your way back to one another. I've always believed you would.'

'Find our way back?' I exclaimed. 'You speak as if Arthur might forgive me, but don't ask if I can forgive him. Why in all hell would you think it's possible?'

For all I had been drawn in, she still did not understand me. I pushed up from my chair, alive with an anger that felt fresh but not new, a slumbering, ancient pain that if I didn't move to shake free of it, might grow too heavy to bear.

Ninianne rose in pursuit. 'You are hurting,' she said. 'King Arthur is hurting too. If you let me bring you to him, face him as a sister to her brother, you may find solace in the pain he carries. There is yet a future before you both.'

'His pain?' I cried. 'How dare you suggest I should care for his feelings. Even if he did admit to his wrongs, it's far too late. It won't bring Accolon back. It won't restore my reputation and give me my son's love and regard. Arthur should crawl to me before I am done with him, because *he does not deserve my forgiveness.*'

I swung away, my façade of calm shattered, but Ninianne stepped in front of me. 'This is not you, Morgan,' she insisted. 'All your life you have sought answers, ways to fix what is broken. You have the chance to harness your skills and start a new part of your life.'

'I don't *want* to fix this,' I said. 'I don't need a new life. All I've ever wanted is the ability to return to the happy existence I once had. Now, thanks to you, I can.'

She stilled at my words, as though I had managed to stop time. 'You're going to use the Shroud,' she said, in a tone of revelation. 'You never wanted it to hold power over King Arthur. You need it for a purpose of your own.'

I stared at her in puzzlement. 'Of course I do.'

She rocked back on her heels. Somehow, in all her wisdom, Ninianne had never understood the reason I wanted the Shroud. Perhaps she did not know I had taken Accolon's heart, or else thought nothing of it. Maybe she never imagined I could attempt such a feat.

'You can use the Shroud?' she said in wonder. 'Do you know what it means, if you have mastered the art of resurrection? For your brother, and Britain?'

'I haven't mastered anything yet,' I snapped. 'And if I did, it's none of anyone's concern. I cannot be treasonous and a saviour, Ninianne. Accolon died because of a lie you all believed. Arthur killed the man I loved to punish me for something I did not do, and you helped him. My life was, and is still, ruined. Nothing you say can change that.'

I picked up my skirts and strode out of the reception chamber. Ninianne followed, calling for me to wait. I wanted her gone but still I paused, drawn by her divine light.

'Morgan, if we have ever meant anything to one another, heed me now,' she said. 'I gave you what you wanted for love of my son, but I am asking you, for your brother's sake, not to use the Shroud. Do not take away the kingdom's future. *Please.*'

'For the last time, *I don't care about the kingdom.*'

Tearing myself away, I went to the side table and picked up the reliquary. A star-tail of vitality glittered through my blood from the miraculous object within, followed by a surge of hope that expanded in my chest, then settled as calm.

This was all that mattered. Once again I held control of my own life.

'You should go, Ninianne,' I said evenly. 'There is nothing more to say. Arthur's future is in your hands, not mine.'

No response came, so I turned back. She hadn't moved, the Book of Prophecies clutched in her arms, glowing with her light.

'It won't last, Morgan,' she said. 'None of this.'

'Nothing ever does,' I replied and left her, vanishing up the turret stairs with the Shroud of Tithonus clutched to my heart.

29

After Ninianne left, I took the Shroud of Tithonus up to my study, removed it from its reliquary, and lay it across my desk. I was still staring at it when Alys and Tressa marched in and asked me what in Heaven was going on. Torn from my reverie, I was surprised to find the room almost entirely dark, only a violet haze drifting through the balcony doorway.

'You missed the evening meal,' Alys said. 'Why are you sitting with no light?'

I snapped my fingers and lit the candles, gathering myself. It had been hours with only the intensity of my thoughts, and that morning felt a hundred years ago.

'Ninianne came,' I told them. 'I contacted her and said I held Sir Lancelot prisoner. She came to answer his ransom.'

Alys crossed her arms in exasperation. 'Morgan of Cornwall,' she said.

'Alys of Llancarfan,' I retorted with a smile. 'I know it wasn't particularly honest to let her believe he was still here, but it was worth it. Look.'

I picked up the folded fabric and they crowded curiously behind the desk. Alys said, 'Is that …?'

I nodded. 'The Shroud of Tithonus. Merlin's last resurrection object.'

Alys put her chin on Tressa's shoulder and they both gazed at the Shroud, as if they could see the magic shimmering within.

'So the Lady of the Lake had it all along,' Tressa said.

'Of course,' I replied. 'Or knew where it was. She played her game perfectly, until I found where she is weakest. Her son.'

Alys tutted at my nonchalance. 'What did she say?'

'Many things. Disapproving words about my behaviour – how acting *this way* wasn't in my nature. Then, true to her paradoxical self, she asked if I was the one who betrayed Arthur, and seemed to accept it when I said I was not.'

'She believed you?' Tressa exclaimed. 'After all this time?'

I shrugged. 'Who can say for certain what she thinks? She asked if we could speak and shared a great deal. How magic is waning here, and eventually she and her elemental ilk will have to leave. She spoke of a mystical island where those touched by fairy magic can go to seek knowledge, expand our wisdom for eternity. *Ynys Afallach*, it's called. Avalon.'

'*Our* wisdom?' Alys queried, and inside I cursed. I had not meant to mention the offer to go to Avalon ourselves, but she was far too astute.

'Yes,' I admitted. 'Ninianne said she would take us with her, if we wished. Our experiences with fairy magic along with our scholarship means we would all be welcome.'

Ever practical, Tressa asked, 'Are we going?'

'No. I mean … I haven't considered it,' I said. 'We have a home here, that you have worked hard to make. I would never ask such a thing.'

Alys reached out and took my hand. 'We will go anywhere with you, *cariad*,' she said. 'You know that. Your future is always our future.'

I smiled at her, absorbing the comfort of her love and loyalty, before drawing away. I could not think about any of that now.

'I highly doubt Ninianne was serious about allowing me of all people onto her wondrous island,' I said dismissively. 'We did not conclude on friendly terms. She lost the means to prevent Arthur's death today, even if she could not have used it.'

Epiphany lit Alys's face. 'Does this mean … Sir Accolon?'

The air changed in an instant, as though a ghost had drifted through the wall. I placed the Shroud back in its reliquary and closed the lid.

'I don't know,' I confessed. 'Such a feat requires much more than this piece of cloth. If I cannot raise a bird, how could I begin to consider using it?'

'But you did raise a bird,' Tressa said. 'The magpie.'

'Maybe, though I couldn't find the reason why, and never succeeded thereafter. Whatever force brought the magpie back, it wasn't from my formula.'

Alys frowned. 'So you're not going to try?'

I made no reply, but instead picked up the reliquary and went to the alcove, placing the blue glass vessel carefully on the top shelf, beside the silver box containing Accolon's singing heart. The Hecate tapestries fell back into place and I regarded the witch goddess for a moment, wondering what she would do. When I turned back, Alys and Tressa were still waiting for an answer, but there was none I could give.

I am asking you, for your brother's sake, not to use the Shroud. Ninianne had entreated me. *Do not take away the kingdom's future.*

I didn't want her voice in my mind, or this responsibility which was never mine to carry. But I could not shake the one desperate word, brief and powerful, that I had rarely, if ever, heard pass her lips.

Please, she had said.

So the Shroud of Tithonus remained on my alcove shelf, dead and alive all at once. Midsummer arrived, with its usual noisy joy and quiet grief, then a few weeks later Belle Garde's unspoken, but much felt anniversary. Our twelfth, without Accolon.

At intervals, my women would enquire about my plans, but after a while with my doing nothing, even Alys stopped asking. Sometimes, when alone, I would draw out the Shroud and contemplate what it meant that I hadn't used it, or sought to find a way.

Summer's abundant green transformed into autumn's burning gold; deer season turned into boar season, and first frost dressed the meadows in crisp white, until the ice thawed and crocuses peeked through the earth once more. Trees budded, shyly at first, then burst forth into spring bloom, birdsong accompanying a chorus of new life. Then May Day again, a year since my journey to Camelot, and my first laying eyes on its champion knight.

Occasionally, I thought of him – Lancelot, in all his shining beauty and inner turmoil, his yearning for miracles and penchant for sin – before forcing my mind away from our time together. In any case, my plan had worked. Elaine reported Yvain's success in finding Lancelot along the Cymri road, and their return to the Royal Court triumphant.

My sister heard less of my son than before, but mined every seam of information for my sake. Tales of his questing home and abroad, his courage and confidence, made my heart grow, the thought that I had found a way to smooth his path, restore his self-belief.

Thereafter, more missives came as another year passed, and another.

Your son rides with a lion now, she wrote. *The story is he rescued the wild cat from danger, and it follows him everywhere, quite tame. This and his knightly success have brought him fame in the Royal Court.*

The stranger details I could not quite fathom, but my son was making his good name and was happy. I tried not to think about how, before his lion, his restoration in Camelot, he had stood at the cusp of my valley and turned away.

I threw myself back into my usual days: healing in the infirmary; making sure the household saw me at meal times; study and work with Alys and Tressa until our writings filled volumes. More seasons came and went, with more self-made distractions from everything I could not face. Accolon was thirteen, fourteen, fifteen years gone.

Every so often, when restless, I bestowed an act of chaos upon Camelot: a week of rain to disrupt Pentecost celebrations; an eminent knight seduced and sent away a rebel. When Arthur did not deign to retaliate, I became bolder, taking the Shroud from its reliquary more often, running the cloth through my fingers, absorbing its symphony of life. I left it on my desk while I read, imagining its power alone might be enough to force my decision.

'If you don't use it, then you may as well not have it at all,' Alys liked to say. 'The time, the scheming, the effort – what was it all for?'

She was right, but only because I had not told her everything that passed between Ninianne and me. Alys knew something was amiss, but my secrets were ingrained, a form of protection for us all. Still, I took the Shroud out often and sent Camelot my renewed vengeance. Occasionally, I would enchant a drinking horn with a 'faithfulness in love' spell, and send them to the court as anonymous gifts, so Guinevere would spill wine down her white gown and reveal herself. Not that she ever did; luck was always with her, a different faithless spouse who drank first and ensured her escape.

Nevertheless, when heralds were reported riding across the boundary bearing Arthur's red-and-white standard, I assumed sanctions were on their way.

I waited on the front green with my arms crossed as the main herald dismounted and approached. 'Lady Morgan,' he said with clerkish indifference. 'I bring a message from my lord King Arthur, which he conveys to you in regret and sadness. May I proceed?'

Their polite arrival was strange enough, even odder his request I consent to hear it. 'You may,' I said cautiously.

He bowed. 'Your mother, Queen Igraine, formerly of All Britain, has died. Gone to God in peace and comfort. The High King sends his deepest condolences. Your brother wishes it known you are not alone in your great sorrow.'

I stood motionless: that my mother had died was no shock – Elaine had told me of her fading health, after many happy years spent in Ireland, and I had come to terms with the eventuality. However, I expected the news to come from my sister, not a brother who could not bear the thought of me. That Arthur had done this, with such ceremony and deference, brought a confusion far beyond the grief I felt at the news.

The herald cleared his throat. There was more.

'His Highness also tells you that a rose garden is being built to honour your lady mother, with a memorial stone bearing her name and that of her children. If my lady agrees, you may choose your own style.'

'I agree,' I said faintly. 'Style me as ... Morgan of Cornwall.'

It seemed the most apt, how my mother had herself named me, and who I was when we spent the best of our years together.

'It will be done, my lady. Any return message, for the High King?'

It struck with even greater force; the herald would only ask for my reply if Arthur himself ordered it thus.

'Y-yes,' I said haltingly. 'Say ... I feel his grief as my own, as both a shared burden and a comfort. And send my thanks.'

The herald gave a deep bow, remounted, and left. From the green, I watched until they disappeared, then found myself walking back up the turret stairs to my desk in a daze.

Your brother wishes it known you are not alone in your great sorrow.
Do not take away the kingdom's future. Please.

I put the Shroud of Tithonus back in its reliquary, and didn't look at it again.

Though the loss of my mother wasn't unexpected, death had its way of casting a raw light upon life's empty spaces. Sixteen years since I had lost Accolon, it would be by summer's end. Five years since I had regained the Shroud, and still could not bring him back. How long I had lived without his love.

When the torture of an empty bed was too much, I would rise and go to my study to read – the ancient tales, the histories, the poets; words of time and trouble, of adversity, courage and a hundred kinds of passion.

One night, Alys appeared in the doorway in her bedrobe. I was sitting at the desk before my old resurrection notes, but had not found the strength to start reading.

'I thought you might be here,' she said, pulling a chair to the deskside. 'Are you working on your formulae again? For the Shroud.'

'No,' I replied. 'I told you, it's too risky. When the Shroud is gone, it's gone.'

She leaned back in her chair, thoughtful. 'I keep thinking back to the magpie you raised. The gold spot on her chest.'

I shook my head. 'When she moulted, the mark came away. It was just a stain.'

'From what?'

'I don't know, but ultimately it couldn't have mattered,' I said. 'Nor did her resurrection, in terms of progress. She's a mystery, an aberration.'

Alys scoffed. 'In all of our work together, you have never let me call something an anomaly. *There is always a reason, dear heart, however rare the cause.*'

I smiled at her accurate mimicry of me; how once my way of learning had been to push every boundary. 'I'm not always right, you know.'

My tone was in jest, but she leaned forwards, her gaze direct, serious. 'Tell me about that day. The magpie – every detail.'

I began to protest that I'd told her before, but her expression was adamant. I thought back, describing how I'd decided to stop trying with birds, how I saw the dead magpie and took her into my hands anyway.

'I was afraid, I remember that,' I said. 'Thinking of her fledglings, the entire tiding and who would lead them. I knew I couldn't save her, and I … panicked.'

'Then what?' Alys urged. 'What was different?'

'I … don't know,' I said. 'I couldn't think what to do, so …' I conjured the sight in my mind, the broken-necked matriarch, how I had felt. 'I did what came naturally – I tried to heal her. Pointless, of course.'

'What if it wasn't?'

A sudden exhaustion washed over me. 'I can't do this. It was fifteen years ago. Why all of these questions?'

'Because you're pushing me away, Morgan,' Alys said. 'Our whole lives we have shared our thoughts, our pain, our hearts, however difficult the truth, and I cannot bear that you feel you need to keep things from me. I am not your duty, an entity to protect. We are in this together and always have been.'

I sighed. 'There's just … nothing to tell.'

She regarded me for a long, expectant moment, then said, '*Iawn*. If that's the way this has to be.'

Abruptly, she stood and stalked away to the worktable. I watched her go, regretful but shackled, as she opened a wooden apothecary box and retrieved something, then turned to me with one hand outstretched. Between her fingers was a small black vial. Without pause, she unstopped the bottle and emptied the contents down her throat.

'Alys,' I said. 'What was that?'

'Wolfsbane,' she replied. 'Pure and strong. The deadliest poison known to us.'

'*What?*' I exclaimed. 'Are you testing an antidote? But you should never—'

'There is no antidote, as you well know,' she interrupted. 'With the quantity I took, I'll be dead this half hour.'

Fear ripped up my spine as I tried to think what I should do first. I stumbled towards Alys, but she swerved out of my reach.

'Before you heal me,' she said, 'cut your hand.'

Her voice was already breathless with pain, her twisting gut crying out to my senses. Panic surged through me like floodwater; once poison got into the blood it could be in the entire body within moments, and wolfsbane killed at speed. Time was everything.

'Absolutely not!' I cried. 'Aconite is no game, Alys. I must heal you before something terrible happens.'

'Not yet.' She feinted sideways again and swiped the falcon-handled knife out of my belt, holding it out to me. 'Take this, now, and cut your palm, as you have done for the sake of experiment many times.'

The knife shook in her hand, her skin chalky, lips turning blue. 'I can't ... not like this,' I insisted. 'Dear heart, just let me ...'

'No,' she said. 'This is what we do, Morgan. We learn, we try, we fail and try again. Curiosity, challenging assumptions, the bravery needed to truly seek knowledge – I learned that from you. I don't want to die in this moment, but if it saves your brilliance and brings back truth between us ... *Cut your hand.*'

How she could be so heartfelt and insistent while her body fought death was a wonder, and it moved me even in the midst of my exasperation.

'God's blood, you are impossible,' I hissed. 'Give me that.'

I snatched my father's knife out of her hand. Its edges caught the candlelight; since girlhood, I had learned to keep it sharp.

Curling my fingers around the steel, I closed my eyes and clenched my fist tight. The blade sunk into my flesh instantly. As pain arrived with its banshee scream, the healing inside me answered, rushing like sunrays towards every part of my damage. I released the knife and the wetness of blood dripped through my fingers, hot and alive.

Alys gasped, the air tearing through her failing lungs. My eyes snapped open; we had wasted too much time. I grabbed her wrist with my good hand and pulled her close, sending the full force of my healing into her body. She stiffened as the wolfsbane fought back, but I persisted, pushing the poison into retreat through her veins, into her stomach, bright shoots breaking apart the dark, twisting tendrils.

As the power balance shifted into my favour, Alys began to cough, exhaling curls of black smoke, corruption leaving her body until her breath was clear air again. I held her to me as her pulse recovered its rhythm, her bloodshot eyes clearing to amber and white.

I glared at her face from a distance of inches. 'Don't you *ever* risk yourself like that,' I told her. 'Not for my sake.'

To my astonishment, she only smiled, no regret on her pale, sheened face.

'As you always say, *cariad*, it was worth it.' She nodded down to my slashed hand, bleeding at my side. *'Edrych.'*

Only then did I raise my arm and saw what Alys's dangerous, valiant experiment had done.

The blood running through my fingers was molten gold.

Resurrection as I had known it wasn't far behind.

Once I understood how to shift my body into its mercurial state, I never failed to turn my blood into a river of bright rushing gold. How right it felt, how obvious that my most beloved skill was what had revived the magpie matriarch from death, and was everything I had been seeking all along. Healing was my peak, my power, and I was its mistress. If I was ever worthy of being called Morgan the Goddess, then this was why.

Alys had suspected the answer lay within me all along, her belief the miracle I most needed. She and I spoke a great deal in the days and weeks later. I told her everything I had kept inside for years, and once I began, it felt like magic, a resurrection in itself.

Within a month, I had achieved more than in years of trying. I raised dead birds again through their heartsong: from finches to song thrushes; a wild and broken-winged goshawk returned to glory; a mangled swan, trampled by a bull so badly it lost a foot and half its beak, restored to its alabaster entirety.

In late summer, when hounds-in-training accidentally took a mother doe out of season, I saved the huntsman's guilt and conveyed her torn-up body from the hanging room back to the forest, where my refined formula set to work. The deer burst forth from her grave of leaves on the second night, fully formed and returned to her waiting fawns.

After that, there was nothing more for me to do. My golden blood had recreated every marvel from my time at Merlin's, and gone beyond. I had the Shroud of Tithonus, and the power with which to use it. I was ready to perform a miracle of my own.

Yet, between my rapid victories and Ninianne's echoing pleas was a question growing louder: *What happens next?*

Failure had been my companion for fifteen years; I knew how it felt, and understood the consequences. As I stood with victory within my grasp, I still did not know what it meant – or what it might cost – to succeed.

So I reverted to old habits. Every day before the household stirred, I went to my study and took out the reliquary and silver box containing Accolon's heart, hoping to find myself feeling differently, or understand why I did not.

One gilded autumn morning, I had been contemplating the Shroud for a while, when footsteps sounded on the stairs and the huntsman appeared, two senior grooms hovering behind him in the doorway.

'A knight has been spotted just outside the boundary, near the chapel,' he said. 'His leg is bleeding, and he's jumpy. We've tried to send him to the infirmary, but he keeps circling his horse and refuses to come any closer.'

I rolled my eyes; some still believed my Vale of No Return would trap knights indefinitely. I went to Alys's remedy cabinet and brought them a small ceramic pot. 'Take him this salve. If he won't come in, this will soothe his cut leg and help it heal.'

No one accepted my offering. 'Unfortunately, my lady, that's not possible,' said the huntsman. 'We cannot get closer than fifty yards.'

A shiver passed through me, the kick of wind before a rainstorm. 'Why not?'

'His ... companion, Lady Morgan. The knight is riding with a lion by his side.'

I had rushed down the stairs and was calling for a horse before they had a chance to ask what it meant.

30

The scene was exactly as they had described: a knight pacing his horse back and forth on the road, his own restlessness writ in his mount's jagged strides.

The famous lion – a lioness in fact – was more sanguine. She had retired to the grass, lying along a strip of sun and licking one giant, honey-coloured paw. I had never seen an animal of her like before; not even Camelot's menagerie contained such a dangerous wonder. But her huge mane-less head, leonine insouciance and the underlying violence in her flexing claws could not compare in fascination to the one who rode beside her.

It was him, strong and handsome in light mail and a fine green tunic, his dark-gold head bowed. So deep was his pensiveness that he didn't notice my approach. Nor could he know that the sight of him left me blinded, like seeing the sunrise after half a decade of night.

'Yvain,' I said.

His head flew up, deep-blue eyes and quizzical brow arresting my heart. He halted his horse and regarded me with a wince.

'You know me?' His voice was almost plaintive. Five years ago, he had merely escorted an unknown damsel. To his mind, I hadn't seen him since he was eight years old.

'You're my son,' I replied. 'I'd know you anywhere.'

He glanced up at the sky, as if it was not the moment. It would never be the moment, I realised, not for him. At best, I was a stranger; at worst, the absent mother whose poisonous reputation had snapped at his gold-spurred heels for his entire life.

'Oh God,' he said to the heavens. 'It *is* you, isn't it?'

The bitterness in his voice speared me, but I stepped closer. The lion paused in her ablutions, fixing me with a stare. I saw her natural possessiveness and felt a flare of the same.

'Yes,' I said. 'It's me.' *Your mother,* I wanted to add, but such a declaration might just make him turn and flee.

'You look exactly the same as when I last saw you,' he said. 'Sixteen years. How can that be?'

He assumed me conceited, probably, obsessed with my own youth, but what could I say? What patience would my distant son have for my pact with fairy magic, or the efforts I made in grief, keeping my appearance the same as the day I last saw my slain lover in case I could magically raise him from death? Some things were rightfully beyond explanation.

'I have my ways,' was the only reply I could make.

My evasion made him flinch, and I regretted it. 'So this is where you live,' he said. 'Your famous Vale of No Return.'

His dismissive tone held a hint of his father, which I weathered as a blow to the gut. 'Those of us who reside here call it Belle Garde. Would you like to come in?'

'No,' he said sharply, then sighed. 'I – I don't know. I shouldn't, and yet …'

'You will not be kept longer than you wish,' I said. 'I give you my word.'

The look he gave me was incredulous. 'How could I ever trust your word?'

Again, I was winded, but could not argue. Despite the fairer view of me he had given the damsel, he had been raised hearing dark stories of his mother, and my actions told no better tale. The last time Yvain had seen me, I was standing over his father with a sword, ready to cut off my husband's head. I had pushed the memory from his child's mind with magic, but who knew how long such a rushed, imperfect charm had lasted.

'You travelled all this way,' I said. 'Take a rest, some refreshment. We can discuss why you have come.'

'I don't know,' he muttered, walking his horse in another restless circle. As he paced, I noticed his left leg dangling free of the stirrup, breeches torn and a wound still bleeding – the injury the huntsman had mentioned. Infection would be a concern if he didn't get it cleaned up, but the leg radiated a deeper issue. Something broken, I sensed, and complex, but I couldn't be sure without laying hands.

'You are injured,' I reasoned. 'At least let me look at it.'

He paused his mount again, glancing down at his leg then back at me.

'Please,' I said. 'Just get off your horse.'

Something within him seemed to give. With a sigh, he dismounted onto his good leg and limped to the low wall that surrounded the chapel. I followed, sitting down beside him. The lioness raised her head, seemed to decide he was safe and went back to dozing.

'So this is your lion,' I said. 'She that you saved.'

He regarded me in surprise. 'You know about that?'

'I admit, over the years, I have sought to hear news of you.'

'Aunt Elaine,' he said matter-of-factly.

I nodded. 'She was being a good sister, as she always has been. Do not think ill of her because of her love for me.'

'I could never do that,' he replied. 'She has been exceedingly good to me too. Nor do I regret anything I learned from her.'

He was speaking of me, and my heart leapt, but too much hope must have shown on my face because he looked away at once. In no circumstances was he going any further.

'Your leg,' I said softly. 'Let me see.'

Unexpectedly, he did, extending his leg straight. Hesitantly, I placed my fingertips either side of his knee, seeking the more complicated damage I had sensed beyond the torn skin and blood. With the barest touch, the affliction leapt out to me: his kneecap was broken.

'I didn't want to alarm him with such a sudden and serious diagnosis, so instead I asked, 'What happened to you?'

'I answered a joust challenge,' he replied. 'A few hours ago, just off the forest road. It wasn't fair, it …' He pulled away from my touch and shook his head in exasperation. 'Why am I telling you this? You don't care.'

I resisted my impulse to argue that of course I cared. Part of being in his company, I realised, was learning when his emotions superseded my own.

'Above all things, your leg needs healing,' I said pragmatically. 'I will stop the bleeding, eliminate any infection, then fix the knee itself. If you come to the house …'

'No,' he said quickly. 'It wouldn't be right.'

'Forget what's right, or the rules you have been taught,' I said. 'This is your health, your future. I can fix this.'

The look he gave me was glassy, angry. 'You of all people cannot fix this.'

The pain of his rejection was so immediate, so great, that part of me wanted to bolt back within my veil of protection and pretend this had never happened; to imagine my son at a distance again, reconsidering his mother in a kinder light, rather than facing his justified disdain. But my child was hurting, and this one small thing I could make better.

'I *can* repair your leg, in a moment's work,' I insisted. 'You needn't come to the house – I can heal you here just as well. This is serious damage – let me help you.'

It was too much. Yvain reared up in offence, staggering away from the wall.

'That's not why I'm here!' he cried. 'Good God, I shouldn't be speaking to you at all. If they knew I had come ...' He stopped and pulled in a steadying breath. 'I don't need your help, or healing. I don't care about the blood or the pain. I just have to tell you ...'

His voice cracked and he put his head in his hands, shoulders heaving but no sounds coming forth. I jumped up after him, assaulted by a rush of shame: grown man or not, if my child was crying I should have felt it in every inch of my marrow.

'Yvain,' I said, but could think of nothing fit to soothe him. I had lost the chance of truly knowing him long ago. 'What's wrong?' I asked.

He looked up at me, skin flushed but scrubbed of any tears. His beautiful face looked as though it might collapse again. 'My father,' he replied. 'He is dead.'

It hit me with white-hot shock. 'Urien, dead?' I exclaimed. 'When? How?'

He stared at me wretchedly, as if it couldn't possibly matter. His father was gone – what difference did it make? 'An accident,' he managed. 'He was hunting near Caerleon and took a violent fall.'

I could marry Accolon now, came the thought: natural, selfish, followed by a futility that seared in my blood like fire. Another freedom gained when it was worth nothing. I looked away, seething, preoccupied, until I felt my son's gaze on the side of my face.

Gathering myself, I met his frowning scrutiny. 'He fell from his horse?' I said, in lieu of anything better. 'That doesn't sound like him.'

'It wasn't,' Yvain said. 'They say a flock of wild birds swooped at his face. He was fending them off when his horse spooked and ...'

He trailed off in anguish, but I had to know. 'How did he die?'

My son squeezed his eyes shut. 'He broke his neck.'

There were a hundred things I had imagined I would feel hearing of my estranged husband's inglorious death, but the sight of Yvain's grief rendered it all impossible. When I looked at his tired, devastated face, the late King Urien of Gore became the proud and diligent father my son had lost, not the vain, self-centred brute who had made my life hell.

'I'm sorry,' I said. 'A father is an immense loss.'

Again, I had got it wrong. 'How dare you say you are sorry,' he spat. 'You *hated* my father. He told me you *burned his face*. Do not insult me by pretending otherwise.'

His viciousness cut through me, though his voice shook as if he had never used such a tone. I wondered when Urien had spoken of my setting him on fire, if he had savoured telling our son of such an intimate horror. The smouldering fury in my gut lit like tinder.

'That's not how it was!' I cried. 'None of it's true – what others claim, what your father said about me. No one has ever admitted the wrongs I have endured. You are my son and should know better.'

At my escalating reaction, the lioness got to her feet with deceptive speed, a rumble emitting from her throat. Suddenly, I understood that her decisions were her own, and she would protect Yvain how she saw fit unless he told her otherwise.

I did not fear her – if she sprung at me I could turn her to ice without drawing breath – but then my son would hate me more than he did already.

I lowered my voice. 'I did nothing wrong, Yvain. And I care about how you feel. You must believe me.'

My son sighed, his gaze drawn to the lioness, poised to defend him, kill for him if necessary. I envied her that presumption.

'Peace, cub,' he said to her, and she stopped, threats in her gullet receding into silence. She studied me for a few more panting breaths, then looped back to her patch of sun.

To me, he said, 'How can I believe what I've never been shown?'

It was a fair question, but my desperation still held sway. 'I have *tried* to show you I care,' I insisted. 'I have been in your life even if you did not realise it. A few years ago, when you were struggling with your reputation at court, you found Sir Lancelot and brought him back from the wilderness, did you not? It restored you in the eyes of King Arthur.'

'Yes,' he said slowly. 'I found him, and my uncle was pleased. What of it?'

'Did you never wonder why you came across him so easily? Why, of all possible routes, you met on the same one?'

His brow creased in the way that was just like my own late father. '*You* made me find him ... or Lancelot find me? How? Were we ... spellbound into meeting?'

'No! I would never do that. I just ... helped you. I heard of your troubles at court and wanted to make things better.'

Yvain ignored my denial and paced away, every limp on his injured leg a dart of distress to my senses. 'It was all a lie,' he said, half to himself. 'I thought my good deeds were my own, and it was lies.'

'No – you don't understand,' I insisted, but he was too distracted by the revelation. I wanted to take his hand, or turn his face to mine, but didn't dare touch him. In the end, as Alys often did to me, I put myself in the way of his pacing and made him stop.

'Nothing was a lie,' I said firmly. 'No one was charmed or bewitched. *You* still found Sir Lancelot – that was all your own free will. I swear upon ...'

He glared at me, waiting for the end of my sentence, and his fierce expectation struck the words from my lips. What could I possibly swear upon that could convince him? My own life, his eyes – god forbid, my *honour*?

'I swear it,' I concluded quietly. 'All I did was ease your way to being in the same part of the country. The rest was your doing.'

'I don't see how that's any better,' he said. 'Not to mention you kidnapped Sir Lancelot in the first place.'

'That was nothing to do with you,' I replied. 'What matters is Sir Lancelot went free and unharmed, and you brought him home.'

Yvain recoiled. 'Is that what you truly believe? You imprisoned my friend, which can never be justified, then used it to meddle in my life. How is that good for anyone?'

'I was doing the best I could for you,' I replied. 'I was trying to—'

'You don't understand,' he interrupted. 'If you knew me, you'd know that all I have ever wanted, from those professing to care for me, is honesty. What you have done – it isn't honesty in any way. Can you not see that?'

I began to protest, but he held up his hands. 'This was my mistake. I shouldn't have come here.'

His declaration was calm, containing a resignation that hurt me far worse than his anger could. My son turned away and limped to his horse, mounting off his uninjured leg, his pain still crying out to me through the air. He beckoned to his lioness, who rose and padded dutifully to his side, her yellow-green eyes fixed on me.

'Don't go,' I said to him. 'Tell me what I can do.'

'What you can do is leave me alone,' he said. 'As you have always done.'

'Yvain, no. I am your—' I began, but he looked at me with such savage hurt that it silenced me at once.

'Do not say it,' he said. 'It only feels like another lie.'

Touching his gold spurs to his horse's side, Yvain cantered off with his lioness loping gracefully in his wake, until the treeline swallowed him and he disappeared. I sat on the low wall and waited until the sun set and night engulfed me, but he never came back.

When I finally returned to the house, I climbed to my empty study and sat at my desk. The Shroud of Tithonus still lay where I had left it, potent and useless, a symbol of my inaction, my wrongness, my inability to become the woman I had once been. Morgan le Fay, whoever she was – everything her name had meant – felt so far away now.

My son had come to me, had ridden up to my valley and this time had not turned away, until I had played all the wrong notes to a tune

I should have known by heart. Yvain had sought me, and found me wanting; he was part of me, yet I couldn't make him stay.

It only feels like another lie, he had said, when I almost called myself his mother.

Worse still, he was right. Everything, each moment, misjudgement and error, lay at my feet. The lies, the scheming and disguises, every selfishness I had invoked had made me become what I never wished to be. Over and again, I had resorted to Merlin's deceptive magic as I swore I never would, allowing the sorcerer's voice back in my head, too obsessed with achieving my vengeance to care what it might cost.

Nor was I the only victim of my choices. Yvain had stood up to his beloved father and powerful uncle for the right to believe there was more beyond his mother's dark façade, and what had I done? I had donned the poisoned reputation the Royal Court had given me and paraded it through the realm as if every word were true.

Yet again, I had taken my son's faith and burned it into ashes. Of all of my sins, failing him was the greatest.

Now, I had lost him forever, but I must still seek to fix it, even if we would always be broken. Yvain must know that he was not wrong to believe in his mother; that it was honourable and good to have hope, and to question the world's accepted truths. He deserved to know he could trust his own judgement, and move on with his life.

The only salve to our wound was to seek my exoneration. And that singular power lay with my brother.

For my son, I would sacrifice my pride, my grief and rage, and ask Camelot for the acquittal I had never cared to receive. For Yvain, my one faultless creation, I would speak to King Arthur, my brother, my enemy, tell my secrets and admit my own wrongs. Whatever it took to free my child of his mother's curse.

No more games, no more concealment, no more lies. I would never be worthy of any miracle until I had told every last truth.

31

I rode with only the magpies for company and left the flock and my horse in a rowan grove just outside the Welsh Gate. Though I was without disguise and unchanged, no one stopped me from walking into the city, or striding up to the castle's main door.

Camelot had forgotten who I was.

There were no signs of congregation near the larger halls, so I took the route Sir Kay had led me last time, past the King's official chambers, to the doors bearing crowned red dragons. A murmur of voices emanated from within. I drew a deep breath and stepped inside.

The private throne room was less austere than when I had last seen it – cushioned benches had been brought in, and large window alcoves had been built out from the wall. A group of people gathered in the farthest embrasure, silhouetted by sun. On the dais, a pair of figures stood talking, apart from the rest.

I saw him first, shining like moonlight in the dark: Sir Lancelot du Lac, his towering presence filling the space between the thrones. He wore riding garb over silver-white mail, and the sight of him after so long shot through my bones like a comet.

Blue eyes locked with mine, icy as the very first time. Our stare held long enough for me to read the tension in his shoulders, the phantom of torment written on his face. The reason, I assumed, was the figure who stood beside him, regarding me with far less calm.

'By the saints! What is that *witch* doing here? In our city – in our *home?*'

Guinevere: still golden and beautiful, dressed in white. I had not expected her.

At her exclamation, the room shifted, seeking the cause of alarm. Lancelot leapt in front of her, his instinct to protect her well-honed yet unthinking, primal. However, she swerved his attempt to be her shield, brushing him aside to glare me down in disdain.

I ignored her and advanced further into the room. I was not here to answer to Camelot's duplicitous Queen, but to address the kingdom's true source of power. I looked to the gathering at the window, seeking a crowned head.

Instead, a figure stepped tentatively out of the group of people. His leg juddered as he approached – the injury he had not let me heal.

'Yvain,' I gasped. Given his grief for his father and unsanctioned visit to my valley, I hadn't considered he would return directly to the court. 'How are you?'

'I am well,' he replied warily. 'Why have you—?'

'That's *enough*,' came a cold, strident voice.

All along he had been there, not ten feet away. He emerged from the sun's slanted shadow and strode forth, Yvain fading into retreat in his wake. His presence as he halted before me seemed to occupy every ounce of space.

My brother, the High King, tall and proud. Furious.

Arthur regarded me with eyes of molten steel, jaw set hard and body poised, as if ready to run towards an opposing army.

'What are you doing, Morgan?' he said.

The confrontation was upon us, exactly what I had wanted, but as I stood before my brother, I hadn't the slightest idea what to say.

'Yes, do tell us,' the Queen piped up. 'I, for one, would like an explanation.'

Her interruption unchained my tongue at once. 'Stay out of this, Guinevere,' I snapped. 'It's a situation far beyond your understanding.'

She recoiled as if I were a venomous snake. I turned again to my brother. 'I need to speak to you, Arthur. Just the two of us.'

'Don't do it,' Guinevere said. 'She cannot be trusted.'

Lancelot stepped forward, close at her side. 'I agree with my lady Queen,' he said unsurprisingly. 'No good can come of this.'

Arthur looked at his wife and best knight for a long moment, a shaft of sun drawing a line of connection between them. As a trio, they were incandescent.

'A curse on all three of you,' I muttered under my breath.

My brother's attention snapped back to me. 'If you want to speak, then *speak*,' he said. 'Why are you here?'

'I have come to tell the truth,' I declared. 'Every last word, under terms that are favourable to Camelot. This is not surrender – I will not yield to your notions of justice, nor am I asking for mercy. But I will admit every misdeed I have ever committed, then vanish back into my valley and never trouble the Royal Court again. In exchange, I request exoneration from the treasons and betrayal I am not guilty of.'

Unease shimmered through the room. Arthur raised a sceptical eyebrow. 'That seems a great risk, given all you have done. You cannot think you will save your reputation?'

'Indeed not,' I replied. 'It is not for the world's good opinion that I seek this absolution, but for my son.'

Yvain's head flew up on hearing himself mentioned, his expression wide-eyed, confused. In our precarity, I hadn't wanted him to witness this, but I had to go on.

'Sir Yvain is held to his association with a mother whose character is only half drawn,' I said. 'My admissions may make my reputation at Camelot worse – I don't care. But it should be the whole truth, if only in the name of fairness.'

It gave my brother pause. 'Sister, I am no fool,' he said, his voice less flinty.

'I know, and this is no trick,' I said. 'I swear on our mother's good grace.'

Again, he stilled, but I could read him; he too was recalling that upon our mother's death, he had reached out to me without rancour. More than that, he knew I would never stoop to invoke her for a lie.

'Let's finish this, Arthur,' I said. 'Once and for all.'

He put his hands on his hips, his grey eyes keen, calculating every possibility. After an age, he said. 'Very well. We will have this over with.'

Abruptly, he spun away and ascended the dais steps, heading towards the door on the back wall. I followed, passing Guinevere, who huffed and stalked off. Lancelot looked after her, hurt shadowing his extraordinary face, then went to his King.

'Sire, I will stand beside you for this,' he said, but Arthur shook his head, placing a reassuring hand on Lancelot's shoulder.

'It's all right, my friend,' he replied. 'Dismiss the rest, would you? Then I give you leave to start on your travels, if you are in a hurry.'

Lancelot covered my brother's hand with his own. 'No, I will be here and directly outside. If you need me.'

Arthur smiled affectionately at his knight, then drew away and opened the door, gesturing me inside.

Beyond, I was surprised to meet the sight of his Great Chamber from a new entrance. Little had changed – most of the furniture remained, the blue-and-gold ceilings, walls still tapestried with Jason and his Argonauts, the dark presence of Medea lending him her skills. When I lived at court, my brother and I had sat talking in this room every evening, until we knew one another so well we could finish the other's sentences.

Of all places, I never expected him to bring me to the centre of our past closeness, and it hit like a hawk strike.

Arthur too was looking around the room and could not choose where to settle, so he turned to me with his sternest regal demeanour.

'Before we begin, I should warn you,' he said. 'I can make no promises where justice is concerned. Depending on what you tell me, I may still have to act. With severity.'

'Spare us both your posturing,' I said scornfully. 'You won't kill me.'

His eyes flashed at my disrespect. 'Don't presume to know me, Morgan. It's been a long time since you have.'

'It doesn't matter,' I replied. 'I understand how you think. Perhaps I did not know you the longest but I knew you best. I will always know you, Arthur.'

He stared at me in challenge, but I held his gaze. I had never been afraid to face him, but there was a time I had deferred to him, believed in his ways, because we loved and respected one another. He would put his hand upon my shoulder and cast down those assuring grey eyes, and I would be convinced, because to be high in his regard felt like being anointed. We were brother and sister, part of one another, two edges of one blade. It was not just to save face that Arthur would never kill me.

Yet now he looked away, as if reading my thoughts and finding them unbearable.

'There is a far easier life available to you, Morgan,' he said. 'I hope you realise that. There are better ways out of the cage you've put yourself in.'

'I'm not in a cage,' I snarled. 'I don't surround myself with crenellated walls and steel-clad men, nor do I live every moment in fear of my own death. Who between us is the most trapped?'

The accusation cut short his sanctimony, at least. He arched to full height like a rising dragon. 'I fear *nothing*,' he said. 'Least of all death. Do you know how many battles I have fought? How many warlike kings I have faced down? I have walked with the shadow of my own demise since I drew the sword from the stone. Powerful as you are, I do not even fear death from your hands – you learned as much that day beneath your own storm.'

'So you've not forgotten it,' I said.

'No, sister. Not that moment, or any other since the day we first met. I never will.' His voice held more heaviness than ire, but before I could wonder why, he glanced to the rafters and sighed. 'Let's not waste time. What do you want from this, Morgan?'

His dismissal stung, the sudden shift to mere transaction.

I want my life back, I wanted to shout. *I want my valley to be a home again, not an empty shell where love once lived. I want you not to have killed Accolon, nor laid him on a bier and sent his lifeless, carved-up body to me. I want never to have seen him dead on the altar in your cathedral, as if you cared about what you did to us. I want the child I never met not to have been taken and hidden from me, and the son I know not to be a stranger, or be tainted by his association with my name. I want to go back in time and change the moments where everything went wrong.*

Grief scalded through me, boiling water under my skin, but I resisted the temptation to react. I was not here to address my own pain.

'I told you,' I said. 'I have come to offer you all of my unspoken wrongs and be absolved where I am innocent. So Yvain will not suffer for his connection with me, or his fair-mindedness, any longer.'

Arthur nodded and put his hands on his hips. 'Enlighten me, then. Tell me something you have done.'

I wavered, then closed my eyes and thought of my son. 'I don't have Excalibur's scabbard,' I said. 'It's gone.'

When I looked again, Arthur's face was hard and pale as marble. 'Gone how?'

'After I took it from the abbey, I got rid of it. Threw it in a bottomless lake to rot. I said it was lost to you, and that is what I meant. It no longer exists.'

'Blood of Christ,' he said. 'Of all the terrible, faithless things you have done ... How dare you take what's mine and destroy it with such disregard! Yet *another* betrayal.'

'No,' I argued. 'It was my first betrayal. One I do not regret, but perpetrated after the treason you accused me of, in the wake of Accolon's killing.'

He fell silent for a long moment. When he spoke again, his voice was low, restrained. 'Why tell me this? Are you trying to make things worse?'

How could things be worse? I thought.

'I'm telling you because after so many years of lies and conflict, the truth matters more than anything. If you cannot acknowledge that, we will never have peace.' I paused, looking steadily at him. 'Isn't that what you want, Arthur – for the kingdom, those you love, yourself? In everything you do, haven't you ultimately been in search of peace?'

My brother's shoulders dropped, his eyes softening. Somehow it had moved him.

'Go on,' he said, and I felt an eternity of tension leave my body.

'Most of it you know,' I began. 'The storms, the birds, the enchanted objects, chaos I have sent to Camelot over the years. No doubt Sir Lancelot told you I kidnapped him. However, I didn't send the deadly mantle. Yvain was right – I am far cleverer than that, and would never risk killing one of my own household. He should not have been banished or punished for merely expressing himself. It's hardly the fairness that you preach.'

I expected offence, but he displayed none. 'Then I owe Yvain an apology, which he will have. Though I will not take a scolding on justice from you, until I have heard the things I do not know.'

I hesitated, and Arthur coolly noted my pause. He well knew it was easy for me to be honest about that which he was aware of, and made me look better than expected. In one move, he had recaptured his moral advantage and it rankled, but if it was to be the truth, then it must be everything.

'I have concealed myself with magic,' I said. 'Worn faces not my own, lied with my body and voice to haunt your courts and further my vengeance. Not often, but enough.'

'You came here and I did not know?' he exclaimed. 'In someone else's skin?'

A flash of defensiveness raised my chin. 'They were Merlin's arts, his strengths and favoured tricks, taught to me against my will. I won't excuse my use of them, but it was out of grief and fury, and you can believe I will never use such methods again. All it did was take me back to my hatred of Merlin and the darkest days of my childhood.'

Arthur considered me, his expression unreadable. He raised a hand to his temple, rubbing a thumb along the edge of his understated gold crown. Old habits, never dying.

'You hated Merlin all that time?' he said. 'I did not know.'

'I kept it from you, not to tear you in two. But I'm sure you can imagine why. He brought death and violence to my father's door, stole the happy life from me and my sisters, our mother's from her ...'

I trailed off, because I saw Arthur flinch, much as he tried to suppress it. The circumstances of his existence were not his fault, but I knew he took the weight of our mother's experiences upon himself in private.

'It seems strange now,' I said quietly, 'but I used to believe that you were the one goodness that came out of that time. The night you were born in Tintagel, I heard you cry, and when we met again I felt as if I had known you from your first breath. Most of all, I will always hate Merlin for what he did to you and me – what he led you to believe, and that I didn't understand why you listened to him. It was so easy for me to mistrust Merlin, I failed to consider how his effect on your life was the opposite to mine, and you could not simply feel the same. For that blindness, I will forever be sorry.'

Arthur nodded heavily, as if he could neither agree nor argue otherwise. Silence fell between us, carrying the weight of several lives, so many paths untaken.

'Do you still dream of the sea, Morgan?' he asked suddenly.

I almost replied, before realising I had never admitted to him what we shared. Yet he looked too certain for me to refute it outright. 'Did Ninianne …?' I began.

He shook his head. 'She confirmed it, but I already knew. That day in the storm, when you claimed I dreamed alone, I could see in your eyes it wasn't true.'

Before I could fathom how to feel, Arthur urged, 'Well, do you?'

The answer, at least, was simple. 'Yes. Almost nightly, when I manage to sleep. It was you who made me realise we were both dreaming of Tintagel.'

'What do you think it means?' he asked.

I knew he must have spent years wondering why; Arthur had been raised to believe in visions and had been on a constant search for meaning since I had known him.

'I can't define what it means to you,' I replied. 'But to my mind, within Tintagel's waves is where we were both born, and where I first lost you. I have come to view the sea as our presence in one another's lives – the times we have parted, then come together again as the tides go in and out. Maybe we are destined to confront one another, over and over, until the whole truth between us is spoken.'

He sighed and drew a weary hand over his face. 'I've had a dozen wise men working on an interpretation for years. Of course you are the one who makes the most sense.'

His honesty thudded into my chest. 'Perhaps all you needed was one clever sister who knows what lies inside of you.'

Arthur's eyes widened, and I hoped my candour had struck him in the same, bruising way. 'We've been in disagreement so long,' he murmured. 'I often wonder – at what point did this all become too late?'

'You know when. There was always a route back, until you killed Accolon, and blamed me. That was the end of us then, and the beginning of what we are now.'

He shook his head vehemently. 'Our trust had been broken long before.'

'Nothing was irreparable until you put Accolon to the sword,' I insisted. 'I would never have destroyed the scabbard if not for what you did to him. It was the cause of every treason I've committed since. Even if none of it has scratched your shield.'

'As I've said in the past,' he said tersely, 'if you hadn't given Sir Accolon the scabbard, I would have had no need to punish you.'

'You hadn't seen the scabbard for years,' I shot back. 'How did you know his carrying it involved me at all? You knew nothing of us.'

Arthur faltered, as if the question had struck the harshness from him. 'When he ... I ... As the duel concluded,' he managed. 'Accolon ... told me of you and him. Your love.'

'That's a lie,' I said. 'He knew of my troubles with Camelot and would never have willingly revealed us. How did you force it from him?'

'No, Morgan,' he protested. 'I would never ... Not from duress.'

I held up my hand, refusing his excuses. 'If there is any honour left in your heart, you will tell me the truth.'

Arthur sighed, so long and deep it pulled his body into a curve. When he looked up at me, his eyes were quicksilver.

'I know because ... with his dying breath he spoke your name.'

It was the truth I had asked for, and it gutted me in an instant. How much I wanted to cry then, for Accolon, for my losing him, every tear I had held back in the years he had been gone. Except I could not do so in front of my brother, his killer. Now, I could not yield.

'The Devil take me,' I said fiercely, and my father's old phrase brought me strength. 'The Devil take *you*, Arthur. You will not distract me with this.'

'Sister, I am not trying to—'

'Save your breath,' I cut him off. 'I came here only to gain the one thing I deserve – my exoneration. Whatever I've done since, I never had anything to do with any betrayal prophecy. Yvain is owed the truth, so he can live free of the mark of my sin. The court, and my son, must hear it from you directly.'

Arthur still looked shaken, but my tirade had restored his regal aloofness. 'I've spent years enduring your treason. Why would I change my mind now?'

'Because after all this time, what reason have I to lie?'

I was almost pleading – for myself, for Yvain, but also in part for relief, from vengeance and all I had carried, the weight of this great golden castle upon my shoulders. Yet for me to show him the betrayal did not lie at my feet, I had to meet Arthur inside his own beliefs. I needed him angry, I needed him righteous. I needed him *convinced*.

'It's not your fault that Merlin interpreted his prophecy incorrectly,' I said. 'But that doesn't mean he was wrong. You *have* been deceived, just not by me. Lancelot and Guinevere are betraying you, Arthur. They are deep in an adulterous love affair, and have been for years. That is the truth.'

He stared at me for so long that this time, I believed my words had found their way in. Then, like water under a winter's night, I watched him turn to ice.

'My God, not this,' he muttered. 'Anything but this.'

He began to pace back and forth, then immediately stopped with accusation in his eyes. '*You* were the damsel at Westminster,' he said. 'It was you who came and claimed Lancelot was dying. When he returned and said he had been in your captivity, I suspected the young woman was under your orders, but it was far worse. All along, you were there.'

'I won't deny it,' I replied. 'I told you about the disguises of my own volition. It doesn't change what I am telling you now. The emerald ring, Guinevere's grief, Lancelot's breach with you after living with her – your wife and closest knight are lovers.'

'None of that is proof!' Arthur shouted. 'Where are the witnessed acts, the written declarations? What have you seen with your own eyes that speaks to anything more than the affection we all acknowledge?'

His point stopped me dead. What *had* I seen, aside from one overwrought exchange before Guinevere's trial? Even in my captivity, Lancelot had never uttered a word of confession. I knew I was right, but my brother's logic was undeniable, and it infuriated me.

'You had instinct once, Arthur,' I said. 'You alone were enough. Now what are you without your adoring public and sycophantic court to agree with your every word? Have you so lost your way that you cannot see what is obvious?'

The insult was his last boundary, and I saw it break. 'Of all your dark acts, this is your worst,' he growled. 'You did not come here for my own good, or to respect the truth, only for your satisfaction. After this, how can I trust a single ... word ... you've ...'

He spun away, hand to his forehead, breathing hard. Pain rang out to me like a reverberating bell, my blood lighting up in response. The air trembled with his sudden, violent headache of old, the affliction so familiar to me I could have almost healed him across the space between us. I resisted the urge to go to him with every fibre of my being, as he staggered to the long table, reaching out to steady himself.

'Arthur,' I said, only to be cut off by a tremendous slam as he brought two hands down on the tabletop. He looked up at me with bloodshot eyes.

'Get out,' he said. 'Before we both do something we regret. Go from me, from Camelot, and never come back.'

32

Between my shock and Arthur's ferocity, I found myself obeying his command. With a last look at his folded, hard-breathing body, I let my anger take control and stormed out of the Great Chamber, healing burning so brightly in my senses I could feel it crackling behind my eyes.

The private throne room was empty, a welcome quiet from the noise and conflicting emotions that came from arguing with my brother. I savoured my solitude for a moment, just long enough to note I was wrong, and for Lancelot's tremendous frame to step into my path.

Masking my shock, I looked up to meet his glower with my own, when another figure stepped out from behind him, distracting me at once.

Yvain, hovering on the dais, a faintly stubborn look on his face.

'Are you … waiting for me?' I asked.

His eyes flicked to Lancelot, stood between us and radiating displeasure. I imagined the insistence it must have taken for my son to defy du Lac's orders and remain in the room.

Before either of them could speak, a hard roar came through the open doorway – Arthur, protesting against his pain. Lancelot glared at me in horror, then ran into the Great Chamber, leaving me and Yvain alone.

My time in Camelot was running out; I had to take my chances.

I rushed over to him. 'Yvain, listen. When you came to Belle Garde, you were right that I was not honest with you, and I should have been,' I said. 'What your uncle will say of me hereafter I don't know, but you deserve the whole truth. I want you to have it from my own lips, however difficult it is for me to say.'

He considered me for a long, doubtful moment, then said, 'Tell me.'

Briefly, I wondered if it would make things worse, but it was speak honestly or fail him for eternity.

'I did hate your father,' I said. 'For good reason, and he hated me in return. Yes, one dreadful day, I conjured fire in my hand and burned his face when he finally pushed me too far. And, when you were eight years old, I came to his bedchamber in Camelot, intending to kill him. It was you who stopped me that night – you caught me with his sword in my hands and your goodness saved us. I tried to make you forget, and I dearly hope you did.'

He looked stunned, as if he had not remembered, but also did not baulk, so I took it as a sign to go on. 'What lay between your father and me was terrible, destructive, and entirely mutual. When he took you away and I didn't know how to fight it, that was the worst failure I have known. To contact you meant risking your knighthood, your entire future, and I couldn't ruin your life, even if it meant never holding you again, or seeing you grow up. But I will always hate myself for not being able to think my way out of the bind they put me in.'

My voice hitched, and I fought to go on. 'None of this – *none of this* – means I ever stopped loving you.'

As I spoke, Yvain's face drained, his hands dropping loose to his sides as if he was deciding whether or not to stay. I changed the subject before he chose to flee.

'Several years ago, when Lancelot was missing, you escorted a damsel who ran from you, do you remember?'

'Yes,' he said slowly. 'We stopped to take a rest and when I awoke she had gone.' His eyes widened. 'Was that—?'

'It was me, in disguise,' I said. 'You were made my escort, and … I just wanted to be in your company, hear you speak, learn more of you. It was weak and dishonest and I never should have indulged it. That it was done from love is no excuse, and I am sorry.'

A murmur of footsteps and voices sounded beyond the dais door, moving closer.

'All you must know,' I hurried on, 'is the belief you held in me was never a mistake. I'm not asking for forgiveness or anything else from you, but please, do not lose that goodness, your willingness to trust, because of my wrongs. Can you promise me that?'

His face shimmered with indecision, lips parted as if he were about to speak.

'Yvain,' came a calm, authoritative voice, drawing our attention.

Arthur stood in the doorway, recovered and standing tall again. He beckoned to my son, his glance at my presence no more than a blink. 'Come, sit with me awhile.'

Yvain took one more long look at me, then ducked his head and went to his uncle, vanishing from my sight. It burned in my chest, the deepest of wounds.

I hardly had a chance to feel what had happened when Lancelot emerged from the Great Chamber, hard-jawed and preoccupied. When he saw I was still there, he shut the dais door and rounded on me like a pouncing tiger.

'What did you do?' he demanded. 'The King was wracked with pain, furious, refusing all comfort. He could barely look me in the eye.'

My fortitude was already shaken by the day's battles, my brother's rejection and Yvain's departure, and his accusation landed on my rawest nerve.

'*You* have done this to Arthur, not me,' I snarled. 'Every day you are by his side, dishonouring the man who loves you best. His pain lies at your feet.'

'Do not say that,' he warned. 'Arthur is my King, my brother-in-arms, my friend. I cannot bear to see him disrupted in any way, especially by the black clouds you bring.'

'Yet you left him to stand here tangling with Morgan le Fay and will soon ride out.' I smiled malevolently up at him. 'What's the matter, Sir Knight? Are you feeling the need to escape Camelot again?'

Lancelot loomed over me, his annoyance bringing the same dark rush as it always did. My pulse quickened, until it aligned with his own racing heartbeat.

'Hear me now,' he said in a low voice. 'I love King Arthur. I swore my honour to him and would give my life for his. Your corrupted mischief, and what happened with your slain lover, has plagued a good man for far longer than the dead knight is worthy of. If I could make him forget it all, I would.'

I should have been better armoured, but his mention of Accolon hit me like a blow to the jaw. 'How dare you speak of what you don't understand,' I snapped. 'Accolon was a loyal knight with a noble heart. Your honour is a twisted lie, your so-called love a treason and an insult. You are not fit to stand in his shadow.'

His look of outrage could have frozen Hell. 'I will not discuss honour with you – it is beneath me. If this knight you loved so much was happy to associate with you, then he was never worthy of King Arthur's favour, much less his grief now.'

I stood incandescent but trembling, anger suffocating in my chest. When I didn't strike back, Lancelot exhaled crossly and said, 'This is finished. I will ensure you leave before I ride out myself.'

'Do not try and escort me,' I said. 'I know my way out of this damnable place.'

I hated to obey, and this was not over, but staying within these walls was being trapped in a labyrinth without end. I would never find my freedom until I released myself from this world.

I turned my back on Camelot's champion and strode away from Arthur's closed door, past the Council Room, across the jewelled-light atrium, and out of the main entrance. In the courtyard, I stopped, looking up at the windows to the King's Great Chamber. My brother was not watching me leave.

So be it. If Arthur never wanted to see me again, he would have his wish, but in turn, I had no choice but to make him feel my absence. Morgan le Fay would leave Camelot and never come back, but I refused to go quietly.

I was half a mile away from the city and waiting beside a wellspring just off the road when Sir Lancelot rode past me on a huge grey horse, armour and lance strapped across his mount's flanks. As I had guessed from his fraught restlessness, he had waited no time in cutting himself loose from Camelot.

Upon seeing him, the plan that had been forming in my mind hardened and shone, as diamonds do in the earth's dark embrace. This era of war had all begun with a punishment from Arthur; if I must let Camelot go, I would end our time with a punishment of my own.

I had promised never to use the liar's arts of Merlin again, so instead I sent the magpies off after the lone knight, following at a distance until they settled on a branch deep in a woodland glade, overlooking a tiny chapel. Sir Lancelot had stopped to pray.

I entered the nave on silent feet. At the far end, Lancelot knelt at a simple stone altar with his back to me, hands clasped together in prayer. As I advanced, his broad shoulders stiffened slightly, as if feeling my presence up the back of his neck. Still, he did not look back, but ducked his head and spoke to the Lord.

I glided closer, listening to his deep, courtly tones intoning in perfect church Latin. He said the usual things: giving thanks for his blessed existence; asking God's grace to shine upon his travels and quest; begging protection for those he loved – virtuous words masking my approaching footsteps until I was close enough to touch him.

With a flourish of my hand, I swept a glittering charm over his bowed form, anointing the great du Lac like the saint he believed he was. His voice slurred, halting in the middle of his prayer, handsome head swinging towards the altar in a dead sleep. I caught hold of his hair and pulled him upright, cradling a hand under his chiselled jaw.

'You should be grateful, Sir Lancelot,' I said to his slumbering face. 'I saved you from breaking your pretty nose.'

His weight pressed against my torso and I savoured it, watching his dark lashes twitch shadows across his impossible face. I could never tire of looking at him, but soon I would give it all up for good.

Grasping his cowled mail collar, I conjured the air to take his weight and dragged him along the chapel aisle by the scruff of his neck, emerging into the wilderness under a violet sky. With magical ease, I slung Lancelot across his stallion's saddle face down, then mounted my own horse and rode a solitary route back to Belle Garde, Camelot's champion borne behind me like the spoils of war.

Though it was barely dawn when I arrived, Alys and Tressa awaited me at the house's main door. They had not been to bed.

'I can explain,' I said, as they took in the sight of Sir Lancelot, dangling unconscious across his horse.

'There's no need,' Alys replied. 'We know.'

After all we had been through these past few years – my concealment of self and my feelings, my secrets and evasions – her faith was a wonder. But I would never keep myself from them again.

'He insulted Accolon,' I said. 'There is more, and I will tell you everything, but I do not quite have the measure of my full plan yet.'

What I knew was I had committed an act of resistance, held to the fire by Arthur's disbelief and tempered with Lancelot's barbs until my rebellion felt forged from steel. Beyond that, logic and reason were yet to be revealed.

'Then that is enough for now,' Alys said calmly.

Tressa put her hand to the knight's jaw, studying his face dispassionately. '*No one* insults Sir Accolon,' she said, and let his head drop again. 'Where shall we put him?'

The most important thing was that Lancelot couldn't know who held him, or where he was. After deliberating on the ride back, only one room in the house seemed capable of holding him, which I was also sure he had never laid eyes on.

'In the long bedchamber,' I replied. 'Mine and Accolon's.'

I reasoned it was in a wing little used by the household, and far enough away from anything my captive might recognise. Later, while he slept under magic, I had the lower shutters locked on the tall windows so he could not see the view of the spring, and had iron bars fixed on the smaller windows overlooking the courtyard garden, leaving those panes uncovered. I would not deprive the Flower of All Knighthood of his light, even if my intention was for him to wither in the dark.

'Are you sure you want him there?' Alys asked, once he was safely shut inside.

'The window bars are solid and the household will be instructed to keep away,' I said. 'He's as secure as he can be.'

'What she means,' Tressa said gently, 'is are you sure that you want him in that particular room? Given … the memories.'

They knew some of what had happened before, but not quite how weak I had been; how much I had been drawn in by Lancelot's charm, beauty and pain, the strange connection we had formed. This time, I would need to be stronger; I wouldn't go there to look upon him, negotiate any deal, nor even face him in challenge to make myself feel alive.

'That's how I know I will keep away,' I said, and meant it.

For now, my main purpose was to bring clarity to those most deserving. If my brother would not believe what I told him, then Arthur could observe his faithless wife's grief over Lancelot's absence with his own eyes, and learn the deceptions at the heart of the realm the hard way. No more would Camelot see or hear Morgan le Fay, but my presence would be felt like knives in their backs.

Still, practicalities needed to be discussed. A knightly prisoner had to be fed, watered, and given occupation, and no effort would be spared on Sir Lancelot's level of comfort. Forever was a long time, and I was not a monster.

'I'd rather not control him with magic, lest he guess my involvement,' I mused, when we returned to my study and Alys asked the question. 'Nor do I want to embroil too many of the household. But Lancelot is clever, strategic, and can subdue any man. Sending anyone into a room with him carries a risk.'

'I'll do it,' Tressa said. 'He won't overpower a woman.'

I shook my head. 'He has talents beyond strength, and he's not above using his charms to spring a trap. I cannot ask you to do such a thing.'

She grinned. 'Why not? I can withstand Sir Lancelot. He's not so irresistible.'

I glanced at Alys, sure she would protest, but she nodded with enthusiasm. 'There is no one better suited.'

'It's the best solution,' Tressa added. 'He's never seen me before, I know how to hold my nerve, and in no way will I fall for his supposed allure.'

Put that way, I had to admit it was perfect. 'Are you sure?' I asked. 'I cannot say where this will end.'

'We are with you, Morgan,' Alys said. 'Wherever this ends.'

I reached out and took each of them by the hand, linking us in an eternal circle. They kept showing me their faith and love, no matter how I tried to keep them at bay. The ballads may have sung of knights and their honour, the lengths men go to for their brothers-in-arms, but there was no loyalty as powerful as the love that existed between women who had lived entire lives together, and survived it all through the bonds of deepest sisterhood. I was a fool to think they needed to be kept from my despair, my failures, my vengeance, when in truth the three of us had always shared one soul.

'Forget endings,' I told them. 'This is the start of something new.'

We embraced as a trio, then they sprang into action, leaving the study to inform the waking household of how things had changed. I was left alone with my thoughts, but there was no pause left inside me – I knew exactly what I needed to do next.

For the first time in months, I took out the glass reliquary and placed it in the centre of my desk. The Shroud of Tithonus still sat within, its pale aspect slightly warped through the glass. I put my hand on the lid, the Shroud's effervescent vitality dancing through my blood, not a flicker of reluctance in its wake.

All game pieces had been snatched from the board and thrown into the fire. It had never been my realm to save.

I went to the alcove again, threw back the Hecate tapestries and drew out the silver box, heavy with the weight of a patient heart. Only one other soul had understood everything I was and loved me, body and mind, as no one else in this godforsaken world knew how. If I never saw him again, it would not be through want of trying.

It was time to go to the lake.

33

The walk up to Llyn Glas was the shortest it had ever been, as if I glided there on newly feathered wings.

The air was warm, a rich ochre light filtering through the forest boughs. So far, it had been a perfect autumn, leaves burning red and gold under cerulean skies. A lively breeze skipped alongside me, giving the moment an air of vitality, the assurance that I was right.

I had hooked a large satchel over my shoulder containing a set of Accolon's clothing and his favourite boots. The Shroud of Tithonus I had placed in my cloak pocket, its life force ringing above the jangle of my nerves as I strode forth.

In my hands I carried only one object – the silver box containing Accolon's heart. Hereafter, it would no longer be preserved in marble, but beat anew in the depths of his chest.

As ever, our lake looked the same – serene, sapphire, ancient – ready to bear witness to a miracle. I passed through the willow tree's drape of leaves and knelt on the lush carpet of grass, where my Gaul and I had lain for so many of our hours, talking, loving, sleeping fast in one another's arms as the stars rose and fell.

Following a process had always calmed me. First, I drew Accolon's clothes from the sack and folded them in a pile beside the willow. Then, I knelt before roots and asked the earth to shift, making a hole as I had done once before, many years ago, when I had failed to commit his heart to its rest, but heard the heartsong that told me everything was not over.

I asked the elements to make the space tall and wide, enough for long limbs and broad shoulders to be remade. In a smaller sack, I had brought swan down and bundles of herbs to line the sides of the cool damp hole until it was soft and sweet-scented.

Next, I took Accolon's heart from its box and blue silk wrappings, his heartsong choral in my senses. With the other hand, I drew out the Shroud of Tithonus, and laid both precious objects in my lap. Pulling my mind inwards, I let the warm shimmer of my healing reach out for the Shroud's crackling silver vitality, until the two forces met and entwined, braiding together in connection.

I want this, replied the pound of my own heart. I *need this*.

I did not have to prick my finger to know. The blood in my veins was gold.

With my father's knife, I slit both my palms. The blood sprang forth, molten, gilded, so full of power it carried its own halo. No pain clouded my senses, only a lively heat and the rush of control. I had time to do exactly as I wished.

I picked up Accolon's heart and held the cool marble to my breast, curving myself around it as I had all those years ago. Returning the heart to flesh was a moment's work, barely a breath before it reverted to its dark-red chamber, as weighty and muscular as the day I had taken it jewel-like from his chest.

The heartsong grew louder than any I had heard, a soaring symphony rising to the invitation of my blood, the threads of his life strong and ready. All I must do was draw them forth and weave his song into the essence of a living person, while the Shroud of Tithonus rebuilt what was missing.

I bore up Accolon's heart before me, hands dripping gold.

Gently, I placed him on the Shroud of Tithonus and drew the bleached linen corners together, weaving and tucking until it was neatly contained, nestled as close to the object of resurrection as possible. One last time, I held my Gaul's singing heart to mine, then committed him to the ground.

The bolt of blue silk followed, a touchstone between worlds. Next, with the help of a marshalled breeze, I gathered the fallen willow leaves into the hole until they formed a silver-green mound. Finally, I lay on my stomach and stretched my hands through the leaves and down into the earthen chamber, pressing my bleeding palms to the Shroud's surface.

As the force of healing joined with the ancient magic of life, I closed my eyes and spoke my chant, cultivated and refined over hours and days and years of work. Words that were clear as Llyn Glas and sharp as a peregrine's talons, and as powerful. The moment felt endless, suspended between the realms of life and death.

And then, it was over. Weakness raced through my limbs, my breath catching in warning that I had lain there too long. My body, my mind, had given as much as it could.

I pushed up to my knees, breathing hard, vision dizzied by magic and exhaustion, the high-noon light dancing off the lake in shards. An ache burned deep in my hands, so I dragged a thumb across each of my palms, fusing the lacerations shut.

It was too much: the excess of blood I had sacrificed and the final act of healing myself combined to overwhelm the last of my strength. My senses reeled into a freefall, and I collapsed sideways onto the soft grass.

My eyes opened slowly, blinking at a rose-gold sky through the parted willow fronds. The sun had begun sinking towards the horizon, painting a coruscating path across the lake's surface to the foot of my prostrate body. Astonishingly, I felt restored. What seemed like fainting had become the deepest sleep I had ever known.

I eased myself upright, remembering where I was and why. My hand rested on the filled hole, but the leaves looked undisturbed, the air around the lake still and silent. Water rustled against the shore in the amplified peace, amidst birdsong and blue-green flashes of the last dragonflies. I could even discern the trickle of the streams that fed the lake from the high valley sides. All seemed to be entirely as it had been.

Rising, I paced cautiously around the willow. Aside from mine, there were no footprints in the soft ground, no living entity in sight beyond an industrious blackbird, picking at fallen apples. The clothes and boots were exactly where I had left them.

I followed the lake shore, trying to stave off the rising tension in my gut, dipping in and out of the empty forest until I reached the rocky valley cliffs and could go no further.

I did not shout his name. If he was there, I would have sensed him. His presence would have swooped through the dusk and alighted on my heart like a falcon to a glove.

If he was here, I thought, *he would have seen me beneath the willow and stayed.*

Halfway back to the burial site, I started running. At the hole, I fell to my knees, scrabbling desperately at the leaves. The formula, my chant, everything was correct, but perhaps it had not fully taken hold. I would retrieve the heart and the Shroud and try again.

The edges of the hole remained undisturbed. My delving hands raked through the detritus to find the Shroud, the blue silk or glinting residue of my blood, Accolon's heart; any scrap of a failed process that could be begun again. Nothing remained but a small pool of water, glimmering at the bottom of the hole from the damp soil and dew.

'No,' I whispered. 'Anything but this.'

Once again, I had failed. Years of work, sacrifice and wavering hope, dissolved without leaving a trace. I had fought and I had lost. The battles, the war, everything.

A choked cry escaped me, and I gave it breath, letting my voice gather strength, until it was a Fury's howl around the valley. Another scream followed, and another, cries of injustice and frustration. I would not weep for this; if I let one tear break free, then it was a kind of acceptance, a pathway beyond my anger and despair. And I would not move on.

Throat raw, I fell to silence, the lake drawing my blurring gaze. It looked tranquil, deep, comforting – a healing place, for rest and peace. The lake would take all of my losses, my failures, the pain from a thousand cuts, and wash it all away.

I moved closer, until my toes touched the edge. If I could not bring Accolon to me, then perhaps there was another place, another realm, where I could find him. An endless blue abyss, where we would meet again, and stay together for eternity.

I took my boots and cloak off and left them on the shore.

The water was still cool and invigorating, but offered no shock to my bones as I waded in up to my thighs, then felt my waist engulfed. Either it was warm for the time of year, or else I was already numb.

When the depth reached my shoulders, the lake bed gave way, a sudden shelf dropping off to its true, immeasurable depths. Without hesitation, I stepped into the deep.

Llyn Glas welcomed my silent plunge, rushing over my head with ease. My skirts, my hair, once a dragging weight, now swirled about me, trailing bubbles. Curling my body into a gentle arc, I let myself drift down, imagining the cool clear liquid in my throat, my lungs, flowing between my bones, until I became part of the water as its essence was already part of me. I too would be of the lake.

But much as I tried to sink, the water would not take me. My body fought against my stillness, limbs churning in resistance, pushing upwards towards air, seeking breath. Years ago, under streaks of sun, Accolon had taught me how to swim in these same waters and I could not unlearn it now, could not forget how he had shown me how to survive.

I broke the surface with a crying gasp. My soaking gown should have been dragging me down, but my legs and arms were strong, the water bearing me aloft in defiance of my giving up.

Treading my feet, I took in my surroundings: the towering mountainside; evening light fiery on the treetops; the gentle sway of the willow fronds. A sudden shadow passed between the tree's arched parting, catching in my clearing vision.

A tall, broad-shouldered figure stepped out from under the willow and stood at the edge of the lake, clad in a vibrant blue.

I blinked, then again, dozens of times, but still the figure stood there, casting its gaze around lazily as if just waking from sleep, the faded sun anointing the sculptural angles of his face. An elegant hand came up and pushed long dark hair off his forehead.

It couldn't be, yet I knew every piece of him, every line and shadow and the way he moved, as if it were written upon my own soul.

Accolon.

34

Calling out would waste time: I immediately began to swim for the shore.

When my feet touched the lake bed, I picked up my streaming skirts and ran to him. It didn't matter that my breath was fire in my lungs, that my limbs were trembling with fatigue against the drag of my wet clothing. There could have been a riptide to overcome, a ravine to scale between us, and I still would have reached him.

At my dramatic exit from the water, Accolon turned, brow rising in surprise, then recognition. So he could see me, and respond. He knew who I was.

The unlikelihood of it all arrested me and I stopped, suddenly doubtful, shivering from my wet clothes and skin. Closing my eyes, I asked the air to make me dry, the sun's fire to warm my lake-chilled body and return my courage.

Once restored, I looked again, half fearing he would be gone, a creation of my desperate hope. Still he stood there, entire and perfect, exactly as he had been on the last day I had seen him alive, striding along Belle Garde's riverbank. He wore the same rich blue tunic belted over a white linen shirt and breeches, a darker mantle and long brown boots, gold spurs at his heels, his demeanour at ease, as though he had just come to meet me from the tilt field or riding out with the huntsman. Everything of him was as it had been.

I moved closer, braver now. Accolon's top lip rose, face opening into a smile – *his* smile. My God, he was beautiful, so very beautiful. I had forgotten how just looking at him made me ache.

'Morgan,' he said, like an answered prayer.

Morr-ganne, as he had since the very first time. No one had ever spoken my name the way he did.

My formula, the long years of study, the Shroud of Tithonus, had worked. Accolon was whole, incredible, returned to life.

Returned to *me*.

'Accolon,' I said. 'You're ... here.'

I wanted to say that I'd missed him, but I had no idea if he even knew he had died, or how alarming it might be for a person to hear they had been brought back from eternity.

'How do you feel?' I asked.

He regarded me with a calm amusement. 'Extremely well,' he said. 'Quite a feat, when you consider I was recently dead.'

It was so casually expressed I thought I'd misheard. 'Y-you know of that?'

'*Bien sûr.* It's not something one forgets.'

Strangely, it made me laugh, but the sound came out choked with tears. 'Where were you ... before this?'

'I couldn't say. I was not here, then suddenly I am again.' He shrugged in his characteristic way. 'If there was an "elsewhere", then I cannot express it further than that. But I know who I am, where I am, and the places I've been. I have my memories, the same knowledge. My feelings.'

'And is that ... good?' I asked.

His storm-blue eyes held mine, another smile rising on his face, quieter, adoring. 'I'm here, at our lake, looking at you, Morgan. There is nothing better.'

Another sob rose in my throat, but I resisted it. I had to touch him, urgently, wanting only to sink into the warm strength of his arms, to feel his lips on mine before I let myself melt into the wonder of whatever this was. I ran to him, arms outstretched, and he came forth to meet me, the falling sun casting its glow in his wake.

Suddenly, he was gone.

'Accolon?' I stopped, squinting into the lake's rippling light.

'I'm here,' he said in a puzzled voice.

His outline reappeared but I could barely see him, his image opaque, re-forming but incomplete. Accolon was there, but so were the lake and valley beyond – *through* him. Sunset glittered within his body, marking out his hazy figure with pricks of silver and gold.

Something was wrong.

It was my eyes, it had to be, extreme fatigue from such powerful magic and my plunge in the lake. I reached out for his hands and he did the same. My fingers passed right through his, leaving a trail of stars.

'I can't touch you,' I said. 'You're … you're …'

For the first time, Accolon regarded me with confusion. I tried to take his hands again, more carefully this time, but the same thing happened. My touch drifted through him, his form shimmering with disruption.

'Oh God, no. Please no,' I said. 'You're supposed to be whole. *I thought you were whole.*' I waved my hands frantically, over his arms, his chest, his edges that weren't there, finding only stardust. 'Why can't I touch you? What have I done … I—?'

I recoiled, air catching in my chest. It was then I realised that Accolon's hair was long, the way he preferred and always wore it at Belle Garde, but not as I cut it before he left for the Royal Court. His attire was similar, but not quite identical to his riding garb of that day. He was not as I last saw him, but as I most often *thought* of him, his ideal image.

'Morgan, it's all right.' His voice sounded through my rising panic – surely I could not be imagining a sound so real? '*Mon cœur, regarde-moi.*'

His deepest endearment landed like salve on a wound. My breaths slowed long enough to steady. 'It's all right,' he repeated. 'I'm here.'

'Are you?' I whispered. 'Truly?'

'Yes. I am real and I'm here, because of you. All is well.'

'No, it's not,' I protested. 'It wasn't meant to be this way. If you are real, why can't I touch you? Are you alive, dead, between worlds? Some sort of shade? I don't even know what I've done, or if this is pure madness.'

He held up peaceable hands. It was a relief to stop talking. 'Perhaps I can prove it to you.' he said. '*Alors*, close your eyes.'

I shook my head. 'I want to see.'

He smiled, as loving and exasperated at my contrariness as he had always been. Hope stretched like a bowstring in my chest; however he was made, this was my Gaul, the soul contained in his heart brought back to life. Maybe all was not lost.

Opening his arms, Accolon stepped forwards and enveloped me in an embrace.

The first surprise was that he was warm. There was no ghostlike chill about him, but a soft, distinct heat, like the balmy cast of a summer sunset. As his presence wrapped around mine, I remembered how in cold-weather times, he would lie on my side of our bed and move aside when I joined him, so I would slip between sheets already warmed by his body, into the love that awaited me there.

No, I more than remembered – I *felt* it. A specific night in a long-ago December, amidst the first snowfall we had ever experienced at Belle Garde: he and I standing at the window, watching the white flakes fall like silence; my fingers, threading through his to lead us to bed; the low roar of the fire and the scent of the wine he had poured. I pushed deeper into the sensations, feeling the linen brush my feet as I slipped them beneath warmed sheets. Accolon's fine hand on my waist, drawing me closer.

A memory, undramatic, inconsequential, known only to us.

I stepped back with a gasp, pulling out of his phantom embrace. Being apart from him brought a bracing chill, as though I had emerged from the lake after a long swim. Accolon too looked startled, his appearance slightly dishevelled, his edges blurred, though the stars within him shone clearer.

'I'm sorry,' he said. 'I didn't mean to ...' He gestured vaguely, unable to find the words. He seemed as breathless as I was.

'Don't apologise,' I said. 'It was exhilarating. Powerful. How did you ...?'

'I don't know. I thought if I could hold you, recall a moment we shared, it would prove something. But it felt as though we were truly back there. Was it the same for you?'

'Yes,' I replied. 'Every part of it, in all my senses. It was incredible. We—'

A yawn cut me off, my body swaying with all that had caught up with me: the spent magic, my lost blood, the lake; the conjured memories he and I had relived so vividly.

'You're exhausted,' Accolon said. 'I know how using your skills can tire you, and what you've done today is extraordinary. You should go, sleep, restore your strength. I'll await you here.'

The idea of leaving him was unbearable. 'I'm not going. You can't make me.'

'As if I could make you do anything, Morgan,' he said archly. 'In that case, come sit here at the foot of the willow, as we used to.'

Tiredness washed through me again, so I let him guide me to the willow roots. Mysteriously, the hole I had dug for his heart had refilled itself, leaving just a square of soil. The pile of folded clothes remained beside the trunk, but I decided not to think of what that – or the fact his heels bore the spurs I gave to Robin so many years ago – might mean. Instead, I sank gratefully down on the soft ground with Accolon beside me, appearing to recline against the tree trunk, his long legs crossed.

I could not rest my body on his as I wanted, but I moved closer and his heat flowed into me, a comfort, an impossibility. I looked up at him and he met my gaze, his face half stars; a tragedy and joy all at once.

'Our memory,' I said. 'Could you … do that at will?'

'I believe so.' He smiled and it held a certain mischief. 'Why – how much further do you wish us to go?'

For the first time in so long, I felt happiness rise in my chest and laughed and Accolon did the same. I could have been imagining it all, I knew that. Whether he was truly there, a shade, a resurrected soul, or if I was dreaming myself into madness, I didn't care. We were together again, and laughing.

I curled closer to his warmth and looked up at him, before sleep overwhelmed me.

'I love you,' I said.

He smiled in the way I loved best, tender and beautiful.

'I love you too,' he murmured, then I did not know if he said anything more, because I had already drifted off on a sea of our memories, vivid and alive; so many, and never enough.

When I awoke, Accolon was gone.

Dawn had broken a few hours since. My sleep had been profound, with dreams of him intense and unceasing, but my mind felt rested and alert. I shifted up and saw the refilled hole had fully regrown with grass, as though I had never dug it up at all.

I rose to my feet, looking around.

'Accolon?' I called. 'Are you there?'

No answer. I tried again, three times, and nothing.

My first thought was that it had all been a fantasy. Perhaps I never went into the lake and was only now waking from my collapse. Worse still, maybe Accolon *had* been there but our embraces – my bathing in his warm, ethereal touch and our memories – had used up whatever magic had fuelled his presence and scattered him back into nothingness.

The idea left me hollow. I stared at the lake, still as a polished jewel under the morning. *What have I done?*

'Morgan?'

He appeared from behind the sheet of willow branches that curtained our view of the water. Morning sun shone through him, his figure casting no shadow.

'Accolon,' I gasped. 'I thought I'd lost you again – that I'd fallen asleep and you were gone, I—'

Unspent fear folded me at the waist. How could I even say that I'd only lost him now, when in truth I had done so sixteen years before when I didn't stop him from riding to Camelot. I put a hand to my chest, gripping the Gaulish coin.

He came to me at once. 'No, *mon cœur*, I wouldn't leave you. I haven't been far, just to the lake edge and around the willow. Your falling to sleep while touching me, conjuring our memories – it … drained me after a while. I felt myself fading, so I moved away for a few hours and now I am restored.'

He didn't reach for me, though I yearned for him to do so, if only to feel the phantom brush of his warmth. Whatever his capabilities, he had become used to them more quickly than I had.

'I didn't know being close to you could do such a thing,' I said. 'It has a certain logic, now you say it but …' I put my free hand up and scrubbed at my face. 'I should have been more careful. I'm sorry.'

'Do not apologise,' he said softly. 'You are learning of this. We both are.'

His low, melodic voice calmed me as it always did. I stood upright and let go of the coin, watching his face soften at the sight of his childhood treasure.

'Yesterday, I got so carried away with seeing you again that I didn't afford us a chance to discuss anything,' I said. 'You must have as many questions as I do.'

Accolon paced over to the willow trunk and leaned beside me, his shoulder resting there as if he were solid. 'I don't think I could ever want to know as much as you,' he said lightly. 'But I would like to hear of my cousin Manassen, if you can get word of him.'

It was a relief to have the answer to something. 'There I already have plenty of news. Sir Manassen is happily married and living back in Gaul, but I receive letters from him and his wife often. At last count, they have five children – three sons and two daughters. The oldest boy is named after you.'

I thought it would please him, but as I spoke, his eyes widened, expression shifting from disbelief to an alarm that was almost horror.

'Five children?' he said tremulously. 'Morgan – how long have I been gone?'

It had never occurred to me that he might not know. 'Sixteen years,' I said. 'This July just past.'

I felt his shock as a shiver through my body. Accolon slid down to the foot of the tree, ground undisturbed by any impact. I sat beside him, and he stared at me, the trio of lines between his brows tugging at my heart.

'But ... you do not look any different,' he said. 'I thought it had been weeks, maybe months. I remember every part of you, Morgan. I remember how Belle Garde's protective charms have some effect, but you have not aged a day in all this time.'

I sighed. 'I know. I look this way for you.'

'For me?' he echoed. 'How? Why?'

'When I brought you back, I didn't want anything to have changed,' I said. 'I wanted your death, and our separation, to feel like it never happened. But it took so long I ...'

I could not finish the thought, or think of the failures I was yet to face. 'There is a great deal to talk about,' I concluded. 'So much, I don't know if there are enough words.'

Beside me, I felt him calm. 'We will find our way, *mon cœur*,' he said. 'There have never been enough words to contain us.'

He smiled, still slightly shocked, but extremes never daunted him for long, and I loved him for it more intensely than I thought possible.

'I've missed you,' I said.

He raised a hand, his warmth trailing my face. 'I've missed you too, somehow. Suddenly, I can feel every one of those days we've been apart.'

'We will make up for it,' I assured him. 'I'll tell you everything, without delay. Some is unexpected – I know so much of Manassen because I saved his life and he swore his loyalty to me. At first, it was just an alliance against Camelot, but we became good friends. You would hardly believe it to see us.'

His frown returned. 'Against Camelot?' he said. 'I know you had your troubles with King Arthur, but …'

Accolon's confusion struck the words from my tongue, another angle I had not considered. Though he knew he had died, I could not be sure he was aware of how it happened, or who was responsible, or how distressing it would be for him to learn. Equally, in the midst of this wonder of ours, I did not want to concede a single moment's joy to the suffering Camelot had forced upon us.

'We should not speak of it,' I said decisively. 'All you need to know is Arthur and I are not mended, and Camelot has no part of this, of us. Now you are here I don't want to give that world any space in our minds. All right?'

He took it in slowly, then inclined his head. 'If that is what you need, then there is plenty more for us to speak on. What of the household – I would very much like to hear how they will take this.'

I only stared at him with wide, guilty eyes, which Accolon read at once.

'They don't know you were trying to raise me,' he said.

'Alys and Tressa knew I intended to, years ago, but they don't know I'm here now.' I put a hand to my forehead. 'My God, how do I even start explaining to them what I've done when I hardly know myself?'

'Don't tell them yet,' he suggested. 'I'll stay here, and no one will see me.'

'Keep you a secret?' I said. 'I can't do that to you. It's not fair.'

'In truth, for now I'd rather no one else knew. While we try and understand.'

It made sense, if creating more lies. Our new necessities settled heavy in my chest.

'All I wanted was for you to simply return home, and now it's a mess,' I said. 'I will try to fix it, but what we need is time, to discover what happened and why. How you can sit on the grass or seem to lean against the tree, why the sun shines through you, and—'

He held up his hands against my stream of anxious talk. '*Mon cœur*, listen,' he said softly. 'Perhaps for the moment, none of it matters.'

I regarded him in disbelief, and he gestured to our view of the lake, then to himself and me both. 'This time yesterday, we were separated by death, yet now look at what we have. The moments we had in life were never enough, and you have afforded us more. We should savour it, just be together for a while. We deserve that much.'

I gazed up at his remarkable face, which I had long lost hope of seeing again. In my years of failure, if a wish-granting demon had offered me Accolon as he was now, I would have taken the deal no matter the cost.

'You're right,' I said. 'Us together is what I want – all I have kept existing for. There'll be time to fix my mistakes.'

'This is not a mistake,' he insisted. 'It is a miracle, Morgan – your miracle – and you should believe in it.'

35

To return to the house was the strangest thing I had ever done, in a life full of outlandish experiences.

When I reached the end of the path and took in the main building and front green, the turret looking exactly as it did when I left it, everything felt absurd, eternally changed. If Accolon was truly at the lake, keeping a secret of this magnitude would not be easy and I had no desire to return to subterfuge, but for now I could not do otherwise.

As expected, Alys and Tressa were in my study, preparing for the day's work on our latest manuscript, and did not question where I had been. To see them smiling, unknowing, looking over pages on women's life stages with their heads bent close, jolted me with a hundred warring feelings. Without realising it, I had split my life in two.

Luckily, Sir Lancelot brought us enough distraction. According to Tressa, when she went in to check on him and take his food, he was awake but not at all angered by the fact he was in captivity.

'All he said was – *I'm a prisoner here, aren't I?* As if it didn't matter in the slightest. I was so taken aback I answered that it was true. I didn't see the point in claiming otherwise – he opened the courtyard shutters and saw the bars.'

'Iron bars *are* rather definitive,' I replied. 'So I expect he is throwing himself against the doors now, is he? Climbing walls, breaking everything he can get his hands on.'

'That's just it,' she replied. 'I expected his reaction to be dramatic, but he merely thanked me and sat back on the bed. I stood outside his door for a while, but he didn't make a sound. The strangest thing is, he hasn't asked a single question – where he is, who I am, who is holding him. Not a word, bar thanking me for his food.'

'How very odd,' Alys said.

I nodded thoughtfully. Before he woke, I had lightly charmed Lancelot's memory so he would not recall our clash in Camelot or immediately suspect me, but assumed his imprisonment would still be met with outrage. In all my dealings with du Lac, I had only known him to react to his feelings outwardly, often in the extreme. Passive and reserved had not so far been within his capabilities.

'It could be a ruse to flush out his captor,' I mused. 'He is a good chess player.'

Alys and Tressa glanced at one another.

'I'm not going to fall for it,' I insisted. 'Sir Lancelot might be acting the lamb of peace for now, but he'll be tearing down the bed drapes and demanding to face his jailer in a duel any moment. Regardless, I'm staying away.'

Instead, I returned to the lake.

By the time I climbed the path the next morning, I half believed I had imagined it all and would find nothing but the leaning willow and still blue water, same as it ever was. But, before fear could take hold, Accolon came, appearing from beneath the tree exactly as he had the day before – smiling and beautiful. The sight was overwhelming.

I ran to him, tracing my hands along his edges. 'I'm so happy you're here.'

'So am I,' he said. 'To look upon you again, to be able to share all we have missed and our memories ... it is everything.'

I smiled. 'It's all I have been thinking about. I want to relive our every moment, everything we have experienced, together and apart. To see and feel it all.'

He leaned forward, reaching out for the embrace I craved like the most terrible hunger. Suddenly, I could feel him within his irresistible warmth, how his body used to fuse with mine with such exquisite ease.

'Where should we begin?' he asked.

I did not have to pause to think. 'At the glen near Tintagel, the enchanted pool we found. Can we go back to that day?'

The look he gave me was stormy, insoluble, and I felt it as thunder along my spine. '*Oui*, if that is what you want.'

'It's all I want,' I said, closing my eyes as his heat swept away my senses. 'Take us there.'

I spent a month going to Llyn Glas without too much scrutiny. The autumn was still ablaze, with unseasonably clear skies and lingering warmth, so no one looked askance at my wandering abroad.

In this shining, unfathomable time, Accolon and I did what we had always done when finding one another again – we rushed together as if the hours were against us, galloping through our past in its full glory. We revisited the glen near Tintagel several times, delving into a memory that had always been too brief. I discovered I could choose to feel our moments as they had happened, or observe on the periphery, but always he and I stayed together.

Mostly, I picked where and when we revisited, but Accolon occasionally found his insistence. 'Today, I decide,' he said firmly, one burnished morning. 'You forget the most important thing that happened in Tintagel. Before the glen or our nights together.'

I raised an eyebrow. 'Which is?'

'I beat you at chess.'

I laughed. 'I "forget" because such a thing never happened.'

'*Alors*, prepare to be proved wrong.'

Immediately, we were in Tintagel's Great Hall, sitting across a table from each other, the household so bare we were almost alone. Relentless rain battered the windows; I remembered it had prevented us from riding out. We were still in the days when our hours were spent together but we could not admit we had fallen back in love.

The chessboard he had given me years earlier sat between us, Accolon's carriage so self-conscious and upright I was afraid it would give him muscle strain. But, as we began, his shoulders loosened, and soon he was smiling: at the board, at me, at my every gambit.

Through the haze of years, I watched his elegant hands, one wavering over his pieces, the Gaulish coin shimmering back and forth across the other. After four swift defeats, he pursued hard and beat me in the fifth, collapsing onto the table as if he had just won a lengthy footrace. His laughter, deep and joyous, rang around the hall like music.

'Of all the competitive triumphs in my life,' he said as we returned to the present, 'that was my greatest one,'

'You were a distraction,' I protested. 'As well you knew.'

We continued that way, revisiting the old and exploring the new until we were even closer, our love deathless, still growing; another miracle. The only impediment was that the process would tire him; too much time conjuring our memories eventually dissolved his shade into silver-gold dust and scattered his essence across the lake. He would always re-form, though took up to a week to return. In the times I awaited him, I would sit at my desk and surreptitiously study for a way to make Accolon whole.

All was well until the weather turned, an abrupt chill driving in with frozen rain. Some days, I used my elemental skills to clear the skies, but Mother Nature fought against too much interference, and the dark and cold could not be escaped.

'These are no conditions for the woman I love,' Accolon scolded, as I arrived in a haze of sleet. 'Come back when the skies and ground are kinder.'

'Will you not be bored?' I asked, and he shook his head.

'Time and weather do not affect me. I am only here when you are.'

As winter passed, the strangeness of my new existence faded, and I returned to my old rhythms – sitting at the worktable with Alys and Tressa, reading and writing, discussing plans for the valley; mealtimes with the household. At Christmastide, they laid Accolon's place at our feasts and it did not hurt as it used to, knowing that on the next clear day, I could tell him of all that was done and said, the songs we sang and thanks we gave. That soon enough, the space beside me might no longer be empty.

So our weeks and months went, my life divided between two planes: Llyn Glas and Belle Garde; Accolon and my household; the Morgan of truth, and of secrets.

All the while, Sir Lancelot, my caged leopard, ate, slept, and kept his claws and teeth to himself. It was several months, and almost spring, before he made a move to acknowledge his own existence.

'He has asked for paints and brushes.'

I looked up to see Tressa before my desk. It was a bright afternoon in early March and I had retired to read in my study, after spending the morning on Tintagel's headland with Accolon until he faded. He had grown stronger over the past few months, but the memory was potent and we had revelled in it, so it would still take days for him to re-form.

'What?' I asked distractedly.

'Sir Lancelot,' Tressa said. 'He's been watching the painter in the courtyard outside his room – the man painting our new murals. This morning he asked him if he could borrow some supplies, though he hasn't asked for anything to paint *on*. The muralist is happy to share, but thought he should ask first.'

I sat back, considering. Lancelot had no way of getting a message out of Belle Garde, and he had already refused parchment and ink in case he otherwise wanted to write. There were more destructive ways to make a mess of his chamber, and he had so far kept the room in perfect order. He even made his own bed every day.

I glanced up at Alys, seeking scrolls on the gallery. 'What do you think?'

'He will paint the walls,' she pointed out. 'It would change the room.'

My pulse quickened, but I had promised not to let the chamber hold sway over me. It was why I had put du Lac there in the first place.

'If you have no objections, then I have none,' I told Tressa. 'Tell the painter I will replace any supplies he uses. Let's see what our eminent guest does.'

By the afternoon, it had become clear – Lancelot truly wanted to paint. After receiving the pigments and several brushes through the bars, the knight went to work on the walls, until the light waned and he ran out of his third helping of colours. When Tressa went in, she reported him as leaning dazed against the wall beside what he had done. He barely acknowledged her when she put down his evening meal, but as she left, she saw him dive for the food, snatching it up in handfuls as if he hadn't eaten for days.

'He didn't even pause to wash the paint from his hands,' she said, as the three of us sat over our own wine in Alys's physic garden. 'The paintings so far are good. He seems to possess a fair amount of skill.'

I rolled my eyes. 'What endeavour exists that Sir Lancelot isn't brilliant at?'

'What are the paintings of?' Alys asked.

'I didn't have long to look,' Tressa said. 'There was a crowned man and lady holding a baby, then a castle besieged by armed men. The last painting seemed to show a child alone in a dark forest, beside a riverbank. He had sketched the next image in charcoal, ready for paint. A robed woman with long flowing hair, standing in the river.'

I shook my head. 'Not a river. A lake.'

And not just any woman; when Lancelot began to paint the next day, her hair would need a pigment of red mixed with gold, and no amount of skill would ever quite capture its sunset shade.

'The Lady Ninianne,' Alys said.

I nodded. 'Waiting to carry her adoptive son off to his destiny. Sir Lancelot has painted the opening scenes to his own life.'

To my credit, I cleaved to my self-control for several months.

Spring stretched into summer, with long days and good skies. I spent my time at the lake, and refused to ask Tressa about what my unpredictable prisoner was painting. Only in bad weather did my curiosity threaten my pledge to keep away from Lancelot's door.

In the end, however, my impulses could not be contained. When Accolon had been risen a year, and the shifting season brought rains so relentless even I could not banish the clouds, I spent my nights lying in the dark, wakeful and restless. As the Hunter's Moon swelled to its fullest, I found myself stealing down the turret steps and through the silent house.

I needed no light to guide my way; nor did I need a key to turn the lock. The door swung open on quiet hinges, and I stepped inside.

The long bedchamber Accolon and I had shared stretched out before me into a profound darkness, air weighted by every joy and intimacy it had seen. Covertly, I struck my fingers across my palm and a flame sprang to life, making familiar the shadows: the window seats and fireplace; the rafters blotched with faded birds; the hulking silhouette of the carved oak bed, hangings half drawn. It felt less like a room than it did an ordeal of emptiness.

But of course, the chamber wasn't empty, and from the bed came the steady push-pull of arduous breaths. I had not seen Lancelot since the day he became my prisoner, and in the cast of my light, the sight of him had become astonishing again. He lay on his front, arms and face still streaked with paint, a dark curl across his brow. Though he shaved his face every day under Tressa's supervision, he had let his hair grow until it was lush and untamed. I brushed the lock back with my fingertip and he did not stir.

I wasn't sure why I had come, but it could not be for him. Leaving him to sleep, I went to the wall nearest the door and held up my flaming hand. True to Tressa's description, his paintings were good, unexpectedly fine for a man more used to sword strikes and crushing joust opponents. Then again, Accolon had lived the same knightly life, and there were no hands more artful than his.

At the thought, a column of memories rose up: Accolon's coin flashing between his fingers; his swift hands lacing – and unlacing – my gowns; his gentle, searching touch on my skin. What lingered in this place was different from the visions we conjured together at the lake: they were darker, made of loneliness, hovering at my shoulder. I pushed beyond their grasp and moved on.

The paintings continued with du Lac's youth – his time in Ninianne's care, images of his knightly training, lessons and conversations with her, nothing particularly interesting. Next came the unmistakable golden castle, and a knight in silver on a long, twisting road. Lancelot – unknighted and hopeful – had come to Camelot.

Smaller images abounded: the young man meeting his peers, embarking upon his first quest, joust and duel of swords. Then came a large portrait of the High King and Queen, resplendent and detailed, the figure of Lancelot prostrate, gazing up at them both.

Other events came and went: knights and ladies; banquets and jousting triumphs; Arthur and Guinevere watching over Lancelot's feats like gods on Olympus. One long mural depicted a silver-blond man marked as 'Lord Galehaut', a figure remarkably tall and handsome as a prince of myth, his importance definitive but unexplained.

Near the end of the paintings, one image presided over the rest: the Queen standing before Sir Lancelot. Innocent enough at first glance, except he was no longer kneeling, and they were gazing at one another with a directness he had never depicted before.

My head cleared as though I had been plunged into a stream. Surely he would never display what must come next.

I held the fire up to his newest painting, expecting allusion at most. What I found was more revealing, more dangerous than any image yet. Before me, in vivid detail were Queen Guinevere and Sir Lancelot in bed together, embracing, as lovers in adultery.

I recoiled in shock. He had rendered the two of them with such boldness that the revelation felt new to me; a confession daunting in its intimacy, its meaning undeniable.

Lancelot had painted his betrayal of Arthur on my walls.

This was the first material proof of what I had long insisted, enough to convince my doubting brother of their treason ten times over. Finally, I had Lancelot's admission, better than if he had put ink to paper. Camelot's champion had placed the perfect weapon in my hands, the undeniable means to bring the great golden castle to its knees.

Yet when I looked again, the passion and clarity in his work arrested me in a different way. No longer did I see a tool for my vengeance, but a message resonating so deeply it was as if he had sketched an allegory beneath the surface, a code for me alone to find. What Lancelot had done was not to provoke, tempt chaos, or even confess his sins. Instead, from within his imprisonment, he had found a way to express his deepest pains and sleep easily, whereas I lay awake every night and had once again chained myself with lies.

Lancelot had painted his treason, his guilt and failures for everyone to see, because he understood what I had forgotten: that the only way to be free was to tell the truth.

36

The next day, I sought Alys and Tressa in their chambers overlooking the physic garden.

'Come with me,' I said. 'There's something I need to show you.'

We walked the lake path in a mix of quiet talk and companionable silence, a balm to the nervous tension that came with great change. All I wanted was for them to have the truth about everything I had done, even though I should have told them months before.

They gasped in unison as we emerged, the lake calm and shining in greeting, showing off its richest dark-blue hue.

'Look at this place.' Tressa pointed excitedly at the pair of apple trees. 'No wonder their fruit makes my very best cyser.'

Alys took her surroundings with a quiet awe. 'I can see why you come here all the time, *cariad*.'

'You will understand even more in a moment,' I said. 'What you will see may come as a shock, but it's long past time you should have known.'

They regarded me in confusion, so I hurried beneath the willow before I could change my mind.

'Accolon,' I called out. 'I'm here.'

I saw Alys grip Tressa's arm, but they stayed silent, anticipation vibrating between us. Under the willow, nothing happened.

Impatient, I walked around the tree, finding only the weeping leaves and the swaying shadows they cast. The wind caught in the hollow of the valley, rattling through the woodland with a low howl. Frustrated, I raised my hands and pulled the gust to a halt, blanketing the lake with a profound silence.

'Accolon, are you there?' I called again.

I listened intently, my heightened senses alert to the soft lap of the water against the lake shore, the skitter of leaves as an alarmed wood pigeon broke free of its roosting place, the faint rasp of a grasshopper in a sun spot.

'If you are in jest, this isn't funny,' I said. 'Come now – it's important.'

Still nothing. The wind tugged away from my grip and I let it go, feeling it careen out of the valley.

'Morgan?' Alys's voice startled me. 'What's happening?'

I sighed and faced them. 'I wanted it to be a surprise,' I said. 'Accolon is here.'

'Here, as in alive?' Tressa enquired.

'Yes. No. It's hard to explain,' I said. 'Last autumn, with his heart and the Shroud of Tithonus – I raised him. As I always swore I would.'

'*How* long ago?' Alys exclaimed. 'Are you saying he's been living up here?'

'That's where it becomes tricky,' I said. 'He's not whole. We cannot touch in any usual way. He has no physical needs. I've yearned to tell you both, but he didn't want to upset anyone in the household, and I haven't yet found a way of fixing what I've done.'

Neither of them said a word. I swung round and called him twice more, my voice a little wilder each time, walking back and forth in rising frustration.

'Why doesn't he come?' I hissed.

Eventually, Alys came and halted me. 'It's all right,' she said. 'If you say he's here, then he's here.'

Tressa nodded. 'It doesn't matter if we can see him or not.'

I recoiled at their platitudes. 'He's here, I swear,' I insisted. 'He looks perfectly formed aside from being intangible. We talk for hours, and he remembers everything. He feels and thinks how he always has. It's *him*.'

'We believe you, Morgan,' Alys said gently. 'Of course we do. Let's go back to the house and discuss it there.'

In their alarmed faces I saw the situation clearly; they loved me and wanted it to be true but were concerned. Never before had I made such a pronouncement of my skills and failed to display proof.

'No,' I said, drawing away from Alys's touch. 'You should go back to the house. Don't wait for me.'

She began to protest, but I shook my head, trying not to sound how I felt.

'I'm fine, dear heart,' I said. 'I just need to understand what's happened. I'll be along in a little while.'

They hesitated, then Tressa took Alys's hand and led her away into the trees. I listened to their footsteps fading, gazing at the sky-tinged lake, the sunlight thick as honey across the water.

'Morgan?'

The voice made me jump, and I spun round to see Accolon emerging from the weeping willow leaves, glowing with love as he always did. When he saw my expression, his smile dropped. 'Is something wrong?'

'Where have you been?' I said. 'I've been calling endlessly for you.'

'I was here,' he replied. 'I heard you and tried to come forth, but for some reason I couldn't. It was strange.'

'I brought Alys and Tressa to see you,' I said. 'I couldn't lie to them any longer. You didn't come and now they think I've invented the whole thing.'

'I'm sure that's not true,' he replied. 'They trust you and know what you're capable of. Bring them again in a few days – I will try harder.'

'So you don't mind that I brought them?' I asked.

He shook his head. 'Of course not. It's been long enough.'

His willingness bolstered my spirit, but it was no good. Twice more, Alys and Tressa returned to the lake with me, and I called for Accolon to no avail. Twice more they had walked away trailing worry for me in their wake, only for him to appear again, bringing both relief and a growing sense of doubt.

Are you real? I wanted to ask him. *All this time, have you been my madness?*

Soon enough, winter loomed again, with its short grey days and long darknesses, spindly trees scratching at the skies as if they would never again bear leaf or fruit. When it became so cold the lake froze over, Accolon urged me to keep indoors once more, but in the wake of Alys and Tressa's abortive visits and the reawakening of my failures, the thought of leaving him was harder than it had ever been. Dramatic action seemed my only refuge.

'I think it's time for you to come down to the house,' I told him. 'I don't want to endure another winter without you, and if you are there, it will be easier for me to seek answers to making you whole.'

I had expected some doubt, but instead he bit his lip and let out a long, guilty sigh.

'I'm sorry, Morgan,' he said. 'I can't.'

'You need not see anyone for now,' I replied. 'But the household will not fear this. They love you, they honour your memory – they will accept you.'

He shook his head. 'It's not that. I would love to come home. In truth, I have always been ready. I can't come with you because I am trapped here.'

'Trapped?' I repeated. 'As in, at the lake?'

'Not even that far,' he said. 'I cannot move much beyond this tree.'

I opened my mouth to argue: surely, in the many months I had been visiting him we had walked the curve of the lake shore, at least stood before our apple trees. But hard as I tried, I could not recall one instance. We had only ever stayed near the willow, mostly between the trunk and the water's edge. All our time had been spent in fascinated talk, or with our essences entwined, travelling only through our memories.

I put a hand to my forehead. 'Why didn't you tell me?'

'I don't know,' he said hopelessly. 'Part of me thought you knew. And another part … thought it might change. If I moved around, practised, became stronger.'

His expression was wretched, but I wasn't ready to let hope slip away.

'I'm here now. Perhaps it will work if you try again.' I hurried off, pausing half a bowshot away, near the path to the house. 'Come here.'

Reluctantly, Accolon ducked his head and walked towards me. A few yards outside the weeping branches, his form faded, edges dissipating into starry dust.

'No, stop,' I said. 'Don't vanish.'

I felt my blood grow cold as he retreated, his image strengthening until he looked himself again: almost whole, but glittering faintly. His face was riven with sorrow.

'I'm sorry, *mon cœur*,' he said. 'I've tried everything, since the beginning, and there is no change. When I stray too far, I begin to fade. It feels as though I am losing hold of myself, that I will cease to be. Until I go back to the willow.'

'The magic,' I murmured. 'The burial site at the roots. The resurrection must have bound you to the tree.'

I went and put my hand on the bark, partly to see if any feeling came from it. None reached me, but my mind was jangling like chains.

'I thought you not being corporeal was terrible enough,' I said. 'But to be trapped here ... Dear God, what have I wrought?'

Panic hit me like a charging horse, kicking the breath from my body. In my desperation to resurrect him, I had gone beyond failure and turned it into an act of cruelty. I leaned heavily against the willow trunk, heart racing and my vision narrowing to darkness.

A sound broke into my racing thoughts: *Morgan, Morgan, Morgan.* Accolon's voice, repeating my name. The calming rhythm of it soaked into me, and when I opened my eyes, he was there, face concerned but his presence reassuring. I let him wrap his warmth around my cold bones, absorbing his love, his assurance, until I felt like myself again – Morgan le Fay, the name I bore because his faith had bestowed it.

We gazed at one another, enraptured, melancholy. 'You've done nothing wrong,' he said. 'Everything will be all right.'

'How can it be?' I replied. 'No matter what I try, I keep finding ways to ruin you.'

'Morgan, no,—' he began, but I could not bear his understanding, his adoring, beautiful face. He had always, *always*, deserved so much better.

I pulled myself away from his presence, the comfort I had no right to claim. 'I'm sorry,' I said, and left him beneath the willow tree, unable to follow.

Hindered by winter and awash with new grief, I returned to the worktable with Alys and Tressa. We had existed within a kind but tentative mood, able to speak on everything but the lake, the question of my sanity hanging over us like a great spectre.

Eventually, as dreary February finally gave way into mercurial March, the news came that my prisoner had relinquished his paints and brushes.

In the months since I had been in Lancelot's chamber, he had continued to paint, working all the hours that daylight and additional candles would allow, though I never asked Tressa what she saw on the walls.

'He's finished?' I said when Tressa told us. 'For good?'

'So it seems,' she replied. 'Though there is still space on the walls. He simply left his supplies in a pile and declared he was no longer in need of them.'

It intrigued me less than I thought it would. As spring blew in, I was once again frequenting the lake, steeping myself in memory with Accolon, but my escape from the world did little to assuage my hopelessness and growing despair. It was as though I had returned to the ways of before, the pain of my long-ago losses renewed and searing, like a dragon rising from slumber. Of course, I told no one, but it was the worst I had felt in a very long time.

However, I had forgotten how things can continue to get worse, until one day near the equinox, when Alys and Tressa came to the turret and stood before my desk. At their concerned looks, I assumed they were finally bringing their doubts on my soundness of mind, and felt immediately weary. I had no recourse, after all.

Instead, Alys stepped forward and handed me a letter. 'From Queen Elaine,' she said solemnly. Their seriousness and ceremony confused me, but upon taking the missive, I saw the reason. Elaine had used her official Royal Seal, and the wax was black.

Pulse quickening, I tore the letter open.

Dearest Morgan, she wrote. *I am so sorry to be the one to tell you this. Our sister, Morgause, is dead. Taken before her time, in terrible, unexpected circumstances.*

I read it, then read it several more times. Morgause was gone, any chance we would someday meet again snatched away forever. How many of those I loved would be out of my reach before I could no longer stand it?

From my grieving heart to yours, these are the worst words I have ever had to write, but you deserve the bald and awful truth, the letter went on. *She was beheaded. Killed by one of her own sons.*

A cry of horror escaped me. Abruptly, I pushed up from my chair and walked away from the desk, clutching the letter to my hollowed heart.

'*Cariad*, what is it?' Alys asked.

'My sister, Morgause ...' I managed. 'She's dead.'

They rushed over at once, but I waved them away. 'It's all right – do not fuss. I just ... need to lie down, be alone.'

Half in a trance, I went to my bedchamber and changed into a long blue robe. I made myself lie on the bed, letter grasped in my hand, but could not keep still, or bear to read the rest of what Elaine had written. Instead, I found myself back on the stairs, wandering various hallways until cool air touched my skin, and I saw I had come to the secluded courtyard outside mine and Accolon's former bedchamber.

It was early evening, and still light enough to show the murals painted a year ago, a vibrant depiction of Aeneas's triumphs and trials. Shuddering, I sank down upon the stone bench where we often used to sit to watch the sunset or stars. Sometimes, Accolon would pour us wine and bring blankets, and we would cocoon ourselves there, talking and laughing, savouring our time alone together as true lovers do. Another time, another life long gone.

I looked at the letter in my hand and made myself read.

From what I can gather, Elaine wrote, *Morgause had a lover, and her son Sir Gaheris took exception. He came upon them together and in anger or jealousy, he killed her. The lover escaped and ran directly to Camelot with the news. One would hope the outcome would be a just punishment.*

I did not share Elaine's assumption. Arthur and Morgause had been at odds for decades due to King Lot's rebellion, but her children were sworn to Camelot's cause. The knightly son would not be sacrificed for the sake of the estranged mother, already dead.

A yellow rose vine had blossomed early along the wall, giving off a sweet evocative scent: my own mother and the rose oil she used in her bath; the feeling of being wrapped in her embrace and the sound of my father's laugh; of Elaine and Morgause and our childhood, when the Cornish sun shone upon us and happiness was all we knew.

Killed by her own son. How could we, as women, exist in a world where such things were possible, without losing every semblance of hope? No matter what we did – whether a shrewd, dutiful queen or rebel witch in exile, however much rank, knowledge or power we held – always our survival was in question.

All my life, I had fought against the world's hostilities. I had tried chaos, strategy, and held the forces of destruction in my hands, but it had never been enough to cause the slightest tremor in the status quo. I had trapped the world's greatest knight in the room behind me to make Camelot suffer, and all he had done was paint its golden image all over my walls. When the game was already decided, there was no victory, or true vengeance, to be had.

But there could be punishment. I looked to the window at my shoulder, its candles already snuffed out, its resident sleeping in undeserving peace. Lancelot had dared sully my domain, but it was my Vale of No Return, its fate mine to decide. Here, I did not have to bow to Camelot's curse. What was done could, and must, be destroyed.

When I rose again, the sky was coal-black, the air woven with textures of night. *Flint on steel*, I told myself, and lit fire in the palm of my hand.

37

I entered the long chamber through the courtyard door, stepping softly inside. The air held a particular quiet, as if Lancelot was resting easier for once, the only sound a steady drip-drip-drip of water, echoing throughout the darkness. A faint thrill whispered up the back of my neck as I closed myself in.

Heart pounding, I paused to think, limbs taut, fire in my hand burning so hot it was blue. Would I be most satisfied scorching the paintings black, or shaking the earth until the plaster came crashing down? Should I ask the spring to rise up in violence, flooding the chamber until it was clean? Was Lancelot to be saved, or carried off on the tide of my rage?

I rushed to the images I had not yet seen. Here were more knightly adventures and lavish feasts, further adulterous trysts with his King's wife; the constant golden castle on its hilltop. I moved along the wall, seeking fuel for my flame, when a different set of images caught my attention, the brushstrokes swift, not as precise: a woman arriving at Camelot with an infant in her arms; Lancelot wandering long-bearded and ragged in the wilderness; the knight's return to court, his figure dogged by shadows and set apart from the others.

In the last painting, Lancelot was kneeling at Guinevere's feet, as he so often was, but his hands were clasped before him. The Queen looked away, pointing over his head, her message clear. *Go away from me*, she was saying. His face was streaked with tears. Lancelot was begging for forgiveness, and Guinevere was sending him out of her sight.

From there, colour abruptly ceased, leaving only charcoal sketches, of himself ahorse on the road, bent with grief, and the chapel where I had found him. I halted, unable to tear myself away from his sorrow, the futility he wore as he tried to keep moving.

The fury in my body cooled, gaining in density until I was made of heaviness. Limbs weighted, I leaned my shoulder against the wall, but for once I could find no bright anger to chase the leaden slowness away, the dark barricade before me too high and solid to surmount. The truth I could never admit, grown so great it had become unignorable; that beyond the distractions of anger and revenge, what I felt most of all was sadness.

Beyond, one large, final sketch covered the wall. With effort, I pushed myself up and paced further to see a man made only of thick black lines, lying prone on a bed – Lancelot in repose, one arm slung out to his side. From his mouth came a pair of words.

Forgive me, he was saying.

I gazed at the agonised regret on his face, the smudged black rendering him deathlike, haunted. Lancelot's abandonment of hope, his inability to pull himself away from his own ruin, was a dark mirror, from which my own reflection looked back.

Suddenly, I would have done anything not to have entered that room and seen what he had done. I did not want to be chained to the same stuck wheel as he was, spinning ever faster, but never progressing onwards. What I wanted was to move on, to exist alongside both my fury and sadness with complete honesty, and keep seeking my future, however long and difficult the road. I wanted to be free.

I turned away from the paintings. There was nothing for me here.

As I did, a flash of colour burned in my light. I pivoted back to the charcoal sketch, and a trail of crimson paint pouring down the figure's arm.

My heart and flame jolted: the man in the bed was not sleeping – he was dead.

In the room, the incongruous dripping grew louder, insistent, like raindrops in a metal bowl. Fear rising in my throat, I made myself turn towards the bed. The first thing it illuminated was an arm, pale and bleak, hanging off the edge of the mattress. The next thing I saw was the blood.

It pooled on the floor, dripping from Lancelot's hand. A shiver glittered through my bones: the healing in his blood, calling out to me.

With a sweep of my arm, I lit the candles in the room and rushed to the edge of the bed. A deep cut ran along both of Lancelot's wrists, performed with vicious precision. His pulse vibrated towards my senses, weak and stuttering, his skin drained of life. The next breath he drew could be his last.

I grabbed his hands and pulled his bleeding wrists to my chest. Torrents of light were already streaming through my body, and when his blood touched my skin it became a blaze, almost beyond my control.

I had to master myself. I pulled deeply on my breaths, mind mapping the damage beneath my fingertips: the slashed skin, torn veins and sliced tendons. His injuries reminded me of when Merlin took a dagger to Ninianne's arm, the method of repair the same: halt the bleeding, seal severed vessels, rebuild the flesh.

So rapidly was it done that I barely even felt the stages. Lancelot's lungs took a great, noisy gasp, pulling in air so hard he reared up from the bed, his eyes still closed. I held him upright until his breaths steadied, then propped pillows behind him and eased him back.

Once he was comfortable, I refocused my senses to any hidden afflictions. He was fighting now, but his blood loss would define this struggle. Settling my hip against his, I drew his wrists into my lap, easing my light through him like a slow-running river. I could not restore his blood without days of further healing, but I could ensure he survived the night.

An hour passed, and another, Lancelot's blood replenishing inside him while all he had lost dried darkly across the sheets, my robe, his bare chest. As the candles burned down, I looked around the room, at the walls, his paintings flickering with shadow as if they had come to life. A glint of silver caught my eye from the table at his bedside, surrounding a circle of gold and green – Guinevere's emerald ring, returned to him and back on its chain, but left aside. He had not wanted his holiest of relics to bear witness to his final sin.

I was half dozing when I felt a frisson of observation over my body. I opened my eyes to see Lancelot gazing directly at me.

'God's blood,' he said. 'Morgan le Fay.'

His voice was oddly calm. How long he had been awake, I could not be sure.

I offered a wan smile. 'Who else?'

Upon hearing me speak, he tore his hands away, scrambling upright in evasion.

'Careful!' I exclaimed, but my warning came too late. His shoulder blades crashed against the bedhead and he slumped there, ashen and panting. His pale-blue glare, however, was at full strength – furious, accusing, and icy as a northern winter.

'What are you doing here?' he demanded hoarsely, before his mind caught up. '*You* have been holding me prisoner? All this time?'

Wordlessness had taken hold of my tongue from the fatigue of healing, or because just then, I possessed neither the ability nor the will for a fight. But weakened as he was, Lancelot was still Lancelot, and he would do battle no matter the circumstances.

'Explain yourself,' he commanded.

His tone awakened something hot within me. 'Explain what, exactly?' I snapped. 'That I saved your life *again*, in far worse circumstances than the last time? Look at me – look at *you!*' I gestured to our bloodied bodies, the stained, damning sheets. 'Not another soul in this world could have brought you back from the grievous state I discovered you in. Perhaps instead of interrogation, you should try thanking me.'

I had never seen a look so wrathful from him. The glow of fury in his eyes could have tempered steel.

'Why did you do it?' I asked. 'And don't say *being in my captivity*. Until a moment ago, you didn't know who held you, and being a prisoner hasn't troubled you at all.'

'What is it to you?' he snarled.

I laughed, but it was a brittle thing. For once, I was too tired to get much pleasure out of sparring with him.

'What is it to *you?*' I replied. 'You are loved and respected, and stand beside a king who adores your very bones, blind to all your sins. You have prowess, accolades, peers who would die for you. What is it about your charmed life that is so agonising?'

I expected a burst of outrage, but my words seemed to freeze inside of him. He glanced down at his hands, twisting bloody around the ruined linen.

'You don't know what it's like,' he said.

His voice was low, and he looked so suddenly lost it struck every retort from my tongue. To stare danger in the eye and keep surviving had always been his greatest skill, but he shrunk from it now, the weight of his sadness like a bull's heart in my hands, huge and cold and heavy. *Why have you given this to me, of all people?* I thought.

I sighed and let my need for answers go. Despite everything, I did not wish to see him this way.

'Lancelot, how long have we known one another?' I said. 'You should realise by now that I am never going to let you die. Your fate doesn't end within these walls.'

He seemed to take in, and then accept the notion, pushing himself up to sit straighter. 'How did you get here in time? Have you been spying on me?'

'No,' I said truthfully. 'Only once before I have come here at night, to see what you were painting. Otherwise I have kept away.'

'Then why come tonight?' he asked.

'I received some bad news and was angry,' I replied. 'At the accepted world and its self-righteousness, the false, barbaric tenets you and your knightly brothers live by. At your paintings of Camelot, daubed all over my walls. I wanted to destroy something.'

He nodded as if he understood. 'What news?'

'My sister is dead,' I replied. 'Killed in haste and violence by her own son. Put to the sword by those who should have loved her – knights of supposed honour.'

His eyes flashed, and I braced myself for his inevitable justification of whatever knightly purpose stood behind such a heinous act.

Instead, he sighed and spoke with a rare softness. 'I'm sorry. No one should have to lose family that way.'

'Thank you,' I replied, and meant it. I considered him anew, still pale from blood loss, propped against the bedhead, his skin marked red from his duel with death. His healing blood meant he carried no scars, but the mark of his pain would remain somewhere, written deep beneath flesh and bone.

'Is it me, who has done this to you?' I asked. 'Is it this captivity for which you want to end your life?'

'No,' he replied. 'My actions have only ever been driven by what resides within me. My own great weaknesses.'

As always, his candour played a chord in my chest. 'There is still much might left in you,' I said. 'Isn't it said Sir Lancelot du Lac has the strength of ten men?'

'I do not speak of my body or sword arm, but my mind – my soul ...' Just as quickly, his eyes went flat, as if I had ceased to exist. 'Never mind. It is not in you to know the truth of me.'

His sudden coldness stung in a way I didn't expect. 'My God, you never stop, do you?' I said fiercely. 'Pretending all we share is the conflict of your virtue and my corruption, when we have journeyed far beyond that. I know things of you that you don't even know yourself. Of wonders within your own body. *Miracles* running through your veins.'

The word sharpened his gaze. 'What do you mean?'

'There is healing in your blood,' I said. 'Restorative powers, natural and strong, lying dormant within you because you never understood. Only I can feel what you have.'

He frowned and held up his red-streaked hands. 'In my blood? All my life, I have been this way?'

'Probably,' I said. 'You said that you heal faster than most and rarely scar. However long that has been true, your blood has been the reason.'

'Lady Ninianne never told me of such a thing,' he countered. 'She has far greater powers than you.'

'She does, though not in physic or healing,' I replied. 'She sensed the same affinity in me when we first met, but could not discern what the feeling meant.'

He sighed in slight annoyance. 'I suppose you will tell me next that only you can show me how to use this ... talent. Except you would not, because it is in your interest to have me weakened like this.'

'That's not true, and beneath you to suggest it,' I said. 'If you had not woken, I would have healed you as much as I could. Whatever has gone between us, if we are to do battle, I do not want you weak, Lancelot. I never have.'

His stern, beautiful face lit with surprise, then an emotion I found hard to read.

'So what now?' he murmured. 'If I am to be fully restored, I must let you ...'

I shook my head. 'I will not lay hands if it causes you discomfort. You are recovered enough that you can heal naturally in a week or two. Or, if you want to be restored more quickly, you have the power to do so.'

'Heal myself?' he exclaimed, and I nodded. Lancelot regarded me in wonder, then dropped his eyes. 'I wouldn't know where to begin.'

I considered him briefly, then looked out at the shadowy chamber, candles burning low, the night turning its gaze away. Anything was possible here, in the forgiving half-dark.

'I can show you,' I said, opening my palms. 'Give me your hands.'

Lancelot looked up at me from under dark lashes. With slow decision, he offered himself up, and lay his hands on mine. His blood across our shared skin was a heavenly chorus in my senses.

I slid my fingers up to encircle his wrists, where his pulse thudded hardest. 'Close your eyes,' I said. 'Gather your mind, and focus on the rhythms within your body, the flow of light where the source of life lies. When you find it, you will know.'

I let my own lids flutter shut, feeling his concentration tighten as he drew into himself, seeking what I had told him. His muscles tensed under my touch, skin prickling with heat, the untrained power of his healing rising to the encouragement of my own golden force.

Gradually, I felt him grow stronger within, then the rush of his affinity came faster, his blood surging in replenishment, internal damage receding until it was no more. In its wake came a burst of glorious fortitude, his power of ten men returned.

Lancelot snatched a hard breath as his exhilaration swept through me, the innate knowledge of healing to fulfilment. I smiled in satisfaction and opened my eyes.

For the second time that night, he was already looking at me, eyes glittering like diamonds. When he moved, it felt as though time slowed; he lifted a hand and trailed his fingertips along my jaw, drawing my face closer. Before my mind could decide what was best, Lancelot reached out, I leaned in to his touch, and he was kissing me.

It was different to how I had imagined it, his mouth yielding against mine in a warm, tentative caress, once, twice, three times. I expected realisation, retreat, but none came, and his touch grew bolder, his kiss searching, hungry, fingers pushing into my hair, then entwined at the nape of my neck. Though it was impossible, he tasted like honey.

Still I waited for his mind to change, but in a swift movement his arms were around me, sweeping my body closer with the ease of his renewed strength. I let myself be taken as he pulled me atop him, my hands at his face, his throat, trailing down to the carved relief of his back, our embrace fervent and abandoned in a way I had only ever envisioned alone in the depths of the night. When he reached up and pushed my robe from my shoulders, I knew then he wouldn't cease; that here, now, he wanted this as much as I had.

Pulling myself away, I caught his hair in my fingers and tugged his head back, so he would see me clearly and understand what this meant for us.

'You have enough regrets,' I said. 'I refuse to be another.'

Lancelot looked up at me, eyes wild and gleaming, a fallen saint glorying in his fate. With a roll of his neck, he twisted free of my grip and kissed me again, a definitive answer.

I could do it, I thought, so easily. I could lay him down and bind us together, amidst his singing blood and the shadows and our furious connection. What we could become together, the potential that could rise from our pleasure and complexities felt limitless, ferocious, a force fit to extinguish the stars.

But that's what we were – an incendiary collision, an abyss, two weapons clashing in sparks. Lancelot did not love me, nor I him, in any way beyond our inner damage. Real love was light, where he and I resided in darkness, our desire mixed with the urge to tear the other apart. However bright we burned, our fascination did not make us fit for one another.

I let myself taste him for two more heartbeats, then arched my body upright and took my mouth from his. Immediately, he reached for me again, but I held myself at bay and put a hand to his blood-streaked, impossible face.

'You are not a faithless knight,' I said.

I watched the words sink into him, invoking the memory of another time, a moment where we had stood on a precipice, and he had chosen who he wished to be.

His hands softened on my waist, so I gathered my willpower and slipped free of his arms. I perched on the edge of the mattress, coursing with want and the soaring song between his blood and mine. Lancelot shifted out of the bed and sat alongside me, his breath still slowing from the intensity of our embrace.

'Was that …?' he began. 'Was I …?' He put his hand to his forehead. 'The thought of doing something unwanted—'

'Of course not,' I cut in. 'It wasn't … unwelcome. Just inadvisable, for us both. I have been to bed with men I did not much know – it's not difficult. But you and I know each other too well, in a way. Nothing good can come of what is so …'

'Tangled,' he concluded with a brief, melancholic smile.

'Something like that.'

We sat for a long moment, still looking at one another. Our peace grew into a pause, then a question; another choice. It was no good, staying like this; for our shared sickness, there was only one cure.

I stood up from the bed and walked towards the door.

'Wait,' Lancelot called after me. I stopped and looked back. 'Don't go.'

'I have to, don't you see?' I replied. 'The way we are, this game we play that we cannot seem to bring to an end – it is bad for us. It always has been.'

He shook his head. 'I don't care. You saved my life, told me about myself. This night cannot be over.'

Slowly, he got to his feet, approaching with delicacy, as if afraid I would fly away. It didn't matter; I was captured, a moth to a flame. When he reached me, his shadow enveloped my body like fine dark silk.

'Please,' he said. 'Stay.'

38

For a moment, his words were exhilarating.

In all of our time together, he had never asked something of me in this way, with such simplicity, its subtle chord of need, and the sound charmed, as if it were a spell of my own making. I could not tear my eyes from his face. Nor could I afford to forget myself.

'And what if I do want to stay,' I said. 'Say I heeded you and did not go – what then? Why, now, in the depths of your heart, do you ask this of me?'

I was not powerless, I knew that, just as I knew this had to come to an end. Yet if Lancelot moved to draw me back to him, I wasn't certain I could resist us a second time.

But, in his unpredictable way, he had heard my voice and decided to save us both. He stepped back and held up acquiescent hands.

'Not for that reason, I swear it,' he said. 'We have parted and so we will remain. But just … stay until dawn has broken. There is so much more to say.'

The light in his eyes, too, had changed – no longer bright with hunger, but beseeching, needful of a different type of connection.

'How can there be?' I asked, but it was more curiosity than dismissal. 'Until dawn, then. Not a moment beyond.'

He sighed in relief. 'I will never ask anything more of you. First, let me wash and put on a shirt and clean breeches.'

Mutely, I nodded, and he retreated to the washstand at the back of the room. I went to the nearest window and sat down inside the embrasure, taking in the deep twilight beyond my reflection. In the chamber, I listened to the splash of water poured into a bowl, the hiss of skin on skin as Lancelot scrubbed his blood away. Soon came the whisper of cloth as he dressed in the clean shirt and breeches Tressa left for him daily. I heard the chime of a chain as he hung Guinevere's emerald back around his neck.

His footsteps padded closer, but he never appeared before me. I reached out with my senses and discerned him through several feet of stone, settling in the window seat just behind, until we were seated back-to-back.

'May I ask you a question?'

The deep, clear voice prickled at the nape of my neck; now cleansed, he sounded like himself again.

'Of course,' I replied.

'The gold coin you always wear,' he said. 'Why?'

'For the same reason you wear that emerald ring. It means a great deal to me.' I drew out the Gaulish coin and clasped it in my palm. 'We are all carrying something.'

He sighed, and I felt it as feathers across my skin.

'How long have you known?' he asked. 'That I have healing blood.'

'Some time. Since we first met, almost.'

I expected a burst of temper, but there came only more pensive quiet. I resisted the impulse to seek his face and see what was written there.

Eventually, he said. 'Why didn't you tell me before?'

'Would you have wanted to hear it?' I countered. 'From me, of all people?'

He considered it awhile. 'No, I would not,' he said slowly. 'Back then, at least. Now, I am grateful.'

That his unguardedness still had the power to jolt my heart was both a revelation and completely expected. Lancelot's unpredictability would always carry a thrill.

'Nevertheless, I should have told you earlier,' I said. 'It wasn't my secret to keep.'

I felt his pause, his nod of acceptance. Then, quietly, 'You called it a miracle.'

'It is,' I said. 'In its potential, at least.'

'Then what does it mean for me?'

'I cannot say, beyond it being the reason you heal quickly from your injuries. I have not much observed you in the outside world.'

'It's your own skill, is it not?' Lancelot said. 'I could tell you how a man might improve his jousting without facing him down myself.'

'But you cannot tell how good a rider he is without seeing him ahorse,' I pointed out. 'Without teaching you, I can only advise from a general point of view. Use what I have already shown you, open your mind to your senses, and go from there.'

A tremor of impatience reached me; he was so used to being good at everything, he could not imagine needing to learn from a position of absolute deficiency.

'Is that what you wanted – to teach me?' he said, a slight tension in his voice. 'To induct me into your ways?'

'I did once, maybe. I wanted to enlighten you, expand your mind, bend you until you viewed the world a different way. Amongst other things.'

'And now?'

'Now, I am done with that.'

I turned my face back to the window. Outside, a sliver of gold had just broached the horizon. Dawn: we were almost concluded. 'But know this,' I added. 'You are more than Camelot allows you to be.'

The word, the place it conjured, hung between us, invasive but unavoidable.

'Even if that's true, it doesn't matter,' Lancelot replied. 'I need nothing more – nor should anyone else. King Arthur built Camelot in honour and hope, for the sake of the greater good. A future where anything is possible.'

'I know,' I said. 'I was there when it began.'

'Yes, and at one time, it was all you wanted too,' he said. 'To stand beside your brother, fighting for his ideals as I do. It is well known.'

'I don't deny it,' I replied. 'Yet unlike you, it was never so simple as falling in love with Camelot's promises, or following my own noble purpose.'

It silenced him for a while, so I watched the light creep up the sky and did not try to sense what he was thinking.

Eventually, he asked, 'What was it like? In those early days?'

'I believed in it,' I said. 'Camelot's ways weren't perfect – what means of government is? But I supported the possibilities because of Arthur.

I thought if he could accept the complications of life beyond the boundaries Merlin had given him, then he could do anything. I loved him – we loved and trusted one another.'

'But you left,' Lancelot said. 'You walked away from the King, his vision, the privilege you held. All of it. You chose yourself above the greater good.'

It wasn't quite a condemnation, but the heat of irritation crept under my skin. 'I never said it was easy to leave,' I said tersely. 'The fact I didn't return – the *reason* I couldn't – is none of your business. My brother made mistakes, I made them – none of that can be undone. Perfect, unquestioning loyalty is impossible, but who knows that better than you?'

I felt him tense beyond the wall; I had dared mention what he had painted so fervently, but refused to ever speak aloud. 'I love King Arthur more than any man on God's earth,' he said. 'Whatever you believe, I will not have my dedication to him questioned. Many things can be true at once, even if they are sometimes opposing.'

There, he had caught me; I could not argue with my own belief in complexity.

'Precisely,' I said. 'Hence, I once wanted my life at Arthur's side, but I was wronged and no one would accept it, so I chose exile. I chose love and freedom, whereas you are too enraptured to break away. The Camelot you can't escape, I have let go.'

Lancelot gave a grim laugh. 'Do not fool yourself. You came here tonight to strike my paintings off the wall because you cannot bear to be reminded. No doubt I was taken captive because King Arthur sent you away for good. You have sought vengeance upon Camelot for years because you cannot abandon the connection with the life you lost.'

It smarted like a whip lash, but I would not yield. 'The reason I will keep seeking vengeance upon Camelot is because my brother murdered the man I loved.'

A sudden silence fell between us, heavy and unexpected. It lasted so long it began to weigh on me like a steel hauberk, as if I were a duelling knight and du Lac stood opposite with his sword drawn. For the first time in my life, I was about to get up, leave, abandon this fight, when his voice came, low and serious.

'No, he did not,' Lancelot said. 'There was no murder.'

His opening strike took the wind out of me, but I withstood him.

'I'm sure you'd call it "God-given justice",' I spat. 'It's all the same lie.'

'Indeed not,' he insisted. 'The act you punish him for, King Arthur is not guilty of. I know what plagues him, everything he blames on himself – about you, your breach, your knightly lover. The beliefs which you have built your vengeance upon are not true.'

My fury, already smouldering in my belly, caught alight. 'I've told you, tread this route with care,' I said dangerously. 'You don't know where this began. You were not a speck of mud on the mantle of Camelot when it did.'

'Yet you believe it,' he said. 'I can hear it in your voice. You *feel* when I am telling you the truth. Because, for our sins, I know you, Morgan le Fay, and you know me.'

Full dawn or not, our game was over. I swept out of the window seat, only to find Lancelot standing in my way, his aspect blazing and extraordinary.

'I don't have to listen to this,' I said. 'This is not confession, and I couldn't be further from your priest.'

He stood unmoved. 'If everyone deserves the truth, then so do you,' he said. 'You have never once thought beyond your convictions, or considered you are not the only one who suffers. That your brother grieves what you grieve, and always has.'

'Where do you get the gall to speak to me about my brother, as if you care for his heart, or are loyal to him?' I snarled. 'You are adulterous with his wife, for God's sake. If he could accept the truth, he would hate you far more than he has ever hated me.'

Lancelot drew up to his tremendous stature, hardening until he looked carved from marble, a towering sculpture of a god on some distant mountain.

'You think you know it all, don't you?' he said. 'About me, about her – about Camelot. About Arthur and how it is between us. Somehow, you are *so certain* you understand everything, when you do not even know the truth of your own life.'

'Do not concern yourself with my life,' I said. 'I know myself, my purpose, and everything that's been done to me.'

He leaned forwards, his eyes clear as winter stars.

'No, Morgan le Fay, you do not,' he said. 'But for the truth you gave me, this I will give you in return. If you really want to know who you are, face your failures, your deepest pain, and seek the whole story.'

I felt it then, as his words struck my body – this was not goading or punishment, or trying to win. Lancelot was being honest. And I was not ready to admit I could hear him.

'Who are you to tell me what I should do?' I snapped. 'When you cannot face what your endless cycle of honour and dishonour has made of you. If I have been living a lie, then you are a heathen far worse.'

Lancelot didn't flinch. 'So be it,' he said. 'But I stand by my word. *Listen to me.*'

There was nothing I could say, no magic that could defeat him, no argument that could force him to withdraw the offering he was determined to sling upon my altar. Much as I wanted to deny Lancelot du Lac, he would never yield. Nor was he lying.

I glared at him, the morning light carving his figure into its brooding archangel form. His blood sang out to mine even from within the pulse in his neck, calling me towards temptation and destruction. It took all of my strength not to let us claw at one another until we were both covered in scars.

'You are a ghost,' I said, and walked away.

39

There was nowhere for me to go but back up to the lake.

I made the journey faster than usual, until my breaths seared in my chest with the satisfaction of pain. *Grief and rage, rage and grief,* I was made of nothing else.

I stopped at the water's edge, lungs raw and gasping. Up here, the morning light was just broaching the cusp of the valley, a crescent of pale gold reflected across the blue.

'Morgan?' Accolon stepped out from the willow's shadow. One look at my face and he knew. 'What's happened?'

'I am sick of it, sick of it all,' I said. 'How will any of us be free while that place still casts its great shadow?'

I charged past him beneath the leaves, pacing back and forth, swallowing tears. I had never been this way before him. I came to the lake to unyoke myself from the world, not carrying it on my back like Atlas's burden. We didn't speak of Camelot for this very reason.

'Am I wrong?' I went on. 'All this time – was I wrong about everything?'

'Mon cœur,' he said patiently, 'if we are to get anywhere, you will have to give me a clue, at least.'

His easy tone calmed me and I looked at him; in the shade he looked almost tangible. New anger sliced through my body like a longsword, that this had all begun with his brutal, unnecessary death, only for me to do worse by refusing to accept he was gone. My efforts to spare us from sorrow had only led to yet more catastrophe.

Face your failures, your deepest pain, Lancelot's hard voice echoed back to me. *Seek the whole story.*

'Do you know how you died?' I asked.

'Yes,' Accolon said slowly. 'Why?'

The answer stuck in my throat, but I managed, 'Could you bear to speak of it?'

He moved closer, his proximity thrilling through me as always, followed by the bone-deep agony of it never being enough.

'Of course,' he said softly. 'It is just another part of my story. I can show you, if you want me to.'

Again, the thought struck with dread resistance, but I had gone as far as I could without facing my greatest fear. Accolon's death was the very last thing he and I had not shared; our final intimacy.

'Show me,' I told him.

In one stride he was with me and I was taken, swept away from our lake and the present moment, until I felt a change in the air. When I opened my eyes, I was standing in a meadow under a blazing summer morning. A buzzard flew overhead, giving its eerie, echoing scream.

I looked around to see a small, shabby keep and half-walled town in the near distance, a scattering of people and horses lining the field. Nothing was familiar.

'Where are you?' I said, but Accolon did not stand beside me as he usually did. I was alone.

Then I heard voices, emanating from a red-and-yellow knight's tent pitched just behind. I edged inside to find two men in conversation. Neither stirred at my entrance – here, I was the shade, an intangible, invisible presence outside of time.

I saw my Gaul first, stood in full armour not his own, helm under his arm. Excalibur's scabbard hung at his hip with his sword within, though the pommel was wrapped in brown leather, concealing the silver horse. He looked strong, poised, his face drawn grave.

My heart jolted to see him that way – handsome and alive, immersed in the serious side of his knightly life. Accolon of the past: ready for battle in this mean, frayed tent, unaware of how his day – and his world – would end.

An unkempt man in lordly clothes stood before him, wringing his hands. 'You are our only hope,' he pleaded. 'This village of good souls has been besieged by attacks from my brother for months. He will not stop until he lays us all to waste, unless a knight skilled enough answers the duel he has demanded.'

Accolon placed a hand on the stranger's shoulder. 'Have no fear,' he said. 'I will answer your brother's challenge and prove victorious. The people will be saved.'

'God's blood,' I whispered, closing my eyes. Had a few simple words been all it had taken? How then did Arthur come into it?

I did not have to wait for an answer. When I opened my eyes again, I found myself back outside in the meadow, standing on the edge of a crowd. At one end, Accolon sat helmed upon a borrowed horse, lance couched and ready.

At the other end sat his opponent, also wearing a narrow-visored helmet and his sword hilt concealed. It didn't matter; I would have recognised the imperious set of his shoulders anywhere.

Arthur, carrying Excalibur.

Before I could begin to fathom how this contest came to be, a shout was made, a makeshift flag thrown down. The duellists spurred their mounts and headed for one another.

Two lances shattered on impact, shards of ash spraying into the air. The violence of the joust charge was unlike anything I had ever seen, both knights unseated by the other's blow. They landed on the ground with bone-crunching impact, their steeds galloping off in shock.

Accolon was first to his feet, but when he turned, I saw the jagged end of Arthur's lance buried in his side, below the ribcage. He glanced down at the injury, then as if it were nothing, put his armoured hand around the splintered end and tugged it out of his flesh.

I yelped, a physician's horror at the careless removal, but the sound echoed into nowhere. Accolon touched his split mail in astonishment; the spear wound was not bleeding, due to the scabbard's power. I felt the shiver of his confusion, his astonishment at his luck. I had only ever told him to keep the scabbard close, not what it could do.

His wonder was cut short by Arthur, charging at him with Excalibur ablaze. Drawing his sword, Accolon parried at speed, staving off blows and landing hard counter strikes, drawing blood. Furious, my brother lost focus, swinging too wildly, with a force that would daunt a lesser fighter, but Accolon knew how to exploit.

An hour passed, then another, and still they fought. Arthur was all but spent, staggering the field and bleeding profusely. Any other knight would have already fallen many times, but my brother had always contained more strength than most men on their best days.

Accolon remained unharmed, unable to shed blood and constantly restored by the scabbard's healing power. I could feel Arthur's frustration, his disbelief. He was trying his hardest, a legendary warrior getting nowhere, and he was not used to it.

In a ferocious effort, he took an ungainly swing at Accolon's helm. My Gaul swung up to meet the flailing sword with two-handed strength, and Excalibur flew out of Arthur's hands, landing several yards away.

The loss of his sword only enraged my brother more. With just his body left as a weapon, he shrugged his shield up and charged. Caught unawares, Accolon managed to batter him back with his blade, grabbing hold of the shield with his free hand.

'Stop,' he said. 'I have fought many men and you are the most valiant by far, but you cannot endure much longer.'

Arthur growled and tried to pull free. 'I can endure for however long is needed. I'm as strong as I was when we began.'

Their voices were muffled beneath their confining helms, unrecognisable to one another, but I could hear them as clear as if they stood beside me.

'Listen to me,' Accolon insisted. 'I don't wish to kill you. You have no sword. Yield now, good Sir Knight, and I will insist the brothers arrange a peace that suits us both. For your honour and mine.'

'I will *never* yield,' Arthur snapped. 'I would rather die a hundred times than act the coward you want me to be.'

With a furious burst of strength, he tore the shield away and lunged forwards again, slamming his entire weight into Accolon's chest. Accolon just about kept his footing as Arthur immediately made another ferocious charge. He missed and Accolon landed a swooping strike to the gut, gouging through his mail.

Arthur buckled, gasping for breath. Blood ran from him like rainfall, pooling in the polished rings of his mail and spattering across the dented shield.

Even with hindsight his stubbornness looked foolish, the defeat he refused to accept. Yet I knew that his sheer determination would once again mean victory in a situation that seemed impossible. Here, in microcosm, was my brother's reign, his rise to power, the undaunted courage and strength which had made him the most formidable High King that Britain had ever seen.

And as I watched him defy the terrible predicament he was in, I felt only understanding. How many times had I been caught in a similar trap – my weapons taken, the opposition stacked against me, resistance seeming futile – and forged on regardless? I had fought just as hard, and in worse ways, to survive. My brother and I charged towards trouble with our tempers blazing and impossibilities damned: it was everything that had once bonded us, and had driven us apart.

Arthur landed hard on one knee, panting as if he was ready to give in, then roared, *'I do not yield!'* and wrenched back to his feet. He parried one, two, three blows with his shield, but it was splitting like a tree beneath an axe.

My mind spun with confusion. Under no circumstance could this duel end without Accolon striking the killing blow. Arthur was riven with blood loss, Excalibur lay in the grass too far away; even with his strength of twenty nothing could help him.

Accolon raised his longsword high, a slow arc of silver carving through the air, about to change everything.

So anchored was I to the battle that I did not at first notice that Accolon's sword had halted, along with the gesturing crowd, while Arthur still struggled to his feet. Nor did I spot the vision of white and violet, approaching ever faster like a swooping dove.

Ninianne. I had forgotten about her.

She arrived on a pearl-bright horse, her arms already sweeping through the air, pushing, resisting, and I knew she was holding time at bay. Marshalling her magic in one hand, she dismounted and snatched up Excalibur, rushing over to Arthur.

'My lord,' she said breathlessly. 'You will live, but quickly, take this.'

She helped him to his feet, and handed him his famed sword. Arthur staggered under the pain of his injuries.

'What good is it, when God has forsaken me?' he protested. 'My opponent has fought well, but I have struck him as much as he has me. *Why does he not bleed?'*

Ninianne looked down at the jewelled sheath that Arthur wore, then back to the blue-and-white miracle at Accolon's belt. I felt realisation travel through her body, entire fates contained within a single moment.

'Excalibur's scabbard,' she said. 'Did you ever tell anyone of its secrets?'

'My sister,' he replied. 'I entrusted her with Excalibur's care and she hid both objects. But I found them, together …'

Ninianne was already shaking her head. 'Your opponent wears the scabbard,' she said. 'Yours is a counterfeit. You have been deceived.'

'*Morgan* did this?' he exclaimed.

Ninianne didn't reply, wincing as the world juddered, the cords of her muscles straining against time's fight to right itself.

'My lord, we must leave,' she urged. 'You are injured, and the magic will not hold much longer.'

'No,' my brother said. 'I have never surrendered in my life and won't start now.'

He lurched to his feet with just enough opportunity to tear the scabbard from Accolon's belt and fling it out of reach, as time defeated magic and the world's awareness rushed back into place. Accolon's sword strike continued to fall, and Arthur ducked away, blocking the blow with a raised Excalibur.

Accolon recoiled; when he had begun, his opponent hadn't even been holding a sword. Again I felt his confusion as a shiver across my skin, and something else for the first time: the hot tide of pain.

My brother surged forwards, raining blows that Accolon barely had time to defend. A brutal strike to the gut winded him, and he fell to his knees, clutching his belly.

Arthur pointed Excalibur at his chest. 'Now *you* yield. Admit you are a traitor.'

'I'm no traitor,' Accolon replied. 'You may kill me, but I will never surrender with those words. I—'

Something stopped him, and he looked down at his arm, still gripping his middle. Gradually, he lifted his hand away. His gauntlet came away the darkest red.

'No!' I cried.

I rushed onto the battlefield – to lay hands, make it stop before it began. I could hear their hard breaths, smell the scent of blood on steel, but I swept through both figures as if they were stardust.

And then, inevitably, Accolon began to bleed.

Every wound he had sustained poured forth at once, spilling through his shredded mail. Immediately, he fell, collapsing onto his side, blood soaking the grass as if he was drowning in a sea of red. I stood helpless, shocked at the volume of it, the amount of life his body held, now seeping away into the earth.

Arthur towered above him, taking a dagger from his belt. Leaning forward, he tugged at Accolon's helm under the chin, and for a horrific moment I thought he was going to cut his throat – vicious, unknightly, the stuff of criminals and madmen. Instead, Arthur slashed the helm's laces and sheathed the knife.

'Before you yield, I will hear your confession, then give you a swift, merciful death,' he said. 'Prepare to make your peace with God.'

In a clean movement, he pulled the helmet off. Accolon's mail coif was up, his face bloodied and battered, half turned towards the rucked-up ground.

'Who are you?' Arthur demanded.

Accolon coughed, spitting blood into the dirt. With great effort, he heaved back onto his elbows, pushed his mail hood down and looked his vanquisher in the eye.

'I am Sir Accolon of Gaul,' he said hoarsely. 'A knight of King Arthur's court.'

It was as if time had slowed again, though this had nothing to do with Ninianne. The High King fell to his knees with a crash.

'Accolon? My God, it is you.' My brother tore his own helm from his head and revealed his golden, bloodied face. 'It's me, Arthur. If I had known, I—'

The crowd cried out at the unexpected sight of their King. Accolon's eyes widened. 'My lord,' he managed to utter, as a tremendous pain took hold. He grasped at his body, groaning in such deep agony it reverberated through my bones.

Arthur pulled off both of their gauntlets and took Accolon's bare hand. 'It's all right,' he murmured in soothing tones. 'You are strong. This will pass.'

My brother looked up, wild-eyed, beckoning to Ninianne at the edge of the duelling ground. She came to his side, her light dimmed and trembling.

'How could this happen?' he said. 'Just yesterday, we were hunting in the woods. How didn't I know it was him?'

She stooped beside Arthur, her voice barely controlled. 'Where did you get your scabbard, Sir Knight?'

Accolon squinted at her gleam. 'She ... gave it to me,' he said hoarsely. 'Morgan ... of Cornwall.'

The name by which he had first known me landed as an arrow in my heart. Ninianne stepped back, aghast.

'My sister gave you the scabbard?' Arthur exclaimed. 'But how ... why? Did she tell you to kill me?'

'No!' Accolon's voice was suddenly clear, his vehemence giving him strength. 'Nor would I agree to such a thing. Morgan ... told me to keep it close so I would be ... safe. She and I have loved one another these long years ... as much as two hearts can.'

Another attack of pain took hold and Accolon collapsed back onto the grass. 'Forgive me ...' he gasped. 'If I had known ... I never would have fought ... you.'

'Nor would I.' My brother's voice was full of tears. 'I forgive you, Accolon, but most of all you must forgive me. You are my knight – my friend. Never for a moment would I have wished to do you harm.'

Accolon nodded, attempting to speak, but the words emerged as a hard cough. He reared up, hacking violently, and a gush of blood came out of his mouth. There was nothing I could do except watch it happen.

'No, no, no.' My brother took Accolon's head in his hands, holding him steady. 'Save your strength. You will survive this – I swear it. God will spare you and me both.'

'My lord,' Ninianne said. 'You are badly wounded. There is an abbey nearby with an infirmary, but we must hurry.'

Arthur looked up at her. 'Good. We will both go there to be tended.'

Ninianne glanced at Accolon, her light draining until she was almost haggard. 'There is no time, my lord. You must sit on the back of my horse and we will ride as fast as we can. This knight would not want to delay us.'

'His name is Sir Accolon of Gaul,' Arthur said fiercely. 'He is good and honourable and did not deserve this. I will see him healed alongside me.'

'Your Highness,' Ninianne pleaded. 'It is no use. Sir Accolon is …'

'I won't hear it!' Arthur shouted, but his voice was laced with fear.

A bloodied hand gripped my brother's arm. Arthur held it, helping Accolon hoist himself up into a sitting position. His eyes shone midnight, bright beyond his pain.

'You must tell her,' my Gaul said. 'Le Fay. She is my life, my heart. She must know how much I love her. Take the news to Belle Garde.'

'Hold fast to your strength,' Arthur urged. 'You will tell her so yourself.'

He held him close, insisting that he was strong enough, that he would live to recount this tale for years if he could just stay with him. But it was far too late, the red lake around Accolon too deep to ever let him rise again. He let go of my brother's hand and lay back on the grass, exhaling beneath the ghost of a smile.

'Morgan,' he said, and closed his eyes.

With his dying breath, he spoke your name.

Through the endless circle of time, I felt part of myself vanish with him.

'No,' Arthur said tremulously. 'It cannot be.' He put his hands to Accolon's face, searching for signs of life, then clutched him to his chest. 'Bring me a horse bier!' he roared to the frozen crowd. 'He will be saved. Bring me a bier *now!*'

Stunned, I watched the tears run down my brother's blood-streaked face, as he shouted and bled and raged even as he weakened, pushing away Ninianne's exhortations to leave. I ran towards him, but the ground dissolved beneath me, the crowd fading to a blur, the crumbling castle fading into the sky.

There was a rush of cool air, then darkness fell, engulfing me in a sudden, profound night. A figure glimmered across the expanse of black. Accolon in outline, translucent with stars.

'Not yet!' I protested. 'I need to see more.'

'I died, Morgan,' he said. 'For me, that's all there was.'

He came closer, his face tender, rueful, but we were still far apart. Of everything we had endured, the fact I couldn't put my arms around him in that moment seemed the greatest cruelty of all.

'All this time ... I didn't know,' I sobbed. 'How could I not know?'

I put my hands over my face and felt the salt heat of tears already there. How long I had been crying I could not remember, but I let them come now, the cloud inside of me finally bursting into a storm, bringing a rain that might never stop.

'Mon cœur,' I heard Accolon say, but the sound faded, his form waning, exhausted by the intricacy of the memory.

I looked up for one last comforting glimpse of him, but my Gaul was gone and Llyn Glas had returned, leaving only the echo of his voice and his silver-gold essence scattered across the water.

40

It took a moment for reality to come flying back.

My senses ground to a halt, scrambling to readjust between where I stood now and the lingering vision until my thoughts felt blurred, exhausted. Staggering back, I put a hand against the willow trunk and drew a deep breath, taking in the rasp of bark against my fingers, the lake's quiet lapping of the shore, and the scent of sweet, dewy grass.

It was no good; the entire world had been turned inside out. Accolon's death rushed back in vivid detail: the clashing metal and growls of effort; the mutual shock as he and Arthur discovered who they had been fighting; my brother's desperate call for a bier, trying to undo what he had done. Arthur cradling my Gaul's dying body, insisting they be saved together, risking himself. The blood; so much blood.

To my losses, it meant nothing, but against the darkness I had lived inside, it was a sliver of light, threading through my cracked heart. My brother had not killed Accolon out of spite, or even intentionally. Nor did Accolon lie in the abbey, alive and in agony for four days, awaiting my healing. He was already dead. I never could have saved him.

Accolon's death at my brother's hand wasn't a rageful, unjust act of war upon his estranged sister – it was an outright, devastating mistake.

Why Arthur claimed he had murdered his knight and friend as my punishment, I did not know. To wear such cruelty when he was innocent, while carrying his guilt and grief, was so far beyond what my brother had led me to believe that everything I had learned seemed suddenly inefficient, a bare accounting at best. I didn't know anywhere near enough.

I looked out across the lake, now under an afternoon like any other. Rich sunlight danced off the water like diamonds, mingling with

Accolon's essence. After the length and intensity of the vision, it would be several days before he reappeared.

Regardless, he could not tell me more. Accolon only had knowledge of what occurred up until the moment of his death, not why my brother had chosen to seal our fate with a different story, nor what he lived with in private. This life-altering truth had been given to me by another, one who observed what came after. He who had seen the scars within Arthur and myself and offered what now felt like an act of mercy.

And I had to know why, even if it meant admitting he was right.

Now, more than ever, I needed to see Lancelot.

The scene when I reached the long chamber was not as I expected. For one, the doors were wide open. Secondly, Alys and Tressa were inside, but Lancelot was nowhere to be seen.

'You're back, thank goodness,' Alys said. 'There's been ... a happening.'

I looked around the room. The bloodstained sheets had been stripped from the bed, but it was otherwise free of signs of disruption.

'Sir Lancelot is gone,' Tressa clarified. 'Escaped this morning. Left the house and took his horse while the stable boys were distracted.'

'Escaped?' I echoed. 'But how? He was locked fast – utterly secure.'

'Apparently not,' she replied. 'He never was.'

She gestured at one of the barred windows nearest the courtyard door. Or at least it *had* been barred. Now it was bare, the iron struts torn free and discarded as if they were kindling. I picked one up and it was solid, without fault, just unable to withstand Lancelot's incredible determination.

'Where the Devil did he get the strength?' I said.

The two other fortified windows were still intact, but in the illumination of day, there was something amiss: the slightest bowing in the iron bars in the middle embrasure, where it had been tested, then left alone.

For his entire captivity, Lancelot had been aware that he could escape, and had chosen not to.

I turned to the wall of paintings facing the bed, where he had sketched the death I had snatched him back from, the trail of painted blood stark as stigmata in the sunlight.

Now it struck me, in the echo of his absence, what he had done. Lancelot's revelation in our final, heated exchange was not argument – it was a reply, a settlement; an oath repaid. In sharing my own honesty – about my brother, Camelot, in telling him of his miracle blood – I had given him the key to himself, so he had given me the same.

You know me, he had said, *and I know you.* In kinship, Lancelot had recognised the grief, fury and deathless love that made Morgan le Fay, and honoured our night-dark bond with the truth I most needed. He had set me free.

'Where do you think he's gone?' Tressa asked.

'I know where,' I replied. 'He's gone back.'

Back to Camelot: to her, his Guinevere, and Arthur, his King, the woman and the man he loved best. He could not be made whole any other way.

I accepted it then, suddenly, completely: that for Lancelot to submit to his heart, to bestow his entire self upon those he loved, was his own form of freedom. Whatever I did not understand about the three of them, I never would. It was not mine to know.

'Take the tapestries from the old Great Chamber,' I said. 'Hang them over the paintings until everything is covered.'

Tressa nodded and hurried off, leaving Alys and me looking at the longest wall, full of colour and skill; the great du Lac's lengthy confession.

'What about him?' Alys asked.

'Let him go,' I said. 'Sir Lancelot does not belong here.'

Eighteen months he had been at Belle Garde, and there would be no resolution to what suddenly made him leave. More than that, I never knew why, for so long, he chose to stay.

Though madness was a waning possibility, there was still no absolute proof that Accolon's shade and the story of his death were not inventions of my imagination. With Lancelot gone, ridden off with my ability to question what he knew, I was left with a need for answers, yet few avenues of knowledge. Arthur had sworn never to speak to me again, and regardless of what I had just learned, I remained too proud to ever set foot back in Camelot.

But he wasn't the only person who had been there that day. What I sought, as it so often did, lay within the water.

After a trip to the kitchen well, I returned to my study with a full ewer in my hand, reached behind the Hecate tapestries, and drew out the silver bowl. The metal sang as I poured, playing its strange note.

'Show me Ninianne of the Lake,' I said.

The water quivered in answer, and barely had time to settle before the surface stilled, reflecting the same white arched ceiling as before. Ninianne's face appeared in the glasslike surface, gleaming with intensity.

'Do you have my son?' she demanded. 'Lancelot is missing. Is he with you?'

'No,' I said. 'At least, I don't have him any more. He's on his way back to Camelot. We are finished with one another, Ninianne, I promise.'

She scrutinised my face, reading me for the truth. At length, she sighed and her light softened. 'Then why are you contacting me?'

At the question, I suddenly wanted to pull away, unable to bear the chance that she might scoff at my wrongness, and inform me my new truth had been some self-made fever dream. But either way, I needed to be sure, and Ninianne was all I had.

'I know Arthur didn't mean to kill Accolon,' I said. 'What happened, the circumstances, everything. I just need to hear whether what I've learned is true.'

Briefly, her eyes widened, then she sat back, rolling a swan quill between her fingers. 'Tell me what you know.'

I reached up and clasped the Gaulish coin in my palm. 'I know that when Accolon and Arthur duelled, they didn't realise who they were fighting,' I began. 'I know Accolon was winning, and Arthur wouldn't yield even when he lost his sword. That it could have been very different until you came and took the scabbard.'

My voice burned in my throat, raw and painful as the truth could be. 'I know that Arthur was horrified when he found out what he had done, and Accolon perished on the battlefield, long before he reached the abbey. I know there was no time, no way, I could have healed him. I know that Arthur held him as he died.'

'Morgan,' Ninianne said, but I held up a halting hand.

'I know there were times when you tried to tell me,' I forged on. 'And so did Arthur, I realise now, in his stubborn way. It didn't matter – I was never going to hear it until I was made to listen by someone who had no reason to speak of it at all.'

Until Lancelot sacrificed himself to give me the truth and refused to let me look away.

'How do you know all this?' Ninianne asked.

I shook my head. I would not tell her – not of the magical means of my discovery, nor who had sent me looking for a revelation. What had occurred between Lancelot du Lac and Morgan le Fay I would never be sure of, but our dark, enlivening connection, whatever it had meant, belonged only to him and me.

'Is it true?' I asked. 'Is that how it happened?'

I felt her quiver, but she didn't hesitate. 'Yes. Everything you describe.'

It felt as though a weight had been lifted from my bones, but the relief was too quick, leaving my body untethered, flailing, like a bird caught in a gale. I staggered backwards, landing in my chair.

'Morgan? Are you still there?'

Ninianne leaned closer to the bowl, her aspect seeking mine. I pulled myself upright and looked down at her again.

'That day,' I said, 'how didn't you know it was Accolon? His helm meant Arthur could not see his face, but what of your fairy intuition? In Tintagel, you told me that you felt my presence about him immediately, and that I carried his when I came to Merlin's. Why didn't you sense him on the battlefield?'

She sighed. 'I am not perfect, Morgan. My instincts are powerful, but they are natural, not unassailable, and are at the mercy of my surroundings just as anyone else. I was in a panic, hurrying to reach King Arthur. There was so much noise and violence – the

King was bleeding, determined to fight to the death but failing. I was overwhelmed.'

I could not argue with her. After all, I knew what it was for one's innermost senses to fail. When I had gone to St Stephen's cathedral to see Accolon's body on his dreadful altar – when I took his heart and swore to avenge him against Camelot's wrongs – there had been too much despair roaring in my blood to discern his powerful heartsong.

'I believe you,' I said tiredly. 'But if he was so upset about Accolon, why did Arthur declare to me and the court that he acted purposefully?'

'I cannot say, beyond that he rightfully believed himself betrayed,' Ninianne said. 'I was not privy to his thoughts thereafter and had no involvement in the bier or his message, but I did not disagree. You and he had been at odds for years. You kept the scabbard, a powerful object that could easily be used against him. He told me that once, you threatened to lay waste to his court and said you could run the kingdom without breaking stride.'

There was no lie in Ninianne's words. *This country deserves better*, I had told him that day in the hawthorn grove. Arthur took threats about as well as I did, with his kingdom's welfare his tenderest spot, yet I had chosen to throw that spear.

'I still don't see how it was enough to damn me,' I said. 'We could have grieved this together, unravelled Merlin's lies, maybe even repaired things. Why could he not have been honest?'

'That is a question for King Arthur, not me,' Ninianne said. 'But you and he have always been the same – stubborn, unrepentant, thinking yourselves correct. Yet I have always believed there is the potential to resolve this, if one of you took the first step.'

I shook my head. 'It will not be me. Arthur has known the truth of Accolon's death all along and has chosen not to put things right. If my brother ever wishes to speak to me, he knows where I am.'

'I would not have expected anything different,' she said with a smile. A distinct ease had come into her tone, new calm settling between us. Ninianne was letting herself understand who I was, and accepting me anyway.

'I prefer us like this,' I said quietly. 'I never enjoyed us being at odds, not able to speak candidly, or share our knowledge these past years.'

'Nor have I,' she said with a sigh. Ninianne's eyes flicked to mine and rested there, and we fell into a contemplative silence.

'Did you let him go?' she said suddenly. 'Lancelot.'

'No – he escaped,' I replied. 'Broke the bars on his window, took his horse and rode off. As he could have done at any time during his eighteen-month stay. Then, one day, something finally pulled him away.'

'What?' she asked, and I offered her a sceptical look.

'You know full well, Ninianne. Camelot pulled him back. Love did. For Guinevere and Arthur he broke loose, one or both of them. There is nowhere else his heart wants to go.'

For a moment, she looked set to argue, then put a hand to her forehead and groaned. 'By the goddess, why could he not have stayed where he was, away from his distractions? Better he be safe there than in Camelot with ...'

She expelled a long guilty breath, more revealing than a thousand words.

'You *knew*,' I said. 'All along. At our last meeting, you insisted there was no proof of Lancelot and Guinevere being lovers, or treasonous, then distracted me by speaking of Avalon and the loss of magic. You knew and were complicit in the lie.'

'No, it did not happen that way,' she protested, then gathered herself. 'When you told me you were not the betrayal prophecy, I believed you and it changed things. Every day since, I have felt destiny's threat hanging over my son. When Lancelot is apart from Guinevere, the danger is small. Now he has returned ... if he stays with the Royal Court, it will end in disaster. My only choice is to try and prevent it.'

'How will you do that?' I asked.

'A quest,' she declared. 'I will arrange an urgent endeavour to separate Lancelot and the Queen.'

'It seems a temporary solution at best,' I said. 'He has been away from the court a long time. How do you know he will agree to leave again?'

'It must be something important,' she replied. 'Godly, glorious. Difficult and lengthy. There is an object I know of – holy and protected. Worthy of his attention. I will ask him to seek this treasure in front of the court. For honour alone he will accept.'

Her matter-of-fact tone struck me with unease. 'What about Arthur?' I asked. 'Are you still loyal to him?'

Her light glittered with affront. 'Of course. As I always have been.'

'In that case, if you believe the prophecy – that Arthur's life is at risk from this betrayal – doesn't he have a right to know? Who chooses what's best for the realm?'

'I *am* thinking about what is best,' she snapped. 'What is right for my son will be right for the kingdom. There is nothing else.'

I could have taken my own offence, but there was more at stake than what I felt, or wanted for myself. Yet again, Arthur was not in control of his destiny, and for once, the thought of Camelot crumbling around him did not bring me satisfaction. Whatever the game, every player deserved to be in full possession of the rules.

'Ninianne, wait,' I said. 'You're not being fair.'

Before I could go on, her image blurred to nothing, and I realised she had thrown the water from the bowl.

41

A few days later, I returned to the lake.

In between, I sat down with Alys and Tressa and told them everything: the full story of Arthur and Accolon's duel; what occurred between me and Lancelot, and how my discovery came from his urging; my conversation with Ninianne that proved what I had seen. After our previous difficulties, it was hard to explain the vision and memory-walking, even as they listened without judgement or qualm, but my fear of misunderstanding was unfounded.

'When we said we believed you the first time, we did,' Alys said, alongside Tressa's vigorous agreement. 'It was your own stubbornness that convinced you otherwise, never anything we felt.'

They were right, of course. My withdrawal from them was by my own design, caused by unspoken sadness and the secrecy I built around it. Those days, I hoped, were over.

However, if any doubts of my reality did remain, they left me when I reached Llyn Glas and saw Accolon.

He stood at the willow's furthest edge, watching the path with a rare impatience, as if he had been waiting since I left. Upon seeing me, he adjusted his concerned demeanour to a gentle smile, and his consideration was so natural, so like him, that my heart was struck by a sudden, expansive joy. He had never been more real.

'Well,' I said as I reached him, 'at least I am no longer insane. You truly are here.'

He did not share my lightness. 'Morgan, *sacredieu*,' he said dramatically. 'My death – I thought you knew. All this time, you believed King Arthur killed me on purpose? I would never have let you think such a thing.'

'It's not your fault,' I said. 'I was the one who decided we should not speak of Arthur or Camelot. In my desperation to preserve our happiness, I only wanted us to remember the good.'

The worry lines between his brows faded, but not altogether. 'Yet what you must have endured, believing such a thing of your brother ... You always said that every cure can also be poison if left unobserved.'

I smiled at his artfulness, knowing I could hardly argue with myself. 'I thought it was all for the best, though I see how it was a mistake,' I admitted. 'If you are willing, we should speak on it all now, until everything is in the open.'

At last, he reached for me with his warmth and I accepted it gratefully, the intangible comfort of his embrace.

'I would like that very much,' he said.

So that is what we did; Accolon and I sat beneath the willow and talked as the sun made its arc across the clear spring sky. First, I told him about my following him to Camelot and everything that happened there: of Guinevere, Urien and Yvain; the fateful bier and Arthur's harsh, lying message; of my arrest, escape and visit to his body in St Stephen's Cathedral. I explained my subsequent confrontation with Arthur in the abbey, before I took Excalibur's scabbard and threw it into a lake.

In turn, Accolon recounted his days after leaving Belle Garde, the overjoyed reception Arthur gave him when he returned to Camelot and the time they spent together in friendship; their long talks during the hunting trip, before and after my arrogant former husband arrived, of whom Accolon had deservedly little to say.

'Away from the court, the King and I spoke freely, candidly,' he said. 'Of course, I did not tell him of us, but the conversation came around to you several times. Your brother missed you, Morgan. That is the first thing I was going to tell you when I came home.'

'But you never came home,' I said quietly. 'To me, it doesn't matter what Arthur felt in the wake of what he did.'

He did not dispute it, so I continued my story in the aftermath of his death: Sir Manassen's oath of loyalty, our plans to disrupt Camelot, every act of chaos and destruction I had committed in the name of vengeance. I had long ago told him of the magpies and storms, and been honest about my searing despair and dark, sleepless moods; the inconsequential knights I had gone to bed with, and how I had held myself remote from those I loved. He had taken it all with his usual understanding, but I had not told him where my actions had originated, the reasons for the war of rage and grief that burned around everything I did.

'I wanted Arthur to suffer,' I admitted. 'True, I wanted Camelot, Guinevere and the entire court to feel my wrath, but most of all I wanted my brother punished. I wanted him to hurt, to regret and never know peace, because of what he had done to you.'

Accolon listened with patient consideration. 'But King Arthur did not do what you thought he did,' he said. 'If we had known we were fighting one another, it would never have happened. Yes, you and he had other troubles, but if your revenge was based on his killing me with a cold heart, then it was never true.'

'Maybe so, but I'm not sure it makes a difference,' I said. 'I still lost you. I bore your death as a punishment, because Arthur lied about his actions. He still went to war with me when he knew full well what he had done.'

'*Bien sûr*, so he did, and you have every right to be angry with him,' Accolon said. 'Yet for some reason, you came and asked about my death, wanting to solve something. If it makes no difference, I cannot help but wonder why.'

His logic struck me with a discomfort I did not expect. Needing to move, I stood up and he followed, watching me rove within the willow leaves.

'Lancelot,' I muttered. 'He was the one who began all of this.'

'Ah yes,' Accolon said archly. 'Sir Lancelot du Lac, Camelot's complicated champion. He looms large in your telling of the past few years.'

'He tends to have that effect,' was my careless reply, but I felt an errant flutter beneath my ribcage. Though I had been honest about my dealings with Lancelot – the kidnappings, the sparring and charged encounters, our almost-consummation – there remained a whisper of a story left incomplete. He was more than simply someone to blame.

'In our last argument, Lancelot told me there was something I did not know,' I continued. 'He told me I wasn't being true to myself and to seek out what happened. Without his interference in my life, I may never have known about your battle with Arthur. Still, I do not know why he gave me the key to the truth, or wanted me to have it. More than that, I don't understand *why* I listened to him. Why I wanted to believe, and do what he said.'

Accolon shrugged. 'It seems simple to me. You felt something for him.'

'Not in that way,' I said quickly, but it was unnecessary; he had never needed my reassurance. 'I mean, yes, I felt *something* – many things – for Lancelot, all of it real, but the way we behaved felt like madness. Compelling, but exhausting. We barely gave one another a moment's peace. Even in the midst of it, I never quite understood our fascination.'

He took a few thoughtful steps towards me, bottom lip caught between his teeth. 'Have you ever considered,' he said eventually, 'that your fascination was not as much for Sir Lancelot, as his connection to King Arthur?'

I frowned. 'What do you mean?'

'Perhaps his closeness to your brother reminds you of what you lost,' Accolon replied. 'You said yourself King Arthur loves this knight despite being wronged by him, yet he could not give you the same grace. In challenging Sir Lancelot, perhaps you were battling your love for your brother, and the pain that came with it.'

The notion gave me pause, a strange and labyrinthine idea, but with the weight of an epiphany. Nothing could quite encapsulate what Lancelot and I had been, but I believed we had been searching for something in one another. The answer being Arthur seemed oddly fitting.

I gazed at Accolon in wonder and his storm-blue eyes captured me back, decades of intimacy contained in this moment of love and enlightenment.

'Once, long ago,' I said softly, 'Manassen said that you would want me to find love, another person to pass my life with.' I lifted a hand and traced his silver-gold edges. 'But nothing, no one, has ever come close.'

His top lip curled into the smile I first saw on him all those years ago, charming, only half modest. '*Oui*, but of course,' he replied. 'It is my curse to be irreplaceable.'

It made me laugh, and our eyes held for so long we almost slipped into memory. There was so much more for us to explore now, and I wanted nothing more than to drift away with him. But Accolon would not let me answer my impulse for distraction.

'*Alors*, what of you, Morgan?' he asked. 'Beyond all of the complexities, there is only one question – where do you stand now, in your heart, with King Arthur?'

To this, I did not have a clear answer. 'In what way?' I asked. 'Why would anything have changed?'

'Why should it not?' he countered. 'What you learned has changed you, cast your life in a different light. In your studies, when you have discovered something you did not know before, did you simply ignore it, or look at your viewpoint anew?'

'It's hardly the same thing,' I said. 'The result of what happened doesn't change, no matter what I've learned.'

'Maybe,' Accolon said, 'But when you flew up to this lake and asked if I would show you my death, you were not seeking the riddle of Sir Lancelot, or even my own story. You were seeking your brother.'

I fell silent, wondering if it was true. If I had indeed gone there and insisted we speak of it all because Accolon was the only one who could make me listen to my own heart when all else was noise. Perhaps that meant something.

'You always said the bond you and he shared went beyond conflict,' he continued. 'Don't you think King Arthur at least deserves to know that you now have the whole truth?'

For the first time, his languid, fair-minded logic struck me with irritation.

'This is too much,' I said. 'Am I simply supposed to reverse how I feel about my brother? Arthur *killed* you, Accolon. How can you not hate him?'

To my surprise, he laughed, as if I had just told him a good joke.

'*Mon cœur*,' he said. '*You* don't hate him either.'

I stared at him, aghast. 'Have you not listened to a word I've said?'

His voice and face dropped to seriousness. 'Every word, Morgan, do not mistake me. There is nothing I wish more than that I had been here, that none of it happened at all. Just because I have no reason to hate

King Arthur does not mean he hasn't hurt you deeply. Nevertheless, you do not hate him. You never have, in your heart.'

I wanted to dispute it, but my feelings towards Arthur had become a blurred, uncertain thing, a sand dune shifting beneath my feet. There was so much he had done to me, damage that a hundred lifetimes might not heal, but the strike that had finally torn us asunder, my brother was not guilty of.

There was always a way back for us, I had told him, *until you killed Accolon.*

What did that mean, now the foundation I based my vengeance on had been shaken into ruins? Did I even want to think of my brother in a different way?

I sighed; it was all too much to contemplate. Possibly, it always would be.

'It's too late,' I said. 'Even if either of us were inclined, there's not enough time in this world for Arthur and me to repair our bond, or rebuild the trust that has been lost. What's more – I swore vengeance on Camelot. For your sake, and my own. The oath I made to avenge you has been my survival, my whole life for years. It cannot be undone.'

I walked to the water's edge and gazed at the lake, now touched with the first gold of sunset. Hours had gone by, and I was no closer to understanding than when we began.

Accolon joined me before the gleaming blue, saying nothing, but I felt his presence deep in my body, his love and loyalty no matter what I chose.

'What are you thinking?' I asked him.

He let out a long breath. 'About us, when we saw one another again in Camelot, after nine years of separation. Of my heart, which you kept safe and returned to life after sixteen years of waiting. I am on your side, always, but it is only too late if you want it to be.'

The truth of it played an aching note in my chest. I turned to Accolon and we faced one another, his calm a cool breeze across my confusion.

'I made a vow,' I said. 'How can I go back on everything I swore to you, to myself? Where – and who – would I be?'

'You will be Morgan le Fay,' he replied. 'Nothing you do can change that. But do not forget everything you are. True, you have done remarkable things with your defiance, but what you do not remember are the wonders that have happened when you let yourself reconsider your own view. A stubborn heart is brave, but change is just as courageous. You and I would not be here now, in this moment, amidst our life together, if you had looked at me in Camelot and not changed your mind.'

He lifted one of his fine, clever hands and I met his fingers with my own, warmth without touch but real now, certain and true. All along, I had known it was him.

'Sometimes,' Accolon said, 'love is greater than the oaths we have sworn.'

42

The Grail Quest, as it became known – Ninianne's attempt to remove her son from the dangers of the court – proved successful, at least for a time.

For a while, the kingdom was engaged only in the quest's outcome, and it seemed she had achieved her aim. Then, news of the deaths began. Knights falling to misadventure, tales of rivalries boiling over and competition so fierce it ended in blood. By the time the Grail Quest had lasted three seasons, some had seen the mysterious object, none had achieved it, and over a third of the Round Table Knights were dead.

I sought to hear news, mainly to confirm my son was alive and well. Elaine, as ever, had the best information, and the rest I heard from the knights who found their way, injured and exhausted, into Belle Garde's infirmary. Occasionally, I heard myself asking after Lancelot: where the errant du Lac was, no one knew, but most expected he would achieve the Grail. I wondered if Morgan le Fay and her Vale of No Return ever crossed his mind.

Too often, I thought of him, sometimes finding myself back in the long bedchamber and taking the tapestries down from the walls to look at his paintings. On the day he had been gone a year, I stood before a depiction of Lancelot and Arthur alone in a forest: riding, hunting, talking. They were happy, but the knight had painted a darkness at his own edges – his guilt ever-present with the man he loved best. That week, I had gazed at the image for what felt like hours, though I could not have said why.

Perhaps Accolon was right: I was fascinated with Lancelot because he had given me the most important truth of my life, and I missed him because I still did not know what to do with it. His intimacy with Arthur illuminated the lost bond with my brother that I thought I had ceased to notice, but now felt more every day. When I stood before Lancelot's paintings, I was seeking the perspective, and the answers, he could no longer give me.

I was re-hanging the first tapestry when the huntsman appeared in the doorway.

'My lady, you are needed urgently,' he said. 'Three knights of Camelot are here. One is severely injured. The knight in charge insisted he see you – he said you are family.'

My first thought was my son. 'Where are they?' I demanded.

'I sent them to the red bedchamber nearest the entrance hall,' he said. 'So the blood wouldn't upset the household.'

'Thank you,' I said. 'Go get Lady Alys from the infirmary – I also need two pitchers of water, vinegar and a pile of fresh muslin. Leave them outside the chamber door.'

He nodded and headed for the kitchens, while I went in the other direction. It could be anyone, I told myself, but most knights would give their name. Pulse racing, I hurried towards the bedchamber.

A sleek, blond youth stood outside, looking at his fingernails. He glanced up at my arrival, casting cool eyes over me with interest. I had never seen him before.

'My lady,' he said smoothly. 'A pleasure to meet you.'

He smiled from an aspect that would have been agreeable if not for his slight but unmistakable sneer. His face echoed vaguely, but I did not have time to discern how because another knight appeared, auburn-haired and large as an oak.

'Aunt Morgan, thank the saints,' Sir Gawain said. 'Come quickly.'

I followed him into the chamber, where he rushed to a long table. Upon it, a third man lay prostrate and groaning, a puddle of blood expanding beneath him on the floor. Relief shot through me; it wasn't Yvain.

'I did not expect you, nephew,' I said to Gawain. 'Much less with a knight on my furniture as if he is a roasted hog.'

'I am grateful that you answered my plea,' he replied. 'We need your help.'

'I don't,' came a voice from the doorway. 'This is a detour I could do without.'

Gawain glared at the younger man, who crossed his arms and refused to look cowed. 'I don't believe you have met Sir Mordred,' my nephew said tersely. 'He is—'

The bleeding knight gave a sudden groan, twisting almost off the table. I swung towards the sound, and Gawain's arm shot out to kept him from falling.

'Someone you've never heard of,' Sir Mordred concluded. 'That is my curse.'

'For God's sake, Mordred, this is serious,' Gawain snapped. 'Leave us.'

'I would gladly do so,' the other drawled. 'If I had anywhere to go.'

I pointed him to the door before the argument could take flight. 'There's a reception chamber just down the hallway – you are welcome to wait there.'

Sir Mordred turned on nimble heels and strode off without a second glance.

Gawain beckoned me to the table, where the patient was writhing, fighting for breath. He had taken several deep slashes to the gut.

'A swordfight, gone wrong,' he explained. 'I tried to stem the bleeding but—'

I rolled up my sleeves and gestured him aside, hands already tingling with the impulse to heal. 'What's his name?' I asked.

'Sir Gaheris,' Gawain replied. 'My brother.'

The golden goodness in my veins turned into a burn. I took a step back. 'I'm not healing him. He murdered my sister.'

Gawain stared at me in horror. 'How do you know that?'

'What knowledge do you suppose is beyond me? News travels, you know, outside of what Camelot can control.'

Suddenly, the injured knight jerked up, back arching, beginning to convulse. Gawain swooped over him, one hand to Sir Gaheris's chest and the other on his forehead. 'Hush, *cuilean*,' he murmured. 'Try to be still.'

My eldest nephew looked fiercely back at me. 'What happened with my mother is Orkney business – no one's concern but ours. I do not condone what Gaheris did, but it has been settled between us as brothers.'

His scolding tone pricked my annoyance. 'It's no one's concern until you gallop into my home, demanding help only I can give. That is, I would have helped, if the victim of his unjust rage wasn't your own *mother*.'

Gawain stood upright, gathering the eldest-son authority he was accustomed to. 'You are a healer, Aunt Morgan. The first rule of physic you taught me was healers heal, they do not harm. That is why I know you won't let him die – because we are family, and fixing things is *what you do*.'

It was a rousing speech, and it struck me in the chest despite myself. Gawain was a natural leader like his father, but his shrewd eye – his quick ability to assess a situation and convince others to his view – came from his sharp, strategic mother, who no longer walked this earth because her sons knew better.

I pointed to Sir Gaheris, juddering and oblivious, foaming at the corners of his mouth. 'Was he thinking of family when he cut off my sister's head?'

Gawain paled, his towering body swaying. He had been there when it happened, Elaine had told me; he watched his brother commit the worst crime imaginable, and was too late, too slow, to do anything about it. Beheadings haunted him, it was said, dogging his heels everywhere he went.

'Please,' he croaked. 'I tried in the forest – my physic skills are strong because of you, but it wasn't enough. I cannot make excuses for Gaheris, but help me now. If there was anything I could do to bring my mother back – if I could give my life for hers – I would, but I cannot. All I can do is beg for your mercy and skill. Please, save my brother.'

The final word choked him, his eyes full of tears. They were dark-blue – like his mother's – as mine were shared with Yvain. I had not seen my beautiful, razor-edged sister for what felt like a hundred years, but I knew what Morgause would have said.

Save my son, fox-cub. You know you will anyway.

I drew my spine straight. 'For her,' I told him. 'Not for you, or the brutal, twisted rules you play by.'

He nodded, and I turned to the table, miring my hands in Sir Gaheris's blood. His wounds were deep and bleeding profusely; traumatic to receive, but he would live.

'Put your hands to his belly,' I ordered Gawain. 'Hold the skin together so I can concentrate.'

He did so, and I let my healing touch roam, seeking lacerations to the muscle and organs, stemming any bleeding, then fusing the skin back to an unsliced state. It took some thought and a little time, but proved an interesting challenge.

Once done, I stepped back and admired my work. 'He can keep the scars,' I said. 'A reminder of the mercy that was shown him when he did not show it to Morgause.'

Gawain sighed and made no argument, so I brought in the jugs and muslin left outside. Taking the warm water, he bathed his brother's bloodied skin, while I chased the burgeoning fever from Sir Gaheris's brow.

Once the patient was restful and clean, Gawain picked his brother up and carried him to the bed. 'Thank you, Aunt Morgan,' he said. 'You have no idea what it means to me.'

'I do,' I replied. 'He is your brother. Just as your mother was my sister.'

He regarded me helplessly and I shook my head. 'Come and wash your hands.'

I heated the remaining water with a snap of my fingers and poured it steaming into a bowl. We submerged our hands in unison, scrubbing the blood from our skin until the water was muddied pink.

'Your brother should feel fully recovered within a few hours,' I said.

'Good. We must continue on our way as soon as Gaheris wakes. Our quest should not be further delayed.'

'Let me guess,' I said. 'You are searching for the Grail.'

Gawain shook his head. 'No, the Grail has been achieved. We are riding back to Camelot to report our adventures to the King, as we swore to. In truth, it will be a relief when it is over. Word is, half of Camelot's knights have fallen, some to their own sworn brothers.'

My stomach turned over. 'Does Yvain live?'

'Yes,' he said at once. 'I hear my good cousin is unharmed and already returned to Camelot. Of all my brothers-in-arms, I am most grateful for Yvain's health, and Lancelot's. We are blessed to return, even if none of us succeeded.'

'Lancelot did not find the Grail?' I exclaimed.

'Oh, he found it,' Gawain said grimly. 'He just could not get close enough.'

So Lancelot had failed his great quest, and now he would be without godly glory and back between the thrones. Ninianne hadn't kept him away for long.

My nephew took a cloth to dry his hands. 'I was the one who suggested we all take part, thinking it a grand adventure. How wrong I was. There will be no more adventures after this. Now all I want is to get home and keep my brothers alive. Even Mordred.'

'Sir Mordred is your brother?' I said. 'But he's—'

'So much younger than me?' he supplied. 'I hear that often. Apparently, I am not as young as I like to think.'

It wasn't what I was going to say at all. *He is nothing like you*, was my first response, then I remembered past gossip, and some of my eldest sister's complications that Elaine and I had discussed in our recent letters. Morgause's fifth child had been the subject of some speculation – the other Orkney sons all favoured King Lot but he lacked the resemblance, so the rumour was Sir Mordred's father was another man.

I wondered if Gawain was aware, but I would not risk sullying my sister's reputation further. She had been unfairly punished enough.

'How is my own nephew not known to me?' I said instead.

'We only came to rediscover our relation recently,' Gawain replied. 'A long, complicated story. Nevertheless, I remember him being born. He is one of ours.'

'Then we should tell him his brother will live after all.'

He pulled a face. 'I wouldn't expect to find him wringing his hands.'

Upon reaching the reception room, we discovered Sir Mordred had strayed, spotted by a kitchen lad in a south wing-hallway. We found my new nephew wandering a gallery near the painted courtyard.

'Where have you been?' Gawain said in gruff admonishment.

The fair-haired knight looked as satisfied as a cat recently fed. 'I was restless, worried for Gaheris. Does he live? Do his guts reside within his body once more?'

The elder brother looked as if he wanted to cleave the younger's chest open, but held his temper. 'He lives and will soon recover, God be thanked.'

'*Lady Morgan* be thanked, rather. Our infamous family sorceress has impressive skills.' Sir Mordred's keen eyes flicked to me; I could see now they were grey. 'I know what you're thinking, dear aunt.'

His over-familiarity did not endear or provoke me, though I sensed he was hoping for one of them. 'What's that?' I said.

'You are wondering why I do not resemble my brothers,' he replied, and his correct guess gave me a shiver of unease. 'I've been told my grandmother, Queen Igraine, shared my colouring.'

Indeed, his face bore shades of her and therefore my sister, but there was a furtiveness about his looks, an evasive quality that belied anything more definitive.

'That's true,' I replied. 'You also have her eyes.'

Gawain cleared his throat. 'Yes, well – we owe our aunt a debt of gratitude and courtesy, which means you should not be wandering around her home uninvited.'

'Perhaps not,' Sir Mordred conceded. 'Though your house certainly is interesting, my lady. Brother, there is something just yonder that I think would interest you.'

Gawain hesitated, but Sir Mordred strode off and we had no choice but to follow. What I was not expecting was to be led through the open door of mine and Accolon's former bedchamber, into Lancelot's once prison cell. The walls were still uncovered from my being pulled away in a hurry.

Sir Mordred gestured Gawain towards the paintings opposite the bed – Lancelot and Guinevere's highly coloured treason.

'You have no right,' I began, but it was too late. My eldest nephew stepped closer, and it did not take long for him to understand what he was seeing.

He turned to me in alarm. 'What is the meaning of this?'

Sir Mordred answered before I could. 'You know what it is, brother. These paintings depict the *deeds* of the great Sir Lancelot du Lac. Signed by the knight himself.'

Gawain stared back at the paintings, blood rising up his neck. 'Mordred, leave us,' he said in a low voice. 'Now.'

His brother scoffed. 'I discovered this. I have every right to hear it explained.'

There were no more words from Gawain; Orkney patience was famously short. With a quiet aggression, he strode definitively towards his brother, who attempted to hold his ground then thought better of it, scowling as he fled the room.

Gawain watched him leave, hard-jawed, then went to the first painting and methodically examined every one. When he returned to me, he looked more battle-worn than when he had begged me to save his dying brother.

'He's right – this is Lancelot's life,' he said. 'But some of it I ... I don't understand. He and I are closer than brothers – he keeps nothing from me.'

'It seems he has not told you everything,' I said.

Briefly, he closed his eyes, then lifted a hand to his neck, pulling out a bronze chain from beneath his tunic. A large silver pendant emerged, embossed with Gawain's five-pointed star. He opened the box to reveal a small, grubby scrap of cloth.

'This is part of Christ's shroud,' he said. 'One of the holiest relics there is. Swear upon it that whatever you are about to tell me is the truth before God.'

I shrugged and curled my hand around the pendant. 'I have nothing to hide, and don't need God to witness that. But if it makes you feel better, I swear to be honest.'

I released the relic, but Gawain shook his head and placed it back in my hand. My entire explanation was to be a holy oath.

'Very well,' I said. 'As I'm sure he's told you, Sir Lancelot was imprisoned here for eighteen months. He didn't know who held him. These paintings are what he did with his time. They prove that he and Queen Guinevere are lovers in adultery.'

Gawain pulled the pendant from my hand. 'N-no, it cannot be. Markings on a wall do not mean anything. There's nothing here to definitively prove he painted these.'

I was about to argue when I saw his face – stunned and sickly, but lacking in surprise. A man caught by a punch he had seen coming.

'But you *have* heard it said,' I countered. 'You have seen things yourself that bring fuel to this fire. It doesn't strike you as wild or impossible.'

'Of course I've heard it,' he said. 'Lancelot has been pursued by rumours his entire life. Any knight as great as he will have unsavoury things whispered about him as he writes his name into legend. There is profound love between the three of them – it does not mean he's known the Queen carnally or they have been treasonous.'

'Don't act the fool, Gawain,' I warned. 'Your mother taught you to be cleverer than that. And your father raised you to be braver than this ignorance and cowardice.'

He stiffened at my invoking his long-dead father. 'What is your purpose here, Aunt Morgan?' he said curtly.

I was about to retort I hadn't intended him to see the paintings at all, but when he did, what I had felt was relief. First, he had come across them naturally, without my involvement. What's more, Gawain was Arthur's nephew, by his side since the beginning of his reign. Apart from Kay, there was no one my brother had trusted as much, for as long. If the truth came from Gawain, Arthur would listen. Perhaps this was the way it must be done.

'There isn't one,' I said. 'I didn't bring you to this house, or into this room. But Lancelot is sleeping with Queen Guinevere. If you cared for your honour, and your uncle's, you would gallop back to Camelot to tell him of this. By your admission, you have sworn to tell Arthur every detail of your adventures, and that now includes what's on these walls.'

Gawain's face darkened with guilt. 'I will never interfere in it. How can I speak of what I have not seen with my own eyes?'

'What about Sir Mordred?' I asked. 'Will he not speak of it if you don't?'

'Mordred will do as he's told,' he growled. 'He will not breathe a word of it in Camelot while I still walk God's earth. That, I can guarantee.'

'Then the duty lies with you.'

'This is Lancelot you're asking me to ruin,' he replied. 'I love no man more than he. How do I begin to choose between my greatest friend and my King – my own blood?'

'I'm not asking you to do anything, but your knightly code should,' I said. 'This is the problem with Camelot and its lofty tenets – you all preach your virtues, declare you are bound to your oaths, until it does not suit you.'

He said nothing but looked wretched, so I softened my voice.

'Can you honestly say Arthur does not deserve to know, and it isn't best coming from you? Because he will find out, Gawain. One day, he will see something he cannot unsee and the shock will destroy him. Where will he – and the kingdom – be then?'

I had done all I could, had gone beyond my doubts and courage to put forth what I could not express to my brother directly. If Gawain carried the truth where I was forbidden, perhaps it would be a step towards something; an ending to a long, painful odyssey.

My nephew only regarded me helplessly.

'I can't,' he said.

43

Thereafter, the kingdom fell quiet, unusually so.

Even Belle Garde felt too tranquil as the warmer weather arrived. After the Midsummer feast, Alys and Tressa went to visit Alys's family in Llancarfan, and the household grew sparse, with others on journeys or busy with summer concerns: high harvest and its accompanying revels; resting in the heat of the afternoon; hunting the woods for game. The infirmary saw fewer people in need of healing, the lodges stood unused, no questing knights rode in seeking hospitality or rest. Gawain had been right when he said there would be no more adventures.

He had also told the truth when he said he could never tell Arthur what he had seen painted on my walls. A year had passed with no rumours of turmoil in the Royal Court, or reports from Elaine of trouble in Arthur's closest circle. That the eldest son of Orkney had chosen to protect Lancelot over his own blood and oaths of fealty was astonishing, yet I could not blame him for his conflict when I had hardly been forthcoming in action myself. As much as I endlessly circled my own thoughts, all I could feel was the overbearing peace around me and the scratch of my own restlessness.

Everything I had started was left unfinished. Much as I studied, Accolon remained trapped at the lake and I had still not found a way of making him whole. My honesty with Yvain went unanswered, whether by his choice or under the pressure of Camelot. Ninianne stayed out of my reach, though her island sanctuary was never far from my thoughts.

'Sometimes, I think I do not belong here,' I told Accolon, as we spent the day together on the eighteenth anniversary of his death. 'That I watch this place grow and thrive while I stand on the periphery in solitude. It it goes on without me.'

'I know,' Accolon said. 'Though I do not believe Belle Garde, or even my absence, has been the cause. I have always loved you for it, but since the day we first met, I have never known your mind or self to be still.'

How well he had always understood me; how easily he accepted every facet of my being without pause or judgement. 'Since the day I was born, I have rarely felt settled,' I agreed. 'The Lady of the Lake herself told me that I belong somewhere else, and I often wonder if she was right. About Avalon.'

He looked puzzled, as if he too had heard the name but did not know why. 'What is it like?' he asked.

'I don't know. Ninianne offered me a place there, but I've never been.'

Yet even as I said it, a vision sprang into my mind's eye, so I described to him what I saw: a sprawling island in the midst of a deep-blue sea; lush forests, groves of apple trees and pale buildings full of books; a profound peace blanketing the air from one golden horizon to another. Ninianne's sanctuary as I imagined it, the place that perhaps I had been waiting for, but could no longer go.

Accolon regarded me with wonder. 'It sounds perfect for you. What you have been seeking your whole life.'

I sighed. 'It is, in many ways.'

'Then you should go, Morgan,' he said, but I was already shaking my head. 'Why would you not?'

'Because you are at Belle Garde, and I won't leave you,' I said. 'Your shade cannot even come to Avalon as other departed souls do, because I have trapped you here, half-made. If this is where you are, then so am I. For all time.'

'You should not promise that, *mon cœur*. I do not ask it of you.'

'It is what I choose,' I told him. 'Where else would I want to be but with you?'

The look he gave me was calm but unfathomable, as if there was much more to say, but he knew I considered the subject concluded.

'Here, at least, we can be together,' I said, and reached for him instead, shifting into his warmth until we were immersed in memories of our first year at Belle Garde.

We had long learned to be artful with his capabilities so he didn't fade as often, but we were in need of distraction and greedy for one another, until we had done too much and Accolon scattered into stars. Once again, I was alone, my existence paused.

The next morning, I climbed to my study, walked out onto the balcony and met the sight of his empty joust meadow, now reclaimed by the long grass and wildflowers. I closed my eyes against the view and saw clearly the path of the past quarter century, old joys and later troubles, triumphs and mistakes, riddles yet to solve. At its centre was the clear but distant figure of Arthur. My brother had called for our game to end, and there were no more moves I was willing to make. In all my days spent amidst our various confrontations, I had never expected for us to come to a halt, but now Arthur and I finally stood still. Our great stalemate, by our own design. All that remained, somehow, was Tintagel's roaring sea, ever-present in my mind, a connection that made less sense as time and our mutual exile wore on.

A disgruntled cawing opened my eyes: the magpies calling to one another in irritation, flocking into the shielding branches of the beech tree. Above, darkness had fallen in the shape of a long cloud shrouding the sun, blue-black and dense, rain rustling within.

I smiled at the sight. Long ago, the same act of creation had brought me back to the woman I needed to be, but I could not remember the last time such a thing had been involuntary. For the first time in years, my churning thoughts had conjured a storm.

The invitation was too tempting to resist. Raising my hands, I captured the warm air and pushed it into the cloud to meet cool water, growing and shaping the elements until a vast iron entity towered over the horizon. Flickers of white streaked across the grey, lightning waiting to be released.

My gaze shifted to the eastern forest, to an expanse of clear sky above the trees. Gathering the breeze, I drove the cloud away from Belle Garde until I could see the entirety of my work at a distance, then unleashed the storm. For hours I stood rapt, my hands flourishing, playing the music of nature until it was a symphony. I watched it rage as the day flew past, feeling each torrent of rain and lightning strike as power in my blood, thunder rattling through my bones until I felt vital, satisfied.

When I paused, it was late afternoon, and I had hardly felt the time. In the sky, the clouds had rained themselves out, the last peal of thunder barely audible as the tumult faded away. Still, it was one of the best storms I had made, and I had always recorded my experiments in writing, so I returned to my study and sat at my desk in front of a fresh sheaf of parchment. I had just finished my first page when an odd thumping noise came from somewhere below, then stopped just as abruptly.

It was strange, but I thought little of it, until the muffled thuds came again, impatiently, before falling silent. I got up and went to the study doorway as another sound echoed up – a creak of hinges distinct to the main door, but too cautious, more gradual than any of the household. Someone else was entering the house.

I did not fear anything, but intruders were not impossible. The blood spilled by the Grail Quest meant I had to ride out twice a week now to strengthen the protective charms, as I had intended to do that day, before the storm and my distraction. The magic should still have held, but things were changing so rapidly perhaps I had left it too long.

On silent feet, I padded down the spiral stairs. Near the bottom, I paused out of sight and listened to the echo of footsteps just beyond – long, confident strides, halting in the middle of the entrance hall. Then, a man's voice came, speaking to no one but clear and commanding, as if it was used to being heard regardless.

'What, is there no lord here?'

The sound rang within me like a cathedral bell.

I rested my shoulder briefly against the wall, steeling myself, then proceeded to the bottom of the stairs. The figure had his back to me, blue-and-gold cloak dripping with the remnants of my tempest.

'No,' I answered. 'But there is a mistress.'

My voice was as immediate to him as his had been to me. A slant of yellow storm-light illuminated him as he turned: pale-gold hair and silver eyes, face gleaming with water and disbelief, and a quick, fleeting emotion that I dared not interpret.

'Morgan,' my brother said. 'It's you.'

What remained of my hope leapt at the sight of his stunned expression, a reaction I thought myself far beyond.

'Arthur,' I replied, holding my voice steady. 'What are you doing here?'

He glanced back to the open door, as if he couldn't recall walking through it on his own two feet. 'The storm,' he said. 'I was wandering the forest when it came. It was so sudden, so alive, my horse threw me and galloped off. I didn't know where I was, or where to go, but I ran. When I looked up, I was here.'

In one way, the story made no sense at all but something inside his telling of it whispered to me as truth. He regarded me with a dawning wonder.

'I think, sister,' he said, 'I was trying to find you.'

In his honesty, the words took up a significance that sparked in my being. He had always known where I was, had come for me many times and failed, but now, beyond magic and chaos and all expectation, my brother was here. The protective charms had not faded; I had created a storm and Arthur had answered it, riding through the veil without resistance. We were here because something deep in our cores had called us back to one another.

I edged closer to him and he did the same, our footfall soft and halting. The last scraps of my soft sister's heart wanted to accept his presence in good will, but years of wrongs and mistrust had buried my faith. Morgan le Fay as she was now had changed too much; she could not afford to let herself be disarmed.

'Forgive me if I find that difficult to believe,' I said. 'But given you are here, if you have something to say, feel free to do so now.'

He stiffened at my formal tone, but did not recoil. Instead, Arthur gathered himself and marched towards where I stood. To my astonishment, the High King of All Britain stopped before me and bowed his head.

'I'm sorry, Morgan,' he said at long last.

'Arthur ...' I began. 'What ... why ...?'

'I am deeply, terribly sorry. You cannot know how much.' He looked up, his eyes silver and fierce, clear as our mother's. 'Please believe me.'

My pulse quickened but I refused to be outwardly moved. 'I don't understand. What are you sorry for?'

'All of it,' he said immediately. 'I have made so many mistakes. Known to me or not, I will apologise unreservedly for anything I have done.'

For a moment he looked so young, the confident and hopeful youth he had been, wanting to solve every problem for the greater good. To his mind, if he could make this apology perfect, then all would be well.

'That's not good enough, Arthur,' I replied. 'I am no innocent, but if I let you throw a cloak of apology over all of our troubles, then that is no more use than pretending we have never met. If you must do this, then give me something, not everything.'

He considered it solemnly, then said, 'Of course, you are right.'

I had hardly taken the chance to absorb his acknowledgement when, in a movement somehow both bold and hesitant, he reached out and took my hands.

'First, and most of all,' he said, 'I am sorry for Sir Accolon.'

At the sound of his name, I buckled, crumpling to the floor. After all this time – even as my Gaul's resurrected shade walked, talked and reminisced beneath the leaves of our weeping willow tree – the thought that Accolon had died at my brother's hands still had the terrible power to bring me to my knees.

In a heartbeat, Arthur was with me, kneeling at my side and clutching my hands tight. 'I didn't mean to kill him,' he said. 'His death has haunted me these long years. I know how unlikely that sounds, but I didn't know, I …' He ducked his head, snatching back tears. 'I was drugged on a hunting trip, held captive. They said it was just me who had been taken, and I would have to duel for my life. I tried to tell them who I was, but they either thought me a liar or didn't care. If I thought for a moment my opponent was Sir Accolon …'

I squeezed my eyes shut, but in the darkness came the vision of the battle as I had seen it: the field, rucked with mud, the hoarse grunts of effort and violent encouragement from the crowd; the deadly music of blade upon blade. Blood on mail, on swords, on skin and the grass. My brother weeping as my lover lay dying.

'You must believe me, Morgan,' Arthur insisted. 'I would have thrown down Excalibur and refused to fight. He was a brave, honourable knight and a good friend – I never would have done him harm.'

I gripped his hands harder, feeling the cool, hard flagstones under my knees, telling myself I could collapse no further. 'It's all right,' I said. 'I already know. I … I've seen Accolon's death. Through magic.'

The idea of my conjuring visions did not rattle him – he was raised with Merlin's ways, and assumed I had learned them – but his face weathered a gust of pain.

'How long have you known?' he said.

'A while,' I replied. 'Since just before the Grail Quest.'

'Two years?' he exclaimed. 'And you never told me?'

I recoiled, pulling my hands from his. 'How many times must I bring you my truth, Arthur, only to be rejected? Last time I came to Camelot, you called me a liar, threw me out and commanded me never to return. To come to you *yet again* was not my duty.'

He did not baulk at my anger but nodded and looked away, his silence inadequate.

'Besides,' I forged on, 'knowing you didn't kill Accolon with cold-blooded purpose isn't enough. What you wrought didn't stop there. You told the world that slaying him was righteous – as my *punishment*.'

He gave a heavy sigh. 'I know. I should never have used his death in that way. Out of every regret I have had, this lie has haunted me the most.'

'Then why did you spend years maintaining it?' I said fiercely. 'Before that, why did you lie to me again in the abbey? Accolon was already dead, and there were a hundred other ways to punish me. Why did you want me to believe you a murderer?'

'I was angry, Morgan!' he cried. 'I thought I had been betrayed by my own blood, made a fool by one of the people I had loved and trusted most, and it tore through me like wildfire. I reacted in the moment, amidst all my hurt and fury, then once it was said, I couldn't take it back. You know how that feels.'

'It is no excuse,' I snapped, but immediately heard the absurdity of my words. Of all the people unsuitable to scold another about acting upon rage and impulse, I was the first who should not throw a stone. I sat back on my haunches and sighed.

'Yes, I do know,' I admitted. 'Fury has been my lifelong companion, both cure and poison. But you were supposed to be *better*, Arthur.'

He echoed my sigh. 'And I should have been. Such a grave mistake was beneath me, and I have borne the weight of my actions every day. Back then, I was unmoored, fearful. I had lost Merlin, I was without *you* – all I was left with were prophecies, warnings of betrayal and treason, the danger I was in, and a kingdom depending on me. My worries had become all-consuming, and I had no sister of wisdom to share it with. I felt entirely alone.'

'That was your *choice*,' I said. 'You chose to believe Merlin. You signed the Royal Decree calling me corrupt. Even when you asked me to come back to Camelot, you insisted I prostrate myself before the court so *you* could save face. You had no sister to share your troubles with because you *threw me away*.'

'I see that, I do,' he said. 'I'm not trying to excuse any wrong I have done. For years I wondered if there was a way forward for us. We are bonded, Morgan – we always have been. By blood, our fury, the dreams of our birthplace. One of your storms began our war, and today, you sent another that brought me back to you. It must mean something.'

I opened my mouth to argue, but could speak no denial. Hours earlier, it had been thoughts of him, after all, the confusion of what I felt, that conjured the elements into chaos.

I shoved the notion away. 'Does it really matter if we have a connection when we have spent so many years at odds?' I said harshly. 'You hurt me, and I have tried my hardest to do the same to you. Even when we were in harmony, I kept things from you. Your wish for me to be taught by Merlin wasn't the only reason I left Camelot. There were secrets, lies.'

My brother recoiled. 'What secrets?'

I shook my head; still I could not bear to say that I was pregnant outside of my marriage, and my desire to protect my brother meant I chose not to tell him, because I didn't want to add to his strain, or have him think any less of his clever sister. Surely, such resistance to speak of it even now held more meaning than an accidentally conjured storm.

'It's part of a river that has long flowed into the sea,' I said. 'If we had found peace years ago, I might have gathered the strength to tell you. But now, facing it all again feels like too much. Maybe I am not fixed enough to be broken all over again.'

Arthur nodded, and we sat for a long moment, without rancour but with little else. Eventually, he said. 'I understand. Perhaps it's best if I leave you.'

I watched him stand and rose in turn, saying nothing but wondering if I should. When I didn't argue, he cast his silvery gaze upon me and smiled with regret.

'When you were at Camelot, it was the happiest time in my life,' he said. 'But though I loved and valued you, I know now it was never as much as you deserved. You were enough, Morgan. I wish I had realised it before it was all too late.'

In truth, I was already breaking, and his words crashed through the pieces that were left. As he turned away, I found myself putting a hand on his arm.

'The sea,' I asked him. 'Does it still come to you?'

Arthur shook his head, and my stomach plunged. He saw my disappointment and gave a faint smile. 'It does not *come* to me,' he said. 'It never leaves. Tintagel and its waves are always there.'

His explanation brought only the sweet ache of relief. Before I knew what I was doing, I reached out for my brother and put my arms around him. He let me, leaning in and resting his forehead against my shoulder, as he used to after I had healed his headaches. As I took the weight of him, I found I had missed it.

'How long were you riding lost?' I asked.

He stood upright, lines of tiredness drawn on his face. 'Oh, not that long,' he said. 'Two days, perhaps, until the storm.'

It raised a bittersweet amusement in me; Arthur had never known how to worry for his own person. There was always something more pressing, a kingdom to put first, endless decisions, a thousand questions waiting for the answers he must give; the same fervency for solving problems and perpetual forward motion that I recognised in myself.

'In that case, before anything else, we will dine,' I said. 'Sensible people say that important conversations should only be had on a full stomach.'

'I see,' he said wryly. 'Is that where we've been going wrong?'

He gave a modest, warm smile, and all at once he had returned to me, the brother I once knew, whom I had talked to, and laughed with, and believed in.

'Possibly,' I rejoined. 'Though our tempers may carry some blame. Come on.'

I turned to lead the way when Arthur caught hold of my hand, staying us.

'I'm glad I'm here, Morgan,' he said.

'So am I,' I replied, and somehow, by some miracle, it was true.

44

We climbed the twisting stair to its very top, and I ushered my brother into my eyrie of a study. A honeyed evening light shone through the encircling windows, the breeze meadowsweet through the balcony doorway.

Arthur stepped inside, gazing all around: at the upper gallery and its circular shelves; my desk and chair carved with birds; at the long worktable covered with parchment, quills and inks; my own quests for knowledge scribed in sketches and words. He rested a kingly hand upon a pile of manuscripts, his face glowing with a subtle pride.

'It's a beautiful room,' he said. 'Bright and orderly, as one would imagine great scholars at their books. I did not expect it to be so impressive.'

'What *were* you expecting?' I said archly. 'Some dark and dingy undercroft, filled with dog bones and bats? A cauldron in the corner, bubbling green? Jars of human teeth?'

He considered it, then said. 'Yes, I rather was.'

The candour of his admission, and its ridiculousness, made me burst into laughter. My brother followed, and we laughed long and hard, until it struck us both that we were sharing a moment of mirth over our rift and we quietened.

'How good it feels to laugh with you again, sister,' Arthur said, catching his breath. 'I have missed that.'

It had pleased me too, but I wasn't sure enough yet to trust in our shared enjoyment. There was still so much to say.

We ate a quiet dinner perched at the long worktable, served by a kitchen lad who had no reason to recognise the High King of All Britain, which Arthur found rather amusing.

'When did we last share a meal together like this?' he asked.

I shrugged. 'I can't say we ever have. Most of the meals when we lived under the same roof were held in public. And I wasn't in your retinue for all that long.'

He regarded me sadly. 'You weren't *in my retinue*, Morgan. What we were to one another was far more than that.'

'Yet it came to an end regardless.'

Arthur put a hand to his forehead, rubbing his thumb along his crownless temple. 'I know, and should not have said that. It is trite, useless. Attempting to redraw the past gets us nowhere.'

His quick repentance moved me despite myself. He was trying his hardest, and if I was willing to let him exist under my roof, I had to afford him some grace.

'It's all right,' I said. 'This won't be easy, we knew that, and it will take more than just one evening's conversation. Why don't you rest at Belle Garde for a few days? Give us enough time to discuss everything we need to.'

My brother looked up, his expression soft, weary. 'Thank you, sister. I am humbled by your generosity and will gladly stay.'

'Then it's settled,' I replied. 'Do you wish to retire now?'

'Not yet,' he said. 'I'd like us to talk a little longer, if it suits you.'

A swell of pleasure expanded in my torso – the joy I used to feel at being in the beam of Arthur's regard.

'Let's take some air on the balcony,' I said. 'I'll call for wine and arrange for your chamber. We make an apple cyser in this valley fit even for a High King.'

Arthur smiled and strode outside, while I called down for the serving lad. When I joined my brother again, he was standing at the balustrade, his strong, upright figure silhouetted against the evening, a rare stillness in his demeanour.

'God be praised,' he said. 'What an astonishing view. When I arrived I was running, head down against the storm – I didn't notice the beauty of the place.'

His youthful wonder amused me, as if he didn't have a hundred castles to stand atop, a view to please the Lord from every tower. I followed his gaze, surveying the glorious expanse of trees, meadows, rivers and hillsides, handsomely lit by the setting sun. The storm that guided him to me had rained itself out entirely, leaving the skies blue-gold and serene.

'Belle Garde, we call it,' I said. 'It belonged to our mother first, did you know? She gave it to me. I think part of her always knew I would end up here.'

'She was a good woman. I wish I had known her better.' Arthur sighed and for once I felt sorry for his lack; being raised by our mother was the one thing I possessed that he never could. 'I have often pondered what she would think of all this.'

I smiled. 'She would wonder, as she often did with me and my sisters, why we couldn't all just get along.'

It cheered him enough to chuckle, and for a moment it was pleasant to imagine all of our troubles explained as typical sibling disagreements.

'I would like to see the rest of Belle Garde, if you have the time,' he said.

'Of course. We will ride the entire valley in the morning. My *Val Sans Retour* as Sir Lancelot liked to call it. Though he returned to you from here more than once.'

I don't know why I brought up Lancelot's name, but I watched keenly my brother's reaction. Perhaps I wanted to see where his attitude lay if we truly began to speak of the things that divided us.

As it was, it didn't stir him at all, but he cast his eyes back to the view. 'Lancelot will always return. He knows when I need him most. When we both do.'

'Both?' I queried.

'Guinevere, too,' he replied. The way he said her name still held a thread of awe.

I bit back on any reaction. Upon reflection, it seemed dangerous to our relative peace to have thrown a light upon the subject at all.

But my brother was far from finished. 'What you claimed, Morgan, when you came to Camelot,' he said quietly. 'The truth you insisted I should know.'

'Arthur, I—'

He held up a halting hand. 'No, I understand it, why you chose to say what you said. But it was a misreading of the circumstances, from not knowing how my life has changed since you were by my side.

Being High King is a lonely place, with a level of solitude and pressure that not many souls can breach, but my wife is one of them, and so is Lancelot. It is unusual, maybe, and there have been troubles between us as with any deep bond, but without them, our mutual closeness, I don't know how I would have endured it all.'

Nothing: not a flicker in his eyes, or a twitch of tension in his jaw. He still loved his wife and best knight too much to believe me, and it stung.

'Then consider me enlightened,' I said bitterly. 'I'm sure Guinevere would be delighted to hear herself vindicated in such a way.'

I expected anger, the cold imperiousness I was used to, but Arthur did not yield to my goading. 'I would lay down my life for Guinevere, no matter what has gone between us,' he said. 'That will never change. It is important you know it.'

'Certainly, if you say so,' I retorted.

He regarded my pique with a grave calm, as a polite call came from within.

'That'll be our apple wine,' I said. 'Excuse me.'

I escaped back inside and called in the serving page, who placed a tray on the worktable with two goblets and a stoppered glass vessel.

'One more thing if you could please see to it,' I said. 'My guest has decided to stay, so will require a good sleeping chamber.'

I glanced through the external door to where my brother stood in profile, hand once again at his temple, worrying his phantom crown.

'Prepare the long chamber beside the inner courtyard,' I added. 'It's the best we have, and he requires a room fit for a king.'

Even as I spoke, I wasn't sure if I was making the right choice, but I let the boy go and poured the sweet drink, carrying the goblets out to the balcony. A crescent moon was just visible above the tiltyard's silver birches, cusps yellow and sharp.

Arthur stood awaiting me, his face serious. 'This ill humour is not what I want for us,' he said. 'Perhaps you are right, and we should not speak of them. I never thought I would stumble through the forest and into our reunion, but here and now, we are what matters, Morgan. Nothing else.'

Again, he had disarmed me, so I let my battle-readiness go and handed him his drink. Its heady scent rose up, taking my mind back to

Camelot and the shaded apple grove outside the Great Hall; of the two of us walking there, companionable, discussing the day. Tentatively, Arthur lifted his cup and I let our goblets touch.

'Do you truly believe we can be reunited?' I asked. 'Despite everything?'

'That's up to you, sister,' he said. 'Though in some ways, you could say we have never been apart. Our joint vision of Tintagel has kept us connected even when we were determined to tear ourselves asunder.'

I sipped my wine, letting my mind travel to the island, and the blue wildness we were born within. The sea, always roiling – except for one significant day.

'I remember the moment you were taken away from Tintagel,' I said. 'The sea was flat, lifeless as I had never seen it, and not a hint of breeze in the cove. Everything was wrong. Then you cried, loud and fierce, proving you were alive, as I knew, but no one let me believe. As soon as your voice sounded, the wind came, gusting across the water with such strength the waves rose up at once.'

I looked at him and saw in my brother's golden, indomitable aspect what had been obvious all along. 'It was you, Arthur. You cried out in defiance and the wind answered, bringing the sea – *my* sea – back to its full power. The two have always been connected, part war, part harmony.'

He met my gaze, absorbing the revelation. 'Exactly as we have, sister. First through our bond, then our visions of Tintagel. Something within us is incomplete without the other.'

Tears rose in my throat at his understanding, this epiphany that was so perfect, yet I wasn't sure I was ready for. We were almost found, but still lost.

'I am the sea,' I said, 'and you are the wind that makes the waves.'

Arthur nodded, his eyes silver with emotion. 'That is us entirely. We are meant to be in one another's lives, Morgan. I know your faith won't be easy to come by, but I hope one day you will trust me again.'

'I'd say it's more important that you trust *me*,' I replied. 'Everything went wrong when you failed to do so. Are you saying you no longer consider me traitorous? I was never at the root of the betrayal prophecy, but I have revelled in my treason since Accolon died.'

He released a heavy breath. 'I don't know what I believe about the past. All I know is I wish to change how things are between us now, and for the future.'

I looked away, across the river. The light was darker blue now, a cloud of starlings pulsing against the sky. The tiltyard had gained in shadow, long grass leaning in the breeze, as if a ghostly horse stepped upon it, pacing back from a charge at the quintain. How many times had I stood here watching Accolon ride, lance in hand, his grace and joy alive in his every motion, doing what he loved?

I closed my eyes, memory aching through my body. 'Arthur,' I said. 'What if I cannot forgive you?'

In my senses, I felt him wince. 'If you cannot, then it is my duty to understand.'

It made me look at him, and he met my eyes with a candid grey gaze, his powerful resemblance to our mother once again to the fore. Our road was long, but he stood before me now, open-hearted and trying, and perhaps I owed it to her to meet him halfway.

'Why were you wandering the forest?' I asked. 'Alone, lost. That isn't like you.'

'I wanted to be free, if only for a few hours,' he said. 'Away from the shadows of the man I should be, and who I have become. My weaknesses, my failures.'

I had not expected him to lie, nor did I anticipate such stark truth. 'Is that how you feel about your life?' I asked.

'I'm not sure.' He turned again to the balcony, hooking his hands behind his back. 'I've held a crown since I was practically a boy, and it has been everything to me, but sometimes I wonder what it was all for. I survived, I ruled, I tried – but I no longer know if I have done any good.'

His regret didn't strike my heart with sympathy, but he wasn't seeking pity, because Arthur never did. He wanted honesty, and I was equal to it, even after all this time.

'This ideal nature of yours has always been as much curse as blessing,' I scolded. 'Everything you've done and still you push yourself too hard. Perfection isn't possible in life, yet you forever yearn after it, as if achieving anything less is catastrophe. You are wrong.'

Arthur stiffened at the idea, then his shoulders relaxed and he gave a rueful smile. 'No one has been that forthright with me for a long time,' he said. 'Except Kay, perhaps.'

'Sometimes, direct opposition is what you need,' I said. 'Besides, you are not being fair. Your reign has been an enduring success. You've brought peace and prosperity to the kingdom, unified nations, fought wars to protect others. You've sacrificed your personal feelings to do what is right. The world you were handed is, on balance, a better place because of you. For the most part, you have been an exemplary High King.'

'And as a man?' he asked. 'Beyond the crown upon my head?'

'King and man cannot be separated,' I replied. 'As much as you wish you were High King on this hand, and Arthur – son, brother and husband – on the other, it all flows together, as the rivers meet the sea.'

He sighed with weary acceptance. 'Therein, perhaps, lies where I have failed. You always told me, sister, that life is complicated, but as a king I never believed it. I thought if I cleaved to my ideals and tried hard enough, every problem would yield to a simple solution. This difference is what tore us apart.'

'I had my own part to play,' I replied. 'Even in Camelot, my certainty that I knew best meant I was not honest with you.'

'Yes, but maybe I did not give you the opportunity,' he said. 'In the midst of our arguments, and the rules I felt you should follow, I never understood the complex truth of you as much as I should have.'

His insistence touched me, our exchange more candid than I could have imagined, but my untold truths were more difficult than this one night could contain.

'We both have a temper, and a stubbornness that has made us foolish,' I replied. 'Perhaps to truly move forwards, we must consider the flaws that brought us into conflict.'

Arthur nodded thoughtfully, then regarded me with an admiration that was youthful, almost shy. 'You are wiser than me – it was ever thus,' he said. 'We must keep talking, and I will listen, seek atonement. All I need to know is that you will let me try.'

'Atonement?' I echoed. 'How?'

'First, you must have the exoneration you asked for,' he said. 'A declaration in public that I made a mistake, with you by my side, so the world sees you how you truly are.'

Again, it was too fast, too straightforward. Arthur's willingness was heartening, but our past would not be untangled so quickly.

'I only ever wanted to be exonerated for Yvain's sake,' I said. 'Otherwise, I am who I chose to become, and I'm not ashamed. There are very few people whose opinion of me I would care to change.'

'I understand,' he said. 'Then Yvain must be enlightened. What I say will change his view – I can ensure it.'

I shook my head. 'My son has his own mind. Much of what he feels about me is justified because I failed as his mother. I have no right to his heart.'

Arthur nodded mutely, then considered me for a long, doubtful moment, as if he had nothing else to offer me and it frightened him.

'Please Morgan,' my brother said. 'Let me begin to earn your forgiveness.'

He held out his hands for mine. Above our heads, a slim blue cloud drifted lazily across the sky, towards the joust meadow – not my creation but an echo, a reminder. I was still uncertain, but in my moment of impasse, I had made a storm and brought my brother to my door, seeking healing of the deepest kind. It had to mean something.

'All right,' I said, and put my palms on his. 'Though it will not be now. You are tired and need to rest.'

Arthur smiled broadly. 'Tomorrow, then?' he said.

'Tomorrow,' I agreed, and with it came a surge of anticipation. I did not know how the future would look, but it was there again, wide and bright, awaiting us.

When the page came, I let my brother kiss both of my cheeks goodnight, and watched him disappear down the stairs to be guided to his rest. By then, I had quite forgotten what I had done.

45

I slept well, which was a rarity, and quite late, which was even rarer.

Dressing in riding clothes, I left my turret bedchamber and went briskly to my brother's room. We would ride the boundaries of Belle Garde that day, as I promised, to start off our new association with a pleasant, uncontroversial pursuit. Thereafter, more talk; I had many questions, and we were both seeking answers.

The door to the long chamber was ajar. 'Arthur?' I said softly. No answer.

Cautiously, I entered. The shutters had been flung wide, letting in great shafts of morning sun. Perhaps he had ordered a bath and was in the dressing room above, though I could not sense any water on the air.

It was then that I saw the mess: piles of fabric, heaped on the floor. The tapestries that had covered the walls, torn down in haste, exposing what lay beneath.

Lancelot's paintings blazed in colour and detail, beautiful and terrible, telling of his life, his love, his shame: observing Guinevere, rescuing her, begging her. Lying in bed with her in adultery, committing the ultimate betrayal. His signature beneath every image, red as knife wounds.

'Brother?' I called again, my voice cracking. 'Where are you?'

Only silence replied. Arthur had seen the paintings and gone.

The stables confirmed what I already knew: the High King of All Britain had appeared there at first light, demanding a swift, strong horse. Naturally, no one dared question this, and as soon as they brought his mount, he leapt astride and galloped away.

Arthur had several hours head start on me, but I couldn't let him leave in this reckless way. He would have to pause somewhere; I would take the fleetest courser in the stables, catch up to him. I would explain everything and make him calm.

I had barely gone beyond the hawthorn grove when a hooded figure appeared before me on the road, riding an enormous chestnut horse. My protective charms hung across the boundary in silver-white wisps; fairy magic, fast coming apart. The rider turned his large mount sideways, blocking my path. I could not see his face, but his heel bore a golden spur.

My courser skidded to a halt. 'You have no right to block my own road, Sir Knight. Let me pass.'

'I cannot,' he replied. 'I am here to stop you.'

His voice was tired, almost gruff, but still known to me. The knight pushed his hood down, revealing his dark-gold head.

'Yvain,' I gasped, and leapt from my horse.

He nodded and followed my lead, swinging out of the saddle. We approached one another with caution, like two knights facing down a duel.

'How are you here?' I asked.

'I was with a few others, seeking the King,' he said. 'We found him riding the road, a few miles away. He knew you would come after him and sent me to your valley to find you. He told me to tell you not to pursue him.'

'Respectfully, I must disobey,' I replied. 'Both him and you. There are urgent matters I need to explain.'

I turned and went towards my horse. As ever, to walk away from my son was the hardest thing to do, but he had his duty and I had mine.

'You cannot!' he called out.

I looked back and saw Yvain almost upon me, arm outstretched as if about to catch hold of my sleeve.

'It's too late,' he said. 'The King already knows about Lancelot and Guinevere.'

The simple way he named them caught my attention. I could not imagine Arthur stopping on his flight back to Camelot to explain the paintings – it was embarrassing, raw, and he was far too proud.

'What do you mean?' I said cautiously.

'Don't pretend you are unaware,' he said. 'Everyone knows you have been singing this particular tune for years.'

'Indeed,' I said. 'Not a soul ever took it seriously.'

'Perhaps they should have,' Yvain replied, and the conviction in his tone washed away my burgeoning offence. I moved towards him and he sighed again, his tall frame deflating so much I thought he might sit down in the muddy road.

'What's happened?' I asked.

'Camelot is falling apart,' he said. 'Every rumour, every suspicion held by those with a grudge, has turned out to be true. Queen Guinevere and Lancelot …'

His voice caught, the notion of his friend's dishonour difficult for him to even utter. He cleared his throat. 'They have been caught together in adultery and treasonous betrayal of my uncle.'

'Caught?' I exclaimed. 'How?' After all these years it seemed impossible they would suddenly be so careless.

'I don't know, only that it involves *damned* Agravaine and his allies,' Yvain said. 'I was going to stay and deal with them, ensure Lancelot was all right, but he's gone and I couldn't let my uncle ride back into chaos and humiliation. But when I found King Arthur, he already knew. I assume you told him and he finally believed you.'

'Not … exactly,' I said. 'But the result is the same.'

Yvain nodded and set his jaw, warding against bad feelings just as he had done as a child. I wanted to reach out, brush it all away, before I remembered where we stood.

'It's of no consequence now,' he said brusquely. 'The King told me to find you, and I have done my duty.'

I felt my heart sink back into its rightful, heavy place. 'So you have, and now I must find him anyway.'

This time, I didn't hesitate, going to my horse and gathering the reins. Yvain moved to stop me, but in his haste his leg buckled as if it could not bear him up. He gave a yelp of pain and clutched at his left knee.

I flew to his side, catching hold of his elbows so he didn't fall. We regarded one another for a long, aching moment. 'The knee injury,' I said. 'It still bothers you.'

A wave of amazement crossed his face. 'You remember?'

'Of course I do,' I replied. 'I've never stopped thinking about the day you came here. What I could have done better. That I should have convinced you to let me fix it.'

'Nothing you could have said on that day would have changed my mind,' he said. 'I wasn't myself.'

'You were grieving,' I said. 'I understand.'

He flinched at the memory and righted himself, so I let him go.

'The injury is old, but feels newly sore,' I said. 'You jarred it when you dismounted, but have hurt it worse recently.'

He regarded me with a sort of wonder. 'Yes. I was chasing quarry on a hunt a few days ago. My horse rightfully objected to jumping a stream too fast and threw me. I landed hard and twisted it. How did you …?'

'When I caught your arms just then – I could not help but sense it. Your knee was broken before and healed badly, and the scarring is inflamed from your fall.'

I said it without thinking, and he gave me an enquiring look. 'The barber-surgeon who strapped it claimed it wasn't broken, but I can still feel it when the winter takes hold,' he said. 'Of course, you knew all along.'

My instinct was to tell him he should have let me explain as much all those years ago and heal it in the first place, but maternal scolding was hardly my right. Yvain sighed as if I had said it regardless, his brow creasing, still so evocative of my own father.

'So you are what they say you are,' he said.

'Some of it,' I replied. 'Not everything.'

'I know,' he said quietly. 'Earlier, my uncle told me that maybe you are not entirely what I have been told. But part of me has always felt … that there was more.'

He regarded me again and I held his searching gaze. I could hardly fathom that my son was looking upon me as who I was, without his anger turning him away.

'Yvain …' I began, but he shook his head.

'Don't follow King Arthur,' he said. 'It isn't safe.'

The note of concern in his voice moved me – how could it not? – but after what Arthur had seen on the bedchamber walls, I was still loath to let it be.

'I have to,' I said. 'One truth about me is that I fear nothing in this world. You won't wish to hear this, but your uncle doesn't always know what's best for him, and—'

'Maybe he doesn't now,' Yvain said, finishing my sentence with wry accuracy. 'He told me you would say those exact words. He also said to tell you that you must stay in your valley. So when he needs you, he will know where to find you.'

It struck me anew, a declaration of faith from my brother that I never thought I would hear again, and still could not quite obey.

'But I cannot just sit here,' I protested. 'If I could at least speak to him—'

'Mother,' Yvain said.

The word rang through the air, striking every word from my lips. That I had lived without hearing him speak it all these years, or that he would be willing to say it now, seemed impossible, yet he had, so naturally.

I stood stunned, and an immediate flush crept across his beautiful face. He knew how much it meant.

'Trust him,' my son said. 'Trust *me*.'

Then he smiled at me, hopeful, quietly genuine, and it was worth any sacrifice.

'I do,' I said. 'I won't go.'

Tentatively, I reached up, and when he didn't recoil, I put my hand to his face, his man's jaw, his bronze-stubbled cheek. Yvain didn't shy away, letting me gaze at him as I absorbed the changes he had weathered since I first held him in my arms. I couldn't bear knowing his next move would be to leave.

'You have done your duty,' I said desperately. 'Yet I would not be doing mine if I didn't offer the help you need. Let me heal your knee before you go.'

'Why would you do that?' he asked.

I wanted to say it was a tiny insignificant teardrop in the ocean I needed to fill to atone; the one paltry thing that I could do for the son I had been forced to leave behind. That it would never be enough, but to save him from one pain was something.

Because I love you, I wanted to say, *and I always will.*

None of those words could I speak. 'With all that's happening, you should be at full strength,' I told him. 'It needs to be fixed, and I'm the only one who can.'

Yvain paused, and cast shining blue eyes upon me, a mirror of my own. Too soon, he stepped away and gestured to my horse.

'We should go,' he said, and it was over.

Courteously, he handed me into the saddle, and in a few quick steps he had left me to mount himself. I took a long last look at him, before inevitably he turned for Camelot, and I lost him again.

Instead, Yvain gathered his reins and nudged his horse forward until he was by my side. He glanced about him with a quiet familiarity, perhaps remembering the times he had stood here, at the edge of his mother's domain, never quite ready to cross that boundary. Suddenly, he looked at me, tilting his head towards the path between the hawthorn trees, through the sun-dappled shadows that led to Belle Garde.

'Lead the way,' he said. 'I'd like to see your home.'

Yvain and I rode along the riverbank as if drifting through a myth – a vison that I had imagined many times, but never dreamed could be real.

'It's beautiful,' he said, as we dismounted on the green before the house's main door. 'I cannot remember when I last heard so much birdsong. To live here must be …'

He trailed off and gave a smile so natural that I could barely withstand the flood of regret that washed through me.

'This place should have been part of your life, too,' I said. 'I wanted it, made plans to bring you, but …'

My words caught and I stopped, but Yvain only shook his head. 'I have lived a good life, God be thanked. The past is not for changing.'

Again, his grace was humbling, unanswerable. I cleared my throat and gestured to the turret. 'Your knee,' I said. 'My study is the most peaceful place, but it's at the top.'

'I've been living on this leg until now,' he replied. 'I can manage a few stairs.'

True to his word, he climbed valiantly to the summit, though I could tell by his slowing pace he had underestimated the amount of steps. When we reached my study, he threw himself onto the cushioned bench and propped his injured leg on a footstool, as if he had always sat there.

I sat down beside him, finding myself unsure of my healing prowess for the first time in decades. Hesitantly, I pushed up my sleeves. 'I will need to lay hands to your skin.'

Without qualm, Yvain prised off his boot and swiftly rolled up one leg of his breeches. His beleaguered knee was criss-crossed with white slashes, cut through by one upraised cicatrix – the cut I had seen all those years ago, badly healed.

He looked at me in expectation, and there I found my courage. I lay my fingertips to the call of his pain, and immediately his afflictions assaulted my senses; a triptych of injuries in varying layers. First, I dealt with the inflammation from that day, its heat receding under my hands, brought back into balance. Then came the jarring sprain from his recent fall; palms either side of his knee, I sent the golden force in opposite directions, causing a harsh, corrective twist which he would feel as though the injury had happened again.

Yvain inhaled sharply, and I had to take my own deep breath to steady my rising emotions. The injury yielded well, but not entirely. It would require his stillness, and another painful effort or two.

'Where is your lioness?' I said in diversion.

'She's with—' he began, then cut himself off, his face sheepish. 'It's just ... you might not know. I ... I am married.'

I nodded lightly. 'I had heard. Your Aunt Elaine told me.'

He seemed relieved, to such a degree he did not feel his joint wrested back into place. 'The lion is guarding my wife across the Channel,' he explained. 'Not that my lady needs protecting – she is ferocious enough. Absolutely refuses to come to court or live in Logres.'

I smiled. 'She sounds like a formidable woman.'

'Oh, she is,' he replied. 'She ensured I became a man deserving of her so we could be happy. To have met her, to be loved by her, has been the greatest gift.'

His final injury – the older, worse affliction – had now revealed itself: a ring of hard tissue, formed by pressure around the inadequate healing of the broken knee; a cage of fault lines grown into an armour of internal scarring, resistant to my exploratory touch.

'And are you?' I asked. 'Happy, I mean.'

His face grew soft, even as my healing probed for a way inside the affliction. 'Yes, very. Except for our separation, of course. I had hoped to take a long time away from the court soon, have children, learn to run a manor. Truly begin our lives.'

'It sounds wonderful,' I managed, filled as I was with happy pride. My son had found a strong woman, and he had not sought to crush or denigrate her spirit. He wanted to be with her, there might be children – a legacy of his own that would in some part be mine. The thought was so joyous, I had to pull my focus back to his knee, and the stubborn rope of scars that refused to uncoil. I worked at them in silence for a while, unpicking thread by thread, the rhythm soothing, productive.

'My uncle says I should forgive you,' Yvain said suddenly.

I looked up in astonishment, and the force from my hands burst into a spray of light, shattering the carapace of affliction. Swiftly, I gripped on to the connection, gathering the sparkling strands back under my control as scars immolated into gold dust. Beneath the rush of repair, a final, unseen fracture revealed itself, long and thin along the bone, never fully healed. My power answered, flowing forth to knit my son's knee back together, restoring the last of the strength he had lost.

I pulled my hands away, euphoric. 'It is done.'

Unusually for a healing act, my son didn't gasp, or leap up to see if my claims were indeed true. He simply sat and looked at me, his face smiling and assured.

'Thank you,' he said quietly.

The thought of his acceptance was overwhelming. My healing had left its feathery, pleasant tiredness behind, but beneath I felt a deeper fatigue, the certainty that all my strength was still not enough to fix all that was irrevocable.

'Yvain,' I said. 'You don't have to forgive me, especially not on anyone else's say-so. It is no small thing, and neither I nor Arthur have the right to advise anyone in this regard. We have only just considered the possibility of forgiving one another.'

'And will you?' His face lit with hope, defying my solemnity. I felt myself smile.

'I think perhaps I already have, for one good reason,' I said. 'You. Whatever else, Arthur sent you to me and brought us together in his most pitch-dark hour. To be here, like this, with you now – it is everything.'

You called me Mother, I wanted to add, but it was too new, too delicate. Yet Yvain's face was open, so I allowed myself one strike of boldness.

'I am glad you've lived a good life,' I said. 'Truly I am. But know that I will always be sorry that it was a life lived without me.'

He looked at me for so long that I felt I wouldn't be able to withstand it. Then, incredibly, he reached out and took my hands in his.

'I know, Mother, and I understand,' he said. 'Yet we are here now.'

We sat joined for a long, transcendent moment, then, in a brisk shift, he released me and got to his feet, testing the weight on his healed knee in great, fluid strides. I rose and followed his path, looking closely at his gait, checking my work.

'By my head,' he said, giving a brisk hop-skip of demonstration. 'Strong as a newly forged blade. As though it never happened.'

We laughed together, and I watched him march around for a few blissful, easy moments. At length, he paused by the balcony door, his gaze shifting outside, as if the great golden city had risen up beyond the trees. We could not keep the world out forever.

'What's happening?' I asked. 'In Camelot.'

'Chaos,' he said. 'When I left, Lancelot had absconded, which is as good as an admission of guilt. The Queen was barricaded in her chambers, with Sir Gawain guarding her door. His brother Agravaine was killed by Lancelot in the aftermath, so Gawain is both devastated and furious, which can be a dangerous combination. Where this will lead, I can't say, but it is nowhere good.'

I nodded, unsure how to reply; I knew what I wanted, but not if I was brave enough to speak it aloud. But my son had already gone beyond what I had hoped, and he deserved the same strength of heart from me. I would not fail him, or myself, this time.

'You should stay here awhile,' I said. 'So I can ensure your injury is truly gone. And, perhaps, for you to see if forgiveness is something you wish to choose.'

To my surprise, my son turned to me and smiled.

'Yes, I suppose I should,' he said, as if it were the simplest thing in the world.

46

So many firsts were due to us, moments of everyday life often taken for granted.

Yvain and I spent the rest of the day and most of the night talking, until the blue aura of dawn illuminated the treetops. The next day and those that followed, I showed him Belle Garde, the full scope of its beauty and all we had achieved there. He met those who lived in the valley and was welcomed; he learned of the infirmary, the lodges, the thriving endeavours that made it a place worthy of renown. My Vale of No Return, as it truly was.

One day, without shame, he told me he was proud, and I could not speak for joy.

We ate our meals together, raised goblets of wine to one another's health. In the evenings, we retired to my study and kept talking. First, I listened, eager to hear of Yvain's every moment, each step, thought and breath he took through his life; his joys and disappointments, his wants and fears, his victories and defeats; who he was within.

With endless grace, my son spoke and answered and let me know him, the greatest gift he could ever bestow. Eventually, in the lulls of his tale, his own questions came, and it was time for me to tell him my long and battle-worn story. Yvain had always heard the worst of me, but now he had the opportunity to ask everything he had secretly wondered or been denied, and see what else his mother contained.

Though it ached, sometimes burned, I loved every word that passed between us, because from the scorched earth of truth grew shoots of trust.

Diligent as he was, however, Yvain would not forget his duty. Upon agreeing to stay, he immediately sent a fast rider to Arthur, bearing news of where he was and why.

'Tell the King if he needs me, I will come, as my oath demands,' he instructed the messenger. 'But my choice would be to stay where I am for as long as I can.'

Soon, the answer came, handwritten and unexpectedly from the King himself.

Stay where you are, with your mother, Arthur said. *It is long past due that you know one another.*

'I'm glad,' Yvain said with a smile. 'Now we have more time.'

This is what my brother had done, I realised. Arthur had admitted his wrongs to Yvain, acknowledged Camelot's truth was not the only version of what he had long been told, and sent him to find me. Arthur said he would work for my forgiveness, whatever it took, and this was his miracle. He had given me back my son.

'There's a postscript,' he added. *'Tell my sister to remember the sea.'*

Where there was more time, there was more to learn, more to give. I did not notice the days passing, and could hardly believe a month had gone by when the messenger returned from Camelot with another missive – not from Arthur's quill this time, but a letter with the Lord Seneschal's seal, in Sir Kay's own hand.

The story was briefly told, but dramatic. The Queen had been put on trial for adultery, dragged out in her shift and bound to the burning stake. Naturally, Lancelot had caught wind of the news and galloped in to rescue her just in time, leaving slaughter in his wake. Lancelot had carried Guinevere off to his castle in the north, taking half of Camelot's knights with him, along with any doubt that he and the Queen had been lovers for years.

'Oh God no,' Yvain muttered. 'Lancelot killed two more Orkney brothers in the melee – Sir Gaheris and Sir Gareth.' He lowered the letter and put a hand to his forehead. 'When he killed Agravaine it was justified, but how could he do such a thing as this? He and Gawain have always been so close.'

I was still wary of my right to comfort him, but his grief overrode my caution. Tentatively, I put my hand on his shoulder. 'It's a terrible thing that sides are being taken, and I know you are torn between your love for them. It's natural to be hurt and confused, but know that it's all right to let yourself feel it – every part.'

It seemed so inadequate that when he looked down at me in gratitude I was astonished. I was even more surprised the next morning, when he arrived in my study and said only good morning, rather than telling me he was about to ride back to Camelot.

After that, when yet more news came, I trusted in my son's will to stay.

'King Arthur has laid siege to Joyous Gard,' he reported a fortnight later. 'Lancelot and the Queen are living within. Sir Kay says I should remain where I am – there is nothing for me to do there.'

Understandably, we had no word from my brother himself, but I visited the connection between us often, the sea around Tintagel's cliffs and its mercurial wind. As long as I could feel him there, I knew he survived.

'It makes little sense,' Yvain concluded, handing me the letter to read as he always did. 'Joyous Gard is a steadfast castle, but my uncle has enough men to overcome its walls. Why does he sit outside and wait?'

'The same reason neither man has called a duel,' I replied. 'There will be no battle, because Arthur and Lancelot cannot bear to kill one another.'

To hear of more chaos was hard for Yvain, but he was pleasantly distracted when Alys and Tressa returned from their travels and fell upon him with unfettered joy.

No one would have believed they had not laid eyes upon one another for a quarter century, or that Yvain had left us at far too young an age to have memories of them. He accepted their attentions with ease, insisting he remembered his time in their care, and it thrilled them even though they knew it was impossible. He let them dote upon him like the fondest of relations: Alys stitched him new shirts with intricately embroidered cuffs, while Tressa refused to allow him the strain of writing his own letters to Sir Kay, and became his faithful scribe. I looked on in happiness, and tried not to think of what could have been.

We had several weeks of peace, then one afternoon, I returned from assisting Alys with a risky but successful childbirth in the northern valley to find my son out on my balcony, leaning on the balustrade with a new letter in his hand.

It was the strangest report we had received yet. Guinevere and her lover had been exonerated by the Pope for their adultery, Arthur had accepted it and his wife had returned to Camelot. For his other treasons – the death of Gawain's brothers at the trial – Lancelot had been banished from court and sent permanently to his lands in Benoic.

'This is a great deal to take in,' I said. 'How do you feel?'

Yvain attempted a shrug, though his shoulders were heavy. 'I will miss Lancelot dearly at court, but he's not too far from where my wife and I reside. It is not as though I'll never see him again. And the rest is good news, at least. Perhaps now my uncle will see Camelot somewhat settled.'

He did not sound convinced; we both knew that what had been released into the world was too great to ever put back in its cage. The real question hovering between us was how long any such peace could hold.

But Yvain carried his own particular stubbornness. He stood upright and said, 'We must not dwell on it. What shall we do instead?'

His good nature never failed to make my heart grow. 'Anything you wish.'

He pondered it briefly, then looked at me with charming epiphany, as if knowing he was about to say the words I most wanted to hear.

'Let's go fly a bird together,' he said.

We took my best falcon to the meadow beyond the tilt field, a peregrine descended from a gorgeous, imperious bird Accolon had won for me in a tournament. This one had refined her ancestral traits to a knife edge: she was twice as beautiful, and twice as difficult. Still, she was my favourite. In honour of Alys's tapestries and the witch goddess herself, I had named her Hecate.

I had sent her up and brought her back a few times, testing her recall. Twice she refused my first whistle, and Yvain admired her the more for it.

'Clearly she is an empress of the skies,' he said appreciatively.

'She's not the easiest,' I agreed. 'Sometimes I think she will simply fly off and never come back. She seems to want the wilderness.'

He nodded thoughtfully. 'Some birds are only ever meant to be free.'

His wisdom struck me, articulating the feeling I always sensed in this falcon. She wore her existence like a beautiful but heavy mantle – with style but not contentment.

'Here,' I said, gesturing to the spare glove he carried. 'Take her.'

'Are you sure?' he said.

'You are my son, as I was my father's daughter. Falcons are in your blood.'

I lifted my hand to his and trailed her leash through his palm. The peregrine assessed him, then stepped onto his waiting fist and let him stroke her breast feathers. Mutual respect established, I watched him walk deeper into the grass and send her up into the sky.

For him, she was ready for her steepest climb, circling high above the long grass, waiting for the evening's prey to emerge. A movement caught her eye and she tilted her path, gliding off over the silver birches. We followed, ducking through some shrubbery and out onto the joust meadow, now overgrown with long grass and wildflowers. The blue-and-white tilt barrier glowed violet in the sunset, almost swallowed by nature. At the field's edge, Robin's *carnedd* still stood, unmoved by weather or time.

'This looks like a tiltyard,' Yvain commented.

'It was, once,' I replied. One day I would tell him the rest, of this place and the *carnedd* and what it all meant, but for now, this time was ours alone.

When we reached the bridge, he leaned against its stone side and I did the same, watching the falcon hover high above the shimmering river.

'I still cannot believe it,' he said suddenly. 'Lancelot and Guinevere were adulterous, betraying the King, yet things will just return to how they were? Impossible.'

I knew the letter had been on his mind, that Camelot's claims of normality had not persuaded him. 'What do you think will happen?'

He regarded me with puzzlement, as if no one had ever asked him his opinion before. 'I am no sage,' he said dismissively.

It saddened me, his lack of faith in his own perception, his mind left unappreciated amidst knightly popularity and an easy nature. As I mulled our silence, Yvain made a swift movement at his side, then held up his gauntleted arm and whistled – two short and one long, as I had. The peregrine landed on his fist in a rustling swoop, snatching at the strip of meat he held. I hadn't even noticed how close she was hovering.

'You have your instincts,' I pointed out. 'Trust them.'

He watched the bird tear at the flesh and grimaced. 'There will be war. Maybe not immediately, but it is coming.'

'Why do you say that?'

'Too much has happened – something will have to be done.' He looked from the bird to me. 'More than that, how it occurred doesn't feel right. Agravaine was no master of intelligence. What he did was too meticulous, too faultlessly executed, to have come from his mind alone. He had little to gain from it, unless conspiring with another. Exposing Lancelot's sin wasn't an accident or impulse – it was calculated.'

'You mean an act of strategy?' I asked. 'Some sort of jealous revolt?'

'I don't know. To act against Lancelot isn't wise, but to weaken his power in Camelot, severing his bond with King Arthur would be the one necessary move.'

Yvain took a few steps and launched Hecate back into flight. We watched her go, dark wings cutting against the sky like swinging swords.

'A kingdom divided is a kingdom in danger,' I murmured.

He turned to me, wide-eyed, and for a moment I saw the child he had been, whom I had held for too little time. 'Can't you help him?' he said plaintively. 'My uncle. The wonders you're capable of – there must be something you can do.'

I wanted to say of course I could help, that I would stop the world for him and lay my hands to Fate's wounds until everything was healed. But I had sworn long ago, when he had looked at me through a glamour and I felt myself scrape the depths of my abyss, that I would never lie to my son again.

'You know as well as I, not a soul in the world can stop your uncle when he is set to a course of action. However, that means one important thing: we can choose what we do next. Be that for King Arthur, some other cause, or ourselves. All we can do is listen to our honour, and answer with a true heart.'

Yvain smiled and I felt my words settle across him as comfort. Finally, I had been his mother at the right moment, and brought the honesty he wanted, when he most needed me.

Hope, in itself, was never a lie.

47

Too soon, the time came when Yvain had to leave.

'King Arthur has declared war on Lancelot,' he said one bright but chilly morning. 'According to Sir Kay, Gawain demanded justice for the death of his brothers. The killings were treasonously done, so my uncle had no choice but to acquiesce.'

We were standing on my balcony under a blue sky, the first crisp scent of autumn in the air. Yvain and I had spent three months together, longer than I ever could have hoped.

I took the letter from him and read the news myself. 'This is how you said it would be,' I replied. 'Your instincts were correct.'

He sighed. 'I didn't want to be right, Mother. I would give anything to be wrong.'

I put my hand on his. 'I know.'

The official royal summons came soon after, calling Sir Yvain up to lead a company into war. He was to gather his liegemen and meet his High King in Benoic, to do battle with his most beloved friend.

'This is strange,' he commented. 'My uncle has left Sir Mordred in charge. I never knew they were so well acquainted. I would not have guessed it in a hundred years.'

I recalled the knight from our one meeting, the sly, golden-haired youth who sneered at his brother bleeding out and found Lancelot's paintings in a room he had no business wandering into. He had also run away like a scolded dog when Gawain had chased him off. Perhaps the battlefield was not for him.

'Mordred is of Orkney,' I said. 'Youngest brother or not, your aunt Morgause's sons have always formed the spine of Camelot. Perhaps the King is trying to soothe Gawain.'

He took it in with consideration but passed no comment. 'There is also a note for you,' he said, showing me a small scroll. 'You are not to read it until I leave.'

Naturally, I reached for it anyway. Yvain grinned, holding the curled parchment out of my reach.

'No indeed – you must master your endless curiosity,' he said, and his playfulness, the ease with which we now knew one another was more than I could ever have dreamed.

When his last morning came, I had not slept at all, so I watched the sunrise and thought of my son, his grace and acceptance, how far we had journeyed in such a short interval. It felt as though we had been years together, but no time would ever be enough.

Inevitably, the moment was upon us. Yvain stood before me on Belle Garde's front green, handsome and rested, but with a crease in his brow that could not be smoothed away. Before I could find any words, he took my hands in his and looked at me directly with the blue eyes of Cornwall I had given him.

'Mother,' he said. I could never tire of hearing it.

'I know you fear nothing,' he continued. 'That you are a woman of great power and you have lived all this before. But the kingdom is about to become very dangerous, even more for those without sword and armour. You should go somewhere safe.'

It was all I could do not to pull him into my arms. 'I'm already here,' I said. 'For a time, no one in this realm was more under threat than I was, and I've kept myself, my valley and my people from harm. It is you I worry for – sword and armour may save you on the battlefield, but they will not withstand if the world implodes.'

'It is a knight's life,' he said.

'Codes and tenets do not apply to chaos,' I replied. 'You are more than a knight, Yvain – you are my son. Stay here. Send for your wife, your lioness, anyone you love, and bring them to Belle Garde. I can protect you.'

Fleetingly, I thought of Ninianne's warnings, of the fading magic and the struggles I encountered as it drained away. No matter, I thought; I would make two walls of charms, three, recast them every hour if needs be. Anything it took.

Yvain ducked his head with genuine regret. 'I can't,' he said. 'Who then will protect King Arthur?'

I had no answer; the same impossible question was never far from my mind.

I put my hand to my son's face. 'I understand,' I replied. 'You are a good knight, and the best of men.'

He gave a sad, grateful smile. 'I will be safe, Mother. I promise.'

He could not promise such a thing, but I would not tell him that. Yvain's strength, his courage, would come from his own bright sense of hope.

'I love you,' I said suddenly. 'I have no right to say it, perhaps, but you must know. I have loved you, always. Since the day you were born.'

His eyes grew wide, alight with confusion, a glaze of tears across the blue.

'Do not reply,' I said. 'You have done enough. Just to hear you call me Mother ... I could die now, and my last moments would have been happy.'

A brief cloud of decision crossed his face, then in a swift, unexpected movement, Yvain held out his arms and let me embrace him. He was so much bigger than me I could not envelop him as I wanted, as I used to when his entire body could be cradled against my chest, but in that moment, I could have encompassed the universe if it meant holding him close.

My son rested his chin on my shoulder. 'Or,' he said. 'You could live, and after all this is settled we can meet again, stay together for as long as we wish.' He drew back, still holding my arms, steadying us both. 'We will carry on.'

A pair of tears ran down my face. 'It is all I want.'

He nodded and kissed both of my cheeks. 'Good. We won't forget.'

Stepping away, he checked his sword, mounted his horse, then picked up one side of his cloak and swept it across his chest and over his shoulder. He looked down at me, beautiful, defiant, ready for the road and battles ahead. My son, the consummate knight, but carrying my essence, entirely himself.

'I will miss you, Mother,' he said.

'I will miss you too,' I said. 'Goodbye, my precious eyas.'

He smiled, his eyes aglow as if he remembered the name from a time long past. 'Until we meet again,' he said, and rode away.

With my son gone, it took me a moment and a tearful climb to the top of the turret to spot the curled parchment he had left on my desk. Wiping my eyes, I pulled the ribbon free and dutifully unfurled the scroll.

Unexpectedly, it was not Sir Kay's hand on the page, but Arthur's.

Morgan, it said. *I feel that you are restless, full of strategy and wisdom. I know you will be desperate to ride out and come to my aid. But if you never listen to me again, do me this one honour – an act of trust between a true-hearted brother and his clever sister.*

Hold fast. You will know how to help me when the time comes.

Within a fortnight of Yvain leaving Belle Garde, speculation was rife, but information was sparse. No one, not even tradesmen or travelling merchants, knew much beyond what was said in the official Royal Declaration – the Round Table was at war, Lancelot would answer for his treasons, and Sir Mordred of Orkney had been left in charge.

There was Arthur's faction, and there was Lancelot's – both had riches, prowess and the love of fighting men. It was impossible to know how it would conclude, but bloodshed was guaranteed.

Eventually, Elaine wrote with the little she had. She was safe in Garlot with her daughters, though her husband had taken his bannermen and gone to fight for Arthur with her sons. Sir Mordred, she said, had not put the realm on a wartime footing, but was at Camelot, throwing banquets for the kingdom's remaining barons – men of old age and even older power – seemingly shoring up morale and reassuring the country's elder statesmen that all was well in the seat of Arthur's power. Guinevere, she added, was notably not present.

However, as a hard winter froze us in, so did the news trail turn even colder. Not even Elaine had much beyond the occasional battle report from Benoic as the conflict dragged on. It was difficult not to hear of Yvain or Arthur, and my mind turned to Ninianne – where she was, what she might know. There had been nothing of her since the Grail Quest.

In my study, I drew out the silver bowl from behind the Hecate tapestries and poured the water, waiting for it to settle, my hand hovering to seek the element's essence.

Find her, I exhorted the crystal liquid. *Bring me Ninianne of the Lake.*

The water would shiver, coruscating with internal light, and I would wait for it to turn calm and reflect Ninianne's matchless face, only for the surface to keep rippling, never settling to its glassy stillness. Her low, sonorous voice did not come.

Some days, I tried multiple times, counting to bring myself patience while willing her to appear. When spring came, I visited Accolon most days, and it was not long before he noted my preoccupation.

'What's wrong?' he asked one morning, as I paused to skim a stone across the lake. That day, I had counted to three hundred over the bowl before I gave in.

'I can't reach Ninianne,' I said. 'I've been trying to communicate with her and nothing. Wherever she is, she cannot answer the call of water.'

'Is that unusual?' he asked. 'You said she is used to being on her own. Also, King Arthur and Sir Lancelot are doing battle – is she not with one of them?'

His measured response eased my tension, but only slightly. 'Maybe so, but it's been months. She should have answered at least once.'

He frowned, trailing gold-dust fingertips across my shoulder. 'You're truly concerned, aren't you?'

'Yes. No. I don't know. Something feels different. I can't explain it.'

His warmth and our time together soothed me, but the feeling of unease persisted, particularly when I reached the foot of the lake path and found the huntsman waiting, looking unusually flustered.

'There are armed men just outside the house,' he said. 'Their leader wishes to see you at once, but alone.'

'Whose men?' I asked.

'I don't know,' he replied. 'I thought I knew every standard in the realm, but I do not recognise their banner from the Devil's.'

It rang as odd, even in unprecedented times. Taking a side door back inside, I marched through the house, out onto the front green and into the towering shadow of a man swathed entirely in black.

Behind him, a row of seven heavily armoured guards stood silently, wearing matching black tunics bearing a fierce, two-headed eagle in gold. The former device of Orkney, when it was a sovereign nation.

'Sir Mordred,' I said. 'Why are you here?'

Morgause's youngest son inclined his bright head. He was dressed in dark silks, more like a lord than a knight, and wore no spurs. A slim ornamental sword sat at his hip.

'Lady Morgan,' he greeted. 'I wish to speak with you on a matter of great importance.' He glanced at the huntsman, steadfast at my shoulder. 'Privately. The news I bring is grave, and sensitive. Only for the ears of those with the appropriate pedigree.'

I resented his snide approach to status in this place that had long shaken off such things. However, he was, if not quite the regent of the country, as close as we currently had. To invoke rank suggested whatever he had come for pertained to the highest echelons of the Royal Court. My brother.

I nodded to the huntsman. 'You may leave us.'

'As you wish, my lady. Though I will not be far.' He bowed, eying the men suspiciously, then stalked off between the house and spring.

'There,' I said to Sir Mordred. 'You have my full attention. What is this about?'

'Forgive the intrusion, Lady Morgan, and for my having to bring you this news at all.' He drew a long breath and regarded me with flat grey eyes. 'King Arthur is dead.'

48

'King Arthur is dead?'

It sounded just as unlikely in my repetition as it had in Sir Mordred's voice. I stared at him in horror, though the accompanying feeling wasn't quite the kick to the gut I would have expected.

'Where – when?' I asked. 'How did it happen?'

For a heartbeat, he looked taken aback, then quickly arranged his face to solemnity. 'In battle, I believe. One of Sir Lancelot's faction, perhaps du Lac himself, struck the blow. Details are scant – all that has been confirmed is that the High King has perished.'

His vagueness was strange – one did not just make the most important declaration to befall any kingdom without precise information. Nor did he follow with *Long Live the King*, but of course there wasn't one – no children or named heirs, no obvious knight to step into the breach, Lancelot having been pinned to infamy by Sir Mordred's own brother.

What Agravaine did was too meticulous, too faultlessly executed, to have come from his mind alone.

Yvain's words flew back to me as I looked at my youngest nephew, keen-eyed and swathed in expensive silks, then at the cabal of helmed, anonymous guards behind him.

'This is a terrible shock,' I said carefully. 'You had better come in so we can discuss it. Your men, however, must leave my land and wait for you beyond the boundary.'

He smirked. 'Do not worry, Aunt Morgan. They won't do any harm without my explicit word.'

'They couldn't draw their swords before I turned them into a pile of ashes,' I replied. 'But you wanted this news kept quiet for now, and the presence of armed men might cause alarm – speculation. Dismiss them, and we may speak.'

I left him to consider and swept away into the entrance hall. I strode directly to the fireplace and extended my hands, under the pretence of warming them. Squeezing my eyes shut, I turned inwards, reaching into my depths where I found the ancient power of Tintagel's sea, fierce and blue, foaming white at its edges.

To see it roiling was enough, but a reply came instantly: a sharp gust of breeze, pulling a wave into a muscular curve. It rose, cresting high and controlled, then the wind slammed the saltwater into the rocky cliff side. My brother had answered me, his presence strong as ever. What my instinct had known was true – Arthur was alive.

In turn, it followed that Sir Mordred was the strategist behind Camelot's chaos together with his brother Agravaine, and he had certainly parlayed the aftermath into his power advantage. But what did it mean, his bringing this spurious announcement to my door?

'My men are gone, as you prefer.' The voice was sudden, looming at my shoulder. I spun round to face my nephew once again. 'Truly, I am sorry to be the one who has to bring you such dreadful news,' he added. 'It is not how I wished us to meet again.'

He cast sorrowful eyes down at me, his face painted into convincing sympathy. Sir Mordred was good at pretending.

So too would I have to be. The protective charms had permitted him entry, but he could not be trusted beyond the severity of the lie he had just told.

'Nor I,' I replied. 'This is so unexpected – I need to sit down.' I made a show of composing myself and gestured to the reception room door. 'We will have privacy here.'

Mordred bowed and followed me into the room. I sat in a fireside chair, but he padded the room like a black-and-gold wolf. When he had investigated every corner, he swept back and settled his wiry frame into the seat across from me.

'I must say, you are taking the news rather well,' he commented. 'The lack of tears, no falling to your knees in prayer.'

I conjured a burst of flame amidst the unlit kindling in the hearth. 'How could you form expectations of my reaction? You hardly know me.'

Sir Mordred smiled, his demeanour smooth and cool as a looking glass, an arresting expression that reminded me of Morgause. The burgeoning flames cut his profile out in shadow, his hair a golden crown.

'Maybe, dear aunt, but what I do know is impressive. You have done much with your life, despite challenges and condemnation. My mother told me of you, the last time we met. She said you were clever, a survivor, unfailingly loyal to those close to you.'

'I am loyal to whoever I deem worthy,' I replied. 'Though I'm pleased my sister thought so highly of me. She was a shrewd, strong woman who knew exactly who she was, and I always admired her for it.'

Sir Mordred nodded into the fire. 'In truth, I barely knew her. Our only conversations were when I was already a man, unfortunately few. As you probably know, King Lot believed me a bastard and I was sent away, so she did not raise me as she did my brothers. I didn't even know I had siblings until I was grown and knighted.'

'I'm sorry that was what happened,' I said. 'Above all things, I know what your mother's children meant to her. To lose you would have broken her heart.'

'Yes, well, she did attempt to explain it,' he replied. 'It seemed to pain her, even though my upbringing was as pleasant and uneventful as any boy could wish for. And she at least told me of my true father, though I suspect he considers me a grave mistake.'

'That is unfortunate,' I said, and he shrugged.

'Regrets have no purpose,' he said. 'There is only what can be done next. Such as at this very moment – a strong plan is required to marshal the kingdom through its grief and bring about the change that is needed.'

The switch of subject was quick, and intriguing. 'If the King is dead, won't stability in the realm be key?' I asked.

'It is questionable what stability there is left after the rupture between King Arthur and Sir Lancelot. Things are already in turmoil.'

'A rupture that you caused,' I said. 'From what I hear, you have done quite enough bringing this *turmoil* about.'

His eyes flashed – he had not expected me to have guessed his part in things. 'An odd moral judgement to make, Aunt Morgan,' he said, less smooth. 'Tell me, for how many years did *you* try and expose the treason at the heart of Camelot?'

'I will not lie, but my only purpose back then was vengeance,' I said. 'What was your reason, Sir Mordred?'

'What I *achieved* was bringing the nation the truth,' he said. 'Since the Grail Quest, most of Camelot has known what was going on behind the Queen's bedchamber door, given the way she and her knight behaved around one another. Except the King, of course. His partiality for them was never going to allow him to believe it without undeniable proof.'

It gave me no pleasure to hear that everything I warned Ninianne of had come true. Clearly, only Arthur's stubborn faith had kept Camelot from imploding sooner.

'So, King Arthur was made a cuckold and a fool,' Mordred continued. 'Everyone knew, but no one dared speak of it, fearing their own position. Camelot's concept of loyalty had become so twisted it was strangling the kingdom. The treason had to be brought to light.'

'A noble cause,' I said drily. 'How pleased you must be to subsequently find yourself in charge.'

My nephew recoiled slightly, as if offended. 'That's not quite fair. I have suffered much loss and sacrificed many things to walk the righteous path. Three of my brothers have been killed at Sir Lancelot's hand, and Gawain in his warlike ways risks the same. King Arthur has fallen. But from terrible tragedy can spring great potential – indeed it must. What the Seven Realms need now is fast, decisive action. Leadership.'

'So it may be,' I said in a bored voice. 'Though I do not see how any of this pertains to me. I have been Enemy to the Crown for a quarter century. I have no armed men, no political connections or standing in the Court. I never cared for the systems of power.'

'*Exactly*, Lady Morgan.' In a sudden jolt, he sat upright from his louche position. 'Your grievances are well known. The kingdom's rules sent you into exile, turned your son against you and destroyed your reputation. They let my mother – your sister – suffer an unjust death and did nothing to punish it. We share a common interest in all that Camelot has wrought upon us.'

I looked at him askance. 'Our paths have not been easy, but you are a Knight of the Round Table, nephew to the High King himself. Before he went to war, Arthur put you in charge of the entire realm. Does that mean nothing?'

'Of course,' he said. 'King Arthur showed great faith in me, and now it is time for me to answer that call to action.' He leaned towards me, steepling his fingers like a priest intoning at Mass. 'Camelot has long been resistant to change. These recent disruptions are more dents in a crown that has been of dubious authority for years. This is an opportunity to address the careless idealism that has made this nation weak, and turn its focus to strength, better control, and true unification. I want you to be part of the new world we must create.'

A coup, I thought. *That's all this is. Just as Yvain suggested.*

A grab at power no different from the many others my brother had defeated over the years. Except now, the Crown's forces were split and warring in Benoic, and his proxy was telling the kingdom he had been slain. Arthur did not know how much things had changed in his own Throne Room.

I made no reply, unsure what was safe to say next. Sir Mordred watched me think, keen to my every reaction. 'I hope I have not overstepped my bounds, Lady Morgan,' he said carefully. 'Or that I am too bold, speaking to you this way.'

He distracted like a master thief, his every word part obfuscation. A chill of unease crept between my shoulder blades, but this was an opportunity, a point of suspension in our conversation so far. Assuming me to be of the same mind, Sir Mordred was overconfident – or as men often did, he just liked to hear his own voice. It was time to push him and see how much he would give.

'Not at all,' I said. 'But I hold no patience for sly, elusive talk. Be frank – what are you asking of me?'

'Then forthright we must be,' he said indulgently. 'I want you to stand by my side as I bring the kingdom to heel. You would lend me your powers, your incredible grasp of magic, to help bring about this realm's next glorious era. Is that honest enough?'

'Somewhat,' I replied. 'However, my life is comfortable, hard-won. What you are offering sounds a great deal of work. Why would I be compelled?'

He gave a short, appreciative laugh then fell serious. 'Why would you not, given what you, and your reputation, has unfairly endured? In the Royal Court, I've heard you called a corrupted sorceress, a spurned woman riven with jealousy and bitterness, a lascivious seducer of men. A liar and a witch. You could change what the world says about you.'

'How amusing of you to think I care for idle talk. What others say has never mattered, and cannot compel me.'

'There will be other rewards, naturally,' he assured me. 'Titles, political status, acclaim, your own feast day – whatever you wish for. If you lend me your powers, I will share the spoils of mine.'

I pulled a considering face. 'Until now, only High Kings have sought to harness magic for their own ends. Is that what you wish to be, Sir Mordred – a king?'

He made his expression modest, forbearing, entirely for my benefit. 'My thoughts have only been for what is needed to make the kingdom grow strong again. But of course, it follows that the realm will expect someone to wear the Crown.'

My gamble upon his nature had succeeded; he liked to be resisted and challenged, the perfect opportunity for him to show off. To gain all I needed, he must want to impress me, and I must keep my composure.

'Why would it be you?' I asked. 'King Arthur has no named successor. When the country hears of his death there will be civil war, of the likes this land has not seen since his coronation. You do not have Arthur's authority, his pedigree or reputation as a ruler. You do not possess Lancelot's prowess, his battle record, or the loyalty of great knights that he inspires. Do you truly believe you have the fortitude to hold the Crown of All Britain?'

Mordred stiffened slightly, but covered it with a mocking smile. 'No one in their right mind would believe this a simple task,' he said. 'That, my dear aunt, is why I need you. I don't want a Merlin the Wise, to worship the skies and order me to fear the wrong star. I want the courage and mastery I saw when you brought my bleeding, convulsing half-brother back from certain death. A force that can help me create my own fate.'

He was more astute than I had given him credit for, as if he had known to be compared to Merlin was the last thing I wished to hear.

'An intriguing prospect,' I said. 'But with great magic comes great cost, and I am only one woman. I cannot control the perception of the entire Seven Realms. How could I trust you would hold a crown upon your head in the meantime?'

'I have ways to bring the kingdom to heel,' he replied. 'These past few months, I have held many meetings with the country's elder lords, which has gained me considerable favour. I have listened, been generous – even if Camelot's former *great knights* rebel, I am confident the barons will stand beside me, with men and swords if necessary.'

Courting them with Arthur's wine, I thought. *Buying allies with his gold. Plotting his demise within his own castle walls.*

Impatience was rising within me like high tide, so I chose to use it. 'Is that all?' I said. 'Do you believe that is enough?'

'It is a great deal,' Mordred said pettishly, then quickly smoothed over his demeanour. 'Indeed, that is not even the most compelling part of the plan. Before anything else, I will marry Queen Guinevere.'

My restless body stilled. 'You'll … what?'

'Marry King Arthur's widow. Yes, she is past her best days and it's almost an act of charity, but it has its purposes.' His voice held a hint of pride underneath the matter-of-fact tone. 'That alone should keep the populace on side, calm the lords, appease the clergy. Perhaps I will succeed in giving her the child King Arthur or her famed knightly lover never could. Even at her age, I'm sure the Lord would smile upon us.'

He grinned conspiratorially, certain he had finally convinced me. Cold seeped into my marrow, a vicarious dread I hadn't felt since my years under Uther Pendragon's monstrous eye. My composure shook, then fractured.

'She will refuse,' I snapped. 'There will be no compelling her to such an act.'

At my mask slipping, his grey eyes clouded. 'She will have no choice if she wishes to live,' he said. 'What do you care, my vengeful aunt? Queen Guinevere and Morgan le Fay have carried a mutual grudge since Camelot's earliest days – surely whatever means are necessary to bend the Queen to my will would be well deserved in your eyes?'

The knowing, amused sneer was back on his face. He knew I could not deny relishing the idea of the Queen's ruin: I had rained on her, disrupted her favourite festivals, sent magpies to fly at her head. I had constantly tried to tell the world that she was adulterous, exactly as

Mordred had succeeded in doing. Her actions had led to the loss of mine and Accolon's child, so I had never questioned my right to seek restitution for my pain.

Of course I had plotted Guinevere's downfall, because she had been the first architect of mine. But I had never thought of her confined, or forced and tortured by men, because the idea made me sick to my stomach.

However, I had to tread carefully.

'A king must do what is necessary,' I said. 'Whatever means used to persuade her to your suit, I cannot say I will lose sleep over it. When will this joyous occasion take place?'

'Very soon. The Queen has been in the Caerleon fortress since her husband went to war, but I have recently called her back to Camelot. When she arrives, I will greet her along with the archbishop. We will be wedded and bedded before she has chance to protest.'

I swallowed a surge of disgust. 'In that case, I hope this is not an invitation. I have little time to attend a wedding, even a royal one.'

'The coronation, perhaps.' He regarded me with a hooded amusement. 'Very well, dear aunt, I have satisfied your questions. Do you agree to join my cause?'

'I cannot yet say,' I replied. 'As you can see, I have this valley to consider, a household to run, responsibilities to the people here. I need time to think.'

His pleasant expression froze. 'What is there to think on? I am in great haste and cannot delay securing this kingdom, protecting its future. If you prevaricate, or make the wrong decision, you might end up with no valley – and God forbid, no people – to consider at all.'

His words were murky, but the threat beneath was clear enough. Immediately, the atmosphere shifted, a tremor shivering through my veins as Sir Mordred's intentions seeped into the magic surrounding the valley. I felt the protective charms reach out like vines, silvery threads drawn to the house and into the walls, through the windows and floorboards.

'The kingdom is crying out for a leader, Lady Morgan,' Mordred went on. 'And I am all it needs – strict, ambitious and fierce in defence.

With or without you, I will succeed. Those who bite my firm hand, or deny my rule, will have no future.'

He gestured to me and my anger ignited, bringing me to my feet, the dragon in my belly awoken by yet another man's refusal to recognise that he was not in authority here. The game was gone; no more would I play.

'*You will have no rule,*' I said. 'Dead or alive, you could never defeat King Arthur. If the world remembers you at all, it will be in the shadow of his name.'

Slowly, Sir Mordred rose and attempted to laugh, but it came forth as a humourless bark.

'Foolish, just like your legendary brother,' he sneered. 'Stubborn, self-righteous, undeserving of such power.'

The first tendrils of fairy magic crept soundlessly around his arms. 'Prepare yourself,' I said. 'You have only a few breaths left on my land.'

He glanced down and shied away from the charms. They dissipated into the air like diamond dust, then re-formed around his body again.

'You may believe you are unbreachable,' Mordred said. 'But I warn you, Lady Morgan – there are always ways to come to harm. A new world is dawning, and if you do not make yourself useful to me, you and everything you love will be fed to its jaws.'

His limbs were corded with silver now, charms hardening into steel rope. Clenching my fists, I drew them taut. He fought against his confinement, but my magic was strong, armoured with fury.

'You mistake me for one who has never had to do battle for her freedom,' I said. 'So hear me, now and for all time. I am no man's weapon to wield.'

49

The first thing I did upon Sir Mordred being dragged out of the house by my protective charms was ensure he left my land.

The huntsman had faithfully awaited me by the spring, so I sent him to track the black-clad men out of the valley. Thereafter, I ran up the stairs to my study and sent a group of magpies to follow the rest of Mordred's journey to Camelot, or learn if he took any detours. I could afford to take no chances with my slippery nephew.

When the birds had gone, I went to my desk and wrote several letters – three identical messages to Arthur, telling him in brief what I had learned, and another to Elaine, warning her of what may come, and urging her to sail to our father's ancestral lands in Ireland at the first sign of trouble.

I sent Elaine's letter and one of Arthur's with my fastest horse messengers, then returned to my turret and tied the two remaining scrolls to the magpie matriarch and her mate, sending them off towards the southern horizon. With luck, magic and the good winds I would conjure, they would reach my brother in all haste and bring him back.

Once done, all I could do was wait for what came next. Inaction wasn't my strength, and I considered chasing after Mordred, but I could not leave without risking the protective veil. In any case, it was knowledge that mattered, and there was little I didn't know from his confession. He would do everything possible to get the Crown of All Britain.

Unease prickled beneath my skin like nettles, but none of this could I change. It was politics, war, the business of realm and royalty within a world I had been exiled from – a system full of my enemies for whom I was not inclined to risk myself. Moreover, I had my own responsibilities: before long, news would spread about my visitor and Alys and

Tressa would be in my study asking what had happened. My duty was to them and Belle Garde; until Arthur asked something of me, nothing else was my concern.

I glanced down and saw the unfurled parchment Yvain had given to me – my brother's last message. For reassurance, I read it again, but the words had shifted, gaining a resonance more immediate. *Hold fast*, it said, but when put before all I knew now, it seemed less a command of waiting than one of resistance. Of the need to do what was right.

I leaned my palms against the desk and sighed, relieved when footsteps sounded on the stairs and the huntsman appeared.

'Sir Mordred and his men quit the valley directly,' he said. 'My lads followed them some way and they're not turning back.'

'Good,' I replied. 'Thank you.'

He bowed in acceptance. 'Is there anything else, my lady?'

I looked again at the note, Arthur's voice in my mind as if he stood beside me.

When the time comes, he urged, *you will know how to help me.*

My brother was right: I did. What's more, in the deepest parts of my being, I had always known what I would do. The nettle scratch under my skin was telling the truth I least wanted to admit, but whatever my reluctance, I could not defy the call of my own honour.

'Ready my fastest horse,' I said to the huntsman. 'I must ride out at once.'

It was a long time since I had been to the Caerleon fortress, and like most of Arthur's important court-holding palaces, it had grown considerably, buildings expanded, windows glazed with jewel tones, gardens formalised and carefully planted.

Nevertheless, the castle held an air of abandonment. The main gates stood wide, no guards in sight until I was almost upon the main keep, and I saw not a single knight until I had crossed the open threshold and found my way into the main hall. A fair few armed men were scattered through the room, perched casually in window seats or leaning against the long tables in conversation. The remnants of a recently eaten meal sat out, a skeleton of servants slowly clearing silver plates and heels of dry bread.

All talk stopped as I entered, every pair of eyes turned upon me. A broad, blond knight jumped up, hand at his sword, which fell again when he saw I was a mere woman.

'I'm here to see the Queen,' I said. 'It's important.'

Not a soul asked my name or thought to announce me to her first, which was a relief; if she knew I was coming, I may not have made it a step further. Instead, the blond knight beckoned and led me into a reception chamber just off the hall. It was bright and sun-warmed by large windows, intricate tapestries draping the walls depicting a fantastical woodland scene: kings and ladies at some mythical revel, attended by nymphs and satyrs, bordered with grapevines full of birds. An image of a time both long gone and never was – a Vale of No Return all its own.

She stood before a long window in profile, still golden and quintessentially beautiful, eyes faraway with thought.

'Guinevere,' I said before the knight could.

To her credit, she didn't swing round with the shock I anticipated, but turned in a slow, controlled manner. Upon seeing my face, her pale-green eyes flashed – a moment of fear, quickly mastered. She drew herself taller, cloaking her uncertainty with regal poise like the High Queen she always had been.

'Lady Morgan,' she said formally, as if presiding over a court as regent. 'I suppose you have come to gloat.'

Her dedication to receiving my presence in the worst faith almost made me want to spin on my heel and leave her to reap what she had sown, but for what Mordred had said. Enemies though we were, it wasn't in me to let Guinevere live that sort of horror first-hand.

'Such things are long since beneath my interest,' I replied. 'I need to speak with you in haste. Though it's best if you hear it in private.'

I indicated her knight at my shoulder. She frowned at me, then nodded. 'Leave us,' she told him. 'But continue preparations for my departure. This will not take long.'

The knight bowed and retreated, leaving Guinevere and me alone together for the first time since she had found me wracked with the sickness of early pregnancy from mine and Accolon's soon-to-be-stolen son. Though she could not have known what would happen to the child (and was still not aware), that night she had told me to leave the court or burn at the adultery stake, and, momentarily, my blood seared with remembrance.

'You have plans to leave here,' I made myself say. 'When, and to where?'

'I am expected at Camelot,' she said icily. 'Not that it is any of your business. Say what you must and quickly – I will not be delayed.'

As ever, she knew how to make my hackles rise, but there was no time for such a joust. I was tired, exhausted with the idea of war in any form, even with her. My heart, my mind and entire spirit had gone beyond.

'Do not go to Camelot,' I told her. 'That is all.'

She had already opened her mouth to dismiss me, but my words gave her pause. 'Why would I trust anything you say?'

'You may not, and perhaps that is fair,' I replied. 'All I can say is I rode through the night to tell you not to go. My only proof of honesty is that your husband trusts me again and he would want me to tell you this. He and I were reconciled – I know he has told you.'

'Arthur told me you and he were seeking to *try* and settle your differences,' she said. 'Just before he vanished off to war. Given everything that has happened in the past few months, what people say means increasingly little.'

I held up my hands; in no world was I about to debate with Guinevere about deceit. 'Take it as you will,' I said. 'I have done what I came for.'

I was almost at the door when she said my name. I paused and turned back to her.

'Arthur is dead,' she declared. 'Where should I be but Camelot?'

Her unemotional tone drew me closer again. Of course, she would not want to show herself upset before an adversary, but her demeanour seemed far beyond inner strength. Her husband was dead, and any life she knew had imploded; her stoicism was not so much admirable as it was missing something.

I considered her, then took a risk. 'Arthur is not dead,' I said.

The truth settled as silence. Guinevere regarded me steadily, threading her fingers together before her in a slow, contemplative movement.

The remaining emerald ring glinted from one hand – twin to Lancelot's precious talisman – and a carved gold band shone from the other, identical to Arthur's from their hasty, lovestruck wedding so many moons ago.

'What do you mean?' she said carefully. 'Have you not heard the news?'

'Yes. The declaration was brought to me directly. Nevertheless, he is not dead.'

'Why? Because in your wisdom you refuse to believe it?'

Her voice depicted anger, but without heat, her heartbeat accelerating across my senses. She did not believe it either.

'Indeed,' I replied. 'And because it's not true.'

I held her gaze, challenging her to bring me a more persuasive show of doubt. Instead, she sighed and looked out of the window, across the tangled vista of what was once an ornamental garden.

'How do you know?' she asked. 'That he lives.'

I found myself wordless, wondering how to even begin articulating the tidal pull that Arthur and I so little understood ourselves.

'I ... I can feel it,' I said eventually. 'I could not explain to you how, but—'

Guinevere turned back, so suddenly it cut me off. 'I feel it too.'

'You do?' I said, and she nodded.

'In a different way, no doubt. Still, I know it in my soul. I don't believe Arthur would ever die while there is more for him left to do.'

The truth of her statement struck me – a declaration of pure knowing from someone who had been closer to Arthur than anyone for most of his life, and resounding in my own heart. For a moment we stood, unified in instinct, reaching beyond years of mistrust and hatred.

'Then take my word,' I said. 'Do not go to Camelot. Disaster awaits you there.'

'Further disaster, you mean,' she said drily, and her grim humour caught me off guard. I tilted my head in acknowledgement, and the tension in the room loosened. 'This is not a meeting that either of us wanted, Lady Morgan, but you came to me. The least you can do is explain.'

'Sir Mordred awaits you at Camelot,' I said. 'It was he who brought me the news of Arthur's supposed death, and spreads the falsehood around the kingdom. His intention is to be the High King of All Britain. To solidify his claim, he plans to marry you immediately.'

'*What?*' she exclaimed. 'How could he imagine such a thing? It is not even an appropriate thought.'

'I quite agree,' I replied. 'I told him you were far too old to be a bride.'

She rolled her eyes at my insult, then shook her head in disgust. 'He is my nephew, my ... close relation by marriage. Even if Arthur were not alive, it would be an abomination to God.'

'From how he spoke,' I said delicately, 'I believe he is thinking less of God and only of a crown.'

Guinevere huffed and put her hands on her hips. 'Even more reason for me to go. Once I am at Camelot, I will sit on my throne and ensure everyone knows that Arthur is alive, and that he will deal harshly with that upstart cur of a boy. I cannot be married off while my husband still lives. I remain High Queen of this country and do not fear Sir Mordred.'

'I commend your bravery, truly I do,' I said. 'It will help you in the days to come. But you still cannot ride to Camelot. Mordred has lied about Arthur being dead, while working tirelessly to control information and curry favour with the barons, gaining access to legions of fighting men. All of this to strengthen his hold over the entire kingdom. You are the most important piece of that game, and he will not let you slip through his fingers.'

'He wouldn't dare,' she began, but I held up a halting hand.

'Listen to me,' I insisted. 'Do you think I'd be here if I didn't believe you were in grave danger? Refusal, illegality, the power you believe you hold – none of it matters in the wars of men. What Mordred is willing to do to you, Guinevere ... You and I have our conflicts, but one woman to another, I cannot watch you ride off to violation and torment.'

The harsh honesty of it found its way through, and I felt the chill across her skin as my own. Guinevere broke away from our battle of wills, pacing back towards the window.

'What would you have me do?' she said in a low voice. 'If I don't go where I am called, I can only assume Sir Mordred will come for me. I have loyal knights here, but you say he has armies at his command.

What choice do I have but to go where I am summoned, resist for as long as I can, and hope?'

I was unprepared for her question; I had come here to warn her, not bring answers. I didn't know how to solve Guinevere's problems, nor did I understand her concession to defeat. Throughout my own wild, troubled life, I had never known how to stop fighting, or defying, or trying to be free. Even if it meant escaping, again and again.

'No,' I said vehemently. 'There is always a choice.'

I went to her and took hold of her silken elbows. 'Take your most loyal knights and ride to your strongest fortress. If Mordred wants to besiege your person, force him to do so outside high, unbreachable walls. Make him weaker, buy yourself time and hold fast.'

Guinevere's breath caught, and she stared at me in astonishment. She drew her arms back, but instead of pulling free, she gripped onto my wrists.

'*Hold fast*,' she said. 'That is what Arthur said to me when he left. I thought he meant it as a warning not to stray any further from goodness, but ...'

I shook my head. 'He told me the same. At first I thought it was for caution's sake, but he was urging us to be strong, keep our heads, until he returns to fix this.'

'But he also said that everything he and I had built – the kingdom, our marriage – could be no more,' she replied. 'That the prophecies of his death spoke it thus, and there was no other way. Why would he come back for me?'

'Because he told me he would need my help, and you are what he had to leave behind,' I said. 'That is the reason I'm here. Fate or not, you must keep fighting, Guinevere. He will come, but afford him the chance. Arthur will never forgive himself if he cannot save you.'

She studied me for a long moment, the uncertainty on her face shifting into a fierce, imperious determination. 'The Tower of London,' she said. 'I will ride there and close the gates. Let Mordred throw himself against those unyielding walls.'

With a brief squeeze of my wrists, the Queen released me and flew into action, summoning her blond knight to relay the urgent new arrangements, and sending a woman for her plainest travelling cloak.

Impressed as I was by her efficiency, if I was involved with these new plans, then I owed it to Arthur to see this all the way through.

'It is still wise to think of what happens beyond,' I said. 'You know the prophecy of Arthur's death – what was your intention if it came true?'

She faltered, her expression defensive. I expected to hear Lancelot's name, a twilight love story lived in guilt and bliss in Benoic, so it was a shock when she said, 'The cloister. Where I will go regardless, after this. I long for the company of women, hours spent in contemplation and prayer. I have much to consider before God.'

'And atone for?' I said, because I could not help myself.

Her response was a look that could have cut flesh, and we were comfortably back to how we should be. Her travelling cloak arrived, and I watched as she swung the rich green fabric about her shoulders.

'You forget, Arthur is not without sin,' she said, fastening gold lion-head clasps with quick hands. 'He has his own sources of shame, even if I barely knew him back then.'

'What do you mean?' I asked, but she was already waving it away.

'Never mind. If you do not know, then it's not my place to air that which has been kept secret. I must keep faith with my husband, and the deep love and regard we have always carried for one another.'

She strode out of the room, defying further questions, so I followed her through the main hall and onto the front courtyard, where her retinue was assembling in a tumult of tossing horse heads and organisational shouts. A pile of red-and-white dragon banners lay across hastily stuffed luggage, waiting for their standard bearers.

'Do not carry those,' I said. 'If you are seen—'

'Then those who see me will know their High Queen is alive and present,' Guinevere cut in. 'That the kingdom still stands.'

I shook my head. 'You cannot.'

No more argument came, but her face clouded, sadness catching up to her at last. What was she High Queen of, in any case? If she reached the Tower of London and Arthur came, what would be left for either of them? Before that, even, she had to survive.

I sighed. 'Be still, Your Highness.'

She looked at me curiously, but obeyed. Drawing a deep breath, I reached within for the river of my serenity and plucked silver threads from the air around her. Here, where men armed themselves and thought of battle, the elemental forces were deeply suppressed, every charm aching in my blood as I drew it forth. Still I persisted, knitting a fairy veil across Queen Guinevere, Arthur's wife, not my first enemy but one of my longest.

'These are protective charms,' I told her. 'They will keep you safe from misfortune for several days.'

Her eyebrows lifted, but she said nothing, watching me work with a muted acceptance. Suddenly, in a quiet but clear voice, she said, 'I do not regret either of them. Lancelot nor Arthur. And they do not regret me.'

Such a declaration was unexpected, but it made a strange sense she wanted to express it to someone.

'That is not my business,' I said, and pulled taut the final shining thread. 'This magic should guard you long enough to get to London. Otherwise, I can promise you clear skies to get there, and bad weather along the Camelot roads. If Mordred tries to come for you, wind and rain will slow him down.'

I gestured to her palfrey and she nodded, mounting swiftly without the hand of any knight. I turned away, to where my own horse stood.

'Morgan,' she said, and I looked back. Her eyes were glassy, though she held firmly on to her poise. 'I am grateful to you. I don't know how to say—'

I waved it away. 'I do not need or want your gratitude. I did this for Arthur.'

My dismissal came as a relief to us both. Guinevere gave the ghost of a smile and I nodded in acceptance, pointing towards the road.

'Go now,' I told her. 'I have done all I can. The rest is in your hands.'

50

When I returned to Belle Garde the following morning, Alys and Tressa were waiting in the entrance hall, arms crossed like knights waiting to be ordered into action. They knew where I had been and why, but did not expect my arrival to be a harried appearance from the direction of the back kitchens.

'Is everyone all right?' I asked breathlessly.

Alys frowned at my worry. 'Of course,' she replied. 'Are *you* all right?'

'Yes, it's just …' I paused, unable to quantify the strange concern I had felt as I had ridden back through the darkened forests. Now I was back in the valley and nothing had changed, it seemed overwrought to describe how I had seen or heard nothing on my journey, but nevertheless felt myself slightly pursued.

'I haven't had time to check the charms,' I concluded. 'And with the news of Arthur's death spreading – things are changing so fast.'

'But the King isn't dead,' Tressa replied. 'Doesn't that mean something?'

I shook my head. 'Not for long, if Arthur doesn't appear quickly to prove otherwise. With mass belief and good faith on Mordred's side, it has the power to eventually become the truth, regardless of fact.'

'What about Sir Mordred's threats?' Alys asked. 'Should we prepare the household to leave?'

'No, we must stay exactly where we are,' I said. 'I've sent three separate messages to Benoic, so at least one should reach Arthur. Until then, Belle Garde is safe, perhaps the safest place in the realm. All we can do is …'

A heavy pounding cut me off. We turned towards it in unison, only for it to stop as abruptly as it began. The main door was still shut from the night before, but it had never been locked and no one had seen the barring plank for years. As we wavered, another bout of knocking came, but weaker, fading to a faint scratching, like a clawed animal trying to find its way in.

Tressa started towards the door, but I grabbed her sleeve. 'Stay there.'

Striding across the hall, I placed one hand on my father's knife and pulled open the door. A person in a dark cloak stood stooped and hooded, face concealed. By the time I realised they were leaning on the doorframe, the figure was staggering towards me, legs buckling. I reached out automatically, catching them before they fell.

As soon as my touch landed, I felt her.

'Ninianne?' I said.

She looked up at me in relief. 'Morgan,' she croaked. 'Thank the goddess.'

Steadying herself against my arms, she took her hood down and I gasped. Her face was wan and dirty, hair tangled with twigs and knots, dull as wet rust. Most shocking was her skin; for the first time since I had seen her in childhood, she gave out no light.

'It's all right,' I told Alys and Tressa. 'Go tell the household what we have discussed and to keep within the valley. I have this in hand.'

They nodded and hurried off, leaving me holding Ninianne upright, her breaths ragged with exhaustion.

'What happened to you?' I asked.

'My lake, my home,' she said. 'It's gone. Men came, sowing destruction until my protection, my magic were too weak to hold. I panicked ... I could not keep it safe.'

'What about Lancelot? Does he know of this?'

'He's under siege,' she replied. 'King Arthur has him pinned, the battles are frequent. I no longer know who is dead or alive, or who I am supposed to ...'

She trailed off, the first tears I had ever seen in her spilling over like rain.

'You didn't know how to choose between them,' I said.

She nodded. 'My indecision meant I was too late to stop either one. Now it's a catastrophe ... the realm, finished.'

The thought rocked through her like an earthquake, and I barely caught her before she hit the flagstones. To see the wise, self-possessed

Lady of the Lake prostrated like this was a shock I hadn't expected, the arcane certainty she radiated something I had always relied upon. If she was no longer in control, what hope was there for the rest of us?

'Come with me,' I told her, gathering my bravery. 'We can talk about all of this, but first you need to rest. Everything will seem different after you've recovered.'

Taking her hands, I sent a bolt of healing through her until she was upright enough for me to slip my shoulder under her arm. She leaned hard against me, her voice weak.

'I don't know what to do, Morgan,' she said. 'All is ruined. I have nowhere.'

For so many years, the thought was inconceivable, but it came naturally now, like the gust of brisk air before it rains. I drew my arms tighter around her.

'That's not true,' I said. 'You have here.'

I took Ninianne to the long bedchamber, where she fell into a troubled sleep.

Since the night Arthur had spent there, I had kept the room open, the tapestries permanently removed to leave Lancelot's paintings on display – more beauty than danger now the worst had happened. After so many years trying to keep its memories at bay, the room felt like part of the house again.

I stayed with her all day, in turns observing and pacing, opening the windows so the spring's watery music would trickle in and soothe her. I tried not to think about how I had never seen her this way, how she had always been so vital and in command; how her condition seemed an augury of something too terrible for words.

When she awoke, the late afternoon light had painted the sky gold. Ninianne blinked slowly as she took in the unfamiliar room, then me standing by her bedside.

'Morgan,' she said. 'It wasn't a dream.'

I shook my head. With unexpected haste, she slung back the coverlet and stood, gliding across to an open window, seeking the spring's song.

'You should keep to your bed,' I protested mildly. 'Even water fairies need rest.'

She ignored me, but did sit down in the window seat. Sighing, I took a jug of water and poured a generous gobletful, clarifying its goodness with the trick she had bestowed for my pregnancy nausea, and I had once used to restore her despairing son.

I handed her the cup and sat down opposite. She took a long sip, a candle's worth of light rippling across her skin.

'Thank you,' she said. 'This water, the elemental magic – it's near perfect.'

Her compliment made me flush with pride. 'I can do more, if you let me lay hands. The boost I gave you in the hall should have lasted longer, but I will try again.'

She shook her head, copper hair faintly catching the sun. 'No matter how you restore me, it will seep out again. Between the destruction, the long journey, and the magic of this land fast disappearing, I am doomed to a fate I cannot control. Half a lifetime lived on this land, and this was the only place I could think of to come.'

'I'm happy you did,' I said. 'I wouldn't have you seek sanctuary anywhere else.'

'Still, this care … it is good of you, Morgan. Given our past …'

'We have long transcended whichever "side" of an argument we were on,' I said. 'What matters is you are here, and we are more in agreement than we have ever been.'

Ninianne nodded and turned her face to the glass, Belle Garde's green hills reflecting in her clearer eyes. I felt her thoughts drifting elsewhere.

'What happened?' I said softly. 'To your home.'

She sighed. 'A group of soldiers came to my part of Brocéliande. They cut down my trees, filled my lake with sewage, celebrating that they were destroying where Lancelot lived. Never mind that it was my home, my place of safety.'

'Whose soldiers?' I asked. 'Surely Arthur would not order such a thing?'

'Of course not. These men were barely an army, in strange livery, but strong in numbers and their hunger for destruction.' She closed her eyes, then looked at the spring again. 'With the damage, the charm concealing the island faded, and the house, the land, my sacred places, became visible. When that happened, they sailed across and tore everything apart. I tried to save it with magic, but I was weakened, the task too great. I had to run. When they set everything alight, I felt it burn as if it were my own skin.'

'I'm so sorry, Ninianne,' I said, though no words were good enough.

She accepted it with a muted nod. 'I managed to escape, and used the last of my strength to summon a boat and ask the waterways to convey me here. But I still feel the men in pursuit, as if they want something. I should not have brought trouble to your door.'

'Nothing can reach you here,' I assured her. 'If trouble comes, it will have me to contend with. We will wait out this conflict together, until Lancelot and Arthur come home.'

It raised a smile in her, and for now it was enough. I poured another cup of clarified water, and she drank it with a steadier hand, her light rose-pink in the falling sun.

'You do not seem surprised at this new war,' she said.

'I'm not,' I admitted. 'In a way, I was part of what started it.'

She looked alarmed. 'What do you mean?'

I sighed and rose, gesturing to the room. 'It will be simpler if you just see.'

Ninianne followed me to the wall nearest the door, where Lancelot's paintings began – images of his happy life with her, leading up to his arrival at Camelot. Light fell in shafts through the windows, making vivid the blues and greens of his landscapes, the golden castles surrounded by red and white, the people in all their vibrant and unflinching detail.

'When Lancelot was here the second time,' I explained. 'These paintings are what he did. His truth as he saw and felt it.'

Ninianne said nothing, enraptured by his work, seeing their time together through her son's eyes. She moved along the walls, lingering at every picture, studying his brushstrokes, her restored light surging with the force of her emotions.

After a while she said, 'This started the war?'

I could have said it was too much for her delicate state and spared myself what was sure to be her reproach, but our differences finally felt settled, and maybe she and I needed one another. It no longer served us to keep secrets.

'Arthur came here a few months ago,' I said. 'Just before Lancelot and Guinevere were exposed in Camelot. It wasn't easy, but we talked for a long time – about the past and our mistakes, what the future holds. He apologised for Accolon's death, the lies and distrust that tore us asunder, and admitted our bond has never really left us. We spoke of the possibility of forgiveness.'

She regarded me in astonishment, the image of her son glowing behind her, a glorious knight reduced to riding in a cart.

'He agreed to stay to talk further, and I ordered this room opened for him to sleep in,' I continued. 'The paintings were covered with tapestries, but he saw what was beneath. He galloped out of here in the early hours and headed directly for Camelot.'

I sighed; confession was harder than I had imagined. 'I cannot with certainty say that my intentions were completely innocent, but I did not want this to happen. That was the start of me knowing the war was coming.'

'Even so, it does not seem like enough,' Ninianne said. 'How could King Arthur be sure of what he was seeing? He loved and trusted Lancelot, and anyone could have painted this wall. Why would he believe it?'

'Because he knew,' I said. 'He saw the paintings and recognised what was already within him. Deep down, he has probably known for a long time.'

I watched my confession settle, weighty upon her fraying hopes. Wearied anew, Ninianne leaned against the wall, resting her head beside one of Lancelot's self-portraits. 'We have all been wrong. In trying to avoid the betrayal prophecy, I misjudged everything so badly. The Grail Quest worked for a while, but failure drove Lancelot back into Guinevere's arms with more fervency than before.'

'There was never anything you could have done to prevent that,' I said. 'I tried to tell you. Camelot is Lancelot's greatest love – he will always go back. It doesn't mean you were wrong to try and protect him. Nor did you know what would happen.'

'But *you* did,' she said. 'You knew it would go wrong, and I should have listened. I was only thinking of Lancelot, but my actions brought grief, jealousy and division to the court and sowed the seeds for this war.

I am supposed to be trying to shift fate away from the prophecies, not accelerate Camelot's downfall.'

I went to her and took hold of her arm. 'Listen to me,' I said. 'There's nothing to be done. It is all of our fault – everyone and everything, since the very beginning.'

She frowned. 'What do you mean?'

'Who among us hasn't contributed to this?' I said. 'I put Arthur in the room with Lancelot's paintings. Lancelot painted them because of his sins. Arthur and Guinevere married in youth and haste, with the world's eyes upon them and the weight of a kingdom on their shoulders. Trouble was inevitable – not because of prophecy, but because it is *life*.'

Ninianne straightened, pushing herself away from the wall. 'I cannot disagree with that. But how can we account for the fact that many of Merlin's predictions were correct? For all his faults, he loved King Arthur and did not lie to him.'

'No, he wasn't a liar,' I agreed. 'At least, never intentionally. Merlin was a brilliant reader of the stars, but his trouble came in interpretation. The prophecies have some merit, but they are too vague, too simplistic to contain such a complicated life as Arthur's. Consider it – my treasons since Accolon, Lancelot and Guinevere, King Lot reneging on the treaty that ended in his death all those years ago, even Merlin keeping Arthur's true lineage a secret until he was crowned – all can be interpreted as betrayals. But everything he predicted was put through the lens of what he deemed most important, and Merlin was profoundly flawed at understanding the chaos of the human heart. And due to his need for control, he never considered the prophecies beyond his own worldview.'

She said nothing, but looked doubtful, so I took up her hands.

'Do you see what it means, Ninianne? Nothing we did alone started this war, and there's nothing we can do to hasten or prevent the future. Arthur has faced a thousand challenges, and death is inevitable, but all of these things have happened and he has survived. There is no reason to believe he won't continue far beyond this.'

I expected at least her relief, but my conclusion did not seem to bring her any respite. Instead, she relinquished my hands, her light dimming back to grey.

'Your logic is undeniable, Morgan,' she said. 'But it doesn't matter, because there is something important you do not know. There is another prophecy, one that no one has ever heard. A prophecy so certain, so specific, it terrified Merlin to his bones.'

'What's another, in a book full of them?' I said, but the seriousness on her face was enough to silence me.

'It is not written there,' she said. 'Merlin feared its meaning so much, he never put it down in ink. This augury appeared to him in the skies and every method of divination he used for months, requiring no interpretation. He only confessed it to me because it disturbed him so badly. That's why I wanted the Book of Prophecies, and asked for your insight. I was seeking any sign of Merlin's unwanted prediction, or if he had managed to find an answer to the question it posed.'

'What did this prophecy say?'

'That King Arthur would have a son, who would bring about his death.'

The words shivered through me, despite my better judgement. 'But Arthur has no sons, legitimate or bastards,' I pointed out. 'In all my years seeking his missteps, I have never heard such a thing. Surely there would have been talk of …'

The shiver became a chill of the familiar, then a cold echo: of careless words, spoken years in the past.

Morgause met the new King in Richmond. It's said they came to a friendly accord.

The last Orkney babe – one not like the others, if you take my meaning.

Then, mere days ago:

She told me of my true father, though I suspect he considers me a grave mistake.

Epiphany fell like an executioner's axe.

'Oh God no – it cannot be.' I put my hands over my face, unable to fathom what I was about to say, everything it meant. 'The son is Sir Mordred.'

How had I been so blind? Mordred's keen grey eyes and pale-gold fairness were not only my mother's likeness: they were Arthur's.

Ninianne's jaw dropped, her certainty instant, as strong as mine. 'Of course,' she said. 'It all fits. The army that came to my lake – they were clad in black bearing an old, abandoned standard – the Orkney eagle. King Arthur left Sir Mordred in charge …'

'... and with that power, he seeks to destroy him and take his crown,' I said. 'Mordred separated Arthur from Lancelot, and now the kingdom will fall.'

The fifth and suspect Orkney son was not only the product of a mistaken union between my sister and her half-brother, but the product of a scandal so damning, so against God, that Merlin had fought to keep it secret. What it had created was a shunned child, a man seething with rejection and rage, who had learned of the father he believed had forsaken him, and turned that knowledge into hatred.

'My *sister*,' I said. 'Morgause and my—'

'Don't think of it, Morgan,' Ninianne cut in. 'By Sir Mordred's age, it was before King Arthur's marriage, or any of you were aware of your relation.'

'Maybe so, but it is still perturbing to contemplate.'

Such a connection perhaps accounted for the unease that crept under my skin when I was in my nephew's presence. But as I thought again of his snide, echoing face, the aversion I felt came from something beyond, a fear ingrained deep in my core so long ago that I had not recognised it. Sir Mordred's sneering arrogance, quick aggression and taste for cruelty was the perfect reflection of Uther Pendragon. His lust for power, too, was the same as his grandfather's – selfish, greedy, concerned with nothing but his own relentless needs.

'He wants one of us,' I said. 'Mordred came to see me, lied about Arthur's death, then asked me to lend him my magic to control the realm. I refused, then he made threats. No doubt his men are pursuing you for the same reason.'

'I don't care,' Ninianne said. 'I must go to Benoic and tell King Arthur of this, convince him and Lancelot to form a peace. They will reunite and save the kingdom.'

I shook my head. 'It's too late for that. I have already sent a bird to Arthur, telling him that Mordred intends to force Guinevere into marriage. He will be on his way back to rescue her by now.'

'By himself, with only half his fighting force? It won't work – without Lancelot, the prophecy is too strong.' Panic gripped her chest and she clutched at it, doubling over in breathlessness. 'How could I have missed this? I have been so distracted, by Lancelot, the dying magic, my mistakes, when the danger was closer than I imagined. Now, Mordred will take the Crown of All Britain and at his hand, King Arthur will die.'

Her voice cracked and she slumped against me. I tried to keep her upright, but her form was elusive, as if I was trying to hold up a body of water, and she slid to the floor.

I put my hands to her heart, her neck and face, trying to sense any ailment. There was none. 'Ninianne, tell me what's wrong so I can heal you.'

'There is no cure for this,' she croaked. 'The world is dying, and so am I.'

Frustration rose up that once again I was failing, my skills not fairy enough to restore one as ancient and powerful as she.

'No,' I insisted. 'I've healed you before. We are not so different.'

Within the words, I felt the truth and the lie, then the soaring sensation that always came with solving a problem. We were similar *and* different, and therein lay the answer.

One as ancient and powerful as she.

I threw my arm under hers and asked the air to help me raise her to her feet.

'Don't give in, Ninianne,' I said. 'I'll fix this, or the Devil take me.'

51

There was no time to walk, and Ninianne didn't have the strength, so I brought her white horse to the courtyard and helped her into the saddle, then climbed up in front of her.

'Hold on,' I said, drawing her arm around my waist.

She had enough wherewithal to obey, letting herself lean into me. Her presence still radiated, but I could feel her warmth fading against my skin. I rode as fast as the horse would carry us up the long woodland path to Llyn Glas.

Halfway there, I felt a new weight on my shoulder and glanced back to see Ninianne's head hanging down.

'Just stay awake,' I urged her. 'All will be well, I promise.'

It was hope rather than confidence; I had no idea if what I was doing would work. Once the willows were in sight, I didn't pause to wonder; I rode the horse directly into the lake until it stood submerged up to its withers.

Dismounting, I brought Ninianne with me, almost sinking under her unconscious form and my soaking wet skirts and mantle. Her body slid beneath the surface without a splash, as if the water wanted her, had accepted her. Still I held her chin above the surface, afraid to let her sink. What if I was wrong?

In the midst of my hesitation, Ninianne took a huge gasping breath and opened her eyes, incandescent green and fixed on mine.

Trust the water, she urged wordlessly.

I let her go, her entire form vanishing into its dark-blue embrace. I didn't want to turn away, but I had to believe. The lake had saved me, and it would save her.

I led the horse out and tied it near the path, then returned to the shore, watching the surface where she had submerged. All was quiet – the breeze had vanished, the willow fronds perfectly undisturbed, the lake glasslike, more still than it had ever been. My skirts dried and I helped them along by toying with the heat in the air. The sun began to fall from the sky, but all I could do was watch and wait, as though Llyn Glas needed me to bear witness.

Then, a ripple in the distance, concentric circles getting wider. Splitting at the curve, the circles turned into chevrons, pointing in my direction. A flash of light competed with the sun, shocking, blinding, but I kept my eyes on the water.

The Lady of the Lake broke the surface, copper hair blazing like fire, her skin brighter than I had ever seen it. She rose from the blue until her feet walked atop the surface, flowing forth to the shore and alighting on the grass like a freshwater wave.

'Ninianne,' I said. 'Thank the goddess.'

She smiled, unhurried and contented, gleaming with restoration. 'You swore to me that I would never see your lake,' she said.

I laughed, and it was all relief. 'Yet here we are,' I replied.

'You saved me, Morgan,' she said. 'More than once. Thank you.'

We stood there for a long moment, absorbing what it all meant. She had saved me in the past, and I had returned the deed in time for the future. We were even.

'Never mind prophecies,' I said. 'Let this stand as undeniable proof that we can never truly predict what the future holds.'

Ninianne inclined her head in agreement, then paused, squinting as if trying to catch the bars of a distant song. 'Something is ... here,' she said.

Before I could question, she had waded back into the lake, skimming her fingers over the surface. 'There is a presence, I am sure of it. What can I feel, Morgan?'

'I don't know,' I replied. 'You are *of the Lake*. How can I say what you feel?'

'You do know.' She strode out of the water and took up my hands. 'I thought so. Whatever it is sings of you, too.'

Around us, the willow leaves stirred, though there was no wind, pinpricks of gold and silver glinting between the green.

Did she mean ...?

He had never appeared to anyone but me. I had mostly accepted it, while never quite shaking the possibility that a great part of my life was based on fantasy. And yet ...

'Accolon,' I said. 'Are you there?'

For a moment, nothing, and my insides trembled with the same plunging doubt I had felt with Alys and Tressa. I looked at Ninianne, but she wasn't paying attention to me, gazing at a cool, gentle light appearing just beyond my shoulder.

A familiar calm swept through me, an arrival I knew so well. I did not need to wonder if Ninianne could see him; I could feel her awareness through our joined hands.

'*Oui*, of course,' Accolon said, stepping out from under the willow.

Ninianne released me and took him in, curiosity shimmering from her body. I had never seen Accolon shy, but he eyed her with an uncertainty he rarely displayed. He too had become used to being perceived by no one but me.

'Sir Accolon of Gaul, I believe?' she said, as if greeting a shade half risen from death was entirely usual. 'We have never properly met. I am—'

'The Lady of the Lake,' he supplied. 'I know.'

'Ninianne, to be precise,' she corrected. 'There are many ladies of many lakes. I am only one of them.'

He nodded with a mild shrug, his eternal insouciance undaunted. It was always refreshing how the stranger parts of my life bothered him so little.

'You were there at my death,' he said archly. 'Though that may not count as a formal meeting.'

I had begun to feel mildly dizzy. 'You can see him?' I asked Ninianne. 'I mean – obviously you can, but ...'

'No one else has but you?' she said. 'That is mysterious, but not impossible.'

I nodded, though it clarified nothing at all in my swimming head. So I was definitively not deluded, but that meant I truly had spent years interacting with my resurrected lover, recreated with my own healing power. Either way, it felt like madness.

'How did you come to be here, Sir Accolon?' Ninianne said.

'I am hardly the one to ask,' he replied. 'Whatever this is, or what I am – Morgan made it so.'

Ninianne turned to me. '*You* did this?'

I had never seen such a gleam on her face, and it made my heart leap to behold. She had not taught me for decades, yet her goddess-like wonder, the idea she might be impressed with something I'd done, was more potent than any other praise I could receive.

'Y-yes,' I said. 'I'd been working on a resurrection formula for years – since Merlin's. Raising Accolon was the reason I wanted the Shroud of Tithonus. I had the Shroud and his heart, and I thought it would be enough. But I failed.'

'Failed?' She stared at me, incredulous. 'He stands here before us like this, and you consider it a failure?'

Accolon gave me an affectionate grin. 'See. I told you. *C'est un miracle.*'

'No,' I protested. 'He isn't whole. What I've done is make a terrible error.'

Ninianne stepped closer to Accolon, walking around him with deep scrutiny, which he allowed with an air of amusement.

'I haven't been this keenly observed by a woman in many years,' he commented. 'Perhaps I should be flattered.'

She said nothing, finishing her circle. Once satisfied, she came to my side once more. 'Morgan,' she said gravely, 'what you have done is *incredible*. You should not have been able to perform such a feat.'

'You don't understand,' I said. 'I've done this before, to greater success. You don't know of the white hart. It was dead, torn apart.'

'What you achieved is known to me,' she said. 'You did remarkable work at Merlin's, but the reason your efforts succeeded was because the creature was buried on the island. I've told you – the soil within the moat holds deep and ancient magic, gathering power for millennia. The white hart would not have emerged alive and complete otherwise.'

The sorcerer, too, had mentioned the land's power, the trio of ancient trees that once stood where his house was, creating a deep intersection of old magic. He had directed us to bury the mangled deer within the potent roots of the remaining oak, but never claimed my success was anything to do with the land.

'Merlin treated the white hart as my own miracle,' I said. 'The credit for which he rode off to steal.'

'He wanted to sweet-talk you, no doubt, keep you with him for longer,' Ninianne said. 'In truth, he assumed the earth caused the restoration. The island was key in his plans for Arthur. His intention was to bring him there when the time came for resurrection.'

I looked at her stupidly and she beamed warmth towards me. 'Don't you see, Morgan – even with your developing work, neither he nor I thought it was possible to perform such a wonder as this.' She gestured to Accolon. 'With only a heart and the Shroud of Tithonus, nothing should have happened. The resurrection of a fully formed shade, with mind, memory and soul – it is miraculous. Everything I thought lost is now open to us again.'

'Do not fix any hope upon it,' I insisted. 'He cannot touch, or feel hunger, tiredness – he has no human needs. He's trapped here, unable to move beyond the willow tree. Magical feat or not, it went wrong.'

I looked at Accolon, pained all over again at what he endured because of my selfishness, my desperation, the grief I could not live with. 'I don't regret a moment I have spent with you here,' I told him. 'But what I did wasn't for the best. I wanted another chance, freedom for both of us. Instead, I have trapped you for eternity, bound to this damned tree.'

He sighed. 'No, *mon cœur*. How many times must we—'

'What tree?' Ninianne interrupted. I gestured to the willow and she shook her head. 'He is not bound to that.'

'He is,' I insisted. 'He cannot move outside its environs. Accolon, show her.'

Accolon obediently strode away from the weeping branches. At once, his image began to fade, but he kept going, as if about to take the path to the house. I opened my mouth to stop him, but he disintegrated so fast I didn't manage a sound. Panic flickered through me; every time he vanished, I still feared it would be the last time.

I turned back to Ninianne, who looked utterly unperturbed.

'There was no need to scatter him,' she said. 'I didn't mean he was free. He is confined, yes, but not by the willow. Sir Accolon is bound to the lake.'

I stared at her, astonished I had not considered it myself. At times, when he was weary, his presence often rippled, but the thought never gained significance.

'I buried his heart at the roots,' I countered. 'The tree makes the most sense.'

Ninianne shook her head gently. 'Weeping willows require a great deal of water. This one is large and flourishing because of what the soil, its roots, draw from the lake.'

She looked at Accolon's stardust drifting across the still blue surface. 'This resurrection makes even more sense now. The water feeding the tree helped to remake Sir Accolon because it is your dominant element. The huge task was beyond what the elements alone can achieve, but it gave him as much life as it could. Which, combined with your healing and the Shroud, was a great deal.'

'So he is ...' I began.

'Of the Lake, yes,' she supplied. 'Not completely, but very much its entity. That is why I sensed him the moment I touched the water.'

As usual with her, it was baffling and chimed with perfect clarity at the same time. Instinctively, I looked for Accolon, but his essence was a distant glimmer now. It would be a while before he was back, and I felt it as a small wave of loss.

I sighed. 'Does it matter what he is bound to? He is stuck, regardless.'

I paced to the lake until my feet touched the waterline, gazing across the darkening pool and up the green mountainside, to where the valley's edge touched the sky. Everything seemed eternal and impermanent both.

'Morgan.' Ninianne's voice was a low song. 'I know what you've done here was not the solution you wanted, but it is a revelation. It could be the realm's saving grace. Even if Mordred succeeds in killing him, King Arthur's deliverance from death is still possible.'

'How?' I asked. 'The Shroud of Tithonus is gone. Say I could perfect a form of resurrection before the magic leaves these lands – if I had an entire body to work with instead of a mere heart – without the Shroud it cannot be done.'

'You are forgetting one important thing. There is another resurrection object. Perhaps not as powerful, but with your skills and the right environment ... this is far from over. Even better, it is in King Arthur's possession, and bound to him.'

'What object?' I asked uneasily.

'Excalibur's scabbard,' she said, and my body went cold. 'If I go to the King and explain everything, he will give it to me.'

So it was true; Arthur had never told Ninianne about his loss of the scabbard. After my exile, he had deemed that the way of a king was to present the strongest, most formidable front, even to those who were sent to help him. It was Merlin's lesson: retain the appearance of power at all costs. Aghast, I put my head in my hands.

'Morgan?' Ninianne said. 'What is it?'

I couldn't bear to speak the truth directly. 'You took the scabbard from Accolon,' I replied. 'You saw it was blue-and-white leather. The one Arthur wears is jewelled.'

She was silent for so long that I looked up, in time to see realisation cast its shadow over her face. 'The King told me he had it restored,' she replied. 'That you had changed its appearance and he wanted it back how it was. Fit for his sword, he said.'

Slowly, unbearably, I shook my head. 'I assumed you knew – I never imagined Arthur would keep it from you. The scabbard he carries is not the one you gave him.'

'Then what is it?' she said in a small voice.

'A counterfeit. An excellent copy that I had made when he entrusted me with Excalibur's care. I suppose, after believing in my betrayal, he had to show the kingdom he had regained his object of great power. He could not very well declare that I had taken it again, when I saw him in the abbey.'

'*You* took it?' she exclaimed, her light returning. 'Then there is nothing to worry about. As long as it is in the possession of one of us when the time comes …'

At my expression, her voice faded, despair dawning in her eyes.

'I don't have it,' I said. 'When I heard Accolon had died and my theft of the scabbard was blamed, I was wild with grief. The object was too powerful, no one deserved it. So I threw it away – for good.'

Ninianne's hand flew to her mouth. 'Where?' she demanded.

'Into a lake near the abbey where Arthur was healing. I spoke to the water, asked it to swallow the scabbard forever, and it responded. It sucked it into a whirlpool and assured me there it would stay.'

I grabbed her arm. 'But you are *of the Lake* – you can go there, find it, ask for it back. Maybe all is not lost.'

Ninianne hung her head. Under my hand, her skin was stone cold. 'I know that lake,' she said. 'It has no guardian, no fairy to reason with. It is ancient, indifferent, and keeps its secrets, which is why you were drawn there. What it took, it will not return.'

'Don't say that,' I pleaded. 'You can do wonders – that can't be all there is.'

She sighed, so deeply it seemed to echo around the entire valley. 'Even if I could, the scabbard's hide was imbued with magic, not formed from it. Twenty years in water and mud – the leather would not have survived nature's decay.'

'Are you saying …?'

'All is lost,' she said. 'Any chance we had of saving King Arthur resided in the Shroud of Tithonus, or Excalibur's scabbard.'

'My brother will die because of me?' I exclaimed. 'I am the cause of his destruction after all?'

She regarded me with attempted calm, but I could sense her bone-deep chill. 'I cannot answer that. Only you know in your heart what your actions have led to.'

The thought struck me like a battering ram, and I fought to keep from falling to my knees. 'We can fix this,' I said. 'I know we can. There must be another way.'

Ninianne looked at me with an indifference I knew she did not feel, then put her back to the water.

'It's over, Morgan,' she said, and glided away, leaving me alone beside the lake.

52

'Where is she going?'

I hadn't realised Accolon had returned; he had never re-formed so quickly before. He stood at the willow's edge, observing Ninianne remounting her horse and riding away.

'She's leaving,' I said, leading us under the tree's swaying fronds where he could appear whole again. 'I told her about Excalibur's scabbard – that I threw it away. All this time she never knew it was gone. I destroyed her last chance of saving Arthur.'

'She'll come back,' he said.

'Why would she? I have just set her final scrap of hope alight with another of my acts of defiance.'

I sank down between the willow roots and sighed. Accolon sat at my side, regarding me directly until I raised my eyes to his.

'Morgan,' he said, the way he often did, as though it were a complete sentence.

In that one word I heard it all: his adoration and belief; his sense of when I was giving up too easily; the grit he carried beneath his carefree demeanour that had driven him to his successes and happiness. The strength to bear my heavy heart when I could no longer.

'What about everything else she said?' he asked. 'About my presence here – what you have achieved.'

'For a moment, it pleased me deeply,' I said. 'That you are real beyond all doubt, and the best of my knowledge and skills brought you forth.'

'But?'

'But it's not deserved,' I said. 'In reality, I was not enough. What I did brought you back only in part. It entrapped you, binding you to the tree – the lake – whichever, it hardly matters. The only thing that makes me happy is … that it's truly you. We have had all this time together. And even that is selfish, because what choice have you had? It's imperfect, craven, yet this has been the most wonderful thing I have done in the past two decades.'

'A wonder I wish you believed in,' he replied. 'Given the chance, I would have chosen this to be with you again. I will never regret that you tried.'

I smiled sadly at him 'The worst part is, I don't regret it either. For so long, thinking that we could be together again was all that kept me drawing breath. I was wrong to do it, but it saved me.'

'Then it was worth it,' he said firmly. 'If I have to be bound to our lake for eternity for you to believe your life, your future, is worth preserving, then I would answer your call from death a thousand times.'

His love, the absences we could not surmount, ached in me anew. How had we endured, found joy, while being deprived of the closeness of touch?

'I know you would,' I said. 'But I have stolen the future of so many – yours, Arthur's, even Ninianne's. If I cannot think my way out of this, then every false charge against my name will be proven correct. I will have spent my life in pursuit of destruction, not healing.'

I looked at him, seeking agreement to my dire pronouncement, sympathy for the hopelessness I alone had created. Accolon's face showed no flicker of pity, but remained tender as he refused to indulge me.

'Then think your way out of this,' he said.

'I can't,' I protested. 'If Ninianne, an immortal water fairy and King Arthur's own Lady of the Lake, cannot see a way through this fog I have conjured, then what chance do I have? She's right – there is nothing left.'

Restless, I rose and paced to the edge of the water again. I knew more of Llyn Glas and its depths today than I had learned in years, but now it yielded nothing.

Before the emptiness could settle, Accolon was beside me, sharing the view of our silver-blue lake as we had done countless times.

'Perhaps it's fine that there are no more challenges to defeat,' I said. 'To relinquish control, accept I have gone as far as I can.' I turned to my Gaul, and he faced me, his sunlit beauty arresting me anew. 'You are my greatest feat.'

Softly, he smiled, but shook his head. 'No, I'm not.'

'Yes,' I insisted. 'You always were. Not just my bringing you back, but in life – the fact that I found you at all. The first time, then what it took to keep finding one another, the impossibility of every moment. That you loved me at all is a miracle I cannot imagine being capable of. Yet it happened – we brought ourselves into existence. If that isn't a feat worthy of legend, then I do not know what is. How lucky I am to have been loved by you.'

Though he never forgot his phantom state any more, Accolon raised his hand to my face as if he could not help it. At the brush of his warmth, I closed my eyes and remembered his gold-dust fingertips as touch, the proximity of his body a memory of pleasure always too hard to bear, but worth the agony.

'And I by you, *mon cœur*,' Accolon said. 'That you loved me is the only blessing I have ever needed. As for the rest of it, you are wrong.'

My eyes flew open in amazement; in our many lives together, I could count the times he had told me I was wrong on one hand. He offered me his most charming smile.

'All right,' I said ruefully. 'Tell me how.'

'It is only what you already know, deep inside,' he replied. 'That our love – powerful and deathless as it will always be – is not your miracle. I am bound to your past, and you are so much more.'

'You will never be in my past,' I said. 'Forever, you will be with me.'

'I will, in some way or another,' he agreed. 'But I am not all there is – I never was. You are not meant to stop, Morgan. There is no world in which you will be finished with seeking, learning, expanding your mind. Always, you will have more to do. What you are, your extraordinary self, goes far beyond me and our love, the time we spent here.'

'Accolon, no ...' I began, but he held up his hand in interruption.

'Do you know what the greatest honour of my life was?' he asked.

A litany of possibilities ran through my mind: his knighthood; the years of joust victories and travel with Sir Manassen; choosing to fight for Arthur and a cause he believed in. Once he had said it was bringing Tressa back to Alys from a hostile Camelot, or taking Robin in and raising him to become the knight, the good man, that he wanted to be. His many successes, achieved on his own terms.

'The greatest honour of my life,' he continued, 'was that here, in this place of ours, you let me stay by your side. You chose to sit and dance and laugh together, to share your quicksilver mind, to lie with me night after night. You fought for us, you sacrificed, you gave over your heart and trusted me to hold it close. The greatest honour I have ever received, Morgan, is that you paused in flight to be with me.'

Tears were running down my face, my heart so tight in my chest I felt it would burst, but this time it was not from despair but something greater – a soaring song, reaching its peak; a blue-bright sky breaking through clouds. Pure joy, without the crushing companion of grief.

'Why are you saying this?' I asked. 'It sounds like an ending, when it cannot be.'

'I say this because I am far from all you have left,' he replied. 'Because you belong in the future, *mon cœur*, creating wonders from knowledge, performing feats of brilliance as no other can. There is more beyond this, and you deserve to find it. But this belief will come only from yourself.'

He was right, but he was also one of the few who could make my mercurial mind stop and listen. 'The future,' I said with a sigh. 'I wish I knew how to get there.'

'You will find a way,' he said. 'That has always been your strength. I do know this – whatever happens, your fate is in your own hands. Do not forget, you are Morgan le Fay.'

I let the music of my name from his lips flow through me, the rush of love and quiet exhilaration that came with feeling myself completely known, by one who had seen me exactly as I was from the very first.

'Morgan le Fay,' I echoed. 'I am. Now and forevermore.'

Accolon smiled and enveloped me, perfect and made of light. I could have stayed that way for eternity, bathed in his warmth and belief, the love we felt so powerfully, even across our veil of separation.

Instead, a high, impatient shriek cut through our lovers' haze. We looked up to see a sleek dark falcon over the treetops: Hecate, my fractious peregrine, jesses still attached but climbing towards the sky in furious haste.

Instinctively, I broke away from Accolon and sent up my recall whistle, before she could soar out of sight. The bird heard it; I saw her falter, and for once she changed her mind. Curving her path, she tilted down and flew a brisk half circle, alighting on a low branch of the left-hand apple tree.

'One of ours?' Accolon asked.

'My own peregrine,' I said. 'She must have escaped the mews.'

On calm feet, I approached the tree, murmuring compliments to the falcon. Eyeing me, she no longer seemed sure of herself, and I remembered why I had named her thus – not because of Alys's tapestry, or my more witch-like interests, but because her namesake was the goddess of crossroads. Clever as she was, this bird had always been caught at one, between comfort, her training, instinct and a thirst for liberation. And I had persisted with her complications until she became my favourite falcon, because I understood.

Some birds are only ever meant to be free, my son had said, with wisdom both inherited and his own. He had seen the conflict in her and considered its cure, whereas I had only made excuses to keep her with me. Maybe I had been wrong.

I took a few cautious steps towards the falcon's branch, low but still far out of my reach. The bird gave a chirp of recognition, so I wrapped my mantle around my upraised fist and whistled again. I didn't expect it, especially without the reward of meat, but the peregrine swooped down onto my clenched hand with a thud. She was trusting me.

With careful fingers, I untied the jesses around her fearsome feet. She kept her sharp gaze on my face as her fetters slipped away, leaving her lighter, unburdened. Tentatively, the falcon extended her wings with a slow elegance, barred black and white beneath, slate-blue top feathers shining; experimenting with her new, unleashed state.

I moved closer to the water and lifted my arm slightly, testing her in turn. Hecate glanced away, out across the lake, then brought her gold-ringed eyes back to mine.

'Fly,' I told her.

And she did; I didn't need to throw my arm or send her into the wind. The falcon went of her own volition, wings catching on the air, gliding over the surface of the lake with bladelike grace. Where she went now, what she did in the wilderness, was undecided, yet to come, but the choice was hers.

Seeing the bird depart, Accolon came and stood beside me. We were just beyond the willow tree, and his edges were starting to blur, but he didn't seem to mind.

'Do you know what the word "peregrine" means?' I asked, and he shook his head.

'Wanderer,' I said. 'She that roams.'

'It suits her,' he agreed. 'Where did you learn it?'

'My father told me, on a day not unlike this. It was the last time we ever spoke alone.'

Then, I heard it again, as if Gorlois, Duke of Cornwall stood by my side on Tintagel's windswept headland: my father's voice, telling me about falcons, and though I didn't know it yet, speaking of life itself.

Do you know what her greatest strength is, Morgan? he had asked of Jezebel, his own favourite peregrine, and now I knew. Not her talons, her sharp beak, or the speed and deadly accuracy she had honed since birth.

Survival, he had told me. *Any moment she can fly away, knowing she can live. That is the greatest power of all.*

A brief piece of wisdom, given from a father to his youngest daughter, a child he would not see grow into the woman she became. Even then, he had known who I was.

True power comes from freedom, and the ability to survive what befalls us.

All along, I had been the bird, the peregrine. She that roams.

Now, at Llyn Glas, my liberated falcon reached the valley's high mountainside on perfect wings and disappeared over the horizon, not a twitch of doubt or pause in her mind. She understood she was free.

In her wake came another memory of my father, crouching before me on Tintagel's headland, his deep-blue eyes on mine, and an oath I had sworn to keep.

You are wise, Morgan, you always were. You must use that wisdom, harness it, learn to wield it. Promise me you will not forget.

'I see it now,' I said. 'I know what I have to do.'

I turned to Accolon, still there, eternally beside me, waiting for what I would say next. His smile for me was as it always had been – charming, beautiful, full of love.

'Alors,' he said. 'Go and do it.'

53

As it was, I didn't have to go far.

When I reached the bottom of the path, I saw Ninianne, dismounted from her horse and standing beneath the beech tree, gazing up into a cathedral of branches. Above her, the magpies swooped in and out, drawn to her shine.

'You're still here,' I said.

She looked at me, her light not as blazing as after the lake, but enough to warm the air around us. Her face, however, was weary, her beauty drawn hollow. She hadn't been crying, but her unnaturally bright eyes suggested she could begin at any moment.

'Are you all right?' I asked. No response.

I moved closer and caught the flutter of her heartbeat, the battle with panic that I knew so well. Softly, I put my hand on her arm, sending forth just enough golden force to make her pulse slow. She exhaled with some relief.

'It is hopeless,' was the first thing she said.

'That's not true,' I replied. 'I know it seems that way, but up at the lake I realised something. There is an answer to this, if you and I both bring our wisdom to it.'

She looked away, but I put my arm through hers. 'Come with me.'

I led her to the top of the turret and into my study, bathed now in soft copper light. Ninianne glided through the room, observing every object, piece of furniture and work area, and it occurred to me that she was seeing me in my entirety for the first time.

'This is where I think,' I offered.

'The perfect place,' she said. 'Exactly how I imagined it.'

She continued to explore the chamber, glow radiating softly, her presence suddenly essential. I felt a strange impulse to keep by her side – perhaps I even wished to embrace her – but we had never been that way, had barely touched even in our closest moments at Merlin's.

She paused by the worktable, fingers drifting across a spray of my anatomical sketches and accompanying notes. I went and stood with her, shoulder to shoulder, watching her consider my work, the healing and physic where I had found my greatest purpose.

Then, in the most unexpected move she had ever made, Ninianne tilted her head sideways, until it rested against mine. I stayed there, letting her essence soak into me, our heartbeats, our individual thoughts and strengths, coalescing into something shared.

'Give me the answers, Morgan,' she said. 'If there is a future, where does it begin?'

'With us, now in this moment,' I said. 'It was true about the magic, how we've changed and our place in this world. To advance our wisdom and be free, we must go where the quest for knowledge leads. Our liberty lies exactly where you said it did – in Avalon.'

She recoiled from me as if it hurt, her eyes green fire. 'We cannot go to Avalon,' she said. 'When I said that, things were different. I thought I would be going to my own fate after saving Arthur from Merlin's unspoken prophecy and assuring the kingdom's future. Now, Camelot is burning, bonds I thought eternal have been destroyed. I have failed and must repair what I've done. I do not deserve Avalon.'

'Don't say that,' I said. 'This is not your fault. Everything that is happening with Camelot – the betrayals, the desires, the jealousies, the need for war – those are all deeply mortal flaws. None of it could have been prevented, nor has it anything to do with you.'

'It's not true,' she protested. 'The hours I spent staring at the Book of Prophecies, trying to find another way, yet I missed so much. Sir Mordred stood in the court for years, vengeful and plotting, and I did not sense it. Even you and me, I got so wrong. All of that time, I allowed us to be at odds when we should have been working together to solve this.'

'We have all made mistakes,' I replied. 'My grief, my rage – they were both keeping me alive and burning me to the ground. If I had sought the truth earlier, listened to you, perhaps Arthur and I would have repaired things. I would have been there to help him. We can never know, but what's important is acting *now*.'

Her eyes were so bright I felt seared, like seeing the sun after swimming underwater. 'How can I leave him, Morgan?' she said suddenly. 'It's impossible.'

'Lancelot?' I said. I should have seen it, I suppose, the pull of maternal love she had found far into her life. I thought of Yvain, what we were just beginning to find; it was not part of my plan to lose him either.

'You told me yourself, Avalon is freedom,' I reasoned. 'We can still visit the mortal lands. That even beyond death, the spirits of those we love can cross between worlds there and be with us again. Lancelot is fairy-raised – could he not come with you?'

'In theory,' she said. 'But I speak not of Lancelot. My son has only ever followed his own heart, and his honour will lead him through what is left of this world. I have done all I can for him, and I am made proud.'

'Then whom can't you leave?'

'King Arthur,' she said. 'An innocent soul handed over to this burden from the moment he was conceived. He has given his whole life, every piece of his mind, body and soul to the impossible task that was thrust upon him. He kept a crown on his head that he did not ask for, carried an entire nation through good and bad and never tried to escape it, or say that he could do no more. He has withstood deep personal pain and still put the kingdom first. Now he must watch everything he achieved fall apart because he is a mortal man?'

She leaned back against the table and put her head in her hands. 'I helped do that to him. How can I leave now his predicament hurtles towards disaster?'

'That is what I'm saying,' I told her. 'You don't have to leave him. When Arthur dies, we will take him to Avalon with us.'

Ninianne looked up so sharply it caused sparks in the air. 'What?'

'There's no reason why not,' I continued. 'You delivered him, and he has often been under your magical protection. He has carried Excalibur, bestowed by your hands. No one has been more touched by fairy magic than my brother.'

'To what end?' she said. 'He is at war with his son. If the hidden prophecy bears out, he will be dead.'

'That doesn't matter. If we take him to Avalon, we can bring him back to life.'

Her interest dimmed, and she looked away. 'No, that is not the answer. The scabbard is gone, the Shroud of Tithonus is gone. We have no way of resurrecting him.'

'Not resurrection – it has never been the solution. But that's not all there is.'

A frown glittered across her brow. I drew a deep breath.

'I can heal him,' I said. 'I'm not saying it will happen quickly. Indeed, it may take years. But it is the right way, I can feel it. I can bring Arthur back from death.'

Rarely had I seen Ninianne unintentionally speechless. She stood up from the table and stared at me, unable to form any words. I reached out and took her hands.

'When I was a child,' I said, 'I made my father a promise, just before he died. I swore I would always try to harness my wisdom, to keep learning and moving forwards. For all the other mistakes I have made, the good and the bad I have done, knowledge has been the oath I have kept, and it has all been leading here. When you told me that raising Accolon should not have been within my grasp, when you said that saving Arthur is impossible, I felt it as potential deep in my being. Healing has been my life's work, and I can use it to change the future.'

Again, she said nothing. I took her hand and held it over my heart, so she could hear the truth beating there. 'You were right, Ninianne – I am more than I was before. I can do this for my brother.'

She looked pained, unable to ignite her hopes. 'I want to believe you, truly I do,' she said. 'But one woman alone, against the forces of death …'

'I'm not alone,' I said. 'I have you.'

Her face changed then, her light growing until she regarded me in wonder. Still I held her hand to my heart.

'I can't do this without you,' I continued. 'I have the skills, but what I need is everything else – the time, the perfect place to work, access to more knowledge than I possess. You give us the Isle of Avalon and its potential, a place of peace and study with magic still flowing through the elements. Most of all, I need *your* help, your counsel, your deeper wisdom. Don't you see? Together, we have already solved this.'

She considered my words for a long moment, then drew her hands away and went out onto the balcony. I followed and stood beside her, hearing, as she did, the clear music of the rising spring above all else.

'How would you do it?' she said suddenly.

'With time and patience,' I said. 'No tricks, no theatrics, no simple solutions. My brother will not rise within a day and charge back off to win this war. But I will heal him, slowly and definitively, until one day, he will be whole again. Then, if Arthur feels that his country needs him, he will be strong enough to return. What matters is that next time, he will have the wisdom, and the choice.'

She gave a slow nod, not quite convinced. 'It is all very well, us making plans, but Avalon is a different life – a way of beauty and enlightenment, but utterly different to how King Arthur has lived. What if he does not wish to start anew?'

'My brother has been told what he should do his entire life,' I said. 'This, he must choose. You will ask him, and if his answer is no, we accept his decision and agree to find our own peace. But if I know him at all, then he will want this. It is the future, given into his hands – the greatest quest he has ever faced.'

'After everything, you would do this for him?' she asked.

'It is not just for him, but both of us,' I said. 'I am the sea, and he is the wind that makes the waves. When our connection was at its most severed, we both dreamed of Tintagel until we found one another again. Our future is inevitable and eternal. Arthur will bring me the most formidable challenge for my skills, and I will give him new life. We will be a family restored, able to make up for the time we lost. What greater act of healing could there be?'

She gazed at me, captured by my belief, the hope she thought turned to dust.

'We are the answer, Ninianne,' I said. 'All you must say is that you will take us to Avalon.'

Her smile was quiet, but with such a gleam it could have lit any darkness. 'Yes,' she said. 'Of course I will.'

Hesitantly, she opened her arms, as if she did not quite know how this type of gesture worked. However, I did; I reached out for her, and for the first time, Ninianne of the Lake embraced me, and allowed me to embrace her.

I had always thought she would feel like being held by the sun, but this was something better – swimming in Llyn Glas on a summer's day, the water both cool and warm, its soothing power bringing me strength and comfort. In return, I could feel her deep satisfaction radiating through my bones. The fairy made mortal and the mortal made fairy, meeting halfway.

'What's next?' she asked when we parted.

'The start of a new era,' I replied, pointing her to my desk and drawing up a second chair. 'We sit side by side and make our plans together.'

When many days had passed and Ninianne was ready to leave to put our intentions into motion, I asked if there was anything left to do. She regarded me with unusual shyness and said, 'I'd like to see Lancelot's story one more time.'

We returned to the long bedchamber and faced Lancelot's paintings, lit by shafts of autumn sun. I stood in the middle while Ninianne paced along the walls, taking in his work, his confession. She paused long at the beginning, absorbing her son's rendering of his upbringing at her lake. The contentment she had brought him, however brief, was enough for both of them.

From my own vantage point, I looked around the room, at Lancelot's images still searing bright, then everything that came before, steeped in memory: the birds in flight painted high up the walls, long faded by sun; the musical trill of the spring always in my ears; the huge oak bed once hung with blue drapes, where I had awoken every morning to Accolon's sleeping face.

The thought of this chamber, what it represented, did not break me as it once could. The room's power was different now – it had seen enough that its significance had changed with the years alongside me. The deepest parts of my life would always matter, written as they were into my core, but there were other things, more ways to exist.

'Ninianne?' I asked, and she turned to me in question.

'Before we leave here,' I said, 'will you do something for me?'

54

Several weeks later, after deep discussions with Alys and Tressa, much planning with the household, and many preparations had been made, Ninianne returned.

Our own arrangements were set – we had our meeting place to sail for Avalon, and an hourglass turned on our departure. With war now on Britain's shores and the magic draining ever quicker, Ninianne said we must leave before the next full moon, or there would not be enough fairy strength left in her to convey us from these shores. She had not yet asked my brother if he would take the journey with us, not to distract him before the time was right.

Otherwise, she brought much news. As I had hoped, Arthur had rushed back to Guinevere in time to break Mordred's siege of the Tower of London and ensure his wife's escape. Rumour had it Sir Mordred, now stripped of his advantage, his political marriage, and the lie of Arthur's death, had ridden to Camelot and destroyed it in a fit of temper.

'King Arthur is furious and battles Sir Mordred's forces wherever he can,' Ninianne said. 'Though it will soon be over. Merlin prophesied his last stand would be at Salisbury Plain, and they meet there in a few days. It seems the prediction will prove true – the King's numbers are depleted without Lancelot's men, and he refuses to ask him for help.'

'Because of Guinevere?' I said.

She shook her head. 'The Queen too tried to reason with him, to no avail. King Arthur refuses to summon him because he says it will take too long for any army to arrive from Benoic. But in truth, after everything, I believe he thinks Lancelot will not come.'

'That sounds like my brother,' I said. 'Stubborn to the last.'

She nodded, her presence enigmatic but soothing. *Lancelot will be here*, her mind said to mine. *He will find a way.*

'Then we are ready,' I said. 'There is nothing left but to wait.'

'Yes, there is,' she said gently. 'Your own request. Are *you* ready?'

'No, and I never will be,' I replied. 'But I must do what is best.'

Ninianne said to meet upon the cusp of sunset and I awaited her at the foot of the lake path. I was watching the light lengthen the shadows across the joust meadow when I felt her warmth, spreading like wings of comfort across my back.

We walked slowly, a lengthy procession I was grateful for, emerging beneath the flourishing apple trees just as the copper-gold sun touched the western horizon.

I did not have to call for him. Accolon appeared beneath the willow, regarding me with his usual contented admiration, as if happy just to look upon my face.

'I've made a decision,' I told him. 'I am not free unless both of us are.'

He glanced at Ninianne lingering behind, then back at me. Over the past weeks we had spoken at length about Avalon, Belle Garde, my future and his. He knew what I meant.

'How is it done?' he asked.

'The water knows,' I replied. *'Oui?'*

He smiled then, in his eternal way, curved-bow lip rising, his eyes dark and tender, so sure of his love. Accolon, my Gaul, charming and beautiful. Mine in life and beyond death.

'Oui,' he said.

As quickly as that, we had chosen. Ourselves, and one another.

I turned to Ninianne, waiting patiently at the lake shore. 'It is time,' I said.

She gestured to the water. 'Sir Accolon of Gaul, you know what you wish to do.'

I frowned in confusion, but he seemed to understand exactly what she meant. In a few strides he too was at the water's edge, the lake's silver-blue sheen glittering through him. He looked back at me and held out his hand.

'Morgan,' he said, and I didn't hesitate. I followed him into the lake as I so often had, until I was up to my waist, the water singing like angels in my veins. Accolon and I faced one another, in this haven we had found, for the final time.

Ninianne watched us from the bank until she was satisfied, then glided into the lake with incredible ease, small waves leaping at her body as if in celebration. When she was half immersed, she put her palms flat to the sapphire surface and closed her eyes.

'Llyn Glas,' she declared in her low, irresistible voice. 'I am Ninianne of the Lake, and come in great respect. Your depths hold the soul of this man – Sir Accolon of Gaul. His heart was given to the water in an act of love and magic, bonded to the elements, and made strong by the lake's grace. He is grateful, and always will be, for your sanctuary, but I ask you now to unbind him, and return his essence to its liberty.'

She held her hands against the quivering surface, listening. Whatever language she and the water spoke, it was beyond my younger skills. For this, I was not yet fairy enough. Nevertheless, I felt the water give, its acceptance of her request.

Ninianne scooped up the clear liquid and threw a scatter of droplets into the air, drawing a pair of waves up either side of her body. As she lifted her hands higher, so followed the lake, roaring but controlled. A smile of pleasure and triumph gleamed on her face and I could feel her exhilaration rippling across the space between us, from the element she loved flowing through her core.

In all our years known to one another, I had never seen her like this, in full command of her magic. I had known many magical feats, but to be with the Lady of the Lake in this moment, at her most powerful, was to be in the presence of an ancient goddess, an experience as humbling as it was transcendent.

In a sweep of Ninianne's arms, a coliseum of water rose up around me and Accolon, a glassy wall shot through with sun and elemental power. Its shimmer surrounded us until we could see nothing but one another, alone again within the lake's embrace.

Immediately, Accolon's image began to change, turning translucent until he was made entirely of stars. Around us, the water shifted, ripples turning to gentle waves, and I felt the lake reach for him, pulling him away and into its depths.

'I don't know if I can bear this,' I said. 'How can I watch you leave me again?'

At the sound of my doubt, Accolon stopped, resisting the lake's pull, and regarded me with a stormy, boundless look, fierce in its love. Above, the sky darkened, clouds gathering close and slate-blue, the scent on the breeze metallic, vital. A thrilling tension gripped the air, waiting to burst.

'You can bear it,' my Gaul said. 'We both can, knowing this is not forever.'

He reached for me, and his true hands landed on my waist. Suddenly, he was whole – his touch, his body as I had always known it, warm and strong and present, cleaving itself to mine. Whatever the water had done, I understood it would not sustain, but I savoured every sensation as he took me into his arms and pulled me to him, no closeness ever enough for us; two halves creating one entity.

I put my arms around his neck as he kissed me, and I kissed him, for the last time in this place of ours, that our love had made sacred. I felt his hands at my back, in my hair, our colliding touch giving way to a cascade of memories, every moment of our life together rushing between us like a river towards the sea. There would be no forgetting; the water would remember us.

Accolon gazed at me as if he could look at my face for all time and never tire, until the sensation of his hands left my body, and his presence once again turned to stardust.

'It's too soon,' I said. 'Promise me this is not the end.'

He smiled again in his particular way, and my heart fluttered as it had the very first time. 'There is no end for us, Morgan,' he replied. 'Nothing in life or death can keep us apart for long.'

Above, the sky split with lightning, clouds meeting in a thunderous crash. Warm rain began to fall, hitting the lake like diamonds, giving rise to a glorious elemental song all around us. The torrent shimmered through Accolon's body, skies alive in the depths of his tempest-coloured eyes. Now and forever, we were a storm.

'I love you, Sir Accolon of Gaul,' I said. 'Too much – far too much.'

'I love you too, *mon cœur*,' he replied. 'Look for me when it rains.'

There were no goodbyes, because it would never be over between us.

Another flash of lightning illuminated the sky, followed immediately by a tremendous crash as the circle of water came down. Through sheets of rain, I saw Ninianne settle the waves, her hands flickering over its peaks and troughs, in complete control of everything around us. She looked at me and I bowed my head in assent.

'*Release him,*' she called, and the lake obeyed her at once.

Keeping his eyes on mine, Accolon's presence receded as the water took him, his form dispersing across the surface as stars, the storm still raging above us. Ninianne dropped her hands, relinquishing her hold; the lake would do what it had promised.

I turned my eyes back to the man I loved and watched him set free.

The water stilled where he had vanished, his essence rippling outwards in bands of light, then rising, rising, rays of silver cast up into rain and across the dark-blue sky. In the lake, I sensed him no longer, and instead, my heart felt him everywhere.

And I remained in Llyn Glas, in the wake of Accolon's liberated soul, with the rain on my face and his touch imprinted on my skin, until the storm had played its last note and was gone.

55

We burned Belle Garde on Accolon's birthday, a blazing final tribute to the life we had all spent there.

Or the house was to burn, at least – the rest of the valley and its buildings had been made secure, protected by a shared enchantment between mine and Ninianne's fairy magic that would ensure no one outside those who had lived there would remember what it once was, or that Morgan le Fay had been its mistress. Mordred, or any other enemies of mine inclined to threaten my Vale of No Return, would find only a beautiful valley inhabited by wise and brave people, and know nothing else.

The household that remained settled into the lodges, with a voted council led by the huntsman holding the keys to the vault and Belle Garde's future. They would continue in their contentment, custodians of the valley's prosperity and memories. The land, the trees and rivers, the wilderness, would be renamed in honour of its native tongue and most steadfast residents and once again be called *Ynys-y-Pia*. Isle of the Magpies.

The flame enchantment I had designed would preserve everything except the house – not a leaf, branch or blade of grass would be touched. The beech tree would remain, and its generations of magpies that had taught me so much, with their chatter, mischief and loyalty. Their matriarch, still thriving, would preside over all. Robin's *carnedd* would endure for all time, a future curiosity for enquiring minds.

Standing on the front green, arms raised, it was easier than I thought to engulf the building in my column of bright-blue fire. We had lived well and happy in this place.

Beside me, Alys and Tressa stood hands entwined, watching our past burn, so we could walk a cleansed path towards the future.

'Are you sure you don't wish to stay?' I had asked them countless times, and again as the flames began to sing. 'There truly is no coming back from this. It is forever.'

Tressa, forthright as ever, spoke first. 'My loyalty is to you, and my heart. Wherever Alys goes, I go.'

With sudden speed, the fire overcame the turret, magic straining within me as it fought with the stones, turning the building into finest ash. Before long, only a patch of earth would remain beside the silver spring, to grow over with wildflowers and tell no tales.

I looked then to Alys, my first true friend. The wisest, most faithful woman I would ever know; the one I loved best.

'And you?' I asked her. 'I cannot promise I will never again cause chaos.'

Alys smiled, the same mischievous glint in her golden-brown eyes I had seen on that very first day in St Brigid's Abbey.

'I swore you an oath,' she said. 'I meant it to be no less than eternity.'

The meeting place Ninianne had set was a stone circle, at equal distance between Belle Garde, Salisbury Plain and the wooded river shore where we would leave for Avalon.

Ninianne would come to us by noon, she had said, after several days following our careful plans. By now, she would have spoken to Arthur and heard his decision, and seen the battle play out. If Avalon was his choice, she would ensure the safe conveyance of his slain body to where we awaited her.

'Will he truly be dead?' Tressa asked, as the sun crept towards its peak.

'If Ninianne's assumption proves true,' I replied. 'Of all the prophecies, she believes this one holds the most weight in Arthur's life. From any viewpoint, it's hard to argue with. Mordred's army is large and unwearied. He has the support of many barons. The Knights of the Round Table were decimated by the Grail Quest and are divided between Arthur and Lancelot's factions. Circumstance, at least, will be in Mordred's favour.'

Even the land had made its prediction: at Salisbury Plain there stood a stone, marked with the declaration that the very place would be the site of King Arthur's last battle. Despite my scepticism, the signs were hard to deny. My brother's destiny within the Crown of All Britain had begun and would end with words carved into a stone.

The thought shivered through me, along with the fact that it was already over. If all had come to pass, the next time I saw Arthur he would be dead. To reverse this would be to pit my healing skills against a fate written into the stars since the beginning of time.

I felt a hand on my arm, drawing me back to the present: dense green grass beneath my feet; the ancient stones made to weather any storm; Alys's face, assuring me I had a part to play in it all.

'You will heal him, *cariad*,' she said. 'If anyone can change the future, it is you.'

It had long been her greatest gift – when she spoke, I listened, and trusted her every word. She always made me believe the impossible was within my reach.

'Look,' Tressa called. 'She comes.'

We spun round to see a figure cresting the hill on her pure white horse, violet robes flowing, her hair aflame under the midday sun. Ninianne of the Lake, perfectly on time.

However, not all was as she had promised. She was alone.

Arthur had not come.

Before we had a chance to form any questions, she had galloped into the stone circle and dismounted, her gleam blinding with haste and fervour.

'King Arthur is alive,' she said. 'The battle at Salisbury Plain was a stalemate. After unexpected blows dealt to both sides, Sir Mordred retreated to his command post at Camlann Field, and his men followed.'

I realised then that my brother's survival was the last report I thought I would hear, and the relief of it knocked me sideways. I put my arm out and steadied myself against one of the stones. His absence was a miracle, not a failure.

'So Arthur has defeated the prophecy,' I said. 'He is free.'

I expected the same elation from Ninianne but she didn't respond, gazing off into the distance, her presence stilled. A whisper of unease cut through my joy.

'And Avalon?' I asked. 'What was his decision?'

'He has not made one,' Ninianne replied. 'Mordred's troops ambushed the King's men hours early, so when I arrived, they were already in the thick of battle. Afterwards, King Arthur rode off before I had the chance to speak to him.' She held up her hands and regarded them helplessly. 'I thought I would have enough power to help him in the fight, but the magic, the conflict and bloodshed ... I could not do a thing.'

I reached out and took her hands in mine; her light still shone, but she was cold. This world, everything she had witnessed, had exhausted her.

'When I heard he still lived, I rode to the woodland where his men were garrisoned, but he wasn't there either. The story was that he ordered them to their place of safety then never arrived himself. I rode around for days, searching and waiting for news, but neither came.'

'Perhaps he's at another castle, preparing his next move?' Alys suggested.

Ninianne shook her head. 'Mordred had already taken control of every fortress and allied castle within fifty miles. That's why Camelot's knights are regrouping in the forest. King Arthur is alive but alone – that's all anyone knows.'

As they continued to speculate, I closed my eyes and reached into my core, to the blue-and-white waves undulating beneath Tintagel's cliffs. The vision came at once, proving my brother alive, but his presence was elsewhere, his response only a whisper of a breeze. He was distracted, sad, alone in the deepest shadows of his spirit.

'What about Guinevere?' I said. 'Could he have gone to her?'

'It's not possible,' Ninianne said. 'The Queen rode to an abbey where she immediately took the veil and went into deep seclusion where no men, whatever their rank, are permitted to enter. The King knows this, and could not see her if he tried.'

'Then Arthur has nothing,' I mused.

Ninianne nodded. 'Nor does he have a compelling reason to go anywhere.'

It was somewhat true, but not what I meant. I paced away from them, into the circle of stones, thinking of my brother and all that had befallen him in such a short few months. Arthur was free of every prophecy – his decisions and future were in his hands for the first time in his life. It was a miracle, and yet ...

From the moment he was born he had never known the pathway of his life to be uncharted, or been unsure of what was coming next. To Arthur's preordained existence, this sudden liberation from certainty must have felt like a confusion so vast and deep he could not begin to see his way through.

Ninianne called across to me. 'Time grows short. We must leave regardless.'

I looked back at her, standing beside Alys and Tressa, all three of them expectant, their bodies tilted towards the direction we must head while I felt rooted, pulled back.

'Go to the meeting place for Avalon,' I told them. 'Await me there.'

'Not without you,' Alys said.

'You have to,' I insisted. 'It is the only way.'

'We must travel before the moon wanes,' Ninianne said. 'The magic will not hold another month. If we miss this opportunity ...'

'You won't,' I insisted. 'If I'm not there, you must sail without me.'

Alys and Tressa began to protest, so I strode across and took one of each of their hands, forming our eternal circle. 'I will come, I swear it. Arthur and I both.'

'This is a great risk to take, Morgan,' Ninianne said. 'Even for the King. He has survived the prophecy and may fight on for years, but your future cannot be delayed.'

I shook my head. 'It doesn't matter. Arthur needs me now, more than ever. I won't leave him, not again.'

Their faces showed only hesitation, but it was the simplest decision I had ever made. I was on my horse and setting forth when Ninianne put her hand on my reins.

'How will you even begin to find him?' she said. 'He could be anywhere.'

'Trust me,' I replied. 'If I know my brother, there is only one place he will be.'

56

Of all the astonishing sights I had seen in my life, the greatest shock I ever received was to find Camelot deserted.

Destruction lay everywhere. My horse picked over piles of wood and shattered lances, past weapons and cloth discarded from looted merchants. Red-and-white banners flashed among the detritus, torn and muddied where they had been pulled down and trampled. Not a soul remained: residents, knights, guards, the visitors who would come from far and wide just to see the golden marvel upon its hill, the kingdom's beating heart. It was an empty carapace now, a place abandoned to time.

As I reached the central crossroads, there came a sudden clatter of hooves and a pair of riderless horses careered into view, one black and the other bright white, sweat-sheened and foaming as if they had been running forever. Blood soaked the pale horse's chest, but they galloped on by, oblivious to anything but their need to flee.

Heart racing, I reached out with my senses to glean any other hidden threats – feral beasts, lurking men – but all was silent beyond the reverberation of hoofbeats fading through the empty streets. I pushed on up the hill towards the castle, across the clogged and filthy moat, and passed under the soot-scorched barbican to reach Camelot's main courtyard.

There too I found ruin: stones streaked with mud and manure, the avenue of cherry trees chopped down. Over the door, the rearing dragon had been slung with ropes and half toppled, bent steel groaning its death throes in the wind. I dismounted under the shadow of its claws and walked into the grand entrance hall.

The circular atrium resembled a badly kept barracks: piles of straw bunched on the tiled floor, rough blankets strewn about, rats picking through scraps of cheese and bird bones. A pyre of blackened wood stood in the centre, built for warmth or a failed burning, I could not tell. I kept moving, along the Seneschal's gallery and past Sir Kay's former Great Chamber, where the doors had been wrenched off their hinges, piles of his carefully organised records dumped from the shelves. I winced, imagining how he would feel to see his diligent work scattered and disrespected, then remembered he was at war anyway with his blood up, fighting for his life and his brother, loyal to the end.

Finally, I reached the enormous doorway, slung open to memories both good and bad. Where the time had gone I could not fathom, but I had not entered Camelot's Great Hall in eighteen years. Those last, desperate days before I learned Accolon was dead.

Chaos greeted my sight: the long tables and benches slung across the room, food decaying on surfaces, knives protruding from scarred and filthy tabletops. An army of jackdaws marched along the rows, pecking at rotting meat. As I walked towards the dais, they flew up in rasping irritation to the nests they had made in the rafters.

Hazy jewel-coloured light still drifted through the tall arched windows and the glazed recess at the back of the room, behind where High Table had always been. A few panes had been smashed, letting in moans of wind that rustled the royal banners hanging from the ceiling, too high for any raging, thwarted usurper to tear down. Nonetheless, Mordred's destruction had been thorough.

Two thirds of my way towards the dais, I found myself blocked by a tremendous barrier – great chunks of curved wood, jagged at the edges and stacked tall. I found a gap between two piles and stepped through, eyes catching upon the once colourful surface, neatly delineated sections painted with knightly scenes, each headed with ornate gold lettering. I moved closer, trying to read what it said.

'My table,' came a sudden voice. 'Broken beyond repair.'

I swung towards the sound and saw the dais behind a forest of discarded furniture. Upon the central steps, fiery in the light, sat my brother.

'Arthur,' I gasped. 'Thank goodness.'

I ran to him, but he didn't look at me, his eyes fixed upon the splintered wood.

'People often expected my Round Table to be a solid circle,' he said in a faraway voice. 'Not many realised that it would need to be a ring to seat so many knights, lest no room be large enough to contain it. Still, how glorious it looked – brightly painted, garlanded with silk and flowers, the Ladies' Table and Queen's Knights on the inner side. Gold plate and goblets placed in precise lines. Perfect, exactly as I had envisioned it.'

As he spoke, my initial relief at his discovery drained away. He still gleamed like a king, but his gold armour was battle-scarred, gauntlets discarded, greaves dented and dragon-head pauldrons missing teeth, mail streaked with dirt. He didn't appear injured, but his aspect was stooped and exhausted, my senses unable to discern his state of mind.

I sat down beside him. 'I never saw the Round Table,' I said. 'I wish I had.'

He tried to smile, but it was weighted with regret. 'For a while, everything happened within this table. When petitions came, calls for help that I would answer, new allies waiting to be made, it was here they stood, in the centre of the kingdom. Quests of wonder and greatness began and ended here. The most magnificent knights the world will ever see sat side by side in great love and friendship.'

I followed his gaze to the pile of fractured wood and saw Arthur's name in gold, bordered with crowns. The name beside his was expected, but still gave me a jolt to see.

Sir Lancelot du Lac, silver and unsullied. At his King's right hand.

'I'm sorry, Arthur,' I said.

'Look at it now,' he said. 'Shattered, ruined, all splinters. My world in pieces.'

His voice cracked and to my horror his face crumpled into despair. Swiftly, I reached for him and pulled his quaking body into my arms, holding my brother as he cried – for his ruined kingdom, his great purpose, for his lost friends, family and love. For himself.

I would have stayed there, bearing him up for all the hours it took, but Arthur never did like to wallow in his feelings for long. He lifted his head from my shoulder, drew back, dried his eyes with the heel of his palm, then put his hand over mine in wordless thanks.

'My God, you're freezing,' I said. 'We need to get you warm.'

I got up and filled a brazier with any wood not from the Round Table. To access magic in this palace of destruction was to feel it dragged through my veins, but there was just enough elemental connection to conjure a flame in my hand. I lit the kindling until it burned steadily, then pulled the small bonfire to the dais steps.

A soft beam of light caught my eye from the floor – the sunlit hilt of Excalibur, discarded in the shadows at his feet. Arthur saw me notice the sword and closed his eyes.

I sat down and took his hands in mine, seeking injury. Thankfully, there was none, but neither was he unafflicted. I sent a stream of warm healing through him, but his core held a profound cold that went far beyond the physical. Within, he was utterly devastated, an ailment not even my miraculous hands could fix.

'Talk to me,' I said. 'How did you come to be here?'

He spoke through chattering teeth. 'I came immediately after the battle at Salisbury Plain. I needed to be alone, to consider everything.' He looked out across the upturned furniture, the holes smashed out of the once-resplendent windows. 'It was the only place I wanted to come, and this is what greeted me.'

There were no words fit to comfort him for the annihilation that lay before us. 'What happened at Salisbury Plain?' I asked.

He gave a tremendous shudder. 'It's over. There was no conclusion.'

'That's good, isn't it?' I squeezed his arm, willing him to feel it through the layers of samite and steel. 'You live and breathe still, against what the stars foretold. You survived your final battle and are unchained from prophecy.'

He looked down at his sword-strong hands. 'What does it matter if I survived, when so many others died? At what cost, my own life?'

'Of course it is difficult,' I replied. 'War is always a tragedy. But your knights fight for you because they are loyal and want to stand by your side. In these uncertain times when faith is bought and sold, those doing battle alongside you chose it, and are proud.'

Abruptly, Arthur stilled and regarded me with a regal seriousness. Firelight illuminated the streaks on his face – mud, yes, but something darker, redder: blood across his forehead, speckled on his cheekbones;

a smudged slash along his jaw, staining his beard. His eyes were silver with tears.

'Morgan,' he said. 'Yvain is dead.'

I felt as though I had been plunged into an ice floe, numbed from scalp to toes. The air left my lungs, leaving me able only to stammer one word.

'How?'

Arthur sighed. 'He had been leading a battalion to tremendous success. They defeated an onslaught of opposition soldiers – Yvain himself vanquished several of Mordred's most powerful allies in hard-fought duels. Then, when dusk began to fall …'

His words caught and he stopped. I wanted to shake the rest from him, but his pause was not faltering or afraid – it was measured, purposeful. In the midst of our despair, I watched my brother pull himself upright, gathering the fortitude he knew I would soon need to lean on. He put his arm around my shoulders and drew us close.

'I was battling three knights with lance and sword, and was knocked from my horse,' he continued. 'Yvain must have seen me from across the field because immediately he came, leaping from his destrier and picking me up off the ground. He was helping me remount when the three knights set upon him, but dealt with them valiantly as I righted myself. We drove them bleeding into the mud, but they had distracted us and …' He swallowed hard, withstanding another shiver. 'I swung round as fast as I could, but …'

I couldn't bear it any more. 'What happened, Arthur? How did my son die?'

He held me tighter. 'Mordred rode up with his sword held high. He was heading for me, but your brave, honourable son put his body in the horse's path to slow him down. Yvain swerved and parried but could not block the blow in time. Mordred cleaved him through the skull.' A single tear rolled down his cheek. 'He fell at once, like a stone, he …'

I let myself lean into him, finding the words to comfort us both. 'It was instantaneous,' I managed. 'He wouldn't have known, or felt any pain.'

Arthur shook his head, as if the notion was intolerable. 'I gave chase, but that godforsaken coward rode off into the trees. My men were crying out for command – I had to let him go. Mordred fleeing meant the battle ended without firm resolution.'

He grabbed my hands and stared directly into my eyes. 'That was the moment, Morgan. Death was upon me, and Yvain stood in Fate's way. I escaped, but I wish it had never happened.'

'Don't say that,' I said fiercely. 'Yvain loved you, Arthur. If you had asked him, he wouldn't have hesitated to give his life for yours. Let his courage, his sacrifice, mean something.'

He nodded, but released me and put his head in his hands, king-like calm fracturing. 'What was this all for? Yvain is dead, Gawain already gone. Kay – who I swore to Mother and Father I would always keep safe – was slain in Mordred's knavish attacks across the Channel, fighting for my sake. What will I do now, without my brother?'

I thought I had no heart left to shatter until he spoke Kay's name. I put my arms back around him and Arthur did the same, holding us together.

'Sister,' he said. 'How are we supposed to survive all this?'

'I don't know,' was all I could say. 'I don't know.'

We stayed that way for a long time, clouds outside scudding across the light as if days and nights were passing without end. I was lost in a trance of grief when Arthur sat up, his eyes blazing with fury and purpose.

'I'm going to kill him,' he said. 'Mordred must die. For Yvain, for Kay and every soul he has slain, and to avenge what he has done to Camelot. I will ride to where he lays his cursed head, wake him from sleep and cut him to pieces. For you and me both.'

The idea ran through my veins like molten steel, searing to hardness as it went. I wanted this – a savage and bloody punishment for the one who had killed my son, denying Yvain and me our hopeful future. I wanted revenge for my first-born child, for Arthur in his grief, and most of all for myself.

My brother stood up, pacing before the bonfire with a febrile intensity, as ready to act as I was. 'Come, we must go. There is no time to waste.' He held his hand out and I let him pull me to my feet. 'You will ride with me, bear witness to the justice I will serve.'

His eyes shone unnaturally bright, our shared rage turning a grief-stricken impulse into real and deadly action. Within a few hours and the ring of blades, this could all be over.

My brother was already striding away, towards his decision. I closed my eyes and released the taut breath in my chest, letting loose the furious need to react, the temptation to choose vengeance over everything, at any cost.

'No, Arthur,' I said. 'This is not how your life ends.'

He stopped and looked back at me. 'What do you mean?'

'You have transcended your destiny once,' I said. 'Right now you are free – a miracle of your will over the chains of Fate. But to keep returning to the moment of your destruction is ensuring the inevitable. The prophecy will come true if you insist that obeying it is the only way your life can be.'

Arthur paused, then shook his head vehemently. 'I have to face Mordred – he must die for what he's done. Prophecy or not, *I* choose this. *I* decide when to stare down my fate. There is no other way.'

'Yes, brother, there is,' I said. 'Avalon.'

The word arrested him, as if he had heard the summoning toll of a bell.

'Avalon?' he said. 'I know the name, though not why. What is it to me?'

'Everything, if you choose your future,' I said. 'Avalon, *Ynys Afallach*, is an island halfway between this world and the other, made from fairy magic. Ninianne of the Lake and I will go there soon to live and study, gain in wisdom. Because of Merlin's prophecy, she believed you would die at Salisbury Plain. She was supposed to tell you of Avalon before the battle and ask if you wished to be conveyed there upon your death, where I would gradually heal you back to life.'

Arthur stood like a statue, his face wreathed in confusion. 'If I had died, I would have gone to this island to be … resurrected?'

I nodded. 'It would have been your choice, but yes. Now, you have defied prophecy, but you can still choose eternity. Sail for Avalon, rest awhile, rebuild your body and mind, and consider your future. You are no longer in a duel with death.'

'You mean … turn away? From my kingdom, my crown?' Arthur stared at me – stubborn, fierce, his doubt and duty galloping at one another in a relentless joust charge. 'If I lose this war, accept defeat, then how will that help the realm?'

It raised a bittersweet amusement in me; he had never known how to lose a fight, just as I had never learned to walk away from one. I saw then that he was being truthful when he told me that he never feared death. My formidable brother was only afraid to die in vain.

'I cannot answer that,' I said. 'I can only advise what I think is coming. The kingdom you built, and the shining era you created with it, is over. All these years you have been fighting for your ideals, and you did everything you could. Camelot was a beautiful dream, and that perfection was why it could never last. It is already history.'

Arthur cast his gaze over the remnants of the Round Table, then dropped again onto the dais steps, hand to his forehead. I sat beside him, unable to read his mood.

'They say he is my son,' he said unexpectedly. 'Mordred.'

I nodded slowly, unsure what was best to impart. 'It looks that way.'

Arthur shook his head and pinched the bridge of his nose, relieving us of the subject. It was too much, in that moment, to contemplate.

'How can this all be happening, Morgan?' He looked up at me with pleading eyes. 'Give me your wisdom, sister. What happens to my country if I go to Avalon?'

Over time, my willingness to tell harsh truths had gone in and out like the tides, but we were one mind now. I put my hand on his shoulder.

'Nothing,' I said. 'The country will survive. Lancelot is on his way. He will lament that he could not come to your aid in time, but will finish what you began, defeat Mordred's remaining forces, and allow the kingdom to start anew.'

In a heartbeat, his face ran through more seasons of emotion than I could count: astonishment, pride, regret, deep affection. 'Lancelot is coming? He would do this?'

'Of course,' I said. 'His honour and love have always resided with you.'

The thought of Lancelot's grace left him speechless, but I felt his spirits rise with his best knight's act of faith. He put his chin in his hand and, for a long time, he sat in contemplative silence, the past and future turning over in his mind like a coin.

Suddenly, Arthur sat upright, decision ringing in the air like a drawn sword.

'Could you still heal me, if I died?' he asked. 'If I choose to do battle one more time and fall, is there a way back?'

'I cannot resurrect you in the way Merlin promised,' I replied. 'There will be no flash of heavenly light, or appearing on the battlefield ready to take back your crown. There is no coming back to this day, this time. But I will heal you, Arthur. It will take many days and much work, for myself and us together, but at my hands you will live again. You will be ready for any future you choose.'

'What will that mean – the future?'

'To do this is to have a second chance, to learn from our mistakes and succeed anew,' I said. 'You will be stronger, wiser, able to answer any challenge. If you wish, you will see your country again, and have the power to return when Britain needs you most. You and I will have all the hours we need to talk and heal and forgive one another. But for that, you have to make the difficult choice now, and bring this time to an end.'

He nodded, though I could feel he was being brave about it. Who would he be in all that time away? What would his name mean to anyone?

'I believe you, sister,' he said. 'I want to choose, to live, to seek wisdom and become better. But if I leave this all behind now without conclusion, will I have done the right thing? How will I know if it is an act for the greater good?'

'Because there is a cost to being extraordinary,' I said, 'and this is the debt. By choosing Avalon, you will be showing the world how to let go of one era, and find its way safely into another. Your legacy will be one of hope.'

'Hope,' he considered. 'I would like that.'

I stood up and held out my hands. Rising, he took them, and I drew us together in the manner of taking an oath. In the quiet of Camelot's Great Hall, we reached into ourselves for the bond that years and circumstance had not been able to sever; the wild blue sea of Tintagel, and the wind that makes the waves.

'We can do this, Arthur,' I said. 'Together, we can be eternal, if you trust me.'

My brother regarded me with new certainty, calm and regal; so like our mother. 'I trust you, Morgan. But in turn, you have to trust me.'

Drawing his hands out of mine, he stepped back and reached down into the shadows beside the dais. When he rose again, he was gripping a sleek blade, golden hilt glowing in his hand.

'Hope can only flourish when I have fulfilled my duty to this realm,' he said. 'No one else must die for this cause. If Mordred is my creation, then I will be the one to right this wrong. For the kingdom, those I love, and all who gave their lives – this ends at Camlann. Then you and I begin again, in Avalon.'

With a long-held proficiency, my brother swung Excalibur up and held his legendary sword before him, the blade gleaming in his serene grey eyes.

'For All Britain,' he said, 'I will finish this.'

And for the first time since the moment of his birth, King Arthur chose his own future.

57

Our final gathering place was near an estuary on a bank dense with trees, a narrow strand of pebbles between us and the river. White fog lay over the water, blurring with the sky, so thick it was impossible to discern anything beyond the quietly lapped shore.

Tressa and Alys stood beside me, gowns immaculate and belted with silver chains, hair braided beneath delicate circlets wrought into ferns. Our mantles were the same dark-blue samite, stitched with stars and lined with vair. They looked like queens of another world.

We brought nothing with us except what could not be left behind. For me, this was little: the chess set and the *Ars Physica*; Yvain's baby curl preserved in a small gold box. My father's ring with its trio of sapphires and my mother's name inside the band. His falcon-handled knife, eternally at my hip.

Accolon's Gaulish coin, laying against my heartbeat.

'When will she come?' Alys asked, her voice amplified by the misty peace. We spoke of Ninianne, of course. After hearing news of Camlann, she had journeyed back to the lake where Arthur had first received the sword that would define the trajectory of his life. She was waiting for the blade to come back.

'Soon,' I replied. 'She is near.'

I didn't know where my certainty came from, but I had accepted the heightened senses that the years had given me, fairy instincts I had been warned of but learned to enjoy. I needed them where I was going, and would let them flourish.

A warm glow lit the forest, growing stronger amongst the shadowed branches, until a tall figure broke the treeline. She was dressed darkly in a forest-green cloak, but her hair was liquid fire, skin back to its enrapturing glow. In her hand she held a gleaming longsword, blade shining bright as the moon, golden hilt infused with the sun itself.

Excalibur, returned to the Lady of the Lake.

Ninianne strode forth in her slow, purposeful way, sword at her side, like a warrior goddess awaiting her next battle. Beneath her cloak she was swathed in layers of deep violet, her waist cinched with emeralds. Long silver cuffs encased her wrists as if she were dressed in armour, but she needed none, her power emanating from every pore as light.

She nodded to Alys and Tressa, then turned her glittering green eyes to me. It was a long time since I had seen her this way – calm, assured, her warmth radiating forth and drawing me close, luminous enough to guide us through eternity.

'My apologies for being late. It took Sir Bedivere a while to return the sword to the lake.' She lifted the blade and considered it, their twin glows reflecting off one another. 'He found it difficult to let go.'

We nodded in understanding: it was hard for those left behind to imagine a world without Excalibur, because it meant there would be no King Arthur to wield it.

'Where is my brother?' I asked. 'Is it done?'

'Yes. He will not be long.'

For once, I felt no sadness, only a deep swell of calm. 'What comes next?'

'My son will deal with what is left of Mordred's forces, and make as much peace as he can,' she replied. 'Though after the High King is gone, there are no guarantees.'

'Will Lancelot not rule?'

She shook her head. 'Such a life is not for him. Once his duty is done, there is only one place he will go. Into mourning for King Arthur, and …'

To Guinevere, she did not say, though it already rang in the air. Prophecy was changeable, the stars inconstant, but some things were inevitable.

'And Britain?' I asked.

'It will survive,' Ninianne said. 'Hereafter, it will be a land like many others – it will fight, fail and thrive, adapt and change, as history requires. Though it will never see another era such as this. When those who lived it are gone, it may seem as if this time never happened at all. Even as we speak, the memory passes into myth.'

I smiled; once again she had returned to her elusive wisdom, scattering confusion like raindrops, and making perfect sense.

'We will know,' I said. 'We will remember.'

She inclined her head, her voice in my mind. *That is true.*

A disturbance sounded in the water, drawing our attention. Through the mist, a long white boat appeared, sleek and golden-prowed, helmed by no one.

'Ah,' Ninianne said. 'Our conveyance. Perfect.'

Like a swan, the vessel glided through the water and turned sideways, bow sliding silently up onto the shore. Inside, the boat was lined with silks and furs, rich feather cushions, and carried several ornate trunks.

The Lady of the Lake nodded in satisfaction, then turned to me, swinging Excalibur up so it lay across her palms. 'Here,' she said. 'Take it.'

I regarded her in doubt. I had been here before, urged to take possession of the weapon and its miraculous jewelled scabbard. I would never know how much of mine and Arthur's troubles began in the moment he had given me care of his legendary sword. It would not be my duty ever again.

Ninianne smiled, reading my thoughts. 'Only for a moment,' she said gently.

Exhaling, I held out my hands and she rested the sword across them, warm against my skin where she had carried it so far. The blade still held its fascinating shine, lustrous and deadly, but it had never captured my senses as it had Arthur. The sword was his, and he belonged to the sword; they would always be bound.

Unfastening her cloak, Ninianne swept it off her shoulders, and folded it around Excalibur with methodical care, in lieu of the scabbard that was at the bottom of a different lake, lost to time at my hands. Even knowing what my furious act had meant, I had never regretted giving it to the water.

Once the fabric was neatly tucked, Ninianne ran her fingers through the air, drawing out diamond-bright threads and laying them across the wrapped sword until the dark silk was netted with light. Charms of protection – tricky, of the fairies, and immutable – the same as she had taught me in one of my darkest moments, when I needed to believe

I could survive. The same charms that had kept me and those I loved safe, and made me more Morgan le Fay than I thought possible.

'There,' she said, taking the blade's weight off my hands. 'Until it is called for.'

She carried the bundle over to the boat and slid it innocuously along the vessel's starboard side. When she turned back, she gleamed brighter than Excalibur itself.

'The High King need not see,' she said wisely. 'The sword will return to him when the time is right.'

There was so much I was yet to understand. 'Does that mean he—?'

A rustle came from the forest, cutting me off, refining into the sound of slow, heavy footsteps, leaves crushed beneath armoured boots. Another figure appeared between the boughs, bright in royal livery, a cool shine of steel and stars.

Sir Lancelot emerged from the trees, stark and beautiful, like a winter moon rising. In his arms he carried a tall, golden figure.

King Arthur, my brother, held close by his most beloved knight.

'Lancelot,' Ninianne gasped and rushed over to him, her light shimmering in surprise. 'I didn't know you would come.'

He looked at her with an expression I had never seen in him – fearful, vulnerable, the light of tears in his pale eyes.

'I had to,' he said, his head bowing towards Arthur's. 'I was too late to fight by his side, but I could at least do this.'

She nodded and stepped back, letting him pace forth, bearing up his King for the last time. Lancelot laid my brother gently on the ground and knelt beside him. Then, with deft hands, he unfastened the red-and-white mantle he wore, snapped the silk in the air and draped Arthur's standard across his body.

For so long, the roaring, rampant dragon had been an enemy of mine, but I saw it for what it was now – a symbol Arthur had chosen because he was seeking a reminder, a representation of ancestral power that he first sought to change and, in the end, surpassed.

When his task was done, Camelot's best knight rose, catching sight of me across the man who had bound our fates together. He gave me a long, searching look, but this time there was no challenge or suspicion in his ice-blue gaze.

'Morgan le Fay,' he said.

'Lancelot du Lac,' I replied.

He bowed his head briefly in acceptance, and I looked long at him, taking in his astonishing archangel's face for the last time.

'Did you do it?' I asked. 'Did you work a miracle?'

He hesitated for so long I thought he would not answer. Then he sighed with the heaviness of confession.

'Yes, I did,' he said. 'Once. I healed a knight of an injury he had suffered for many years. But it didn't matter in the end. I failed to save what was most important.'

We looked down at the man he had carried, the King he had served and loved.

'You didn't fail,' I told him. 'Saving him was always my duty.'

He nodded but it pained him, that a quest's conclusion was out of his reach. Unexpectedly, he reached out and took up my hand, pressing his lips to my fingers. Raising his celestial eyes to mine, Lancelot gave a sad, beautiful smile, and let me go.

Then, with the same elegance that made him a master of the swordfight, he stepped back and swung away, and went to his waiting mother to say their goodbyes. I watched her draw him aside, put her hand to his face, but would not see Sir Lancelot of the Lake leave. The next time I looked up, he would be gone.

Instead, I knelt on the ground beside my brother, Arthur, High King of All Britain. He was breathing, just, and when I took his hand his eyes fluttered open, bright steel in the filtered light. He fought for twelve hours, it was said, ferocious as he always had been in defence of his kingdom; stronger than he ought to be.

Mordred's spear was still in him, its shaft broken off, deep in my brother's heart.

His pain called to me, and I sensed the pointed steel head pinning down the major vessel. If removed, Arthur would die immediately, but even if it stayed in place, death was assured. A fate that could not be escaped for now, but would, in time, be changed. Fixed.

I leaned over him, brushing the hair from his brow. Despite everything, being in his presence again brought only happiness.

'Brother,' I said. 'Why did you tarry so long?'

Arthur smiled at my jest. 'Apologies, sister. It was not ... an easy ... battle.'

Suddenly, he half sat up, his eyes wide on mine. 'I avenged you, Morgan – for Yvain. I avenged myself, for Kay, Gawain and the rest. For Lancelot and Guinevere, everything. For Camelot. It is done.'

'I know,' I said. 'You did what you needed, and now you are free.'

I tried to ease him down, exhorting him to be gentle on himself, but he shook his head in stubbornness. 'No, the sight of you has brought me strength. I can walk.'

Needing no hand to lean upon, my brother rose to his feet and looked about him, standing tall as if he were in the Great Hall of Camelot, about to raise a cup to the kingdom's glory. In him, as myself, I felt it: possibility, opening before us, vast and endless. Our future awaited, and we were ready.

Arthur cast his grey eyes down at me and lifted his sword arm, palm upraised.

'Together,' he said with a smile.

'Together,' I agreed, and put my hand in his.

In unison, we walked across the stony bank and stepped onto the boat. A bier lay in the middle, cushioned and draped in red-and-white silk. Arthur regarded it with a flash of doubt, but fatigue had caught up with him, his breaths heaving in his chest, the effort of his courage sacrificing the last of his incredible fortitude.

He looked back at the shore to his beloved kingdom, no more to touch the land of All Britain until he was restored to strength, called upon as its saviour, and chose to return.

'Arthur,' I said, and he turned, eyes clear but darkened, tired. 'It's time to go.'

His nod was full of sadness, but accepting. Keeping hold of my hand, my brother lay down upon his bier and I sat beside him once again, easing him back until his head rested in my lap. Armour and all, he was heavy, but I bore his weight with ease.

As he settled, the true cost of his battles took hold, the final flare of vitality he had conjured burning down to its last ashes. He tried to speak, but his voice was a croak, his mind cloudy with the pain and his fading life. I laid my hand on his chest and he gripped it close.

'Hush,' I told him. 'All is well. I'm here.'

Still he fought, his hand tight on my wrist, silver eyes on mine. He was not afraid, but his body was failing him in a way he had never known.

'Morgan,' he said hoarsely. 'Is this the end?'

I shook my head, putting my hand to his face.

'No, brother,' I assured him. 'An ending, but not the end.'

At my words, his body relaxed, calm determination falling over his face. Raising his free hand, he curled his fingers around the broken shaft and, with the last of his strength, wrenched the spear out of his heart and threw it into the water.

Arthur exhaled, long and final, and let himself go.

His hand fell to his side, grip on my wrist loosening. I drew my fingertips across his eyes, closing them, and kissed his untroubled forehead.

'Rest now,' I told him. 'We will see one another again.'

His gold crown was cool at the edge of my lips, modest for a king of his greatness, but still the Crown of All Britain and Seven Realms. It would never be worn again, in the same way, by anyone, even if he returned. By then, the world would have changed in ways broad and small, obvious and unimaginable.

King Arthur, and the age he had created, would be the first and last of their kind.

A corona of light beamed across us: Ninianne, standing on the shore. At her gesture, Alys and Tressa embarked beside me, sitting serene amongst the cushions, eyes on the water and their arms about each other.

Our fairy guide alighted last, gliding to the boat's high stern. As she took her place, she glanced back at us and gave a rare, broad smile, her aspect aglow with peace.

'To Avalon,' said the Lady of the Lake.

The vessel moved off, smooth as water on glass, golden prow carving a path through the white clouds. Towards Ynys Afallach, her immortal island, where we would study and heal and live, and seek wisdom that knew no bounds.

There, at the seashore, lakesides and forest rivers, as the water flowed and the veil between worlds disappeared, the souls once lost to death came forth to walk again beside us, to be loved and heard and better understood, and there was always enough time.

Avalon, where on clear days, I could stand before the waves and see the cliffs of Tintagel.

For now, I looked down at Arthur's face, resting, peaceful, awaiting the miracle that I would bring. What we would be known as in eternity was yet to be decided, but it no longer mattered. Whatever tales were sung of us – however our lives changed in the telling and our characters shifted as we were unravelled and rewoven; whether the words were spoken, or rewritten in ink, as years passed and complexity was elided, until only legends of good and bad held sway – the truth would find its way through. As my brother and I vanished into myth, our voices would remain, waiting in time, ready to tell our story anew.

King Arthur and Morgan le Fay. Fierce and furious. Formidable and clever. Revered and reviled. Light and dark.

Once and future. Brother and sister.

We would always be here.

I did not watch the shore retreat, or see the land slip out of sight. My gaze was set only forwards, on the limitless horizon, as we left the river and broke through the mist, and reached the deep-blue expanse of open water.

The vision of it enveloped me in a heartbeat, a yearning long held that was now fulfilled. Amidst the scents of salt and foam, the ancient roar of tumult and tides, the brackish taste on my lips, I felt my greatest truth deep inside: here, within the chaos and wisdom of the wild blue sea, was where I belonged.

Morgan of Cornwall, Morgan le Fay; Morgan, sea-born.

I was home, and free.

ACKNOWLEDGEMENTS

My first and deepest thanks are forever reserved for my agent, Marina de Pass, for being the guardian of my writing career, my greatest advocate and my light in the dark when things were at their most challenging with this complicated book. Every writer needs a champion, and she is my knight in shining armour.

Many thanks are also due to my editors and managing editors, who helped marshal my manuscript into a proper book: Jenny Parrott and Wayne Brookes, Robin Morgan-Bentley and Oliver Grant, and their Canadian counterparts, Amanda Ferreira and Stephanie Alleyne. A huge debt of gratitude is also owed to the brilliant teams at Oneworld Publications, Audible UK and Random House Canada, who work so hard across sales, production, marketing and publicity to get my words into the world. As always, particular thanks to Francine Brody for her copy-editing eagle eye, and for her patience with my tendency to edit up until the very last minute.

A special thank you to Matilda Warner (the Duchess of Bloomsbury), for being such a great supporter of Morgan, a wonderful bookshop wandering companion, and one of the best people I've met on this journey. I will miss working with you, but am so happy to have made a new friend.

Life as an author would not be possible without the support and endless enthusiasm of the many bookshops, booksellers, fellow authors, bloggers, reviewers who shout about books, celebrate them, and stoke the fires for us writers every day. A massive, heartfelt thank you to every single one of my readers for buying, reading and listening to my books, attending my events, writing thoughtful reviews, or otherwise taking the time to share with me that you have enjoyed the stories I tell. It is my privilege to have been embraced by such a dedicated and lovely bookish community.

However, before a book gets anywhere near a shelf, there is the long and solitary time writing it, and the conclusion to Morgan le Fay's trilogy was a deeper, more difficult and much more complex task than I imagined. I would not have kept my belief in my capability to bring this book to life if not for those who walked beside me while the work was done. To Jess Lawrence, for her early reading and feedback, and the accountability, process chats and steadfast support that underpinned the entire project. And to Emma Hinds, my coven sister, for her presence and patience, the wisdom and the laughter, whose courage makes me find my own again when I am lost. There are not enough thanks in the world for either of you, but I hope you know how essential you are.

Continuing appreciation is due to my parents and extended family for their ongoing love, pride and enthusiasm, and for still asking me how the writing is going, even though a writer rarely has a satisfying answer to that question. I am so grateful for the check-ins and understanding when I enter the various 'hermit' stages of the process and disappear from view. Thank you.

Last, but never least, I reserve the greatest of my thanks for those who are here, living with me, the stories I talk of endlessly, and my artistic temperament, and still love me for it. To Milo, my best ever creation, but entirely himself – you inspire me every day. Finally, I owe a lifetime of gratitude to Jason, my husband, best friend and partner in all things. I know how to write about love because of you.